Praise

"*High Hopes* tells a rapturous story. If Bruce has taught us nothing else, it's that 'it ain't no sin to be glad you're alive.' Abel takes that lesson deeply to heart, and her book reaffirms it for us. It is a true inspiration."

—**Anthony DeCurtis, contributing editor at *Rolling Stone***

"*High Hopes* traces the story of one woman's unexpected journey to Australia at the age of sixty, and a series of life-changing insights she could never have imagined. With the Boss's humanism and boundless energy as her guide, Abel discovers a renewed sense of self in the wake of years of depression. A story of inspiration and rediscovery, *High Hopes* is the perfect tonic for our troubled age."

—**Kenneth Womack, author of *Bruce Songs* and *John Lennon 1980***

"Anne Abel is a survivor of severe depression. She finds the route to emotional healing at the age of sixty during a solo, twenty-six-day trip to Australia to follow Bruce Springsteen, displaying enormous courage and perseverance on the road to her own empowerment. She turns her doubt and hesitation into a travelogue of faith and commitment as she slogs through the days, becoming stronger and more determined each day. *High Hopes* is an authentic, gripping, heartfelt read. If you're new to Anne Abel and/or Bruce Springsteen, you'll come away as a fan of both!"

—**Jane Seskin, LCSW, author of *Older, Wiser, Shorter: The Truth and Humor of Life After 65***

"Anne Abel's memoir, which began as a winning story at a Moth StorySLAM in Chicago, is a lyrical account of the resilience of the human spirit. It shows how Anne's gritty determination, tempered by an open mind and an open heart, enabled her to find her long-silenced voice."

—Lee Ann Gullie, Director of Development, The Moth

"Anne's 'Come to Bruce Springsteen' moment, and the vibrant stories that unfold from it, is the most unusual path I've heard about, and I've heard about quite a few. But this isn't really another book about Springsteen; this is an inspirational book about Anne's self-discovery. Whether you have never seen Springsteen perform or you just exited the stadium of his last sold-out show, Anne's storytelling will resonate."

—Donna Gray, founder of Bruce Funds

"Reading this book as someone who is both a psychologist and a major Springsteen fan, and who has done my own work researching what matters to women fans of Bruce Springsteen, was compelling. Anne's psychological and physical journey, and the validation she felt through her experience of the Springsteen concerts and her time on the road, was a very fitting example of what many women in our study spoke of as seeing Springsteen as a therapist, teacher, or guide. You don't have to be a psychologist to appreciate Anne's journey, as the book is written for all fans."

—Lorraine Mangione, coauthor of *Mary Climbs In: The Journeys of Bruce Springsteen's Women Fans*

"Central to her journey, and her memoir, is a candid exploration of her lifelong struggle with depression and the ways in which becoming a Springsteen fan fuels her healing. Many aspects of her story are unique—not least her sudden discovery of popular music in late midlife—but the meaning, inspiration, solace, and joy she finds in Springsteen's music and performances will resonate with many longtime fans."

—**Donna Luff, coauthor of** *Mary Climbs In: The Journeys of Bruce Springsteen's Women Fans*

"What a pleasure to accompany Anne Abel on this beautiful journey of personal growth as she shares the saga of growing a new identity and freeing her soul by summoning the courage to say yes to one bold thing. There's a message for all of us here: Never be afraid to have new experiences. Sometimes, the best way to change our internal world is to be bold and take steps to change our outer world. It's also a testament to the power of art to open hearts and minds and free the soul."

—**P. Shavaun Scott, LMFT, author of** *The Minds of Mass Killers* **and** *Game Addiction*

HIGH HOPES

HIGH HOPES

A Memoir

Anne Abel

SHE WRITES PRESS

Copyright © 2025 Anne Abel

All rights reserved. No part of this publication may be reproduced, stored in a retrieval system, or transmitted in any form or by any means, electronic, mechanical, photocopying, recording, or otherwise, except for brief quotations in reviews, educational works, or other uses permitted by copyright law.

Published in 2025 by
She Writes Press, an imprint of The Stable Book Group

32 Court Street, Suite 2109
Brooklyn, NY 11201
https://shewritespress.com

Library of Congress Control Number: 2025909426
ISBN: 978-1-64742-972-0
eISBN: 978-1-64742-973-7

Interior Designer: Andrea Reider

Printed in the United States

Names and identifying characteristics have been changed to protect the privacy of certain individuals.

No part of this publication may be used to train generative artificial intelligence (AI) models. The publisher and author reserve all rights related to the use of this content in machine learning.

All company and product names mentioned in this book may be trademarks or registered trademarks of their respective owners. They are used for identification purposes only and do not imply endorsement or affiliation.

For Andy, of course.

1

I WALKED TO the middle of the semicircle of desks in my Developmental English classroom at the Community College of Philadelphia.

"Scott, please close your dictionary. You cannot use a dictionary during a vocabulary quiz," I said to my twenty-six-year-old Iraq War vet student.

I waited a moment. I waited two moments. I waited three moments. He was so big that that even with him seated and me standing, if he had looked at me, we would have been eye-to-eye. But he did not look at me. He continued to write on his quiz paper, his Webster's dictionary open next to it. In my peripheral vision, I could see the eyes of the other students jumping from me to Scott, from Scott to me. This was better than any reality TV show they had ever seen.

"Scott, if you don't close your dictionary now, you'll have to leave," I said calmly.

Scott stood up from his seat so suddenly that even he seemed to be taken off guard by the move. His dictionary fell to the floor. His white, blue-lined quiz paper floated down after it.

"Fuck *you*." He stared down at me, his brown eyes locked on mine. "*Fuck* you."

It was Monday, the fifth week of the fifteen-week semester. The previous Wednesday, after our last class session, I had gone to the head of the English Department to ask for advice on how to deal with this difficult batch of students. It was the first time in the five years since he had hired me that we had spoken.

"Why do you think we have those beige phones on the wall at the entrance to every classroom?" he said. "As soon as you lift the receiver, Security will come on the line. Give them the room number and hang up. They will arrive within minutes."

I nodded. In my entire time teaching there, I had never wondered about the beige phones. More importantly, I had never needed them. Now, sitting across from the department head, I wondered why no one had told me about them when I first began teaching.

"Another thing you need to do, immediately," he said, "is to begin writing behavior reports for every out-of-control student and submitting them to the dean of students. The dean's office will review them and set up a date for you and the student to appear before a judiciary hearing board. Be forewarned, it is time-consuming to complete those forms."

"Thank you," I said, standing up. "I've never had a class like this before."

"It happens," he said, smiling in commiseration as he walked me to the door of his office cubicle. "Remember, that's why we've got those phones."

After that meeting, I'd spent two hours writing behavior reports for four students in my class. A few days later, on Sunday, I'd received emails from the dean's office with four judiciary hearing dates. I'd been shocked to learn that each of the hearings was in the first week of December, six weeks away. What was I going to do with these students for six more weeks?

And today, Monday, things had gone from bad to worse.

"Yeah, fuck her," I'd heard someone say outside the classroom before class began.

I'd looked up from my desk. Scott and the three other students for whom I had written behavior reports were standing together in the hallway outside of my classroom, nodding at each other.

"Yeah, fuck her. Yeah, in December when we have our hearings, we'll see who's gonna win," one of the others had said, and they'd glared at me.

Not only had the dean's office set the judiciary hearing dates late in the semester, but apparently they'd also emailed each of the students to let them know. At the very least, they could have also assigned me two bodyguards.

Now, two hours later, as I stood staring at Scott and he stood staring back down at me, his dictionary and quiz paper still on the floor, I could feel the tension between us coursing like an electric current.

Finally, slowly, he picked up his dictionary and quiz paper off the floor and sat back down at his desk. He began to fan through the dictionary, searching for the next vocabulary word on the quiz.

I was now regretting having given each student one of those dictionaries on the first day of class.

I walked backward to the door of the room, picked up the receiver of the beige phone, and pressed it to my ear. It sounded like the phone was dead. I waited. With the students' eyes following every movement I made, I pushed down on the lever at the top of the phone, hoping to jiggle the phone to life and make a connection with Security. The receiver remained silent. I tapped the zero on the keypad. The receiver remained silent. The beige phone did not work.

I put down the receiver and walked back to the middle of the room.

"Ten more minutes and then I'm collecting the quizzes," I said.

Reluctantly, one student after another picked up a pen and put their focus back on the quiz in front of them.

I didn't care if I was admitting defeat by allowing Scott to continue to use his dictionary. My only goal now was to remain unharmed for the next fifteen minutes, until the bell rang and class was over. I just hoped I could make it to the safety of my car without being attacked verbally or physically by Scott or the other three students for whom I had written behavior reports.

When the ten minutes were over, I began collecting the quizzes from each of the students. Robert, another student about whom I had sent in a behavior report, was the last student to hand his in.

"Thank you, Robert." I took the paper and added it to my pile, then turned and walked back to my desk. As I put the quizzes down, my back to the class, I heard a crashing, screeching noise.

I whipped around to see Robert's desk with its attached chair careening toward me. It landed just short of hitting me.

"I told you I hate these desks," Robert screamed at me. "I want *your* desk."

It was not the first time he'd hurled a desk at me.

In my peripheral vision, I saw on the circular wall clock that it was 11:55.

"Okay, everyone—that's it for today," I said. "I'll see you back here on Wednesday."

Within moments, the classroom was empty. I waited until the bell rang. Then, with my heartbeat quickening, I stepped out of the classroom. In the safety of the crowd of students and teachers, I walked along the corridor and down four flights of stairs before bursting out the door into the noontime October sun.

I stopped. The sun's soothing warmth on my face and bare arms was so unexpected, so wonderful, so different from anything I had experienced in a long time. I stared at the blue sky, the white clouds, and the leafy, colorful autumn trees. The muscles throughout my body softened. I took a deep breath. I felt a space open up in my tight, overcrowded head. The agony that had accumulated within me during the five weeks I had worked so hard to teach these students—so often angry, belligerent, and even violent—dissipated. I felt so good, so very, very good.

After a few sun-warmed moments at the top of the stairs of the main building of the Community College of Philadelphia, I thought, *I deserve better. I am* never *coming back here.*

I took another deep breath, stood up straight, and walked down the steps to my ruby-red Volvo station wagon. I threw my canvas totes with books and papers into the trunk and slid into the driver's seat. I clicked my seat belt, turned my key in the ignition, and threw the car into gear.

But then, as I pulled out of my parking spot, I pictured my empty six-bedroom house. My three grown sons were living on opposite coasts and my husband was away on business trips more than he was home. My breaths became quicker and shallower. The surge of self-empowerment I had felt moments earlier was quickly turning into panic.

I had struggled with depression since I was sixteen. As an adult, I had tried over twenty antidepressants in as many years. I'd been an inpatient at a psychiatric hospital twice.

I'd undergone three regimens of electroconvulsive therapy (ECT). I'd also tried transcranial magnetic stimulation (TMS), a treatment that sends magnetic currents through the skull. None of these modalities had ever given me any significant relief from my depression.

Teaching at the community college had helped to keep me out of the abyss. Each previous semester, I had found one or two students who'd hoped that my class would be a stepping stone to a future they envisioned for themselves—students for whom it had been so fulfilling for me to help along their way.

One such student was Mardoche. In the two-page writing sample required of all students in my Developmental English class on the first day of the semester, Mardoche had written about his release from prison two months earlier and his hope of getting a football scholarship to Alabama State University. At the end of class, I offered to meet with anyone who wanted to work with me one-on-one to improve upon their essay.

"I need any help I can get," Mardoche told me as all the other students raced out of the classroom. "My dream is to play football for Alabama State."

Two days later, after class, he followed me to my pale-yellow cinderblock office and sat down catty-corner from me at my industrial metal desk. I pulled out his writing sample and put it on the desk between us.

"I know it's not good," he said, shaking his head and slumping backward against the chair. "I got my GED in prison."

"Mardoche, this is a first draft. A first draft you didn't have much time to do. No one writes a finished story the first time."

He sat up straight, resting one arm on the desk and picking up his essay with the other. "Really? You think *I* can write something?"

"Absolutely. Absolutely for sure," I said, smiling.

Excitement ran through me. I could feel myself filling with energy.

Twice a week, we worked on his life story, crafting it into a personal essay. At the end of the semester, he won first place in a developmental English writing contest and read his essay at the awards ceremony.

Joe was another student who lifted my spirits and helped me stave off a deep depression. In his first-day writing sample, Joe wrote about his family and online gambling. I read the two pages, and when I got to the end, I turned over the page, hoping there would be more. And more and more. His fast-clipped pacing, energetic prose, and insights—far more mature than those of a typical eighteen-year-old—had me awed.

"Joe, would you be interested in expanding your writing sample?" I asked him at the beginning of our next session. "If you are, I would love to help you. From what I read, though, I don't think you need my help."

"I don't know if I could write more," he said.

"Don't think of the length," I said. "Just think about what you want to say about your gambling. About your family. About your life. Just sit down and start writing whatever comes into your head."

"Really?" He looked doubtful.

I nodded enthusiastically. "Try it. Set yourself an amount of time, if you think that will help, and try to write until the time is up."

A week later Joe returned with five typewritten pages. They were even better than the two he had written in class.

His voice was like nothing I had ever read. Engaging, sincere, irreverent, hopeful. Vulnerable, arrogant, insecure, honest.

Over the course of several weeks, Joe showed me his progress. His voice and his story were mesmerizing. Occasionally, I sensed there was more he wanted to say about a topic than what he had actually written, and I'd point to the piece in question. "Joe, is there something more you have in your head about this?"

"Yeah," he'd say, tentatively. "But I didn't think it would be interesting."

But then, at the following class, he'd bring in his expanded version, and it was inevitably interesting—incredibly so.

It was gratifying and energizing for me to be able to encourage and enable students like Joe to be the best they could be, and to feel proud about their work and themselves.

Joe ultimately submitted his essay to a writing contest that was open to all CCP students, and he won first place. At the award ceremony, he gave me an expensive bottle of Russian vodka. I never opened it, but it sat in a prominent place on my bookshelf. Every time my eyes rested on it, I thought of Joe and felt myself smile.

Triumphs like these invigorated me. Working with students like Mardoche and Joe had lifted my spirits in a way that no antidepressants or treatments had ever managed to do. But this latest class had been horrendous; not only were many of the students disrespectful and aggressive toward me, but not even one student in this group had seemed to want anything from it. Or me.

On this sunny October day, as I navigated the narrow streets toward the expressway home, I realized I needed a new focus. If I was no longer going to teach at the community college, I needed a plan.

As I merged onto the expressway, I thought, *I know. I'll go to Australia in February and see Bruce Springsteen.*

2

THIRTEEN MONTHS before the sunny October day when I quit my teaching job—on Labor Day weekend 2012, at the age of fifty-nine—I agreed to go to my first concert ever. A Bruce Springsteen concert. A musician I knew nothing about.

I had just finished my daily sixty-minute stationary bike ride to nowhere that Friday when Andy walked into the room holding his iPhone to his ear.

"I have Robert on the phone," he said. "He wants to know if he and Lindsey can come to Philadelphia this weekend."

My son Robert and his wife, Lindsey, lived in Boston.

"Are you kidding?" I said, my feet still anchored into the toe clips of my bike. "The whole time I was working out, I was feeling sorry for myself because we don't have any fun plans for this holiday weekend."

Andy, a professor at the University of Pennsylvania, and I had been planning to spend the long weekend preparing for our semesters, which would begin the day after Labor Day—not exactly exciting stuff. My favorite thing in the world was to spend time with my children; I was thrilled Robert and Lindsey wanted to visit.

"They're going to a Bruce Springsteen concert here on Sunday night," Andy said, taking the phone away from his ear. "They want to know if we want to go with them."

I shook my head no. As much as I wanted to see Robert and Lindsey, I did *not* want to go see someone whose music I didn't know in concert. I'm sure I had heard of Bruce Springsteen—who hasn't? I might have even been aware that he was a rock star. But that was the limit of my Springsteen knowledge. I was brought up in a house devoid of any kind of culture, pop or otherwise. When my mother bought a white Plymouth Valiant in 1964, she was proud that she did not get a radio. Music was never played in our house.

Besides, these days, I was typically dragging myself up the stairs and collapsing onto my bed, grateful that another day was over, by seven at night. I couldn't imagine heading out of the house for a rock concert that would likely start even later than that.

"Your mother doesn't want to go, so I won't go either," Andy said into the phone. "But thank you for asking." He listened for a few seconds, then looked at me again. "Lindsey wants to know if she should bring her wedding dress for you to see."

I smiled. "Absolutely!"

Robert and Lindsey's wedding had taken place six weeks earlier—halfway through my five-week regimen of ECT. It was my third regimen in four years. Terrifying as it was, I had agreed to do it because I hoped it would bring some relief from my debilitating depression. Instead, not only had the depression remained equally suffocating, I'd also developed severe pain in my upper left jaw. And lost my memory. In fact, I couldn't remember anything from the beginning of May until the middle of August. I did not remember going hours, sometimes days, that summer without saying a word. I didn't remember Robert and Lindsey visiting us over the Fourth of July weekend. I didn't remember going with them to buy a rehearsal dinner dress for Lindsey, and I didn't remember them going with me to buy a green, sleeveless A-line dress to wear to the wedding.

In one photo from their wedding day, Lindsey is flanked by her mother and father, and Robert by Andy and me. Lindsey and Robert are beaming. Lindsey's parents are smiling. Andy is smiling. I am staring directly into the camera—trancelike, vacant. I am not frowning; I am not smiling. I am not there.

I didn't remember anything about their wedding—the ceremony itself or any of the guests. I didn't remember waking up the morning of the wedding and saying to Andy, "I can't wait until tonight, when I will be able to crawl back into bed."

So I was looking forward to Lindsey bringing her wedding gown to Philadelphia for me to see.

Getting off my exercise bike that day, I felt better than I had since well before May. Robert and Lindsey were coming to visit! It didn't get better than that.

The next day, at exactly four o'clock, Lindsey and Robert's gray Saturn appeared at the top of our driveway. Andy and I ran out the back door and got to them just as they were tumbling out. I hugged each of them.

"Here's my wedding dress," Lindsey said, pointing to the satiny white dress spread out across the back seat. "I love it. But, after I put it on for you this weekend, I can't imagine when I'll ever wear it again."

I smiled.

Then she picked up a *New Yorker* magazine that was lying on the floor of the car.

"Yesterday I finally had a chance to go through the *New Yorker*s from before our wedding and I found an article about Bruce Springsteen. I grew up listening to him. My parents are fans. I read that he's sixty-two and I figured I'd better get to a concert soon."

I didn't know how to respond. Did she mean she thought Bruce Springsteen was likely to die soon? If so, at fifty-nine, I wasn't far behind. Or did she mean he would soon retire? I didn't want to think of myself nearing that stage of life either.

The following morning, I woke in a better mood than usual and went straight to my exercise bike. I didn't want to waste valuable time working out after Robert and Lindsey woke up.

As I pedaled away, I felt my mood lightening even more with each advancing minute. Suddenly I thought, *Why not go to that concert tonight?*

I jumped off my bike and ran into the family room, where Robert and Lindsey were sitting on the couch, staring into their iPhones.

"I want to go with you tonight," I said, startling them not only with the content of my declaration but also with my exuberant delivery.

They looked at each other. They looked back up at me.

"I'll go ask Daddy," I said, taking their silence as an okay.

I found Andy in the basement, finishing his workout.

"I decided I want to go to the concert tonight," I announced. "I want to spend the time with Robert and Lindsey. Do you want to go?"

"Yes," he said in between breaths and smiling.

I ran back upstairs. "We're in!" I told Robert and Lindsey. "But I want to sit with you guys, so we need to buy four new tickets."

"Okay," Robert said. "I'll go to StubHub and get new tickets."

I sat down in a chair across from Robert and Lindsey. I needed to shower but I didn't feel like moving. I could already feel my energy beginning to drain.

"Do you want to read the *New Yorker* article I was telling you about?" Lindsey asked, lifting the magazine off her lap and holding it out to me.

I took it from her and forced my lips into a polite smile.

What had I done? After my workout I really did feel happy and energetic, but now, an hour or so later, my endorphins and my energy were dissipating. Sitting on the chair with the *New Yorker* on my lap, all I could think about was how horrible the evening was going to be.

I was not feeling any better when the time came to leave for the concert. And by six o'clock, as we arrived at the first lot of the ballpark turned concert hall only to find that it was full, I felt my heart sinking into my belly.

The next lot was full too, and the one after that.

Finally, Andy found a spot in a remote lot. I sighed with dread as I rolled out of the car.

In each lot we walked through on our way to the stadium, people were tailgating. It had never occurred to me that non-sports people would arrive early to do this. Everyone was attired in easy, summer fashions. They were sitting on beach chairs, picnic chairs, blankets, and the open tailgates of pickup trucks. No one was alone. Everyone was with someone. Wisps of smoke spiraled up from sizzling kielbasas, hot dogs, hamburgers, and ribs on small backyard grills, creating an array of familiar smells.

Music sounded from radios on the ground near the chairs and blankets and from speakers inside the cars and trucks. It wasn't blasting, blaring, or annoying music. It was soft enough that I couldn't make out the words, but I could hear the rhythms as we walked by. Instinctively, my feet seemed to keep step with the changing beats.

People were swaying to the music. Many were singing. I had walked through many tailgating sessions on my way to baseball games, but this version of it was different. Unlike baseball tailgaters, who would be disappointed if their team lost, these concert tailgaters would all feel like winners at the end of the evening.

We stopped in front of a man who was grilling hot dogs on a hibachi grill and wearing a gray T-shirt with an etching of Bruce Springsteen on the front.

"Help yourself to a dog," he said, rolling the hot dogs over with a spatula.

The four of us looked at each other and smiled.

"Thank you," Andy said to the man. "We're holding out for the hoagies inside. Enjoy the concert."

I looked at the man. "Yes, thank you," I said, smiling at him spontaneously. "Have fun at the concert."

A few steps later, we came to a woman in a black Bruce T-shirt with a guitar on the front and "Wrecking Ball 2012" on the back with a list of cities. She pointed to pretzels roasting on her grill.

"Can I interest any of you in a soft pretzel?" she asked, holding a salt-coated twist out to us.

"Thank you so much, but we're saving our appetites," I said with a smile.

Farther down the row of tailgaters, we were even offered beers. In all the years I had walked past tailgaters on the way to baseball games, no one had ever offered us anything. It was so pleasant to be surrounded by such generous and kind strangers.

Everyone seemed so excited and happy about seeing Bruce Springsteen. And their excitement and happiness were contagious. I wasn't as excited as they were, but in the presence of their good cheer I could feel the heavy tightness that typically resided in my gut loosening and lightening. Walking to the stadium, I absorbed enough of the happiness exuding from the tailgaters that I felt my mood elevating back up to its post-workout, non-depressive state.

Suddenly Andy, who was walking a few steps ahead of me, stopped, and I walked right into him. I was so caught up in the moment-to-moment sights and smells and sounds that I hadn't realized we had already arrived at the ticket booth.

When we entered the stadium, I was surprised by my sudden recall of stadium geography. All my years of going to baseball games with Andy and the boys were paying off. I had not been there in the three years since Ross had left for college, but stepping along the familiar shiny gray cement concourse, the familiar smells of spilled beer, popcorn popping, and butter melting overtook me.

Looking out toward the daylight of the baseball field, I was overcome by a sense of nostalgia. There were a lot of things I didn't enjoy about the many, many games we'd come to here. But they were far outweighed by the comforting wholeness, the soothing togetherness, I had felt from the moment our family piled into the car and headed to the stadium for a baseball game. I loved being with my family.

I loved hearing their voices. I loved hearing them banter. That was enough for me. More than enough. As much as I hated sweating in the summer sun, watching a game I could see and understand far better on the television in our family room, I loved the feeling of utter peace that filled me when I was with my family.

I glanced at Robert and Lindsey in front of me, and then Andy beside me, and smiled with contentment.

Our seats for the concert were directly in front of the middle of the stage, high up in the third-tier section of the four-tiered stadium. I could make out the microphone but it looked really, really small.

While we waited for the concert to begin, we ate our hoagies and looked at pictures of Robert and Lindsey's wedding on Robert's iPhone. Robert and Lindsey filled me in on the backstories of guests at the wedding who I didn't know.

Lindsey was in the middle of telling me a story about her sister's boyfriend when suddenly everyone around us mysteriously rose in unison. I looked at my watch. It was nine thirty. I had been worried that it would be difficult for me to stay awake for a concert that began at seven thirty; it had never occurred to me that it would start late. *Two hours* late.

Usually, there is nothing I hate more than waiting. But I had not even been conscious of waiting, I was having such a good time listening to the kids' stories.

I felt myself rising to my feet as if I were being lifted by the energy of the crowd around me. Down on the stage, I saw a man with a guitar, strumming and strumming and strumming. Singing and singing and singing. And tapping the heel of his foot with such energy that it radiated from down on the stage all the way up to me.

On the giant screen to the left of the stage, I saw the face of a man with the biggest, kindest, most effervescent smile I had ever seen. His bursting smile seemed to fill the entire screen. His white teeth were as sparkly as the tiny diamond stud glistening in his left ear. The energy of his tap, tap, tapping foot and strum, strum, strumming fingers filled me with energy. His smile embraced me. I felt my heart opening for this man.

I took my eyes off the giant screen and looked directly at the stage. Even from my bird's-eye view, I could sense that the man who was strumming and tapping and singing and dancing down there was having so much fun. I could sense that right here, right now, there was no place else in the world this man wanted to be. It felt so good to be with someone who was so happy and excited to be with me—and the forty thousand people around me. And all of those forty thousand people seemed as happy and excited as I was.

I couldn't make out the words of his songs. It didn't matter. His smile, his energy, and his enthusiasm traveled on every note that emanated from his guitar, on every sound that left his mouth and filled my soul. His humanity lifted me. I was clapping. I was swaying. I was smiling.

A thirty-something woman in front of me who had been jumping and dancing from the moment the man appeared onstage turned around, looked at me, and smiled. I smiled back at her. And then, suddenly, in the six inches of concrete in front of my seat, I was not only smiling and clapping and swaying but also jumping and dancing. The energy of the man at the microphone in the middle of the stage had somehow gone from him to the woman in front of me and then up to me.

I was standing, I was dancing, I was swaying and clapping and smiling. I. Was. Not. Sitting. I was not even thinking of sitting. I was not conscious of the pounding my feet took each time a dance step or a jump landed me back on the unforgiving cement floor. The man onstage—a man who, at sixty-two, was three years older than me—did not stop. From the drawn-out last note of one song to the anticipatory "One, two, three" of the next, this man was giving us everything he had. He didn't want to waste even a second pausing to catch his breath. And if he could keep on going like this, so could I.

I was captivated each time his face spread across the giant screen. I could not take my eyes off his smile—a smile that, no matter how big, seemed to somehow expand each time it appeared.

Finally, after two encores, the stage went dark. I just stood there, butterflies fluttering inside me, staring down at the microphone in the middle of the stage. I could feel myself smiling. I could feel myself shaking my head in disbelief. Disbelief that it was possible to feel so good. So happy. So energetic. So alive. So very much the opposite of anything I had ever felt before.

I looked at my watch. It was one o'clock in the morning. I had been smiling and clapping and swaying and jumping and dancing for three and a half hours. For three-plus hours, this man's energy, humanity, and empathy had lifted me up. For three-plus hours, Bruce Springsteen had made me feel like I had a chance.

I turned to Lindsey. "Thank you. Thank you so much," I said, giving her a hug. "I have never experienced anything like this. I am so glad I could share it with you."

As I floated my way out of the stadium, I saw someone selling T-shirts. They were light gray and had a black sketch of

Bruce Springsteen wrapping his arms around his guitar and pressing it tightly to his torso. I bought one for each of us.

It was two thirty by the time we found our way through the crowd to our car and then home. But I was not tired. Not at all.

I was bursting with energy. I was happy to be alive.

In the next six months I went to six more concerts.

3

I WAS never the depressed mother whose children found her in bed under the covers when they came home from school. Quite the contrary; being with my children always invigorated me. When I was with them, I didn't need to pretend that I was okay. My goal of nurturing them with support and encouragement kept me in the moment. It buoyed me and gave me purpose and energy. I was interested and engaged in helping them navigate their worlds and getting them where they wanted to go.

Even so, I had to work hard to be emotionally present and available for my kids. Each morning, after I dropped them off at school, I drove to the local Y and swam a mile. I dreaded getting into the cold water, but I knew that when I was done, I would feel better—at least until midafternoon, when my mental and physical energy would drain and I would feel like dropping to the floor and curling up into a ball. That's when I would change into my workout clothes, go down to the basement, and ride an exercise bike for sixty minutes, bringing my heart rate up to 148 beats per minute. When I finished, I had energy again. I had energy to happily pick my sons up at school and ferry them to one after-school activity or another. Being with them, listening to them, advising them, and laughing with them was the highlight of my day.

Then my oldest moved to Florida; and then three years after that, in September 2007, within two weeks of each other, the other two left—my youngest son for college and my middle son to San Francisco.

And yet the empty bedrooms of my house were not what sent me into the pit of depression.

The morning after we moved my youngest into his dorm at Swarthmore, one doctor put my left foot into a cast for acute plantar fasciitis and another diagnosed me with cutaneous B-cell lymphoma, a rare type of skin cancer. Though, admittedly, the three weeks between the day I learned I had cancer and the day I got back the PET scan results showing that it had not spread were rough, *this* was not what sent me into an emotional spiral either. Once I learned the cancer was isolated and that I would undergo four months of radiation, I felt fine. I had a goal: *Get better*. Every day I showed up at the hospital and sat in the radiation waiting room. I talked to other women. I talked to the radiation technicians. Being with people, talking to people, sharing with people gave me energy. During those four months, I was actually happy.

It was afterward, in February, when I felt myself begin to slip. My steps got heavier. My mind began to feel numb. My heckling inner voice turned into a muted drone. I stopped reaching out to friends. By the end of the month, for the first time in my life, I couldn't even motivate myself to work out. I just sat.

Andy stayed home with me when he could, but it was difficult for him to tend to me as I dropped further and further into the abyss—he had responsibilities at school, a schedule to keep up with. At the beginning of March, he called the psychiatrist at the University of Pennsylvania Cancer

Center, who recommended inpatient psychiatric treatment at The Retreat at Sheppard Pratt, a private psychiatric hospital in Towson, Maryland.

I was terrified of going to The Retreat. I was terrified of being alone. I was terrified of missing Andy. I was terrified of being thrown in with a group of equally miserable and unhappy strangers. I was terrified I would be told that I needed ECT.

If I could have just disappeared from the world like a wisp of smoke, leaving no one sad behind me, I would have done that. But as terrified as I was of going to The Retreat, I wanted more than anything to feel better. For me. For Andy. For my kids. So, when the University of Pennsylvania psychiatrist suggested I go, I agreed. I never *didn't* try to do what was good for me, even when it terrified me. But I didn't have much hope for The Retreat; I simply didn't believe that feeling better was possible.

Six days later, clutching my pillow, I was in the passenger seat of Andy's Lexus SUV for the two-hour drive to The Retreat at Sheppard Pratt. I didn't speak any more during the ride than I had for several days, so Andy turned on SiriusXM. Elvis would be the soundtrack of my final hours of freedom.

At 10:30 a.m., we pulled up to a sprawling, Gothic-style brick building with pitched roofs and eaves and pointed arches. The Retreat's director, Lois, and a member of her staff were waiting for us out front with a brass luggage cart worthy of a first-class hotel.

"I'll take you upstairs while Andy shows my staff what to bring inside," Lois said when I got out of the car.

I looked at Andy.

Immediate separation was not what I'd had in mind. I knew that at some point Andy would have to go home—that at some point, I would be alone in this strange place. But I had not thought concretely about when that sometime would be. I knew I would see him again inside, but I was scared to be away from him for even a minute as I committed myself to being a patient in this mental hospital.

Andy has many admirable traits, one of them being that he always does the right thing. Even if it hurts him. If he could have absorbed my pain and borne it himself, it wouldn't have been *my* belongings we'd just unloaded at Sheppard Pratt. But he couldn't. So, with an apologetic grimace, he nodded me toward Lois, and obediently I followed her through the automatic glass doors and down the green-plaid carpeted hallway.

Lois pressed a button at an entryway, and after a buzz she pulled the door open. On the other side, a woman stood facing us.

"Anne, this is Kathy, one of our head nurses," Lois introduced us.

I reciprocated Kathy's handshake but not her smile.

"Your room is in the East Wing and I'm the head nurse of that unit," she said as she led me down a hallway. At the nurses' station was a twelve-paned glass door. "The door is locked," Kathy said, pulling on it as if I wouldn't believe her. "When you need something, you just knock, and someone will come out immediately."

I recoiled internally. Was every door in this building kept locked?

We continued down the hall. As if reading my mind, Kathy said, "There are no locks on the doors of the residents' rooms." She stopped. "This one's yours."

I stepped through the doorway and surveyed the cavernous, high-ceilinged room. On the far wall were two large multipaned windows with fire-retardant dark-green drapes. Despite the tall windows, the room seemed dark, cold, and dreary. Between the windows was a low, round wooden table flanked by two upholstered armchairs covered in a worn, tweedy green fabric. It was as if someone had wedged a bed into a tired, musty conference room.

I began to feel worse. Something I had not thought possible.

"Every Tuesday fresh flowers are brought in," Kathy said.

I remained silent.

I heard Andy enter behind me. Kathy smiled at him. "I'll check back with you in a bit. Finish unpacking. No need to rush. When you're finished, we'll still have plenty of time to tour the unit."

She started for the door but then turned back to us. "You have a one thirty appointment with Doctor Quaytman. It would be best if you could go too," she said, looking at Andy.

Andy and I exchanged quick glances. I knew what he was thinking; he knew what I was thinking.

Some years back I'd heard Kitty Dukakis, the wife of Massachusetts governor Michael Dukakis, speak on NPR about undergoing ECT to treat her depression. At the time, I'd felt sure I'd never be willing to undergo something as frightening and drastic as ECT to relieve my recurrent depression.

Now, at The Retreat, my biggest fear was that I'd be ECT'd.

When the nurse was out of sight, Andy did a 360-degree inspection of the bedroom and bathroom. "This is nice," he said. "Who'd expect stone and granite in a psychiatric hospital bathroom?"

By the time he turned around, I was plopped on the bed, picking up where I'd left off at home. Showing no signs of unpacking. Showing no signs of doing anything.

Andy settled the two garbage bags full of my belongings in the middle of the room and began to pull my clothes out. "I'll do this for you if you want," he said. "But it might be better if you do it so you know where everything is, and you can put things where you want them."

He had been wife-sitting for weeks—buying my food, preparing my meals, feeding the dogs, and deflecting phone calls. So it didn't surprise me when he began removing my balled-up clothes from the garbage bag and folding each item, like I'd watched him do so many times with his own clothes.

But I had neither the patience nor the heart to watch him unpack for me here at The Retreat at Sheppard Pratt.

"Let me do it," I said, rolling off the bed and speaking for the first time since we'd arrived. I pulled a red "Life is Good" T-shirt from his hands. As I shoved it into the top drawer of a chest near the bathroom door, I appreciated, even in my catatonic state, the pink heart above the hopeful, if ironic, lettering.

Within seconds, my T-shirts, sweatpants, J.Crew sweaters, and cargo pants were stuffed away. With my last bits of energy and motivation, I ripped the blanket and bedspread off the bed and tossed my own pillow and comforter onto it. Then I threw myself face down on the bed, with no intention of ever getting up.

"You're quick," I heard Nurse Kathy say some minutes later.

I rolled over and looked up at her. Did she *ever* not smile?

Andy looked at me, the veins in his long, skinny neck popping. Aside from having to worry about my depression and leaving me at The Retreat, he also had to worry that I'd be rude or inappropriate to Kathy.

But I cope with my depression not by abusing others but by internally abusing myself. So, with a glance at Andy, who heaved a visible sigh, I followed Kathy out the door.

As we walked through a doorway into a room filled with desks and computers, I heard deep moans coming through open French doors at the other end of the room. It was impossible not to think of *One Flew Over the Cuckoo's Nest*.

"This is our computer room," Kathy said, not acknowledging the morbid sounds. Then she led us through the open French doors. Lying on a black leather couch, covered with a blanket and clutching an ice pack to her forehead, was a hefty woman in her late twenties.

"Why can't I go to my room?" the woman said.

"Because you'll just get into bed and sleep," Kathy said, standing over her. "It'll be lunchtime soon, Marianne. You need to eat."

Leading Andy and me back out of the room, Kathy said, "Marianne had ECT this morning."

"ECT?" Andy repeated, eyes wide. He was clearly shocked to be meeting an ECT patient so soon.

I was too. Stumbling across Marianne so early in the tour was not a good omen.

We continued our tour of the facilities. Toward the end of it, Kathy identified the art therapy room and said, "That's where the residents are now."

One of my many fears about coming to The Retreat had been meeting the other nuts in this high-class nuthouse. Now that I was here, I wanted to see them and get a sense of who they were. I've never been one to put off the inevitable.

"Can I see it?" I asked.

Kathy opened the door and motioned us in. I took a few steps. In the center of the room, four long tables were pushed together, forming a large square. Covering the surface of the tables was an expanse of brown paper, a mural in the making. A rainbow stretched from end to end. Some patients—some *residents*—were standing, some were sitting. All held colored markers. And *everyone* looked happy.

Kathy introduced Andy and me.

"You all look so happy," I heard myself say.

"Don't worry," said a brown-haired woman in her fifties from one of the tables. "We aren't all so happy. And when I first got here, I looked as sad as you do, and I cried for three days straight."

Kathy, through her relentless smile, said, "That's very compassionate, Alison, for you to share your arrival experience with Anne." Then she stepped forward to inspect the mural. "This is a very interesting poster. Very colorful and cheerful."

She spoke to the residents like a kindergarten teacher.

Not a good sign, I thought.

At the end of the tour, Kathy left Andy and me in the dining room to await the others for lunch.

I was silent. What was there to say? In the past six days, in the rare times I *had* spoken, I'd said to Andy, "Why do you have to send me away? Why do you *want* to send me away?"

But I hadn't really meant it. And I hadn't put up a fight. As much I dreaded leaving my home, I dreaded even more being a burden—physical or mental—on Andy. As brain-dead as I had become, I still noted the tightness in Andy's face and the popping veins in his neck every time he walked into a room and saw me. So, here in the dining room at The Retreat, with nothing left to do but accept my fate, I looked up at him and forced my lips into a smile.

During lunch, Marianne, the woman who'd wanted to go to her room after ECT, came shuffling in, wearing her bathrobe and slippers, and hoisted herself into the only empty seat, which happened to be next to me.

"Hi," I said when she was situated. "I'm Anne. This is my husband, Andy. We saw you earlier in the living room."

"You did?"

"Yeah. You were begging Kathy to let you go to your room?"

"I was?"

I didn't think too much about Marianne not remembering me from the living room. I assumed she had been distracted by her discomfort. But I found it disconcerting that she didn't remember wailing to Kathy about returning to her room.

I was sure I too was headed for ECT, so I hoped Marianne's memory loss was the reason she was at The Retreat, rather than an ECT side effect. "You don't remember?" I asked gently.

After a swig of 2 percent milk from a school-lunch-size carton, she said, "Since I started ECT my memory has gone to shit."

I was already beginning to view Marianne's story as my own. Terrified to hear the answer but unable to resist posing the question, I asked, "Why are you having ECT?"

"I suffer from depression. That's why I came here. And nothing else was working."

I slumped in my chair.

"Is it helping?" Andy asked.

She frowned. "Today was my sixth treatment, and as far as I can tell, the only thing it's done is wipe out my memory."

"That's not true, Marianne," said a man with a deep southern accent from a few seats down. "You're much peppier now than you used to be. The ECT patient is always the last one to notice the difference. I had ECT the last time I was here."

The *last* time he was here? He'd had friggin' ECT and he was back again? I couldn't help myself: "How many times have you been here?"

"Three."

Horrified, I quickly deflected by turning back to Marianne and asking, "Where are you from?"

"Philly."

"So am I," I said, glad to be able to offer information about myself, as I had solicited so much already from her.

"Where in Philly?" Andy asked.

Marianne looked up from her plate, put down her carton of milk, and stared at Andy. For several long moments, she said nothing. I began to worry she was annoyed by all the questions.

Finally, she spoke: "You know, I don't remember where I live."

No one at the table said anything.

"And it really pisses me off," she added.

"Don't worry, Marianne," the southern man said. "The memory loss really is temporary. It happened to me too, but after a few months almost everything came back. Not the stuff that happened while I was having the treatments, but everything else. And when you think about it, why would you want to remember getting electroconvulsive shock therapy?"

I grabbed the arms of my chair, fighting the urge to flee. "Does it hurt?"

"No, not when they do it," Marianne said. "But afterward . . ." She swept a hand downward over her face and body. "Well, look at me."

She was right. She was not a pretty sight. The bathrobe she was wearing over her pajamas was rumpled, her wavy black hair was knotted and gnarled, and she was slumped forward, keeping herself upright with the support of her elbows on the table.

I pushed my plate away. Andy pushed it back.

"Anne, you've got to eat," he said. "You're not going to feel any better if you're starving." He looked around the table and leaned closer. "Besides"—he lowered his voice—"how many people on the Main Line of Philadelphia can say, 'Been there, done that' about being a resident in a nuthouse? Think of the story this will make." He gave me a prodding stare.

I stared back. "Andy, I'll be lucky to leave this place remembering my own name."

After lunch, Kathy led us to a balding mid-fifties man in a blue button-down shirt and yellow tie. With a twinkle in his eyes, Dr. Quaytman shook my hand and then Andy's. His movements were quick and sharp. He had a sly, impish smile and an easy, irreverent manner. He reminded me of a pixie—like someone who wouldn't follow the rules just for the sake of following them.

"Let's go to my office," he said. "It's downstairs, outside The Retreat."

Off we went. Silently. Nobody, thank goodness, made small talk. We walked out the locked door of the west wing, down a flight of stairs, past the still-bustling cafeteria, then down a long corridor with yellow walls and a blue carpet. From there we followed Dr. Quaytman into his office, and the three of us sat.

I studied the wall-to-wall bookcases, scanning them to see what I could learn about Dr. Quaytman. There were a lot of art books, a scattering of Greek drama books, and one called *The Golden Cage*. That one sounded like it could be about The Retreat.

"Andy wrote a textbook with Ben Bernanke," I said, shamelessly name-dropping. I thought it would make good conversation and take the focus off me.

"Oh, really?" Dr. Quaytman said, looking toward Andy with interest.

He and Andy chatted for a few minutes about Bernanke and the state of the world economy. It was a familiar shtick for me, and I felt myself relaxing slightly as it went on.

This helped me to muster an answer when Dr. Quaytman asked me to tell him, in my "own words," what had brought me to The Retreat. I told him about my long history of depression. I told him about the reprieve of the previous four months while I underwent treatment for lymphoma, and then about my recent inability to function.

"I need ECT, don't I?" I asked, unprompted, at the end of my monologue.

"It's a possibility," Dr. Quaytman said softly.

"See?" I said to Andy. "I *told* you."

"He said it's a *possibility*," Andy said quickly.

He wasn't convincing anyone.

Two days later, at my first ECT appointment, I followed a Retreat nurse through a maze of corridors and into a waiting room with a television in the corner. The entire walk, all I could envision were bolts of lightning striking my head, passing from one temple to the other. How could the idea of volts of electricity shooting through your skull not be frightening?

After about a minute, a cheery nurse in dark blue scrubs called me in. I stood up and, somehow, walked toward her and through the door.

Inside, the ECT doctor asked me to lie down on the examining table. I was surprised not to have to change into a cheerfully patterned hospital gown but instead be allowed to climb onto the table in my cargo pants and T-shirt.

The doctor introduced the anesthesiologist to his right, and then Anita, the nurse, put an IV in my arm. I could feel my heart pounding against the wall of my chest and the vertebrae of my spine.

"Okay, I need to put this bite plate in your mouth," Anita said, showing me a flat blue plastic device. "This is to prevent you from clamping down on your tongue."

More visions of *One Flew Over the Cuckoo's Nest* raced through my helpless mind.

"Now I'm going to put these on your forehead," the doctor said, spreading some gel on both temples and holding up two round patches about two inches in diameter.

My entire body jittered with nervous energy. I was surprised the IV didn't fall out of my arm. I envisioned pulling it out and bolting from the room.

"Okay, take three deep breaths and begin counting down from ten," said the anesthesiologist, putting a plastic mask over my nose and mouth and pulling the rubber band around my head.

I was taught at an early age to do as I am told, with severe consequences if I did not. My parents were unrelenting in their demands, and I tried to accomplish every one of the tasks they set for me. I never stopped hoping that *this* accomplishment, *that* achievement, would be enough to convince them to love and accept me fully. Nothing I did mollified them. Nothing I did kept them from abusing me verbally and emotionally. But still I tried.

And now here I was lying on a table, hooked up to an electric current, doing exactly what the ECT doctor told me to do. *Ten*, I counted silently. I inhaled deeply. It worried me that I was still aware of everything around me. *Nine . . .* things were getting fuzzy. I felt my body loosen. *Eight . . .*

The next thing I knew, I was in a wheelchair being rolled back to The Retreat. I was famished. The only thing on my mind was finding something to eat.

"Can I walk?" I said to the nurse as soon as we passed through the locked Retreat door. "I'm fine."

And I was! I really was. Unlike Marianne, my only residual effects of the ECT were hunger pangs.

I underwent sessions Mondays, Wednesdays, and Fridays. By the second week, my energy level had rebounded, at least to the point where I was eager to get back to working out. Dr. Quaytman gave me permission to go to a nearby fitness center and exercise on non-ECT days.

Still, it was daunting to lie on a table and have a plastic mask strapped over my face. It was frightening to think in any detail about what was being done to my brain. It was terrifying to contemplate losing my memory. It might happen, I was told. It might not. It might happen after one treatment. After two. No one could say for sure.

I tried not to think about what it was that I was doing.

During treatment, small electric currents are passed through the brain to intentionally trigger a brief seizure. Anything over twenty seconds is good.

The way people at The Retreat spoke about their seizure lengths reminded me of those advertisements during baseball and football games for erectile dysfunction drugs. Tom, a fortyish Retreat resident, was practically an ECT stud. He regularly had seizures of ninety seconds, which meant he would need fewer than the standard eight to twelve treatments. My seizures only ran from twenty seconds to forty seconds, so I was slated for a total of nine treatments.

Six weeks and two days after dragging myself to The Retreat, I went home. When I walked into our kitchen, I thought about how bad I had felt the morning I walked out the door headed for The Retreat. I remembered dragging my feet as I followed Andy. I remembered hugging my pillow to my chest. I remembered looking at my three dogs for the last time until . . . until when, I didn't know.

As much as I could remember the images of myself that morning, I absolutely could not conjure the desolate despair and remember how bad I had *felt*. And for that I was very grateful.

A year later, my depression returned. That is, after all, how recurrent depression works.

When it happened, I went back to Sheppard Pratt for another regimen of ECT. This regimen of ECT also successfully treated my depression without any side effects.

4

IT HAD BEEN five years since my second stay at Sheppard Pratt. I was determined not to go back. So, even though I hate to travel, and I hate to be alone, as soon as I got home from CCP on the day I decided to quit, before even taking off my coat or saying hi to the dogs pouncing on me, I sat down at the kitchen table and googled "Australia Travel Agents." I emailed the first five that popped up on my screen.

Then I called Andy.

"I quit," I said.

"What?"

"I quit," I repeated. "I walked out the door and that's it. I'm never going back."

There was silence. Andy knew how difficult the last five weeks had been for me. He also knew what can happen if I'm not working or engaged in something substantial.

"Don't worry," I said. "I'm not going back to Sheppard Pratt. I'm going to Australia instead. In February, to see Bruce Springsteen's 2014 High Hopes Tour."

If he thought I was joking, he didn't say so. In fact, he didn't say anything at all.

"Do you want to go with me?" I asked. "To Australia?"

Andy was on sabbatical from his job as a finance professor at the Wharton School. If he wanted to, he could come.

"I know it's been rough at CCP," he said slowly. "I can see why you quit. And if you think going to Australia is what you want to do, you should do it. But I don't want to go. I don't like Bruce Springsteen and I don't like the stadium seats. They aren't good for my back."

What could I say? The man had had back surgery two years earlier.

I'd be going to Australia alone.

The next morning, I got a call from one of the travel agents.

"All I want to do in Australia," I told her, improvising my plans as I spoke, "is go to eight Bruce Springsteen concerts, work out, and write. All I care about is having access to good health clubs and having as few hassles as possible. I'd like you to arrange everything: my flights and my transportation from airports to hotels, as well as to and from concerts."

The fact that working out was on my Australia to-do list didn't surprise me. Exercise had become my one reliable relief from my spiraling moods.

However, I was taken aback to hear myself say that I wanted to write in Australia. I had given up on that pursuit. Whenever I tried to write, I heard a derisive voice in my head—usually my mother's. And for years, teaching had been enough to distract me from the desire to write. But driving back from CCP on the day I decided to quit, my instinct to survive had ramped itself up into a full-force operation. My will to live had pumped itself up to shove me away from the edge of the abyss. My will to be happy had felt deep and strong.

And all that, it seemed, had brought my desire to write back to life. I wanted to write. I wanted to be part of a conversation.

"Yes, I want to go to Bruce Springsteen concerts, work out, and write," I repeated to the travel agent.

Finally, I knew what I wanted to do.

Every day for a week, the travel agent called trying to sell me add-ons: Chef's tours, penguin tours, helicopter lunch trips. A jaunt to the Great Barrier Reef, kangaroo safaris, koala pettings. A day trip here, an afternoon trip there.

"No," I said, over and over. "Linda, even when I went to Paris with friends after college, I sat outside the Louvre while they went in. I don't like sightseeing and tourist things."

Eventually she gave up, and a week later a FedEx envelope arrived, my itinerary inside.

I didn't open it. I was not one bit curious. I had done what I needed to do, and now I wanted to forget that in three and a half months, I would be traveling alone to the other side of world.

I carried the unopened FedEx envelope upstairs to my desk and dropped it into the bottom drawer. *I'm doing it*, I thought as I pushed the drawer shut with my foot.

The deal was sealed. I was doing it.

You're doing what? a voice in my head demanded as I walked away. *Anne Abel, you are so pathetic you have nothing better to do than chase an aging rock star to the other side of the world.*

I was caught off guard by how hostile and derisive the voice was. In one sentence, it had attacked not only me but also an unsuspecting Bruce Springsteen.

Over the next few months, the voice became a continuous soundtrack running in a loop through my head—sometimes louder, sometimes softer, but always there. It was the first thing I heard in the morning and the last thing I heard as

I wrestled myself to sleep each night: *You are pathetic. You are pathetic. You are pathetic.*

Despite this, I didn't question my decision. I couldn't help but listen to the voice in my head, but instead of succumbing to its message, I simply lived with it. I had made my plan.

One night at the beginning of December, five weeks before my trip, I was lying in bed reading when Andy came into the room with a boarding pass for a business trip that he was taking the following morning. He carefully folded the boarding pass into thirds and slid it between the folds of his wallet. Then he pulled his suitcase from the closet and laid it open on the bed next to me. I watched him walk briskly back to the closet and choose a pair of pants and two button-down shirts. On the bed, with a packing board like they use at the Gap, he folded the pants and his shirts. Next, he folded a maroon V-neck sweater, then three pairs of white underpants and undershirts. Methodically, swiftly, Andy folded, packed, and filled his suitcase. He carefully put his shaving bag into the side mesh section of his carry-on roller bag. Then he set a pair of underpants and an undershirt on his dresser with a pair of socks to put on in the morning.

This was for a three-day trip! I tried to imagine his packing ritual if he were coming along with me to Australia.

And then I wondered why he wasn't going with me. For almost thirty-five years, Andy had been taking care of as many of my physical needs as humanly possible to try to make my sad life a little better, which meant often putting my needs above his. Why was he backing away now?

I got out of bed and stood in front of Andy in the middle of the room. Looking up at my six-foot-two-inch husband from my five-foot-four-inch vantage I said, "Andy, I don't understand. You would do anything for me. You always have. But now, even though you have a year off from teaching, you won't go with me to Australia. I just don't understand it."

Andy looked down at me. After a few long moments of silence, he said, "Okay. I'll go."

In an instant, a short and very cognizant instant, I imagined a mad dash of Andy following me from one airport and plane to the next, one alien airport to another. Onto a plane. Off a plane. Packing his suitcases. Unpacking his suitcases. Packing and unpacking again. And again. And again. I pictured him tired and haggard. Too tired and haggard to even think about his research papers. He would be miserable.

I'm going to have enough trouble worrying about myself and keeping myself afloat, I thought. *I don't want to have to be worrying about Andy being unhappy too.*

After this short and illuminating moment—during which neither of us moved a muscle—I said, "That's okay. I'll go alone."

Since booking my trip in October, even though I had been listening to the heckling voice in my head telling me I was pathetic, I'd somehow been able to keep myself from thinking about the fact that I was actually going to Australia in February. Now it was the first of January, and as I sat on the couch in the family room, I could no longer ignore the fact that in exactly four weeks I would be boarding a plane alone to travel to the other side of the world.

The clock was ticking. The countdown had begun. I was terrified.

To make matters worse, I could no longer remember what I liked about Bruce Springsteen. So, I sat down and googled him.

At the top of my screen appeared an NFL YouTube video titled, "2009 Half Time Show Super Bowl – Bruce Springsteen."

I had no expectations. I just clicked.

Bruce Springsteen appeared in the middle of the stage, surrounded by a football field full of cheering, clapping fans. He took the microphone out of its stand.

"Ladies and gentlemen," he said, holding the mic to his mouth. "For the next twelve minutes we're gonna bring the righteous and mighty power of the E Street Band into your beautiful home."

He pointed into the camera and implored, "Turn your television all the way up. And what I want to know . . ."

His face filled the entire screen as he stared directly into the camera.

Directly at me.

"Is there anybody *alive* out there?"

Pause.

"Is there anybody alive out there?" he asked again.

All of a sudden, I felt every single one of the cells in my body shaking awake. I felt every cell in my body filling with pulsing energy. Every cell within me was 100 percent in the moment. Every cell in my body was 100 percent having fun.

Bruce Springsteen held the microphone into the crowd for them to sing. Back and forth he went. He sang. They sang. It was a group effort. He leaned into the crowd; he made eye contact as he sang his lines. He was having a conversation with his audience. They were listening. They were answering. He loved us. We loved him. He led. We followed. And boy oh boy did he look like there was nothing else he would rather be doing than leading us, waking us up, and making each one of us feel alive.

Some of the songs I recognized; some I didn't. But I knew the smile, the energy, the enthusiasm of The Boss. The infiniteness of these Bruce Springsteen characteristics rendered my musical ignorance inconsequential; I was under the spell of the magic created by this man.

He shimmied backward into the bowels of the stage, took a running leap, landed on his knees, and slid down a ramp into the audience. The show was everyone and everything. It was Bruce Springsteen. It was the band. It was the audience. It was all of us. We were all in the moment, each and every moment. We were all having a good time. We. Were. All. Alive.

The stage darkened. Bruce Springsteen, flanked by Steve Van Zandt and Patti Scialfa, began singing, "I'm working on a dream . . ."

Other than the chorus, I couldn't make out the words. It didn't matter. I *felt* the words.

Yes, I thought. *Everyone is striving, everyone is trying. I am not alone.*

I heard Bruce Springsteen sing, "I'm working on a dream, and I feel that I will make it real someday."

A sense of peace flowed through me.

The stage brightened. The introspectiveness of the previous song was a distant memory. The band was wild, the crowd was wild. Bruce Springsteen flung his guitar around his body three times.

He looked into the camera and bellowed, "I'm going to Disney Land."

The stage went dark.

I stood there in my family room looking at the quiet screen. Chills were running through me. Goose bumps were popping on my arms. Boy oh boy, did I feel alive.

I tapped the screen of my computer and watched the twelve-minute video again. And again and again and again. Then one last time before I went to sleep. Doing so, I remembered with every ounce of my being *why* I liked Bruce Springsteen—why the day I quit CCP, intuitively, in my desperation to keep myself from falling into the abyss, even though I hate to travel and I hate to be alone, I'd decided to go to Australia to follow Bruce Springsteen.

5

THE LAST DAY of anything is difficult for me. The last day before my children go home after visiting me and Andy. The last day before *I* leave after visiting *them*.

Richard, my oldest son, long ago dubbed these final countdowns the Cavern of Sorrow and our last dinners together the Last Supper. As I counted down the days until my departure for Australia, I grew terrified of the Cavern of Sorrow. The day when I would look at the clock and say to myself, "Tomorrow at this time, you won't be here. Tomorrow at this time, you will be all alone."

But an unexpected phone call from my friend Deborah spared me this agony.

"Anne, they're predicting snow on Saturday," she said when she called. "You'd better change your flight to LA and go out on Friday, so you don't miss your connection."

I was terrified of my upcoming trip. I didn't want to go to Australia, but I was determined to go. This was the way I had decided to fight off my depression. If I didn't go on this trip, the alternatives were bleak. So no snowstorm was going to stop me. I needed to change my flight to LA. Time was of the essence. I had a mission.

I hung up with Deborah and found my Australia itinerary in my desk drawer, where it had been since I had received it in October. I picked up the phone and called USAir.

"I'm sorry," the USAir woman said, "we don't show any weather in our system. I'm going to have to charge you a change fee."

I had not bothered to confirm Deborah's weather forecast before making the call and I did not feel like arguing with the agent. "That's fine," I said.

I was feeling the way I imagine nondepressed people feel when they are doing regular, normal things. I was sitting up straight. I was listening to the USAir woman clicking away, doing whatever it is airline people do.

"Yeah," I said as she clicked, "I'm going to Australia to see Bruce Springsteen."

"Really?" she said, dropping her more formal airline voice. "I'm from New Jersey."

"Where are you now?" I was curious.

"I'm in Texas. You know, my sister still lives in New Jersey, and once she went to a Bruce Springsteen concert."

"Really? When?"

"Oh, decades ago. But she still talks about it."

"Yeah, he's amazing," I gushed. "I didn't know who he was eighteen months ago, and now look at me. I'm going all the way to Australia by myself to see him, even though I hate to travel and I hate to be alone."

"Just a minute—let me put you on hold," she said abruptly. "I'll be right back."

I didn't know why she was putting me on hold, but I wasn't annoyed.

"Okay, I'm back," she said when she returned to the phone a few minutes later. "I just spoke to my manager. She's a Bruce Springsteen fan too. We're going to waive the change fee."

I thanked the USAir woman in Texas as chills ran through me.

Just by saying, "Bruce Springsteen," I had become a link in a chain reaching from Philadelphia to Texas by way of New Jersey.

6

TWO DAYS LATER, it was time to go. For the month leading up to this day, I had felt more and more dread. I was terrified of being alone for so long, so far from home. As someone who suffers from depression, I wasn't anticipating that the trip would be "fun"; I was just hoping it would keep me out of the abyss, and that it would be better than ECT.

Andy put my two oversize suitcases in the trunk. Suddenly, I wasn't nervous or anxious, because I now had a mission: *Be at the airport in time for my 12:10 p.m. flight to Los Angeles.*

As Andy and I headed toward the airport, he uncharacteristically took his eyes off the snow-covered hill in front of him and turned toward me. "I'm going to get your car washed while you're away," he said. "I'm even going to have it detailed. You won't recognize it when you get home."

I looked at him and smiled. I knew it was something he felt he could do for me even while I was away. I also knew he understood me well enough to know that talking about my future return might distract me from my present departure.

We kissed goodbye curbside at Philadelphia International Airport. I checked my black Tumi suitcases and walked through the sliding glass doors into the terminal. I didn't think about being alone for the next twenty-six days in a foreign country on the other side of the world. I thought only about following the arrows to security and finding my departure gate. I was putting one foot in front of the other. But not as I do when I am feeling slow, lethargic, and depressed. Here, in the airport, I had a destination. I had a goal. One foot in front of the other, I stepped—through security, then down the windowed concourse toward my gate.

I'm doing it, I thought. *I'm on my way. I'm all alone, and nothing bad has happened.*

I felt fine. I wasn't frightened. I was alone and I didn't feel bad. In fact, I felt buoyant.

An hour later, I boarded the plane. As I settled into my seat, I remembered what one of my teachers had said before I went to Israel at the age of sixteen: "You must begin speaking Hebrew the moment you land in Ben Gurion Airport. You have to jump in and do it. If you wait, you'll lose your courage and never do it."

I pulled out my computer and began to write. I didn't want to wait and lose my courage. I began an email to twelve people—family members, friends, and acquaintances—who had asked me to write and let them know about my trip. With their assurances that they *wanted* to hear from me, the critical voice in my head—my mother's voice telling me I had nothing worth saying—disappeared. These twelve people wanted to hear what I was seeing, doing, and feeling. I imagined them looking forward to my emails. My fingers began dancing across the keyboard.

When the flight attendant announced it was time to put away electronic devices, I looked out the window at the terminal. I had no critical thoughts cycling through my head. My mother's voice remained quiet. I was managing, and managing quite well. All I had to do was keep doing what I was doing.

For the next twenty-six days, all I had to do was go to eight Bruce Springsteen concerts, work out, and write. Then I would be back home. Mission accomplished.

7

WHEN THE Qantas check-in agent at LAX asked me if I wanted to be first or last to board the flight to Melbourne, I remembered that not only was I traveling first class, I was also traveling as a Qantas White Glove VIP. Linda, the travel agent, had convinced me that if I did not like hassles, White Glove VIP was the way to go.

It sounded good to me. First class, even with White Glove VIP, was a lot less expensive than a return visit to The Retreat at Sheppard Pratt.

"Boarding first would be great," I said.

Immediately, a blonde flight attendant took my red Longchamp totes and led me to my seat.

"What brings you to Australia?" she asked.

"I'm going to see eight Bruce Springsteen concerts," I said, still standing. As soon as I said the words, I felt embarrassed. Would she think I was pathetic because I had nothing better to do with my life than to chase an aging rock star across the world?

"Are you . . . meeting someone there?" she asked, not looking at all aghast but rather excited.

"For better or worse, I'm going alone," I admitted.

"Oh my, good for you," she said. "I'm so impressed. You're very brave. I've never met anyone who's done something like that. I think it's remarkable."

My eyes popped open in surprise at her enthusiastic response. She sounded as if she were talking to some kind of superstar—*me*.

"The shows will be terrific," she said. "I saw him in Melbourne last year." She leaned in closer. "You know, he flew with me on this very flight. In the same cabin you have now."

I looked at the cabin. It was hard to imagine Bruce Springsteen in this very spot where I was about to spend sixteen hours. Just as it is difficult for students to imagine their teachers anywhere but in the classroom, it was hard for me to imagine Bruce Springsteen anywhere but onstage.

"This year," the flight attendant said, "he and his entourage are traveling on a private jet."

It was my turn to lean toward her. "Did you speak to him?"

"Oh yes," she said. "He is *so* kind. He asked me about my job, about my life. He seemed sincerely interested. It was remarkable. *He's* quite remarkable, isn't he?"

"If I didn't think so, I wouldn't be doing this," I said.

"I really think it's wonderful what you're doing," she said again, smiling.

I tried to see myself through the eyes of this Qantas flight attendant. As someone *remarkable* in my own right. What was remarkable to me was the wide net of kindness cast by Bruce Springsteen. Once again, just by saying I was going to Australia to see him, I'd opened the door for a fellow fan to treat me as if I were special just for being me. And for the briefest of moments, I'd caught a glimmer of myself as someone doing something brave and wonderful.

I sat basking in that feeling for a while. Then I heard the pilot say, "We're number one for takeoff," so I clicked my seat belt and nestled into my plush cabin seat.

The plane rushed forward, the wheels skimming against the runway and then rumbling as they lifted, as we in our aluminum tube lifted—hurtling forward, hurtling up. The sixteen-hour countdown had begun. I felt my adrenaline surge, as if I were responsible for navigating this speeding bullet toward Melbourne.

You're doing it, I thought. *You are on your way. Good for you!*

Big deal, I heard my mother's voice say. *You got yourself on a plane, where you'll be alone, disconnected from everyone you know, for sixteen hours. And for what?*

When the cabin lights dimmed, I managed to drift off to sleep. Sometime later, my eyes popped open. I lifted the window shade. Sunshine streamed in and lit up my space. When I had lowered the shade what seemed like moments earlier, there had been nothing but blackness.

I looked at my watch and was shocked to see I had been asleep for eight hours. Eight hours! I was halfway there already.

When the pilot announced that we were beginning our descent into Melbourne, I got up to use the lavatory one last time. Minutes later, as I pushed the paper towel into the trash bin with one hand and unlatched the lavatory door with the other, I caught a glimpse of myself in the lavatory mirror. I turned to face my reflection.

I did not see the drab, brown-haired woman with mousy eyes and downturned lips that I usually saw. Instead, I saw a woman with chicly short brown hair and hazel eyes. A look of wonder spread across my face as I stared at this person who was staring back at me. The muted pulsing of the Qantas air jets moved in soft waves from the soles of my feet up through my calves, my torso, my neck, and my brain. I felt a fluttering inside me. I realized I was excited.

I looked deep into my reflection's eyes. "You can do this. You are doing this. Anne Abel is going to Australia to see eight Bruce Springsteen concerts."

I went back to my seat and gazed out the window at the cotton-ball clouds and dazzling blue sky. I pictured Bruce Springsteen looking at me from high above and smiling. A sense of awe came over me and I thought, *Because of this man Bruce Springsteen, a man who doesn't even know I exist, I, Anne Abel, am about to land in Melbourne, Australia.* For the first time in three and a half months since I'd quit CCP, the voice in my head was *not* telling me I was pathetic for chasing an aging rock star across the world. My mind was not mutilating itself.

On the contrary, it was cheering me on.

As I stared at the vast, infinite beyond outside my window, the voice in my head repeated its new mantra: *You can do this. You* are *doing this.*

8

I HAD NO idea where I was going when I stepped off the plane in Melbourne. No idea at all. Just that I was *going*. My right foot was still planted in the Qantas jumbo jet and my left foot had just touched down on the jetway when I heard a man say authoritatively, "Anne Abel."

I turned my head and saw a mid-thirties, slightly balding man in khaki pants and a blue polo shirt with the Qantas logo of a leaping white kangaroo surrounded by a red airplane wing.

"I'm Ben, your VIP White Glove escort," he said.

Well, this was a surprise. When the travel agent had told me that being a VIP White Glove passenger would eliminate hassles, I had taken her word for it without asking for any details. I'd been willing to pay for anything that might make my trip easier. Apparently, that included an escort.

"I'm here to guide you through immigration and customs and take you to the gate for your flight to Adelaide," Ben said. Before I could say anything, he lifted the straps of my two red totes from my shoulders and gestured me forward.

"Wait, what!?" I said. "Melbourne is not my final destination? I have to get on another plane now?"

In the weeks and months leading up to the trip, I had never thought past the daunting sixteen-hour flight. I knew I was attending two concerts in Melbourne. I had assumed they would be my first two concerts after I landed in Australia.

I'd been wrong.

I had not paced myself for a layover. I had purposely not gone over my itinerary because knowing the details would have made the trip seem more real and triggered my dread and fear of being alone for so long, so far away.

A cacophony of voices exploded in my head: *You're irresponsible. You're careless. No one goes on a trip without knowing where they're going. What were you thinking?*

I wanted to drop to the shiny, white-tiled floor and collapse into a heap. I wanted to disappear into nothingness.

I concentrated on my footsteps and coordinated them with my breathing, simulating a workout.

"How long is the flight to Adelaide?" I asked Ben, trying to sound casual and curious.

"It's eighty minutes," he said. "It's three hundred kilometers, about two hundred miles, northwest of Melbourne."

I knew that Philadelphia is about three hundred miles from Boston, where I grew up. So that gave me context, if not comfort, about the next leg of my trip.

"No worries," Ben said in his Australian accent, "you only lose fifty minutes because Adelaide is in a time zone that's thirty minutes behind Melbourne."

I had never heard of a thirty-minute time zone differentiation. I did know that China—which is the same size geographically as the continental United States—has only one time zone. Lawmakers do not care if farmers west of Beijing, far from the cities, wake with the dawn at 10:00 a.m. and toil till dusk arrives at midnight. I wondered if Australia's thirty-minute time zone meant that the country's politicians were more caring about their citizens' daily lives.

Ben and I did not slow our gait until we got to the front of an immigration and customs line. Ben smiled at the couple first in line, and, without being rude or obnoxious but instead seeming somehow solicitous of them, he paused their approach to the customs window and passed me by in front of them. At the customs window, he smiled at the agent, stepped aside, and motioned me forward.

I handed my passport to the agent and smiled weakly. He flipped through the blue pages. When he came to an empty one, he placed it flat on the counter between us. *Thwack.* He stamped his seal unequivocally in the middle of the page.

"Welcome to Australia," he said, his lilting Australian accent making his words sound as welcoming as his smiling face.

"You have two hours before you need to be at the gate for your next flight," Ben said as he ushered me away from the customs window. "Is there anything you need or want to do before then?"

I shook my head. "I think I'm all set."

"No worries. We'll be off to your gate."

"What's your job?" I heard myself ask.

"To escort first-class passengers," he said obligingly, though he clearly thought the job was self-explanatory.

I was still wearing the heavy black-and-gray-striped wool sweater I had put on in 14-degree weather in Philadelphia. As we walked, I was getting hotter and hotter. I tried, unsuccessfully, to ignore my discomfort by disconnecting my mind from my body.

"I need to stop a minute," I finally said. "I need to take this off."

"No worries," Ben said. "We have plenty of time. The summer heat wave we're having has been tripping up everyone, especially with the Australian Open and all."

He put down one of my totes so I could stuff my sweater into it.

"Yeah," he said as I stood up. "It was pretty interesting with the tennis players here just a little while ago."

"Who did you escort?" I asked, wide-eyed.

"Serena Williams," he said, looking excited. "She had ten pieces of luggage and no tennis rackets. That was something."

I was surprised that he seemed so regular, so unpretentious. I would have expected someone who escorted VIP passengers to be guarded and circumspect.

"Was she nice?" I asked.

"Oh yes, very nice," he said. "So, why are you going to Adelaide?"

I was embarrassed to say. I was glad that I was wearing a wedding band, so he would know that at least there was one person in this vast, lonely world to whom I was connected.

"I'm going to see Bruce Springsteen," I said, unable to think of an answer other than the truth.

He beamed. "A couple of the girls who work here escorted him last year. They were so excited beforehand. And they were even more excited afterward, because they said he was really nice."

I was relieved to hear that the aging rock star I was following across the world was a decent human being.

9

I BOARDED THE not-so-jumbo Qantas jet for the eighty-minute flight to Adelaide. I am a newspaper junkie. At home I read four papers every morning: *The New York Times*, *The Wall Street Journal*, *USA Today*, and *The Philadelphia Inquirer*. When I travel, I love to read the local papers. I scan the news-story headlines and read every story in the Arts section. Then I turn to the real estate and classified listings.

So, when the flight attendant offered me a selection of reading materials before we took off, I eagerly pulled a newspaper from the pile.

I opened *The Australian*, "The National Newspaper," to the Arts section. In the lower corner of the middle inside page was the headline "Live Music." On that page was a review by Sean Sennett of the concert Bruce Springsteen and the E Street Band had performed the previous night in Perth.

"Bruce Springsteen returns to Australia to deliver what really is the greatest rock 'n' roll show on earth," Sennett wrote.

The fine hairs on my arms stood up. It felt as if butterflies were fluttering within me. I could feel my heart quickening.

"There are no pyrotechnics or sleights of hand. A show built on the intensity of one man's physical presence and a songbook stretching across his entire adult life."

I paused and looked up from the newspaper and out the window. The plane was still motionless on the tarmac.

Not me. I was soaring.

"The musicians bring to life Springsteen's vision of fusing rock, folk, and gospel, with a large dose of soul, into a revue that clocks in at more than three hours . . . An important artist of his or any generation, Springsteen remains the most vital front man of the modern era."

I had never thought about Bruce Springsteen's place in the continuum of music genres or about his place in history. Music and, more generally, fun, were not things I experienced growing up or even as an adult. Bruce Springsteen was the first and only musician I had not only seen live but even listened to. I had just been caught up in his energy, his enthusiasm, his humanity, and his fun. After reading the review, I had so much more to work with in thinking about Springsteen and exactly why I, along with so many others, liked him so much.

When the plane began its descent into Adelaide, my mood descended too.

You are so naive and gullible to be excited about that review, I heard my mother's voice say. *Of course Sean Sennett wrote a good review of the concert. He's a* nobody. *If he didn't write a good review, he'd be sitting in the back row with no press perks.*

I slumped forward in my seat and rested my head in my hands. Reading the review, I had felt as if were soaring. Now, I felt like a naive, gullible loser.

I took a deep breath and bolstered myself. *On the other hand*, I heard my own soft voice saying, *it is Sean Sennett's artistic license to write what he wants and* my *job as the reader to consider the source. And I have to assume that* The Australian *doesn't want to lose its credibility by having self-serving, dishonest writers.*

Despite my best efforts to combat my mother's words, I felt my mood and my energy continuing to spiral downward during the fifteen-minute ride from the airport to the hotel. I felt like a pathetic loser for believing what Sean Sennett had written.

By the time I arrived at the hotel, my mood was lower than it had been in days.

10

I STOOD AT the front desk at the InterContinental Adelaide facing Siddharta, a lean, mid-thirties Indian man, and watched him copy information from my passport onto a hotel form. I looked at the wall clock behind him. It was seven o'clock, Monday evening. I was more jet-lagged than I could calculate. I had not showered or worked out or changed my clothes or talked to anyone at home since Saturday afternoon. I was a wreck. I was wasted. It took everything I had to keep myself from keeling over as Siddharta checked me in.

"You're all set," he finally said, handing me my passport and smiling.

He exuded competence and compassion, two of my favorite traits.

"Do you think you could sign me into the hotel internet?" I asked. Making the request, I felt totally incompetent, but the thought of going to my room and syncing my four mobile devices—iPhone, international flip phone, iPad, and laptop—to the hotel's Wi-Fi was overwhelming.

"Of course," Siddharta said.

I dug my devices out and laid them on the counter between us, then watched as he moved deliberately from one to the other.

"You're all set," he said when he was done. "Is there anything else I can help you with before you go upstairs?"

"No, thank you," I said gratefully. I picked up my totes and turned to follow the valet to my room. Then I stopped and turned around again. "I have my workout clothes in this tote," I said. "Would it be okay if the valet takes my suitcases to my room, and I find the fitness center and work out?"

"Of course," he said. "Absolutely. Whatever you prefer." He caught the valet's attention. "Will you show her to the fitness center?"

The valet nodded and gestured for me to follow him.

One of the problems of my depression is that when I am coming down with the flu or a virus and feeling slow and lethargic and overall crummy, I always assume it is my mental state that is the cause. So, every day, I push myself to get on my bike and work out. I cannot give in to my body. If I were to stop every time I felt sluggish at the beginning of my workout, I would never even make it to ten minutes. So, each day, I get on my bike and focus my mind on the countdown and pedaling.

On the days when I actually am getting sick, it becomes increasingly clear as I pedal that I cannot sustain the effort. Begrudgingly, I tap the console on the bike and lower the level. It bothers me to do this. I feel as if I am mentally weak. I feel as if I am giving in and sliding down the slippery slope to becoming a sloth. A sloth who no longer works out. A sloth who cannot work out to achieve even a few moments of relief from the heaviness that weighs on me every moment I am awake. It is terrifying to me that I might lose the only way I know how to fight my depression. So, even as my body is weakening from whatever virus or bacteria has invaded me, my mind pushes me to carry on physically as best as I can. It's actually a relief when I find out that I have a physical ailment. Only then does the negative voice in my head stop telling me that I am on my way to becoming a sloth.

Trudging behind the valet, feeling horrible physically and mentally, I didn't know if I should hope I had some kind of flu or if I was just worn out from my travels and needed a workout boost or if I was becoming deeply depressed. Some people might unpack and shower and go to the bar for a drink or the restaurant for dinner when they arrive at their destination after a long trip. Some people might disregard travel advice on beating jet lag and crawl into bed. But I needed to work out. I needed to change the channel running though my head from a commercial-free barrage of negative self-reflections to one with a buoyant flow of hopeful possibilities—or, at the very least, silence.

Repeatedly, I had told Linda that the only hotel amenity about which I cared was the fitness center. I had never followed through to make sure she had taken these critical instructions seriously. Now, as I pushed open the door of the InterContinental's fitness center, my fate at stake, I was anxious about what I would find.

I stepped into the room and saw two upright bikes and two recumbent bikes, the latter being what I ride at home. I let out a full-bodied sigh of relief. In under one hour, if I could just get through this workout, I was going to be a new person. A better person.

As I approached the recumbent bikes, however, I saw that each bike was missing a pedal—and I felt the last remnants of energy inside me drain out.

I really needed my fix of aerobic exertion, and I needed it now. I walked over to the upright bikes. I had not sat on an upright bike in decades. I cringed as I imagined how my butt would feel after an hour on one of them. But I was desperate, so I did what any professional workout person would do: I mounted the upright bike and began pedaling. I kept pushing the level up until I felt my hamstrings and calves quiver. I put on my headphones and tapped on *Wrecking Ball*.

Minutes after I began pedaling, I felt the seat gouging into my butt. I wanted to stop. I wanted to tumble to the floor and curl into a ball. But that was not an option. I kept going.

My butt hurt, my crotch hurt, my legs hurt. I was huffing like a pack-a-day smoker. One minute, another, one minute, another.

Sixty painful minutes later, I was done. I had accomplished what I'd set out to do. I felt energized. I felt great.

11

I WOKE UP at seven the next morning and *jumped* out of bed. Almost twelve hours had passed since I'd worked out, but it seemed as if the endorphins were still surging. I felt nothing like the downtrodden, travel-weary me who had arrived at the InterContinental the previous evening. I felt nothing like the me who wakes up each morning with a thud and then begins my trudge, one heavy step followed by another, through the day. Instead of a heavy dread in the pit of my stomach, I felt an open lightness throughout my whole body. I was curious about what was waiting for me when I walked out the door of my room, headed for a new fitness center—one with working recumbent bikes, located a mere five-minute walk from the hotel.

I put on my Wrecking Ball T-shirt. My lips turned into a smile. A bevy of butterflies fluttered through me. I had been so busy thinking about how good I felt—except for my sore butt—that I had forgotten that tonight was my first concert. No wonder I had woken up with coursing endorphins!

As I found my way back from the fitness center to the hotel two hours later, I saw more and more people wearing Bruce Springsteen T-shirts headed in the same direction I was. I seemed to be the only one who was not part of a pair or a cluster in this thickening crowd of Springsteen fans.

When I got to the hotel, I stopped and watched as the steady advance of fans disappeared through the doors into the lobby.

"Is Bruce Springsteen staying here?" I asked a forty-something man who had paused beside me. He was wearing the same gray Wrecking Ball T-shirt that I was wearing.

"My buddy is an Uber driver," he said. "One of his passengers said this is where Bruce is probably staying because it's the nicest hotel in Adelaide. I like your T-shirt," he added quickly before running after his friends.

I'd told the travel agent repeatedly during our conversations, "If I do anything other than go to concerts, work out, and write, it will be to sit in the hotel lobby and be a fly on the wall." It had never occurred to me that I might be sharing a lobby with Bruce Springsteen. Being a fly on the wall suddenly seemed a lot grander.

I walked inside and up three shallow stairs to the marble lobby. The entire circumference of the space was lined three people deep with hushed fans wearing Bruce Springsteen T-shirts. They were all aiming their smart phones toward the bank of elevators.

I started to head across the lobby toward Siddharta—Sid, he'd said I could call him—who was standing behind the concierge desk.

"Excuse me, ma'am," a man wearing khaki pants and a blue InterContinental polo shirt said, stopping me. "You have to stand against the wall with the other fans."

"I'm staying here," I said.

"I'm so sorry," he said, stepping back. "I saw your T-shirt and assumed . . ."

"No worries," I said with a smile. "Is Bruce Springsteen staying here?"

"I hope you enjoy your stay with us," he said, as if I had not asked the question.

I walked over to Sid.

"Is Bruce Springsteen staying here?" I asked as soon as his eyes met mine.

"Mrs. Abel," he greeted me with a smile. "How was your workout?"

"It was great. Thank you. Is Bruce Springsteen staying here?"

"If there is anything else I can help you with, please let me know."

On the fly, I came up with a ploy to help me find out what was going on. "Would you help me log in to my devices again, please?"

"Of course," Sid said.

As he worked, I watched a hotel security guard stop a man and a woman in Wrecking Ball T-shirts as they entered the lobby. "You're welcome to come in and stand to the side here," he said. "But please don't approach any hotel guests. If you do, we'll have to ask you to leave."

Most of my knowledge about fans was from movies and television. I had a vision of them reaching and screaming for autographs and, these days, selfies. But I did not think of myself as that kind of fan. I was a fly-on-the wall fan. A fan who just wanted to observe.

"So, tell me," I said to Sid, who was now on device number two. "I just heard a hotel security guard tell some fans coming into the lobby that they shouldn't approach any hotel guests—but no one said that to me. Not that I'm thinking of doing that, but . . ."

"Yes, that's our policy for people who are not staying with us," he explained. "Before we initiated this policy, we had some situations that got out of control. We don't want to spoil anyone's fun, but the comfort and safety of our guests—celebrities and noncelebrities—are top priority for us. We leave it to the discretion of our guests how to behave, and it's never been a problem."

I saw Sid look at a hotel security guard across the lobby by the elevators. Their eyes met. The guard nodded. Sid handed me my iPhone and iPad, which he had already hooked up, and then his eyes did a sweep of the room. He put down my international flip phone on the desk and, with his hands still on it, scanned the whole room again. I looked down at his hands and saw that they were shaking. I began to feel nervous myself.

"How 'bout if I take the two you haven't done yet and go to the banquette and see if I can do them myself?" I asked. I'd just realized the banquette would be a much better place for seeing whatever was going to happen next than my spot at the concierge desk was.

"Yes." Sid looked at me distractedly for a moment, as if he had forgotten I was there. "That sounds like a grand idea."

I turned and walked to the banquette, where I sat down, opened my laptop, and pretended to try to connect it. Meanwhile, I quietly shifted my focus back to the security guard and Sid.

The elevator door opened and two thirty-something men, dressed in black and carrying black guitar cases, stepped out and began walking across the lobby. Without hesitation, without a moment of thought—and abandoning my notion of myself as a fan who only wanted to admire and observe from a distance—I dropped my laptop on the banquette and ran toward the two men.

"Are you with the E Street Band?" I asked.

"Don't we wish," one of them said in an accent I did not recognize. "We're with a band from Italy."

I looked over at Sid as the two men walked away. He smiled. I wondered if he was amused that I had traveled across the world to see Bruce Springsteen and the E Street Band but did not know the difference between them and an unknown Italian band.

My brush with the Italian band members had gotten my adrenaline going. Maybe they were the warm-up band for tonight's concert. I sat, alert, on the banquette and waited. I was not sure what I thought I would see. The ring of Bruce Springsteen fans along the lobby wall was now six people deep.

My eyes circled the lobby. At the elevator, I saw a Black man with curly, shoulder-length hair who was carrying a black guitar case. He looked familiar. He looked like the E Street Band's saxophonist. I wondered if the guitar case was a decoy. I did not remember his name, but I did know that he was Clarence Clemons's nephew. Stepping out of the elevator, he looked much less dramatic and younger and smaller than he did onstage.

I jumped up and ran over to him. "I came all the way from Philadelphia, Pennsylvania, to see you and Bruce Springsteen," I said.

He stopped and looked over his shoulder at the elevators behind him. Then he looked back at me.

"I didn't know who Bruce Springsteen was eighteen months ago. Now I like him for so many reasons. Besides his music, I like that he is about my age and has so much energy," I said, holding his gaze. "Can I please have my picture taken with you?"

He looked disconcerted, surprised. Maybe he had not expected to be accosted by a fan. Maybe he did not know that hotel rules allowed guests to use their own judgment about approaching celebrities.

From somewhere behind me I heard someone say, "Philadelphia, Pennsylvania."

I did not turn around. I kept my eyes on the young saxophonist.

"Okay," he said, sounding defeated.

I slid my hands into the pocket of my pants and pulled out my iPhone. I had no idea how to use the camera function. Even if I had known, I was too shaky to do it.

"You probably know better than I do how to do this," I said, handing my iPhone to a twenty-something man in a Bruce Springsteen T-shirt who was standing behind us.

I took my place beside the saxophonist. He put his arm around me and rested his hand on my shoulder. I grinned.

"Got it," the photographer said.

"Thank you so much," I said to the saxophonist as he picked up his guitar case.

From the crowd I heard someone shout, "Tom Morello!"

I ran to the man the crowd was pointing at. He was dressed in black and wearing a brown leather cowboy hat.

"Can I please have my picture taken with you?" I asked, darting in front of the guitarist so he was forced to stop.

"Okay, but I have only thirty seconds," he said, not seeming surprised by my request.

"Thank you so much," I said.

Then I remembered my "I ♥ Bruce Springsteen" canvas tote on the banquette.

"Wait! Please, you have to wait until I get my 'I love Bruce Springsteen' bag that a friend gave me. It's right over there." I pointed toward the banquette, already running in that direction.

I was in the moment. I was focused on getting myself a perfect picture with Tom Morello. I was so in the moment that I did not think about making Tom Morello wait, even after he had given me a thirty-second window. But wait he did. By the time I ran back to him, Sid was standing beside him, waiting for me, also.

"If you give me your phone, I will take the picture for you," Sid said, holding out his hand and smiling.

I took my place beside Tom Morello, who put his arm around me.

Sid took not one photograph but three. Tap, tap, tap. Then I thanked Tom Morello, and he went on his way.

I looked at Sid, who was standing beside me, still holding my iPhone. "Have you ever seen Bruce Springsteen up close and personal?" he asked. "Or maybe I should ask, how many times have you seen Bruce Springsteen up close?"

Between the adrenaline and all the running around I'd just done, it took me some time to catch my breath. "No," I managed to say, finally. "I've never seen him up close."

I walked with Sid back to the concierge desk. When we got there, I collapsed onto it, my arms stretched across the desk, and rested my head on my arms.

"So, this made your day?" Sid asked.

I lifted my head and looked at him. My heart was still pounding. "After this I don't think I *want* to meet Bruce Springsteen. I don't think my heart could take it. It already feels like it's maxed out from meeting Jake Clemons and Tom Morello." I was surprised that I had spontaneously retrieved Jake Clemons's name from my memory bank.

Sid nodded.

"Actually," I said, after a quick scene of me running up to Bruce Springsteen as I had done with Jake Clemmons and Tom Morello played in my head, "I wouldn't want to meet Bruce Springsteen in person because I don't know what I would say to him. There's so much I would want to tell him about how he has helped me. I wouldn't know where to begin."

I looked at Sid, waiting for him to respond. But he was not looking at me. He was looking around the lobby as if he were searching for someone. His phone rang. He picked it up, listened for a minute, and then hung up.

"Well," he said, looking me in the eyes, "you will have more time to think about what you want to say to him. He's leaving right now through the garage downstairs. But don't worry, we'll try to get you a photo with him before you leave tomorrow."

I stared back at Sid and imagined Bruce Springsteen slipping out through the garage at that very moment. I was not disappointed. Clearly, I was not ready to meet the man.

I had perched myself on the lobby banquette, planning to be a fly on the wall. Instead, in the moment I saw his band members enter the lobby, it had been as if someone had snatched the thinking, self-conscious me and replaced her with one who was controlled only by emotions and feelings—emotions and feelings that until that moment I had never experienced. I hadn't concerned myself with what people would think about me. I hadn't questioned my motives. I hadn't worried about anything. Instead, I'd *reveled*.

And I was still reveling, though I was not even sure what, exactly, I was reveling in. My heart and soul were simply in the moment. Reveling.

12

AFTER THE excitement of being a photo-seeking fangirl, I remained in the lobby and let my heart rate return to its customary slow rate. With only two hours remaining until I had to leave for the concert, I decided to go outside and let the February heat wave warm me up.

I joined the quiet, orderly exodus of my fellow fans. It was as if we had all received the memo at once that Bruce Springsteen had left the building.

Outside, the warm air swaddled me. I closed my eyes and let my body soak and luxuriate fully in the soothing comfort of the late-afternoon sun. There was nowhere else I wanted to be. There was nothing else I wanted to be doing.

Then, from behind me, I heard a woman's gravelly voice, perhaps a voice made this way by age, ask: "Do you like my dress?"

There was a pause.

I did not turn around. I did not move.

"Yeah," I heard a man say.

From his voice, I imagined the man was a generation or so younger than the woman.

"I got it down in the square just now when I went to get my grandson's T-shirt," the woman said in a breezy voice, as if the man had indicated he wanted to know more. Or maybe she simply wasn't good at interpreting social cues.

She sounded so animated, I decided that she was just happy. Happy that she was going to see her grandson. Happy that she had found herself a new dress. I imagined that she did not care if her companion wanted to hear what she had to say or not. I imagined her being so happy, she just wanted to hear herself say the words out loud so she could hear them.

As much as I wanted to see the characters in the play that was going on behind me, I did not turn around. I did not want to give up my invisibility.

"I think I'm gonna head out," the man said.

"Okay, I'll see you later," the woman said, not sounding disappointed.

I looked over my shoulder and saw a forty-something man, dressed in black and carrying a black guitar case, hurrying away. The woman was standing with her back toward me. We were so close that if I had reached behind me, I could have tapped her on the shoulder. She had straight, shiny shoulder-length black hair and was wearing a boxy black mid-calf linen dress with a black cardigan.

I turned toward her. "*I* like your dress."

I spoke tentatively. I did not want to sound declarative or bossy. After all, she had not asked my opinion.

The woman turned around and looked at me. "You do?" she asked, reaching for a tuft of material and pulling it out as if she were about to curtsy.

"Yes, I do."

It was not a dress to like or not like. It was a dress that did not call attention to the wearer. It would have looked good on a big person trying to hide her body or a smaller person who wanted to be comfortable. Like me, this woman was about five foot four inches, and though she was bigger boned than me, she was also slender. She looked like she could have been the mother of one of my kids' friends. She looked like she could have been one of my friends.

I wasn't sure why I was reaching out to her. Perhaps because I was intrigued by this grandmother who sounded so happy to have found a new dress and so happy to have been shopping for her grandson.

"I like your sweater too," I said.

"You do?" she repeated, letting the side of her dress fall from her hand and looking down at her cardigan.

"Yes. Did you get it with the dress?" I wanted to keep the conversation going.

"No—I know it looks like I did, but I brought it from home. It's Eileen Fisher."

"That's amazing," I said, smiling and nodding in knowing acknowledgment.

The woman looked at me. She seemed as interested as I was in continuing the conversation.

"I heard you mention your grandson. How old is he?" I asked, but what I was thinking about was the man in black with a black guitar case who she'd been talking to a few minutes earlier. I suspected she was not just another hotel guest hoping to glimpse Bruce Springsteen. So I'd chosen not to ask her the obvious question, "What are you doing in Adelaide?" I realized that if I asked this and she was someone of note, it would lead to a short and not very interesting conversation. She would be famous. I would not be famous. And after a few minutes of chatter, she would be off. So I'd decided to focus on her being a grandmother.

I was not yet a grandmother. But from friends and acquaintances, and in waiting room conversations, I constantly heard that being a grandparent was "the best thing in the world" and "the payoff for having children." I did not feel that I needed payoff for being a parent. Nevertheless, I *do* believe that something *everybody* says usually has some truth to it. So, the topic seemed a good one for my conversation with this stranger in her new black dress.

"He's three," she said, absolutely beaming.

"I found out right before I left for this trip that my son and daughter-in-law are having a baby in August," I said.

"Will this be your first grandchild?" she asked.

I nodded.

"I only have Weston, and he means the world to me. He and my daughter live three miles from my husband and me. When I'm in town, I see him every day. Actually, my daughter is meeting us in Sydney with Weston."

"That sounds great. When is she meeting you?"

"We have six more nights. And, yes, I'm counting. One more night here, four nights in Melbourne, and then we go to Sydney, and they arrive the same day."

"Your itinerary sounds like mine," I said.

"We started in Johannesburg a week ago, then we spent two nights in Perth, and now we're here."

I knew that this High Hopes Tour I was joining in Adelaide had begun in Johannesburg and then gone to Perth. I thought of the man in black with the guitar case. My hunch that she might be connected to the Springsteen tour was seeming more probable. I thought of solving the mystery by asking her who "we" meant. But I did not want to be that that direct.

"Are you following Bruce Springsteen's High Hopes Tour until the end? Until New Zealand?" I asked, remembering that when I went home the tour was continuing.

"Until the very end," she said, nodding.

"I guess that makes you more devoted than I am," I said. "I'm just starting now, in Adelaide, and I'm ending in Brisbane."

"We aren't off to a terrific start." She made a face. "We flew together from Johannesburg to Perth, and we all got sick. A doctor came to the hotel in Perth and put everyone on antibiotics."

We all? I thought. *Everyone?* I was getting more and more hopeful that this story would have an unusually interesting ending. But I was not ready for the end quite yet.

"Being sick when you're traveling is the worst," I said. "I always wish I were home in my own bed when I get sick on a trip. Actually, I pretty much always wish I were home when I'm traveling. I don't like to travel."

Her eyebrows lifted. "If you don't like to travel, what are you doing here?"

"I don't like to be alone either," I said, hoping to pique her curiosity and keep her with me a bit longer. "But I'm here alone."

"Where are you from?" she asked.

It was working! "Philadelphia."

"Really? You came all the way here alone?" Her eyes widened. She sounded impressed.

I looked at her for a long moment. "I'm sixty-one and a half, and eighteen months ago I didn't know what a Bruce Springsteen was," I finally said. "But then I went to a concert with my son and daughter-in-law, and I became a fan. A few months ago, when I quit my job and didn't know what do, I decided to come here and go to eight of his concerts. Eight concerts in twenty-six days. And you?"

"I'm also in a sense following the High Hopes Tour—although, 'following' might not be the right word."

She was feeding me clues. It was time.

"Who *are* you?" I said, hoping that only a modicum of my growing curiosity was apparent.

"I'm Barbara Carr," she said with quiet definitiveness.

I nodded unenthusiastically and didn't say anything. I had no idea what this meant.

Undoubtedly, my ignorance was visible.

"I'm Bruce Springsteen's manager of thirty-four years," she elaborated, her voice low-key and matter-of-fact. She could have used the same voice to tell me she was an attorney at a run-of-the mill law firm.

I was impressed. Not just because she was connected to a cultural icon for whom I had traveled solo across the world, but also because of what she had achieved in a chauvinistic industry. She was a thirty-four-year veteran who had risen to the top despite the hostility so many women had faced in the music business. I was also awed by her ability to work for one rock star for thirty-four years. She had been with him from when he was just one among many wannabes all the way until he was *one* in a field of stardom all his own.

As impressed as I was by Barbara Carr and the longevity of her position, I also could not help but think about what this said about Bruce Springsteen. I had been married almost thirty-five years. I knew the kind of empathy, respect, and openness required for a relationship to survive and thrive for that long.

Barbara Carr was looking back at me with the same focused, uninterrupted eye contact we had maintained comfortably since the conversation had moved from her black dress and sweater to grandparenting to this.

"Thirty-four years is an impressively long time for any relationship," I said, smiling and nodding.

"Yes, it is," she said, nodding with me in unison. "Bruce is a great person to work with. He's very thoughtful." For the first time since we'd started talking, she took her gaze from mine and scanned our surroundings. "Well, I guess I really do need to get going. It was very nice talking to you."

"Thank you," I said. "I hope you have a wonderful time with your grandson and daughter."

She smiled. "And I hope you enjoy the concerts."

We smiled at each other, and she started to walk away. Then she stopped and swiveled back toward me.

"I'm sorry. I just realized I don't know your name."

"Anne Abel," I said.

"It was nice meeting you, Anne Abel," she said, slowing down half a beat when she got to my name, as if she were trying to commit it to memory. Then she disappeared into the crowd of departing fans.

I shook my head in disbelief. So much had happened on this first day of my trip. It had been surreal and wonderful.

I ran into the hotel and dropped my tote in my room.

I had a concert to get to.

13

IT WAS ONLY a ten-minute ride from the hotel to the Adelaide Entertainment Center, the venue for the concert. Getting out of the car, I felt the way Cinderella might have felt getting out of her chariot to go to the ball. I had arrived!

I had not wondered what the venue might look like. If I had, I never would have imagined the ethereal white hemisphere tethered to the ground with giant cables and wide, arched openings. It looked like a building that might be constructed on Mars someday.

Neither the travel agent nor I had bothered to find out how far the venue was from the hotel. We had allowed for an hour traveling time, aiming to get me there thirty minutes early. This meant I now had well over an hour to wait.

It was too hot to walk around and explore. I also wanted to get past the ticket takers sooner rather than later so I would not have to worry about losing my ticket. So, despite how early I was, I kept going and held out my ticket to the woman at the turnstile.

She scanned the ticket, and I followed the point of her finger toward my seat.

Although the outside of the 11,300-seat Adelaide Entertainment Center looked futuristic, the concert hall itself was anything but. The floor in front of the stage behind the pit—which became a hockey rink in the winter—was divided into sections with rows of wooden folding chairs. Above, two tiers of balcony seating lined the room.

I found my seat in the middle of the second section and sat down. I let my eyes close. I let my shoulders slump. I breathed in. I breathed out. In and out. I did not have the energy or wherewithal to do anything more. In and out—I felt my breath moving. I sat in silence and let myself be.

I heard some noises from the front of the room and opened my eyes. Six men in black, carrying clipboards and wearing earpieces, were walking back and forth across the stage, stopping at speakers and microphones and jotting notes down on their clipboards. Two men shimmied up towering metal structures topped with speakers that bookended the front of the stage.

People in T-shirts and shorts sauntered in, staking out their seats. Most were carrying oversize plastic cups full of sloshing beer. There seemed to be as many women as men, and a range of ages from late teens to my age. Unlike me, everyone was with someone, in pairs or small groups.

I stood up and headed for the restroom.

The concourse was abuzz with swarms of jovial fans. The lines at the beer concessions were wrapped like coils around the perimeter of the lobby. Bolts of energetic excitement seemed to ricochet through the air.

It was *showtime.*

That is, it was seven thirty, the official start time of the concert—but when I got back to my seat, even though the technicians had finished their sound and lighting checks, the stage was empty and lifeless.

But not the audience. People were talking, laughing, filling the stadium with noise. A number of them were calling, "Broo! Broo! Broo!"

I smiled, remembering when I had turned to Robert at my first Springsteen concert and asked, "Why is everyone booing?"

Robert had laughed. "They aren't booing, they're *Broo*ing."

The seats on my right and left were still empty. Two people sitting up in the side balcony were holding a sign that said, "We sold our cow to be here." I had a feeling it was not a joke.

A man in his early twenties with blond, shoulder-length hair parted in the middle and turned up at the bottom in a classic flip hairdo squeezed his way through the people seated in my row until he reached the empty seat on my left.

He dropped into the seat and gave me an easy smile. I tried to reciprocate.

"Thirty minutes ago, I was at my desk working when a coworker offered me his ticket. And now, here I am!" He pulled himself up from the slouch he had collapsed into and smiled.

"That's amazing," I said.

"Yeah, one of his kids is sick and he thought he should get home."

"Well, you won't believe this," I said. "I left home four days ago to get to this concert. And I'm not thinking about what I paid for my ticket. So that pretty much makes us opposites."

He asked where I was from. I gave him my elevator pitch for how I had come to be his neighbor for the evening.

"That's quite an adventure you're on," he said, shaking his head. "You're very courageous. I can't get my mother to even visit her sister in Sydney. Good for you!"

"Are you a Bruce Springsteen fan?" I asked. It seemed like a fair question. After all, he had gotten his ticket for free and run down the street to get here just in time.

"Sure," he said. "I've never seen him in person. But I'm in a band and we do Springsteen covers all the time. It's what people want to hear."

The bellowing streams of "Broo" suddenly amplified into surround sound, accompanied by unbridled shrieks of joy. Everyone was standing. I was standing. Chills were running through every part of me.

One by one, members of the E Street Band appeared at the back of the stage, then trotted down the middle to the front with their arms high in the air. They stopped at the edge of the stage and beamed big smiles before sliding off to the side and into position behind their microphones.

I had come so far for this moment without ever daring to imagine it.

After Steve Van Zandt took his place up front, beside the empty microphone in the center of the stage, Bruce Springsteen ran from the back, his arms held high, a guitar in one hand. On the giant screen I saw the face of the man with the biggest, kindest smile I had ever seen. My heart swelled. I felt it pushing against my ribs.

Bruce Springsteen took his microphone and, looking into our collective eyes, said, "Adelaide, why is it so fucking hot here?"

Tears dripped down my face.

In one graceful, fluid movement, he wrapped his guitar strap around his neck, slid the guitar across the front of his body, and nodded to the band.

"Summertime Blues" began to shake the room.

And we were off.

I was familiar with only a fraction of the enormous discography of Bruce Springsteen and the E Street Band, but I excitedly recognized "Summertime Blues" from driving with Andy. He loves golden oldies. Until I discovered Bruce Springsteen and E Street Radio, golden oldies was the soundtrack of all our car rides. Dancing and jumping and clapping to "Summertime Blues"—my first song at my first concert in Australia—it seemed to me that Bruce Springsteen was doing everything he could to keep me from feeling lost and out of place. I also knew the next three songs of the setlist: "Devil With a Blue Dress On," "Good Golly, Miss Molly," and "C.C. Rider."

I clapped and tapped and swayed and jumped. I thought about Andy and realized how much I missed him and how much he would have enjoyed the concert so far. For a moment, even in my exuberance, I felt homesick. But the feeling did not last more than a moment. It was hard, even for me, to feel anything but uplifted and happy as Bruce Springsteen and the E Street Band hurtled through these songs, grinning and tapping and looking like they were having a grand time doing it all for us.

I felt a tap on my shoulder. I turned to see a forty-odd-year-old woman in a black High Hopes T-shirt settling back into her seat directly behind me.

"Would you please sit down?" she said. Her request sounded like a command.

I stared at her. I thought maybe I had misheard her. I looked around the concert hall and saw that only a handful of people in the room were standing. It seemed crazy—and odd. By this point, I'd been to six other Springsteen concerts in the US since my first one in Philadelphia. Often, Bruce Springsteen had implored the audience, "Get up off your arses and dance!"

Ordinarily, I do not let random people boss me around. Especially if I think the person is being unreasonable. But I did not know what Australian concert rules were. And I did not want to take the time to find out. Concert time is precious. Minutes or seconds squandered going to the bathroom or arguing with a seatmate can never be recovered. In the interest of getting back into this concert that I had come so far to see, I stepped into the aisle at the end of my row and continued my clapping, tapping, and swaying.

An usher was standing in the aisle two rows ahead, facing me. I looked her in the eyes. She stared ahead, not changing her blank expression, as if she did not see me. Other people came into the aisle in front of me. Two twenty-something girls danced an arm's length away. When I heard the beginning of "High Hopes," I forgot about everything except what was happening in front of me onstage.

My brain was processing the concert on several levels: On one level, I was totally absorbed in the moment, just soaking in my surroundings. This was the part of my brain responsible for my dancing and clapping and tapping. Another part of my brain was listening to the words and thinking about their meaning. On yet another level, I was watching Bruce Springsteen and all the members of the band and trying to figure out how they communicated with each other and worked together.

Then, apropos of nothing, the usher told me to go back to my seat.

"Is it okay for me to stand up and dance in front of my seat?" I said, feeling annoyed to be looking at her when I could be looking at Bruce Springsteen and the E Street Band.

"Of course—this is a concert, not a classroom," she said before continuing on and sending everyone else back to their seats.

I sat down in my seat. Immediately, I stood up. I. Did. Not. Want. To. Sit.

The people behind me seemed to tolerate me as an obstruction through enough songs that I forgot about them and the usher. I forgot about everything except what was happening onstage. Then I felt the tap again.

I really did not want to start a ruckus. But I also did not want to sit. So I danced my way back to the aisle and danced for two or three songs before the usher sent me back to my seat. She did not seem annoyed that she had to speak to me again. I took that as my cue that it was okay to dance in the aisle, in moderation. So, I got into a rhythm. I danced at my seat for a few songs. When I felt the tap, I danced back into the aisle. After two or three songs there, when the usher sent me back to my seat, the cycle began all over again.

The third or fourth time I was dancing in the aisle, I felt a tap from behind. I turned around.

"I just want to thank you for being so brave and standing up and dancing," a woman in her thirties said to me, her face damp with sweat. "I'm sitting a few rows behind you and I'm following you. I was afraid to do it on my own."

I felt a big smile spread across my face. I gave her a hug before turning back to the stage.

I was *not* alone. I was with eleven thousand members of the Springsteen family of fans. We'd gathered in this stadium to be infused with Bruce Springsteen's pulsing humanity. I felt a comforting sense of familiarity with the people onstage and the fans surrounding me. Bruce Springsteen took our needs and our wants to heart and made it his mission to give us what we came for. I felt enveloped in a mix of joy, gratitude, and awe.

Each moment was as wonderful and perfect as the one before it. Yes, perfect. Bruce Springsteen left the stage, wading into the crowd. Suddenly, he was standing on the stage again—with a ten-year-old boy perched on his shoulders. Together, the two of them began singing "Waitin' on a Sunny Day."

I turned to the young man on my left and said with a giddy grin, "I know this is a tacky song, but it's my favorite."

"It's a good song," he said, giving me a kind, knowing smile.

My ever-expanding heart opened even more to make room for this empathetic young stranger.

I had read that music critics deride the bubblegum tenor of "Waitin' on a Sunny Day." And I didn't doubt that they were correct in their analysis. But I loved the song. I loved everything about it, especially when Bruce Springsteen sang it at this concert: the lyrics that I could hear and understand; the twinkle in his eyes as he sang; the pluckiness of the child sitting on his shoulders, belting out the words off-key; the image of that child's beaming parents projected on the giant screens; the vicarious delight of the audience.

At the end of the song, Bruce Springsteen returned the boy to his ebullient parents, then sprang back onstage.

The lights dimmed. The trill of a piano began. On the giant screens on both sides of the stage were the hands of Roy Bittan, dancing over the keys of his piano. He was playing the introduction to what I now know is "Jungleland."

I had heard the song before as a full-band piece. Never had I heard it played like this, with only one instrument. Roy Bittan's grace and dexterity and speed overwhelmed me. How was it humanly possible to move one's fingers as if they were ballet dancers? How did anyone learn to create such aesthetic pleasure out of nothing? I considered the creative genius of Bruce Springsteen, the man who'd put together those notes that Roy Bittan was sending out into the world.

It took my breath away.

After the encore, when Bruce and the E Street Band walked off the stage, the audience began bellowing, "Broo! Broo!" again. Everyone wanted more. As if Bruce Springsteen had not already given us everything one human being—even a mega human being—might have to give.

From the back of the stage, from the same place he had come at the beginning of the concert, Bruce Springsteen ambled to his microphone, stage center, and positioned his guitar across his body.

I was shocked. I was such an amateur Bruce Springsteen fan that I did not know he ever performed without the backup of the E Street Band. I had never heard him play an acoustic guitar. There was a single stage light on him. He began to strum and sing:

> *We said we'd walk together baby come what may,*
> *That come the twilight should we lose our way*
> *If as we're walking a hand should slip free*
> *I'll wait for you*
> *And should I fall behind*
> *Wait for me*

I had never heard this song before. By the end of the first stanza, tears were spilling from my eyes. I pictured Andy and me on the bimah on our wedding day and telescoped our many years together. Over the decades we had stumbled and fallen in ways that I could never have imagined or even believed possible on our wedding day. As Bruce Springsteen crooned to the reverberating sounds of his guitar, I saw myself falling behind and Andy turning to hold out his hand. I saw Andy visiting me in Sheppard Pratt, days after he had had back surgery. I saw him holding my hand as we walked together into the hospital the day that I had my CAT scan to see if my lymphoma had spread through my body. And I saw him sitting down on the kitchen floor with me as I lay face down, sobbing in emotional agony, after another one of my Sunday phone calls with my mother.

And then I saw Andy faltering. I remembered the day I called Andy's father and began the intervention on the life-long alcoholism of Andy's mother. I thought of the painful memories of childhood abuse he had repressed until then, and the estrangement from his family that ensued.

Standing there in the Adelaide Entertainment Center among the hushed crowd, listening to Bruce Springsteen and thinking about Andy and me, I felt I had never heard a song as beautiful as "If I Should Fall Behind."

After the song, Bruce Springsteen waved goodbye. He did not return. I smiled at my seatmate, then watched him disappear into the crowd.

Never in my life had I felt this happy. On my own, I had been able to take what The Boss and his band had given me and lift myself up. I felt strong. I felt in control. I felt empowered.

14

ON THE ten-minute ride back to the hotel, my driver clued me in to the fact Bruce Springsteen and the E Street Band had stayed at the InterContinental the previous year when their tour visited Adelaide, and that after the concert they'd gone to the hotel bar to unwind.

There is no question that watching Bruce Springsteen and his band hanging out in a bar is an opportunity few fans would want to miss. Certainly not an inveterate fly-on-the-wall fan like me, who had lifted her wings and traveled thousands of miles to find interesting walls on which to perch. But it was twelve thirty in the morning. I was leaving the hotel in eight and a half hours, at nine o'clock, to go to the airport and onward to Melbourne. Between now and then I would have to pack and work out. It would not be bad if I could fit in some sleep as well. So, all things considered, I decided it would be okay, this once, to let an opportunity pass me by. It was okay to let Bruce Springsteen and the E Street Band hang out in the bar without me as their witness.

Just as I stepped toward the elevator in the lobby, however, I remembered that I had put my valuables—passport, concert tickets, airline tickets, cash—in a lockbox in the bowels of the hotel vault. So I about-faced and headed for the hotel desk—but then I could not resist veering off course and looking in on the hotel bar.

Steve Van Zandt and five other band members whose names I did not know were lounging together, beer bottles in hand, on a round banquette in the middle of the room.

Seeing them kicking back as pseudo civilians was, I realized, a lot less interesting to me than watching them onstage, working together to create magic. And I was tired. So I turned around and continued to the hotel desk to retrieve my belongings.

"I'd like to get my things out of the hotel safe," I said to the lone woman on duty.

She looked at me, concerned, and did not say anything for some moments. Then, finally, she picked up the phone. "Let me call the hotel manager."

A minute or so later a man appeared from a door behind the desk. A pin embossed with the name "CHARLES" was affixed to his lapel.

"You want to get your things *now*?" he asked, blinking repeatedly.

I did not answer. I had taken it as a rhetorical question, although it did not sound like one. It did not seem at all unreasonable that I would want to get my things from the safe now—or any other time, for that matter. It seemed like a standard request, easily accommodated.

But Charles stood there staring back at me, clearly waiting for my answer.

I felt as if I was imposing on him by requesting my things. I did not want to impose. If I did not think that I would be rushed in a few hours when I had to leave for the airport, I would have backed away and planned to get my things then. But I did not feel comfortable leaving something so important until the last moments before my departure.

"Yes, I need to get my things now," I said. To make myself feel less bad for being so demanding, I added, "I'm leaving for the airport at nine o'clock."

Charles gave me a half smile, unlocked the gate at the end of the check-in desk, and gestured me inside. When I walked through, he locked it. He punched numbers into a keypad on one door and opened it. I followed him through. The door slammed shut. He punched a code into a keypad on a second door. It opened into a room with a desk and a computer and two chairs.

"Please have a seat," he said, motioning me toward the chair in front of the desk.

He sat down across from me in front of the computer. He looked at his watch. He looked at me. I thought he was going to say something. He did not. He looked at his watch again. Then he tapped a few keys on the computer keyboard.

"What is your mother's maiden name?" he asked.

I told him.

"What city was she born in?"

As I gave my one-word answer, he again looked at his watch. He did not type in the city. He looked up at me. But it did not seem that he saw me. There was something more important than me and my valuables occupying his mind.

A hypothesis occurred to me: Bruce Springsteen was going to be joining his buddies in the bar, so Charles and hotel security were on alert.

I felt adrenaline start pumping through me. Now that The Boss's appearance was causing a full-blown tactical operation, I suddenly wanted to be part of the excitement. I let Charles bumble his way through retrieving my belongings, and then I returned to the bar.

Steve Van Zandt was still slouched with his bandmates, bantering between swigs of beer. There was a white baby grand piano abutting a wall outside the bar entrance. I staked out my spot, leaning against the piano to give my tired legs some relief.

As I waited and hoped for a Bruce Springsteen sighting, I watched Steve Van Zandt and the other musicians. They looked like *real* people. Real, tired people who needed to let their minds settle down and synchronize with their bodies so they would be able to get to sleep. Seeing them as people, unwinding after an exhausting day at work, now made me feel reverential toward them. Admittedly, they were talented people, well practiced at what they did. But they were not creatures from another galaxy, blessed with magical superpowers. They were flesh-and-blood people—and thinking about them as such made it even more awesome that they could get together onstage and do what they do.

I turned my head away from the bar and saw a mid-thirties man in black jeans, a form-fitting white T-shirt, and flip-flops approaching.

"Are you waiting to see Bruce?" he asked with an animated grin.

"Yes," I said. "But I don't know how much longer I'm going to hang around. Especially since there's no guarantee he's going to show."

"Trust me, he's going to show," he said, grinning and nodding with his whole body, dancing back and forth on his feet. "My buddy works hotel security here; he called me about a half hour ago, saying they'd just gotten word that Bruce would be going to the bar."

So much for hotel security.

Suddenly, the eyes of my Australian informant bulged. He jumped away from the piano and me.

I turned to see what he was seeing.

Fifty feet away, strutting down a narrow corridor that opened into the room we were in, I saw a man in tight white jeans, a tight white jeans jacket, and sunglasses.

Sunglasses? I thought. It was close to one o'clock in the morning.

As the man got closer, I saw that he had a mischievous smirk. And he was short—nothing like the persona Bruce Springsteen exuded onstage. He was so close to me that when he passed, I could have touched his arm. I did not. I was not even tempted. As I watched him continue his strut into the bar, I thought, *Who does he think he is, Elvis Presley?* (Musical neophyte that I was, I had no idea then that when Bruce Springsteen first saw Elvis Presley on *The Ed Sullivan Show* in 1957, he was "transfixed," and the very next day he convinced his mother to rent him a guitar.)

I watched as Bruce Springsteen in his Elvis Presley costume sat down beside Steve Van Zandt, and then I said goodnight to my informant. I had occupied the same airspace as Bruce Springsteen. That was enough.

I went upstairs and drifted to sleep.

I woke up with the image of Bruce Springsteen as Elvis floating in my head. I did not regret that I had not tried to touch him or get a selfie with him. It was his stage persona—his unfailingly kind smile, his humanity—that pulled me in and gave me hope.

I wasn't naive. I didn't think Bruce Springsteen jumped out of bed in the morning, threw open the window, and shouted, "Is there anybody alive out there!?" I knew he put on a show for his fans. I knew he had a public persona. But it was reassuring to me that people who had met Bruce Springsteen spoke about his compassion and thoughtfulness.

If I ever heard that he was rude or abusive, his spell on me would be forever broken.

Meeting The Boss was not at all the same to me as meeting members of the E Street Band, as I had the previous afternoon in the lobby. Even though they were part of Bruce Springsteen's magic, they were more like line dancers for the main act, backups for the big talent. They were fun to watch. They were good at what they did. But not one of them was a magician. Not to me. I liked watching them watch Bruce Springsteen. I liked watching them watch him for cues on when to come in, when to stop. I liked watching him work with them to create his magic. If any one of them was unkind or surly to me, it would not have had any long-lasting effect on me. It would not have hexed the magic spell cast on me by Springsteen himself.

The fact that I could come under his spell in any kind of sustained manner was miraculous in and of itself. My entire life, whenever I experienced something positive, whenever I had a happy thought, whenever I forgot myself and became excited or happy about something, the voice of my mother in my head had always interrupted, saying, *You are pathetic. You are being duped. You are a loser.*

It amazed me that Bruce Springsteen had muted this voice in my head. And I did not want to get too close to my magician. I was afraid I might learn that—like the wizard in *The Wizard of Oz*—my magician was just a small, curmudgeonly, blustering man. I needed to believe that Bruce Springsteen was a decent person. If I met him and he didn't seem like he *was*, I would find myself depleted, disappointed, depressed, and feeling stranded—all alone, so far from home.

15

THE FLIGHT from Adelaide to Melbourne was blissfully uneventful. I already felt so much more confident than I had when I stepped onto the plane in Los Angeles. *Experience*, I thought as the wheels of the plane rolled along the runway, *is a wonderful thing*.

It was six o'clock on Wednesday evening when I arrived at the Park Hyatt Melbourne. I would be staying here until Monday morning. The only things on my itinerary were the concerts on Saturday and Sunday evening.

I walked into the lobby and toward the check-in desk feeling as if I had stepped into an alternate universe. The lobby was surrounded by a curved wall of floor-to-ceiling mirrors. I did not see elevators. I did not see restrooms. I did not see a restaurant. I did not see people. All I saw were mirrors and an infinite reflection of images that seemed to ricochet around the room.

Stephanie, a mid-twenties blonde woman in a khaki skirt and jacket, checked me in and handed me a plastic room key.

"Where are the elevators? And where is the fitness center?" I asked.

"Of course, let me explain where things are here," she said with a smile. "The restaurant is down that hallway. The restrooms are behind the mirrored doors on the right over there. The business center is behind the mirrored doors on the left. The fitness center is on the second floor, and I will take you to the elevators."

I followed her.

"I believe that originally the design of the lobby was for aesthetics," she said. "As it turns out, it is helpful for hotel security to know who belongs here and who doesn't. When they spot someone groping the mirrored walls, unsure which mirrors open and which ones don't, hotel security makes sure they have a key to show that they are guests and belong here."

I thought of the big, open lobby at the InterContinental Adelaide, filled with Springsteen fans. Even if Bruce Springsteen were staying here, it seemed obvious to me that fans would not be welcome, even if they stood up against the mirrored walls.

The elevator doors opened; I left Stephanie in the lobby and stepped inside.

I stopped on the second floor to check out the fitness center before going to my room. It looked like a large, converted closet. It had no windows—or mirrors! It had only two treadmills and some free weights. But I had found a terrific fitness center outside of the hotel in Adelaide. Melbourne was a much bigger city, so I was confident I could find someplace acceptable here too. And an excursion to a health club would be a good way for me to see the city.

I got to my room just as Robert, the valet, arrived with my bags. He swiped the key for me and motioned for me to go in. I took five steps into the room—and was hit with a rush of very hot air.

I stopped, thinking that the rush of heat would pass as my body acclimated from the air-conditioned hall and lobby. It did not. As I walked toward the thermostat, the air felt even denser and hotter.

The thermostat read 90 degrees Fahrenheit. Robert and I tried to adjust it. The lever would not move.

He shook his head. "I'm sorry. Let me go down to discuss this with the front desk."

"It's not your fault," I said. "Thanks for helping. I'm going to wait in the hall."

Standing in the hall, I felt not only hot but also sleep deprived and jet-lagged.

Ten minutes later, Robert returned with a key to another room down the hall. I followed him in. Suddenly, goose bumps popped up on my arm and I began to shiver.

This thermostat read 62 degrees Fahrenheit. Again, Robert tried unsuccessfully to move the lever. This time I called down to the desk.

"I'd like to speak to the manager, and I would like to speak to him or her right now," I said.

Five minutes later, Dani Butler, the night manager, arrived.

"Yes, it does feel cold in here," she said as she walked over to the thermostat, her blonde ponytail swinging. She peered at the screen. "It says it's 17 degrees."

"I *know* what the temperature is," I said. "I need another room."

"I'm sorry, we're fully booked," she said. "As a matter of fact, this room was part of a block of rooms for the group that's checking in now. We had to separate two of the guests from their group and put them in the room you were in first."

I imagined these guests pulling their clothes off in the 90-degree room.

"Let me bring my engineer up here," she said.

I turned on the light on the desk and looked around the room for the first time. Even though the room was still dark, my body, already tight from the cold, tightened even more as it recoiled at the thought of having to *touch* anything in the dimly lit room. The maroon-palette room had a floral bedspread, a dirty maroon-and-gold-swirl carpet, a glass desk with hand smudge marks, and, like the lobby, mirrored walls. I pushed one of the mirrored panels and found drawers. I pushed another and found a closet. Behind the third was a bathroom with a handprint on the glass vanity.

The metal-and-mesh nylon desk chair looked like the item in the room least likely to collect germs, so I dropped my body into it. As I did, there was a knock at the door.

It was Krisham, the engineer, a fortyish Indian man wearing tan pants and a work shirt. As soon as he was through the door, Dani's pager beeped.

"The thermostat is stuck at 17 degrees," she told Krisham. "Can you take a look?"

He nodded; she left.

I smiled at Krisham from my desk chair. He smiled at me. Then he pulled out a device that looked like a plastic label embosser and held it up to a ceiling vent above the desk. A red dot appeared. "Sixteen degrees," he said. He held it up to a vent above the bed. Another red dot. "Also 16 degrees." He went into the bathroom.

"It's 24 degrees in the bathroom," he said when he came out. "That's 75 degrees Fahrenheit."

For a brief moment, I considered sleeping on the floor in the bathroom. Then I remembered the smudge on the vanity. I did not want to think about what lurked on the floor in there.

"I'm sorry," Krisham said. "The HVAC system in this hotel is antiquated. There really is nothing that can be done to make this room comfortable without updating the system."

I appreciated his honesty. Before I could respond, there was a knock at the door.

Dani Butler was back.

Krisham shook his head at her. "The thermostat is not responding, as you know," he said. "Although it is warmer in the bathroom."

Dani nodded in commiseration with Krisham, then turned to me. "I agree it's too cold in here."

I waited for her to say more. She did not.

I stifled a sigh. "Could you get me a clean comforter for the bed?"

"Of course," she said, smiling for the first time. "Is there anything else I can get you? Would you like to go to the dining room, compliments of the hotel? Or I could send up room service?"

I smiled wanly. As hungry as I was, I was even more tired. More than tired; I felt ravaged from within and without.

Then I had a thought.

"I looked at your fitness center and was disappointed," I said, standing up from the desk chair. "Would it be possible for you to recommend an outside health club and pay for me to use it during my stay here?"

"Yes, of course," she said, looking relieved by my request. "I will leave a note for the day manager to look into this for you. Are you sure you don't want to have room service, at least?"

"I'm fine," I said.

"Okay, then," she said. "I'll have the duvet sent up immediately. I'm really sorry about the less-than-adequate welcome we have shown you. I'll touch base with you tomorrow afternoon when I'm back on duty."

When Dani left, I looked at Krisham. He shrugged and shook his head, as if he were now commiserating with me. He seemed like a gentle man.

"What brings you to Melbourne?" he asked.

"I'm here to see Bruce Springsteen. He has two concerts here this weekend." Just saying this, I felt a little better.

Krisham gave me a sly smile. "I shouldn't say this. Please don't repeat it. But Bruce Springsteen and some of his band checked in here this afternoon. They stayed here last year, also."

"Wow! Thank you so much for the heads-up," I said, feeling energy bubbling up in me. "They stayed at my hotel in Adelaide too. I even saw him walking into the bar last night. He was so close I could have touched him."

"One last thing before I go," Krisham said, making no movement toward the door. "I heard that he doesn't use the fitness center here. He goes to a health club in town called Virgin Active. It's owned by the man who owns Virgin Airlines. Anyhow, I'm really sorry we couldn't make your stay here more comfortable. But I hope you enjoy the concerts."

Before I could say anything, he bowed his head and walked out the door.

I thought about Bruce Springsteen. Somewhere in my hotel, again. I thought of going to the same health club as him. Krisham's thoughtfulness to stay behind for a few minutes to try to bolster my sunken spirits had in fact helped me—not so much because of his inside scoop on Bruce Springsteen, although that was a fun side note, but more because he had seen my despair and cared enough to take the time to try to help me.

I stumbled around, flicking on any light switches I could find in the room, and still it was dark in there. Undaunted,

I unpacked my suitcase and laid out my warmup pants, a sweatshirt, and Lululemon workout clothes to slip into the following morning.

Just as I pulled the bedspread off the bed, there was a knock at my door. I opened it to find Robert outside, holding *two* folded white duvets.

After thanking Robert and closing the door behind him, I tossed the duvets over the bed and—still wearing my jacket, my clothes, and even my shoes—I crawled between the cold sheets and passed out.

16

THE FOLLOWING morning my eyes opened to see a small, round, dimly lit, Roman numeral clock on the night table beside me. It was seven thirty. I had slept ten and a half hours. I was on my way toward adjusting to jet lag.

Feeling joyful, I sprang from the bed, kicked off my shoes, and yanked off the jacket and clothes I'd been wearing since I left Adelaide the previous morning. Was it really only five days ago that I had been in LA? At home I often said, "The hours go slowly, but the days fly by." In Australia, the hours flew by but the days seemed to go on forever.

I headed for the hotel restaurant. I had not eaten anything since lunch on the flight from Adelaide to Melbourne, and I was ravenous. But as I was about to walk inside, I stopped mid-step. A waist-high maroon velvet cable the same color as the dirty carpet in my room was blocking entry into the dark, silent room. There were no people inside the restaurant. There were no people sitting at the tables. There were no people setting the tables in preparation for the breakfast rush.

I turned from the restaurant and walked across the black-and-gray marble floor to the check-in desk.

"I'm sorry," the thirty-something Asian man standing behind the desk (his gold pin told me his name was Mark) said when I asked him why the restaurant was closed. "Our coffee and breakfast service don't begin until six o'clock."

I waited for Mark to continue to speak to make sense of this situation for me. He looked at me with a pleasant smile.

"It's not quite four o'clock here in Melbourne," Mark said gently, as if he were reading my mind. He held out his wrist, showing me his watch.

I stood, catatonic, and stared at Mark. Why had my clock read seven thirty?

"Give me a moment, please," he said. "Let me see if anyone is in the kitchen early. If I can find someone, what would you like?"

His gentleness brought tears to my eyes. I tightened my brow muscles and created a dam to keep them from spilling out.

I stepped back ten feet or so and fell backward into a round black leather swivel chair.

The old, familiar, derisive voice in my head returned: *What am I doing here? Why am I following a sixty-four-year-old singing guy and buying into his money-making ridiculousness? If I had* anything *to do at home, I would not be here. I would not need Bruce Springsteen. I am pathetic. And frankly, so is he. I embarked on this endeavor to avoid the abyss. But I am my own worst enemy. I cannot run from the abyss because I bring the abyss along with me, deep in my soul. I am a loser.*

I lowered my head. Tears dripped down my cheeks and onto my hands in my lap before I could even try to stop them. They were warm when they landed on my hands but turned cold quickly.

Suddenly, between my wet cheeks and my wet, cold hands, a square box of tissues appeared. Before I could think or do anything, I felt an overwhelming sense of gratitude. I pulled out a few tissues and dropped my face into them. When I looked up, there was Mark.

How had he known? How had he noticed? Why did he care?

"Thank you. Thank you so much. Thank you for noticing," I said, unable to contain my appreciation and my words. "Thank you for being so kind to me. How did you know?"

"We have all been there," he said. "Alone and far away from home. It isn't easy. But sometimes it's what you have to do."

He smiled, bowed his head, and went back to his desk.

The humanity of Mark's simple words palpated deep within me. Holding my wad of wet tissues, I felt the cold emptiness that had hollowed me out minutes earlier fill with the gentle warmth of his empathy for me. Mark saw me in a way I had not been able to see myself just a few moments earlier—as a person struggling with difficult circumstances, not unlike circumstances with which he and many others struggled. I suddenly saw myself not unlike Mark and all the other travelers in this world who had at some point found themselves jet-lagged, disoriented, lonely, homesick, and sad. And as I felt empathy for Mark and the other homesick travelers, I also felt empathy for myself. For some moments, I saw myself as someone with an intrinsic value all my own, worthy of the compassion this kind stranger had bestowed on me.

I watched Mark leave the lobby and his desk. I closed my eyes. I wanted to try to hold on to the gentleness I was feeling toward myself.

Some minutes later, I sensed someone standing in front of me. I opened my eyes. It was Mark. He was holding a tray with a silver pot of coffee, a mug, a carafe of milk, and two blueberry muffins.

"Room service was not open, but I was able to find someone who could put something together for me—I mean, for you!"

My body relaxed. I jumped up and beamed at the kind, wonderful man before me. I wanted to hug him—but I did not. Instead I said, with all the feeling I would have put into a hug, "Thank you so much."

He smiled. Then he put the tray on the table beside my chair and hurried away to help a weary traveler in cargo shorts and sandals coming in with a suitcase from outside.

I sat back down and prepared my mug of coffee. I took a sip and closed my eyes as the hot liquid slid down my throat. At home one of my favorite things is my first sip of coffee. It is the most delicious part of my day. Sitting in the lobby of the Park Hyatt Melbourne, my first sip of Mark's coffee was better than any first sip I had ever had at home.

I took a second sip, and a third. I leaned back in my chair and exhaled a deep, calm breath. Life was good. It was very, very good.

As I was finishing my second muffin, I overheard the man in cargo shorts speaking to Mark.

"I'm interested in having a car service to take me back and forth to the concert Saturday night at AAMI Park."

AAMI was the venue for the Springsteen concerts. I also had a car service taking me back and forth from the hotel to the concert—a car service with many empty seats. It would be fun to share a ride with this man, and to talk to him and learn about his connection to Bruce Springsteen. Had he come all the way from the States to see the concert, as I had?

My heart was beating hard and fast. My feet felt light on the ground, ready to step toward Cargo Shorts Man. In my head, the words I would say to him lined up, waiting for the green light to go. But for all my readiness, I could not move forward. As experienced and disciplined as I was in getting my inert self to put one foot in front of the other, I could not get myself to move even one inch toward Cargo Shorts Man.

Why would that man want to share a ride with you? the voice began, each word sounding louder and harsher. *After traveling all this way, he is not going to care about saving money with a free ride from you. If you speak to him, he will think you are a loser. A loser who came to Australia alone because no one wanted to be with you.*

With this maelstrom of negativity swirling vigorously in my head, my well-crafted first sentence receded farther and farther into the background and eventually broke into aimless wisps of syllables that fluttered into oblivion.

Somewhere in my consciousness, I saw Cargo Shorts Man move.

Missed opportunity! a different, cheering voice inside me called. *It's now or never.*

Finally, one foot quickly followed the other toward Cargo Shorts Man as he lifted his backpack and grabbed his suitcase.

"Excuse me," I said to his back.

He turned and looked at me.

"I couldn't help overhearing you ask for a car service to AAMI Saturday night."

Cargo Shorts Man nodded.

"I have a car reserved to take me. You're welcome to come in my car."

"Thank you, that's generous of you," he said. "But my wife is here, and so is my son. He's beginning his semester abroad here. Things are pretty hectic with us. I think it's best if we get to the concert on our own."

Okay, I thought. *I asked. He said no. He did not make me feel like a loser.*

"Where are you from?" I asked when he did not hurry away.

"Potomac. Potomac, Maryland."

I knew one person in Potomac: Sarah Stern, a woman I had met when we were both inpatients at The Retreat at Sheppard Pratt in Towson, Maryland. So, when Cargo Shorts Man told me he was from Potomac, Sarah's name popped into my head. The odds were virtually zero that he would know her. It seemed stupid to play people geography with one person's name. But still I heard myself say, "Do you, by any chance, know Sarah Stern?"

"Are you kidding?" Cargo Shorts Man said, suddenly animated. "You know Sarah?"

I nodded, wondering what I would say if he asked me how I knew her.

"I live two doors down from Sarah. We belong to the same synagogue and country club."

I was stunned. I wondered for a moment if I was a luckier person than I'd previously thought. I wondered if I should play the lottery.

"I'm Anne Abel," I said.

"Jeff—Jeff Blum," he said, extending his hand.

"It's good to meet you, Anne. When I see Sarah, I'll tell her we bumped into each other." He hoisted his backpack over his shoulders. "Have fun at the concert Saturday night."

I watched Jeff Blum disappear into the elevator, and then I sat down in my black leather swivel chair to finish my coffee.

I opened my laptop. I wanted to write. I had so much to say to my group of friends at home who'd asked me to keep them updated on my journey.

Suddenly, once again, Mark was standing in front of me.

"These newspapers just came in for you. I thought you would want them here, rather than delivered to your room. And I know it isn't quite six, but I just called the restaurant, and it's open now."

What a gem of a human being. "Thank you so much." I grinned at him. "You've helped me so much."

"I'm happy I could do it," he said, handing me the folded newspapers.

In the restaurant, I savored my oatmeal and berries and read my four newspapers. Then I wrote and wrote and wrote my daily email to my twelve readers back home about everything that had happened since I landed in Melbourne. I was shocked when I looked at the time on my iPhone and saw that it was ten o'clock. Not once during the four hours I was typing had I heard the voice in my head say, *So what? Who cares? This is boring.*

I typed my last words feeling the opposite of depleted.

Heading back to my room to get my workout gear, I noticed I was feeling okay. If I had been more familiar with the sensation, I might have realized that I was feeling *good*. Jet lag and sleep deprivation notwithstanding, I felt full of energy—and this was *before* working out. I was excited to find my way to Virgin Active.

17

WHEN I arrived at Virgin Active, two beautiful women in their twenties with long, straight blonde hair and a man, also beautiful, blond, and twenty-something, were sitting behind a high counter. They smiled in unison when I stepped in from outside. Behind them was a wall of glass, and behind that a café with sun streaming through its floor-to-ceiling windows.

I was not hungry, but I love sun. I felt myself being drawn toward the café like metal toward a magnet.

"Hi," one of the blonde women said, interrupting my impulse to follow the sun. "Are you from the Park Hyatt?"

I nodded, too surprised to speak.

"You're Anne?"

I nodded again.

"Terrific, the Park Hyatt manager called to say you were on your way. John will give you a tour of the facility."

I wanted to get going before my energy drained from me. But I was curious. I felt as if I had entered a workout temple dedicated to disciples willing to pay for the best.

Before we had gone ten steps, I stopped.

"What's that?" I asked John.

Through a wall of glass, I saw a purple-hazed room that was at once both underlit and iridescent. It was filled with plastic modules that made me think of something I might have seen in George Jetson's futuristic living room.

"Those are sleeping pods," John said matter-of-factly. "Our members sign up for them in twenty-minute time slots."

"There's no one in there," I said. "Do people actually use them?"

"Oh my, yes. Stop here around lunchtime. On Mondays we usually have a waiting list."

"What's the purple light?" I asked, shaking my head in amazement.

"It's a special-frequency light ray or something like that. It's supposed to be soothing."

To me, the pods looked like space-age electroconvulsive treatment tables.

"What brings you to Melbourne?" John asked as we walked up the stairs to the first of four floors of equipment and studios. "Business or pleasure?"

Each time someone asked me this, I was stymied anew. Neither before nor after signing on the dotted line for this trip had the idea of pleasure entered my mind. My entire purpose in planning it had been to avoid feeling the opposite of pleasure—to avoid feeling pain. Soul-crushing, mind-numbing psychological pain.

But this would be too much information for John.

"I'm here to see Bruce Springsteen this weekend," I said.

"Lucky you!" John said.

"Actually, I quit my teaching job last fall and didn't know what to do with myself," I said between deep breaths as I followed one stairstep behind John. "The students were out of control, and I got fed up."

"I get it, totally," he said, stopping at the top of the stairs and turning to me. "My mother was a ninth-grade math teacher for twenty-five years. Last year *she* got fed up with *her* students. She said she was tired of looking out at the class and seeing all the stoned faces staring into their laps at their phones. So she took early retirement."

"Sounds familiar," I said, feeling validated.

John did not say anything more as we stood together at the top of the stairs. He did not seem to be in a rush to finish the tour. It seemed he was waiting for me to say more.

I hesitated for a beat, then added, "Good for her."

"Are you doing this trip alone?" he asked.

"I am," I said, surprised by his question.

"Does Bruce Springsteen know you're doing this?"

If only, I thought to myself. On the flight from Adelaide to Melbourne, a flight attendant had asked me the same question. Then as now, I thought that my smiling, hopeful questioner did not understand the magnitude of Bruce Springsteen's iconic status *or* did not understand that I was one of countless others.

"I wish *my* mother would do something. We were all supportive of her retiring"—John began to lead me around another floor of bright, windowed workout space—"but my dad still works, and all her friends work too. She seems pretty bored. We can't get her to do anything or go anywhere. She won't even volunteer at our church's rummage sale like she used to when she was working. I don't think she leaves the house all day."

He stopped and looked me in the eyes. "You're traveling alone across the world to see Bruce Springsteen, and we can't get my mother to even go by herself to a movie. You're so courageous. Good for *you*," he said with a smile and a declarative nod of his blond head.

I tried to see myself from John's perspective. Not as a desperate sixty-and-a-half-year-old woman with nothing better to do than this but as a courageous sixty-and-a-half-year-old woman up for adventure. It was difficult to see myself this way. The best I could do was see myself as a woman trying as hard as she could to help herself. My mind paused a beat—and then I realized a woman trying as hard as she can to help herself is another definition of *courageous*.

In the days since I had left home, so many strangers had said positive things about my traveling to Australia alone to see Bruce Springsteen: the USAir woman who'd changed my ticket; the Qantas flight attendant; even Barbara Carr, Bruce Springsteen's manager, had seemed impressed. Others, like Ben, the VIP airport escort in Melbourne, had accepted my trip as a perfectly reasonable thing to do. The image of me that these strangers had reflected back—as admirable, even *enviable*—had taken me by surprise. Each time I heard one of these favorable remarks, I stopped and imagined myself through their eyes—not as a desperate, frivolous loser but as a brave, bold adventurer. And I tried to hold that novel image in my mind. Periodically, I even scrolled through my memory bank and retrieved one or another of these upbeat perspectives of myself and let it settle in the front of my mind for a moment or two. Or three or four.

In this case, I was also struck by the compelling, articulate way that John spoke about me. He didn't just tell me about my courage, he also *showed* it to me. His story about his mother pulled me into another world. I felt myself relating to this woman, a teacher who, like me, had quit her job because of unruly students. As John spoke, I pictured her standing in front of her classroom as students texted and played games on their phones. I pictured her walking out the door, filled with relief that she would never go back. I pictured her, next, alone on the living room couch watching television. I imagined this woman who had once been active in her church sitting at home, unable to motivate herself to get up and get out.

I knew what it felt like to feel unable to propel yourself forward. I knew what it was to feel aimless, despondent, and alone, disconnected from the world. Listening to John talk about his mother, I imagined myself quitting CCP and feeling clueless about what to do next. I could see myself collapsing on the couch in my family room, disconnected from the world. I remembered the terror I felt driving home from what I knew was my final class. And I remembered the moment, only a few minutes into the ride home, when my instinct to survive surged up and I grabbed it.

Thinking about John's mother quitting her teaching job and unable to get up off her living room couch, I knew how close I had come to doing the same. If I had not decided to go with Robert and Lindsey to the concert eighteen months earlier, if my heart and soul had not been uplifted by that man onstage with the biggest smile I had ever seen, I too would now be sitting, inert, on my family room couch.

And yet what I found most compelling about John's image of me as courageous was that he did not attribute my courage to Bruce Springsteen—he spoke of my courage as something intrinsic to *me*. I realized as I stood with John that it wasn't because of Bruce Springsteen that I was in Australia. It was because of my own resolve, my own strength, that I had chosen to launch myself into the unknown in the Land Down Under, on the other side of the world from home, rather than let myself fall into the abyss. And now I was beginning to feel like I had something to say, something to add to a conversation.

After working out, I stopped at the front desk to inquire about the cost of a Virgin Active membership.

"We don't have that information," one of the blonde young women replied. "If you're interested, we can arrange for you to speak to one of our member coordinators. I'll give Liz a call. Her office is right here. She'll be here in a flash."

Before I could respond, she picked up the phone, said a few words, and hung up.

Suddenly another young, blonde, smiling woman appeared before me and held out her hand.

"I'm Liz," she said as we shook. "I'm happy to talk to you about membership."

"I don't want to take up your time," I said. "I'm just visiting Melbourne for a short time. I'm not going to join Virgin Active. But it's a beautiful club and I was just wondering how much it costs to join."

"No worries," she said. "Follow me and we can sit down and talk."

I'd started this; I might as well see where it went. I nodded my agreement, and off we went.

"What brings you to Melbourne?" Liz asked as we sat down across from each other on two love seats in her small but sunny office.

I did not feel like being absolutely honest. I had already told her I did not want to join Virgin Active, that I was merely curious. I decided to answer her as breezily and superficially as I could.

"I'm here to see Bruce Springsteen concerts this weekend," I said without blanching or blinking.

"How fabulous!" Her face lit up. "You must be quite a fan."

"A new one, but a true one," I said, smiling.

"Then I'll let you in on a secret," she said, leaning forward. "Bruce Springsteen works out here when he's in town. He came here three times last year when his tour came through Melbourne. The young trainer who worked out with him said he could barely keep up with him."

"Wow!" I said to Liz, impressed but not surprised by Bruce Springsteen's strength and stamina.

"And . . ." Liz sat forward even farther, then suddenly stopped and pulled back.

I looked at her, my eyes widening in suspense. This conversation was already better than anything I could have anticipated. I edged toward her a bit.

"Well, this is confidential. But you don't seem like a wild fan," she said before hesitating again.

I shook my head gently, hoping to offer subdued reassurance that I was not a wild anything. My composed demeanor must have allayed any trepidation she had, because she rocked forward again and continued.

"This afternoon at four we are closing the club and he is coming here with some of his entourage."

As she was finishing her sentence, I was already estimating how many hours were between me and four o'clock. This could be my chance to meet Bruce Springsteen. But when I pictured myself meeting him at four o'clock, I hit the same mental block I'd run into when I'd seen him in the flesh in the hotel bar. I knew I couldn't possibly say to him in just a few words how much he and his music uplifted and helped me. And if I couldn't say something meaningful to him, I didn't want to say anything at all. For me, the enchantment of Bruce Springsteen was that, in the guise of a rock star, he was part motivational speaker, part spiritual leader. I did not pretend that he was a saint. I did not pretend to know what kind of person he was in private. But for me, his public persona—the one I felt entitled to judge—was that of a hardworking, well-meaning person. He didn't come onstage stoned or drunk. He did not come onstage as if he were punching a time clock and counting the dollars represented by every screaming fan in front of him. Quite the opposite.

Bruce Springsteen had suffered from depression. He knew what it was like to feel dead inside. He came onstage to help us, his audience, feel alive. He came onstage to help us feel good, to have a good time. He gave all that he had inside him to lift us up.

"I cannot give you life everlasting," he often told us. "But I can give you life in this moment."

And he did. In that moment, and the next and the next and the next.

Sitting with Liz in Virgin Active, I realized once again that I did not want to meet Bruce Springsteen. I didn't want to risk an encounter with the real man that might destroy the magic energy he created for me onstage.

18

WHEN I returned to the Park Hyatt Melbourne, the room was no less grimy or cold than it had been when I'd checked in twenty-four hours earlier. I walked into the bathroom, where it was a few degrees warmer.

On the glass shelf above the sink were my daily medications in twenty-two days' worth of pill organizers. Several of my medications were to manage jaw pain I'd developed eighteen months earlier during my third regimen of ECT. In the months leading up to my trip, I had been pain-free. In my last visit with the doctor, he had said I could begin weaning myself off the drugs whenever I felt ready. If the pain returned, I could re-up the dose.

Standing in the Park Hyatt Melbourne bathroom, staring at the pill organizers, a thought popped into my head: *What if you started weaning yourself off the drugs now?*

I had not considered doing this for even a moment before this. I had been too terrified of reliving the trauma of the chronic pounding of my jaw. The pain had made it difficult for me to function mentally and physically, even more so than usual.

But now here I was, on a trip that had so terrified me; I had taken a leap and landed on my feet. As long as I was leaping and landing okay, why not try leaping a bit higher? Why not cut my topiramate in half for three days and see how I felt? If I were to relapse into pain, I could up the dose.

And if that didn't work I could call my pain doctor at home, as he had told me to do. With the image of my kind, wise doctor in my head, I opened the pill boxes for that night and the following two and broke the topiramate in half. I was going to do this. At the very least, I was going to try.

Invigorated by my newfound resolve, I wiped down the glass desk across from my bed, opened my iPad, googled "Bruce Springsteen," and clicked on the YouTube video at the top of the screen.

Written in white on a black background was a quote from a Bruce Springsteen song: "I'm working on a dream though sometimes it feels far away. I'm working on a dream and I know it will be mine someday."

My breathing stopped for a moment or two. I did not recognize the words, but they resonated with me. I did not have dreams, literal or metaphorical. At least none that I ever let myself think about. Perhaps that was because I was already disappointed enough with myself, and I did not want to set myself up for further disappointments by dreaming of my life's possibilities. Possibilities I would never achieve.

But watching Bruce Springsteen, listening to Bruce Springsteen, validated me. He courageously and honestly put himself out there in front of his audience. Watching and listening to him, I realized I was not the only one struggling. He put his heart and soul on the line, telling everyone who he was. He was unafraid that people might not like him. He was unselfconscious about showing the world who he was. Onstage, you could feel him becoming comfortable with you, his audience. You could feel him coming to trust you. You felt him falling in love with you, as you were falling in love with him. His onstage openness, his transparency, gave all of us, his audience, the courage to emulate him and take ownership of our feelings, our insecurities. It showed us that we too could be hopeful for ourselves. It was okay to be unsure. It was okay to not feel okay. We could feel these things and still have hope.

After the quote, the video continued with a story about Scott Fedor, a thirty-seven-year-old fan from Cleveland, Ohio. Scott had heard his first Bruce Springsteen song when he was eight, and he was immediately "hooked." When he was sixteen, he and his best friend went to their first Springsteen concert. "He had this uncanny way of telling a story through his music," Scott said. "In a few short minutes he makes us fall in love with a character and associate ourselves with the journey the character is on, which is usually someone up against the odds overcoming obstacles."

In the summer of 2009, Scott broke his neck in a diving accident. When he finally woke up three days after the accident, he was completely paralyzed. Hooked up to a dozen life-support machines, he was unable to speak, eat, or even swallow. Doctors told him that he would never walk again. That he would spend the rest of his days in bed, however long that would be, and that all he should worry about was being as comfortable as possible.

While he was still on life support, three friends came to his room every day and played Springsteen songs on their guitars. As the days and weeks went on, Scott could barely breathe. But day after day, he sang along—barely audibly, because he was so weak.

Month after month, Scott blasted Bruce Springsteen through his headphones as he tackled one hurdle after another. "Springsteen motivated me every step of the way," he said.

Tears streamed down my face as I watched this video.

In 2012, three years after his accident, Scott was able to sit in a motorized wheelchair. He and the best friend who had gone to the concert with him when they were sixteen got tickets for the Wrecking Ball concert in Cleveland. The day before the Cleveland concert, Scott wrote to Springsteen's "camp" about how vital his music had been in his recovery process. Midway through the Cleveland concert, after playing "Trapped," Springsteen stood in front of the microphone and said, "This is for my friend Scott." Then he began playing "We Are Alive."

After the concert, Springsteen invited Scott and his friend backstage.

The power of Bruce Springsteen to help someone he had never met touched me. I scrolled through the comments below the YouTube video:

"I had cancer and listening to 'We Are Alive' is how I had the strength to beat it."

"In 1986 I was in an abusive relationship. I played these songs over and over and got myself out."

"Mental illness builds walls that are sometimes tougher to break down than real ones. I listen to these songs to give me strength to keep on trying."

I closed my iPad and sat back in my chair. There could not possibly be another singer, another rock star, another human being who had lifted as many people from the abyss as Bruce Springsteen.

19

LATE ON Saturday afternoon I arrived at AAMI Park, an outdoor stadium, in Melbourne. I walked up the fenced maze that wound from the sidewalk to the entrance of the thirty-two thousand–seat stadium and arrived at the ticket turnstile just as they were opening for business.

I found my way to the entrance of my section and stepped from inside the dim, low-ceiling cement concourse into the sky-high stadium. My eyes widened and I stopped to take in the vastness, intricacies, and details of the structure.

The seats were configured in a U shape, with the stage spreading across the top of the U. On what would have been the playing field if that day's event were a soccer game were two corralled sections for standing only. Men were shimmying up the speaker towers. Men were darting back and forth across the stage. Men high above the stage were adjusting lights. If it takes a village to raise a child, it takes no less to help an audience rise up and have fun.

I found my way to my section, stage right, and then to my seat—midsection and eight rows up from the field. Two couples were already seated on either side of my chair: a man who looked to be about forty-five with a woman who looked like she could be his mother, and a woman a bit older than me with a man I assumed was her husband. Both pairs were engrossed in conversations I could not hear. Neither pair seemed to take any note of me.

Eventually the middle-aged man glanced my way.

"Have you been to a Bruce Springsteen concert before?" I asked.

"No, never," he said. "But my mother loves his music, so I got tickets for her birthday."

"I think you're in for a real treat," I said, trying to seem cool and calm and not like a crazy, lonely old lady chasing an aging rock star.

He nodded, smiled, and turned back to his mother.

When the woman on my other side glanced at me, I asked *her* my question.

"No, actually, we haven't been to one of his concerts. We were busy last year when he was here and couldn't go."

"Wow! I think you're going to love it." I said this as if Bruce Springsteen were some unknown performer yet to be discovered.

"Yeah, I like his music and I hear he's quite a performer," she said, smiling. Then she turned her back on me.

I slumped back in my seat. I heard the man and his mother saying something about watching the bush fires caused by the heat wave from the deck of the mother's house. The woman on the other side of me said something similar. Before I knew it, the two couples were leaning across me and animatedly discussing the fires and then Melbourne politics and then Australian politics. I stared straight ahead and watched the spots directly across the stadium from me fill as people found their seats.

"I'm really looking forward to this concert," I heard the older woman beside me say to the mother and son.

"We are too," the son said, nodding and smiling.

I could not contain myself. Maybe they did not want to talk to me. But I was not thinking about that. I was thinking only about how amazing the concert was going to be and how much the people beside me were going to love it.

"Oh my God," I said, popping up between them. "You guys are going to love this. He's absolutely amazing."

I was off. Before I knew it, I was telling them about googling Bruce Springsteen and watching the YouTube video of his 2009 NFL halftime show.

"I watched the eleven-minute video five times in a row the first night, alone." I shook my head, excited all over again. I remembered the goose bumps I got every time I watched it. "Each time the video ends, I think, *I can't believe this man's father wanted him to get rid of his guitar*."

I looked at my seatmates. They were smiling at me, but just barely. I felt like an absolute jerk. I leaned back in my chair, put my hands in my lap, and stared straight ahead. I sat there breathing in and breathing out, careful not to look out the corners of my eyes so I wouldn't have to see their nonverbal communiqués with each other.

Finally, they turned back to their respective companions and became engrossed in their own conversations again.

I escaped to the bathroom.

On the way back from the bathroom, I saw an usher in her mid-forties standing at the end of my row.

"Excuse me," I said to her. "I'm from the States. Is it okay for me to stand and clap and dance during the concert?" After being hassled by the people behind me at the Adelaide concert, I wanted to know the rules in Melbourne.

"Of course," she said, smiling. "Enjoy yourself. Have a good time. Isn't that why you're here?"

"Thanks—that's my plan," I said. "I just wanted to make sure."

When I sat down in my seat, I noticed a woman on the field directly in front of the stage. She was walking toward the edge, pointing at me. She was dressed all in black and was wearing a lanyard.

Concert lanyards, I had learned in my short time as a fan, indicated that the wearer was someone special—either a VIP fan or a staff person connected with the band or venue. This woman in black with shoulder-length black hair and a lanyard, I suddenly realized, was Barbara Carr. And she was not just pointing at me, she was beckoning me toward her.

Even though the stadium was now full, there were no people sitting in the seven rows between me and the stage, so I was certain it was me she was gesturing toward. But there were thirty-two thousand people in the audience. How on earth had she spotted me? Why on earth did she want me to come down to her?

For a long moment, I did not move. Then, to make sure she was pointing at me and not someone behind me, I turned around. I didn't want the embarrassment of getting up to go to her and finding out she was not looking at me. I was still trying to feel okay about being rejected by my seatmates. I did not want to feel rejected anew by Barbara Carr.

No one behind me was standing or moving forward. I looked back at Barbara Carr. She was waving at me even more vigorously now.

I stood up and climbed, row by row, over the seven sets of chair backs in front of me until only the waist-high paneled fence that separated the field from the seats was between us.

"Anne, I'm Barbara Carr. Don't you remember me? We met in Adelaide?" She said all this as if we were at a cocktail party and she had recognized me from across the room.

I was stunned. She not only recognized me among a crowd of thousands, she also remembered my name.

"Of course I remember you, Barbara," I said, trying not to gape at her. "You're a celebrity."

"Well, I knew you'd be here somewhere, so while I was down here checking on things, I thought I would look for you."

"That's amazing. Thank you so much." I did not know what else to say.

"Well, I hope you enjoy the concert. It should be a really good one." She smiled, and then she walked away.

For a moment I was disappointed that she had not invited me to come over the fence and join her backstage. It seemed a bit odd for her to single me out just to say hello. On the other hand, she was working. And it was pretty cool that she had even thought to look for me, and *really* cool that she had actually found me.

I turned around and climbed back over the seven rows of empty seats. When I got to my seat with my back still to the stage, I stopped to catch my breath. As I did, I looked around. Every single person nearby, including my less-than-friendly neighbors, was staring at me, eyes open wide. I sat down and with just a hint of a smile I met the starstruck gazes of my seatmates. They would never know if dissing me had been a missed opportunity for them.

Everyone was standing now and calling, "Broo! Broo!" As if summoned by the chant, he appeared from the back of the stage and ran to his microphone. As he did, a guitar-carrying man about twenty years younger ran out from backstage to join him. The already-excited, wild crowd erupted as the two began to play.

"Oh my God," the older woman said to me, "that's Eddie Vedder. I can't believe I am seeing Bruce Springsteen and Eddie Vedder."

I had no idea who Eddie Vedder was.

"Oh my God," she said a moment later, "they're doing 'Highway to Hell,' I love this song."

I did not know the song either. But that did not make what was happening any less amazing to me. Whoever Eddie Vedder was, he seemed really happy to be sharing a microphone with Bruce Springsteen. And Bruce Springsteen seemed happy to be making Eddie Vedder and thirty-two thousand fans happy. His smile seemed more avuncular than rock star–ish.

I had never been to a lovefest, but all the positive, adoring, gleeful energy I was witnessing was every bit what I imagined one would be like. Bruce Springsteen and Eddie Vedder and the band were going full throttle. I was loving it. I was electrified.

We were all loving it. We were all electrified.

That hypercharged electricity did not stop flowing through me for the next three-plus hours. I was so electrified, so charged, so in the moment that I remember almost nothing but feeling nonstop euphoria and having nonstop fun. I was completely in each and every moment, not analyzing or thinking or trying to remember it. I let each moment fill me and carry me into the next one.

After a many-song encore, Springsteen and the E Street Band waved and left the stage.

"Broo! Broo!" everyone was calling. We were calling and calling and calling. No one was moving out of their seats or out of the stadium. We were all just standing there, calling, "Broo! Broo!"

I did not know what we expected. We'd already been granted a generous encore. Maybe, like me, everyone felt as if they'd been put under a spell. A spell that had erased the dimensions of time and the existence of gravity. We were suspended in air, floating free and untethered. There was no place we needed to go, no place we needed to be, but right here, right now. All together, as one. With Bruce Springsteen.

He appeared. Springsteen walked onto the stage, alone, with his guitar and a harmonica hanging from his neck. The stage lights went dark. When he reached his microphone, a spotlight appeared. He lifted his guitar and began a mournful rendition of "Thunder Road."

It was all I could do to catch my breath and steady my breathing. I had heard this song before, but always with the rousing accompaniment of the band. This time, the sounds of his harmonica, his guitar, and his voice landed deep inside me. They rocked me slowly back and forth, from side to side. I felt lulled and at peace. I was overcome by the beauty and soulfulness on the stage in front of me. Tears welled up and dripped down my face.

After Bruce Springsteen sang his last word and strummed his last note, he looked up at us—all thirty-two thousand of us.

"Thank you, Melbourne," he said—slowly, with an appreciative smile and a slight nod, sounding like he meant it. "We'll be back here tomorrow night." He turned around and walked off the stage. Then the lights went dark.

Not thinking anything but *Wow!* I instinctively turned to the man on my left.

"Wow!" he said, looking at me with amazement and shaking his head. "Wow! You were right."

20

FIVE DAYS earlier, in Adelaide, after I met Barbara Carr, I had googled her. All that came up was a singer, a different woman with the same name. After that, I had assumed she was one of many managers in the Springsteen organization. Not a no one, but not a someone either. Simply a nice woman with a three-year-old grandson.

But in Melbourne, the morning after the concert where she sought me out, she was the first thing I thought of when I awoke at six o'clock. I jumped out of bed and sat down at the desk, where Marc Dolan's *Bruce Springsteen and the Promise of Rock 'n' Roll* was resting, not yet opened, beside my computer. It had been a going-away present from a CCP colleague.

I picked up the book, turned to the index, and located "Carr, Barbara."

I broke the spine of the 512-page book, flipped to page 300, and read, and reread, and reread again about Barbara Carr, my heartbeat quickening with each reading. Then I put down the book, shut my eyes, and sat back in my chair.

Barbara Carr was indeed Bruce Springsteen's manager—more precisely, his comanager with Jon Landau, who in 1974, after seeing Springsteen open for Bonnie Raitt at the Harvard Square Theater in Cambridge, wrote the now-famous line in *The Real Paper*, "I saw rock and roll future and its name is Bruce Springsteen."

In January 1993, at the age of twenty-one, Barbara's daughter, Kristen Ann Carr, died of liposarcoma. She was engaged to be married, and Bruce Springsteen and his wife were going to sing "If I Should Fall Behind" at the wedding. Instead, they sang it at her funeral. Soon after, Barbara and her husband (Dave Marsh, a music critic and *New York Times* bestselling author) founded an organization named after their daughter to fund sarcoma research. In June 1993, Bruce Springsteen played at the Meadowlands to raise money for the organization.

With my eyes shut and my body rigid, I tried to reconcile the Barbara Carr in Adelaide with whom I had chatted about her black dress and her grandson with the Barbara Carr who had lived every mother's worst nightmare.

It seemed sadly prescient that Kristen and her fiancé had chosen "If I Should Fall Behind." When I heard it for the first time in Adelaide, I had thought of it as a ballad for seasoned lovers and couples. Sitting at the desk in the Park Hyatt Melbourne, I googled the lyrics again. This time I read them as a twenty-one-year-old woman about to be married.

> *We said we'd walk together baby come what may*
> *That come the twilight should we lose our way*
> *If as we're walking a hand should slip free*
> *I'll wait for you*
> *And should I fall behind*
> *Wait for me*

Kristen had been diagnosed only six months before she died. It seemed unlikely that she'd known she would soon be fighting for her life when she and her fiancé chose the song.

I tried to imagine Bruce Springsteen and his wife singing this song at their wedding. Then I tried to imagine them singing it at her funeral. I tried to picture Barbara Carr in the front row, facing Bruce Springsteen and his wife. I could not make out her face. Her head was bent and her black hair covered her face.

This was as far as I let my imagination go. I opened my eyes. The people working behind the stage to lift us up were also trying to make their way, stepping through this world one foot in front of the other.

21

ON SUNDAY I returned to AAMI Park for the second concert of the weekend. The driver had picked me up at four fifteen for the seven thirty concert. The stadium was not even open yet. I decided to go to a pub down the street.

I sat at a high round table near the door and watched as people came in and quickly filled the room with a buzz of shoulder-to-shoulder energy and excitement. Two twenty-something women perched on stools across from me, forehead to forehead, were cackling and taking absolutely no notice of me.

I took out my iPhone and checked my emails. Nothing. I checked my texts. I checked again. And again, and again, and again. Suddenly, my heart stopped and dropped into my stomach. Adrenaline began coursing through me. Nausea, a symptom I rarely experience, roiled inside me. My head, another part of my body that rarely causes me physical pain, started pounding. Pounding and thumping.

I looked at my iPhone again.

A very long, detailed text I had written to a friend two months earlier, venting about my daughter-in-law, Rebecca, was now showing up as a text I had just sent to my son, Richard!

How could this have happened?

It was almost five o'clock in Melbourne. It was two o'clock in the morning in Philadelphia. I could not call

Andy or anyone back home. It was only 11:00 p.m. in San Francisco, where Richard and Rebecca lived.

In fight-or-flight scenarios, I am a fighter. I needed to do something.

I tapped on Richard's name; his number was two below Andy's in my iPhone's list of "Favorites." I had no idea what I was going to say to him. I felt my heart thumping and thumping and thumping. I could feel bile rising in the back of my throat.

One ring, two rings, three rings, four.

"Hi, this is Richard Abel."

My heart stopped.

"Please leave a message and I will get back to you."

My heart resumed beating. I tapped the red dot on the screen and put down my phone. I looked around the maxed-out pub. I looked at the giddy girls across from me. I so wanted to tell someone, anyone, what had happened to me. I needed to talk. I needed not to be alone. I needed help. I searched the pub for someone, anyone, who . . . who, who, *what*? I didn't know.

I closed my eyes. I felt stranded, alone, and troubled, very troubled, in a pub mobbed with bursting ebullience.

I had tried to fight by calling Richard, hoping to somehow talk my way out of this mess. Now, without moving a muscle, without budging an inch, I took flight. My mind fled to where there was nothing but blackness and silence. I did not hear or feel or see. I was not here. I was not there. I was not anywhere.

I opened my eyes. Except for a few servers wiping down the bar, the room was empty. Everyone else had vanished. I looked at my watch. It was seven thirty. I felt for the concert ticket in my pocket. I did not feel like going to the concert. I did not feel like doing anything. I wanted to disappear from the planet. I was terrified. Things had been strained between Richard and me since he had married Rebecca two years earlier—but I had always assumed that we would work things out.

Once he read that text, however, our relationship would have no hope of someday improving.

That last thing I needed to do was go to a Bruce Springsteen concert. It did not matter that I had traveled thousands of miles to see it. If attending the concert was going to make me feel worse, I did not need to add insult to injury and subject myself to *more* anguish. I had been to the concert the previous night. One concert at AAMI Park was enough. I'd had the experience. I. Did. Not. Want. To. Go. Tonight. I just wanted to go back to the dismal Park Hyatt Melbourne.

I had completely and totally fucked up with that text.

I slid off my stool and walked out the door. I looked up the street and down the street. The sidewalk was empty. The road was quiet. It was as if the world had been evacuated and I was the only one left. There were no cars. There were no taxis.

A solitary car came along. I thought of putting out my thumb, but I did not. Not because I was worried about my safety; in that moment, I did not care what happened to me. But in my catatonic state, I could not coordinate my limbs with my thoughts. So I just stood on the sidewalk in front of the pub and stared ahead at nothingness as the car passed me by.

Then I turned my head and looked at the stadium. It was so close. I had my ticket. I could just begin walking there. I could change my mind and stop at any point. Maybe I could find a taxi in front of the entrance.

I set one foot in front of the other, as I was so accustomed to doing. One step. Another step. When I got to the stadium, there were indeed a few taxis. I looked at the taxis. I looked at the stadium. I was so close. I had come so far. If I went in, I could always leave. This would be a true test of Bruce Springsteen's magic.

I shuffled up the deserted ramp, held my ticket out to be scanned, and walked into the concourse. From inside the stadium, I could hear the familiar bellows of "Broo! Broo! Broo!" I stopped in the bathroom. I found my way toward my seat. This time it was on the aisle, higher up than the previous night but more in the center.

It was almost eight o'clock. All the seats except mine were occupied. I sat down, but when the eighty-year-old man beside me stood up moments later, I instinctively followed.

I looked at the stage. I looked around at the *Broo*ing fans. I took a deep breath and said to myself, *Whatever is going to happen with Richard is going to happen. There is nothing you can do now to change it. Just be here in the moment. Whatever will be will be.*

I looked at the eighty-year-old man. "Have you ever been to a Bruce Springsteen concert?"

"I have not. I'm here with my son," he said, smiling at the forty-five-year-old man beside him.

"You're in for a treat," I replied.

The stadium erupted with excitement and joy. One after another the members of the band trotted onto stage, followed by the man himself. I jumped into the moment.

But from the first song, "Born in the USA," I felt something was off. I told myself I was just imagining that Springsteen was not performing well. I told myself I was projecting my own personal turmoil.

But song after song, he continued to drag. Song after song did not seem right.

I glanced at the eighty-year-old man.

"This is not impressive at all," he said to me, shaking his head.

The songs stopped. Bruce Springsteen sat down on the edge of the stage and started talking. I had seen him do this before. But not for this long. Tonight, he kept talking and talking and rambling and rambling. He started talking about watching television past his bedtime as a kid, back when the television went dark for a couple of hours late at night—"Back," he said, "when our hopes and desires were not so scattered, and we actually went to bed at night and got some sleep."

He talked. He stopped. He talked. He stopped. He sounded like he might be drunk. Or very tired. Or really down.

The eighty-year-old man looked at me, and again he shook his head.

Bruce Springsteen talked about aging and dying. He talked haltingly about the isolation of new technology. People sat down. I sat down. I thought it would be inconsiderate to continue standing. I did not want to seem as if I were waiting for entertainment when Bruce Springsteen was so visibly drained of energy.

Finally, after a monologue too long and rambling to have been scripted as part of the evening's show, Bruce Springsteen let out an audible sigh. "If you had told me an hour ago that I would be here now," he said, shaking his head, "I would have said no way."

There was a collective gasp from the audience. The stadium went silent. Even the drunk revelers in the pit froze in place. I looked at Bruce Springsteen, sitting on the edge of the stage. He seemed so small. He seemed to be curling in on himself as he continued slowly sharing with us about how he was struggling.

We waited and watched. We waited and listened. His words began to come faster, his tone grew lighter. Then, he was standing. He was smiling. He was grinning. He was tapping his foot and saying, "One, two, one, two, three, four."

We were all standing. We were all cheering. Within minutes of his standing up and tapping his foot, the stadium was shaking. We were rocking. We jumped and clapped and danced. We turned to each other, smiling.

Collectively, we had hit rock bottom. If we had not felt it ourselves in the moment with Bruce Springsteen, we had all, every one of us, been there at some point. We knew how he felt. So many of us counted on him to get us through. We were happy to be able to return the favor and help *him*. It made our relationship with him, with each other, stronger, more meaningful.

At the end of the three-and-a-half-hour concert, Bruce Springsteen returned to the stage for a solo second encore. Then he bowed his head.

"Thank you, Melbourne," he said with a gentle smile.

He walked off the stage and the lights went dark.

I looked at the eighty-year-old man beside me.

"This was the experience of a lifetime," he said, beaming.

I floated out of the stadium, letting the sea of exiting fans propel me forward. Snippets of music and phrases of songs mixed with a sense of euphoria inside me.

If my feet made contact with the cement concourse, I didn't notice.

It wasn't until I walked into my room and took my iPhone out of my pocket that I remembered Richard and my toxic text about Rebecca. I shook my head in amazement. Bruce Springsteen's magic had indeed cast a spell on me and lifted me from my preconcert despair. Even now, alone in my hotel room and remembering my predicament, it did not feel as dire as it had hours earlier. I still felt that if Richard received the text, it would not be good, but I did not feel fatalistic the way I had in the bar and then trudging toward the stadium.

My euphoria from the concert had settled into a sense of equanimity. I would deal with the situation one thing at a time. The first being to text Richard, *I think I sent you a text earlier today, but I'm not sure. Nothing important, but did you get it?*

In a matter of minutes, he texted back, *No. What's up?*
Nothing. I love you. And goodnight!

Wherever the errant text went, it had not gone to him. All was good with the world. At least for now.

Midnight came and went. I was one day closer to completing my mission. Minute by minute, hour by hour, day by day, I was doing what I had set out to do.

22

THE FOLLOWING morning, Monday, I was on my way to Sydney. It was the third of five cities to which I was going.

Leaving the dingy Park Hyatt Melbourne and knowing I could check two cities off my list gave me a feeling of accomplishment.

I did not look at my itinerary often. My plans were not that complicated. I had eight concerts. I knew the cities in which they took place and the dates when they were occurring. It was not until I was picked up at the Sydney airport and headed to the hotel that I looked at my itinerary to see where I was staying—and panicked. I was staying at the Park Hyatt Sydney.

For eight nights.

The moment I walked into the lobby of the Park Hyatt Sydney, however, my fears subsided. Unlike the cavernous, dark, mirrored lobby in the Park Hyatt Melbourne, the one in the hotel in Sydney was just barely a lobby. It had one couch in front of floor-to-ceiling windows that were situated across from the four-person check-in desk. Beyond the check-in desk was a lounge with more floor-to-ceiling windows, these overlooking Sydney Harbor and the Sydney Opera House. Everything seemed bright and *clean*.

As I waited for the clerk to check me in, I turned to watch the smattering of people flowing through the lobby. They were primarily blond, middle-aged Australian couples in expensive cotton clothes, the women carrying Louis Vuitton bags in various shapes and sizes. Then, out of nowhere, a little boy who looked to be about three came running through the lobby. Chasing behind him was a very haggard-looking Barbara Carr.

She caught the boy by his hand. He was obviously the grandson for whom she had bought the T-shirt in Adelaide. She turned with him to return from whence they'd come, and her eyes met mine.

"Hi, Barbara," I said with a big smile.

I had not been in the hotel five minutes and already I'd seen someone I knew. And not just any someone; Bruce Springsteen's manager. I was *that* cool!

"Hello, Anne," she said with a wan smile and continued on her way.

Any disappointment I felt about her lack of friendliness was far outweighed by the thrill of learning that I was once again staying in the same hotel as Bruce Springsteen and his entourage.

On the way to my room, the valet showed me the hotel fitness center on the third floor. It was small but perfect. It had a bank of windows that looked out onto a sunny park. And in my hotel room there was an entire wall of sliding glass doors that opened onto a balcony overlooking Sydney Harbor and the Opera House—the same view as the lounge, but a little higher up. Even the white stone and marble bathroom seemed designed to allow natural light from the main room to stream in.

The next concert was on Wednesday night, at a venue not far from the hotel. The next two concerts after that were in the Hunter Valley, a vineyard region two hours away. By the time I had booked my trip, all the rooms in Hunter Valley had been filled, so I had decided to stay at the Park Hyatt Sydney all week and travel the two hours each way to the concerts on Saturday and Sunday.

I sighed with relief as I unpacked my bag, grateful that this Park Hyatt bore so little resemblance to the Melbourne one.

At six o'clock, hungry, I went down to the lounge and sat at a small round table. Across the table, I could see through the Chinese-motif scrim with accordion slats that separated the lounge from the small lobby. I prefer people-watching to nature, so I preferred this view to the one from other side of the table, which overlooked the harbor.

Immediately, through the scrim, I saw a familiar, burly man in his late sixties. I had seen him sitting in the bar at the InterContinental Adelaide with Steve Van Zandt. A few days later, when I'd read about Barbara Carr, I had learned that this man was Jon Landau, her comanager. And standing beside Jon Landau now, in the lobby, was Tom Morello.

I stood up, walked slowly into the lobby, and rested against the edge of the check-in desk. A woman who looked exactly like Barbara Carr, minus thirty years, ran by me, following her son.

"Don't you want to go to the beach?" she called to him, pleading.

I went back to the lounge to put my sweater and iPad on my chair. As I was setting them down, I heard a commotion in the lobby.

By the time I returned, the room was empty. I walked toward the sliding glass doors that opened onto the hotel driveway. As they opened, I saw a Mercedes van pulling away and a valet closing the back door of a green BMW with opaque black windows.

The BMW drove off, following the van.

I turned to see a young man with an earpiece giving a thumbs-up to the hotel staff at the check-in and concierge desks. "Thank you," he said to a man in khaki pants and a white button-down shirt.

I could not read the name on the pin on the man's breast pocket, but I saw that it said HOTEL MANAGER.

"Of course," the manager said. "If there's anything you or Mr. Springsteen or anyone in your group needs, call me directly. And of course, you have the direct number for our security manager."

They nodded and walked off.

Then I was all alone. By turning my back for just moments to put my things on my chair in the lounge, I had missed an opportunity. It had all been so perfectly orchestrated: Springsteen's people had created a deliberate commotion with the rest of the entourage, allowing him to sneak out of the hotel and into his car unnoticed.

23

THE NEXT morning, I woke up thinking about Richard. Until he got married, there was not one detail of his life that he did not hash out with me. In middle and high school, he would sound out ideas with me for an English paper. If someone looked at him the wrong way, we would talk about how he could handle it. When his girlfriend at Harvard asked him if he loved her, he talked to me for over an hour about how to answer her. And after he met his future wife, Rebecca, on the first day of his first year at Stanford Law School, he called me daily in a quandary about her. One day he liked her. The next day he did not. This went on for some time.

I did not know Rebecca. I just tried to listen to what Richard was saying and help him sort out what he was feeling. If he wanted her, I wanted her. If he didn't, neither did I.

By February, he seemed to be feeling more serious about her. When he told me she'd invited him to have dinner on Valentine's Day, I'd suggested he bring flowers. I'd also suggested that he look at the Sundance Catalog online and get her a gift. He had. And when they'd gotten engaged some months later, they'd also gotten her engagement ring from Sundance.

Richard was happy. I was happy.

But almost immediately after that, our relationship had begun to deteriorate.

I did not realize it, initially. They were on the West Coast; I was on the East Coast. My son loved Rebecca. And I loved him. So, I loved her. If she was not happy, he would not be happy. And his happiness had been my driving force from the moment he was born.

The way I saw it, we were all on the same team. I was on *her* team. So when I started to sense a shift, a tension, between us on phone calls, I hoped it was only that our relationship was experiencing growing pains, and that as long as I kept doing my best to please her, things would improve.

As the months went on and we visited each other in person back and forth, I refrained from addressing Rebecca's mistreatment of me directly. But after each encounter with them, I would turn to Andy and recount every transgression I had suffered during our time together.

"Did you see?" I would ask. "Did you see?"

"Just forget about it," Andy said time after time. "Just let it go. It's not like they live next door—we don't see them much."

The summer before I quit CCP, before my trip to Australia, Richard had called me to say he and Rebecca wanted to spend July with us at our beach house in North Carolina while they studied for the California bar exam. Hope springs eternal. I was elated. I thought only about how wonderful it would be for all of us to be together for an entire month. I had already invited other guests to visit us that month, but we had enough bedrooms for everyone. It would be fun to have a full house.

Richard and Rebecca arrived at our house the day after we got there. They took over two of the four guest bedrooms, using one as an office. We took them out to dinner. We bought the groceries they requested. We cooked the meals they wanted. They studied in their rooms all day, venturing out only around dinnertime. Things seemed harmonious enough. I liked knowing they were near.

Rebecca's birthday landed on their second week with us. I made a reservation at one of our favorite restaurants. It also turned out that our first houseguests would be arriving that evening. Adrian was my officemate at the community college. I did not know her well, but she seemed pleasant, and I liked having guests, so I'd invited her, her husband, and their eight-year-old son to visit.

I asked Rebecca if it would be okay to invite them to join us for her birthday dinner at the restaurant.

"No," she said. "I do not want them at my birthday dinner."

It did not occur to me that I should not have even asked her permission to have my houseguests come to dinner. Adrian and her family had been invited months before Rebecca and Richard had said they were coming to study for the bar.

I love being a thoughtful hostess and making people feel comfortable. But at that point, nothing was more important to me than pleasing Rebecca. So, although I felt uncomfortable doing it, I emailed Adrian that we would not be home when they arrived, and they should find dinner somewhere along their eight-hour drive to our house.

We returned from the birthday dinner to find Adrian and her family sitting on our porch, waiting for us to come home.

Things went more or less smoothly for a few days after that. Richard and Rebecca spent most of the time sequestered in their rooms. Then one night, all seven of us went out to dinner at a restaurant overlooking the beach.

There were too many of us to go in one car, so I drove Adrian and her family and Andy drove Richard and Rebecca. On the way to the restaurant, Adrian, who was sitting up front with me, quietly told me that although her son, Oliver, had social anxiety, he seemed comfortable with me. "Would you be willing to make conversation with him at dinner to help him work on making eye contact?" she asked.

I do not think of myself as particularly good with other people's kids, so I was surprised to hear that Oliver liked me. Mostly, he and I ate breakfast together. I am an early riser and so was Oliver. I would be in the kitchen, ready to dig into my oatmeal and berries, and he would appear in front of me.

"Hi, Oliver," I would say, "it's so good to see you."

Then I would give him whatever he asked for, and we would sit at the table together and talk. About the beach. About our dogs. We just seemed to go from one thing to another.

I was touched that this meant something to him.

"Of course I don't mind," I told Adrian.

We were seated at the far end of the restaurant. Andy sat at one end of the table, across from Richard and Rebecca. I sat beside him. Next to me was Adrian. Oliver and his dad sat across from me.

I started right in talking to Oliver. It felt different than talking to him at breakfast; in the morning, when it was just the two of us, it just happened naturally. I did not feel compelled to talk to him. He did not feel compelled. We just did. There were pauses while we chewed or thought. But here, at the restaurant, I could feel Adrian's eyes boring into me, and I could see her husband's eyes going back and forth between us in my peripheral vision. I do not like being watched. I felt a lot of pressure trying to dupe Oliver into a performance for his parents.

Thankfully, as we began talking in the restaurant, he eventually seemed to forget that his parents were observing us and he settled into nice, easy eye contact with me. But man oh man, was I working at it. I was so in the moment and so focused on Oliver, I had absolutely no idea what Andy and Richard and Rebecca were talking about. Actually, I'd forgotten they were even there.

Out of nowhere, I heard the loud ring of a cell phone, and my trance with Oliver was broken.

"It's Jason," Andy said to me. "I'll text him and tell him I will call back later."

Jason was Andy's college and graduate school roommate. He lived in Cleveland, where he was a dean at Case Western Reserve University. He'd never married and was like an uncle to our kids. He and Andy talked regularly. There was absolutely no need for Andy to text Jason. Often, they missed each other for weeks at a time before connecting.

I looked at Andy and, in a quiet monotone, said, "Put your cell phone away."

Andy always takes flight when given the choice of fight of flight. For some unknown reason, though, that night he decided to fight.

"I don't like how you said that," he said. "Say you're sorry."

"I'm sorry," I said, although I absolutely was not.

"Do you mean it?" my flight-prone husband of thirty-four years asked as five pairs of non-blinking eyes, in addition to his, focused on me.

I wanted to say, "No, you fucking asshole, I do not mean it. There was no reason for you to have your phone on the table, ringing or not. And, actually, I really, really could use some help here with Oliver; the two of us are stuck on a specimen slide under his parents' microscope."

Instead, I said, "Yes, I'm sorry."

The moment I finished speaking, Rebecca stood up, thrust her arm across the table toward Andy, and said, "I want the car keys."

Andy pulled them out of his pocket and handed them across the table to her.

Clutching the keys in her fist, Rebecca stomped all the way across the restaurant to the door—creating as much noise and commotion as she could create with her five-foot-one-inch, one hundred–pound body (which turned out to be, amazingly, a lot) as she went.

Adrian stood up. As she did, Oliver and her husband stood up also.

"I think we'll go for a walk," she said, pointing to the beach across the street from the restaurant.

Our salads, which had been served as this was happening, were on the table.

"Be sure to come back for dessert," I said. I am not sure why I chose that course for them to return. I was not imagining our eating dinner without them. I was not imagining anything. I was mortified.

Adrian smiled, and they left.

I looked at Richard across the table. He was sitting there as if Rebecca had just excused herself to go to the bathroom.

"What's going on?" I asked.

"What?" he said.

I could not imagine what he was thinking. I did not know what to say.

Suddenly, I felt someone behind me. I turned. Rebecca was standing erect and looking down at me in my chair. She seemed so tall that I wondered if she had grown in the minutes since she'd stormed out.

"You are never, *ever*, to do that again," she said slowly, wagging her index finger at me as she spoke. Then she turned with a swoosh and thundered across the length of the restaurant and out the door again.

I took a deep breath and, shaking my head in disbelief, turned toward Richard. After this last performance by Rebecca, it was clear to me that she was nuts. But my son just sat there calmly, as if nothing whatsoever had happened.

Adrian and her family returned. Andy and Richard and I stood up to leave. I was shaking, visibly.

"Would you like me to drive home?" Adrian asked me.

"No, that's okay." I was trying to act like everything was all right.

But I was not. As I drove the twenty-minute trip home, I had trouble staying on my side of the white-dashed lines.

When we got home, Adrian and her family hurried off to the beach to look for lightning bugs. Richard and Rebecca were upstairs. Andy was in our bedroom.

"I cannot fucking believe what Rebecca did," I said to him as soon as I closed the door behind me. "I absolutely did not deserve it. She was as out of line tonight as a person can be—"

"Just forget about it," Andy interrupted me, as if Rebecca had not said "please" at dinner when she asked me to pass the salt.

JUST FORGET ABOUT IT?

A few minutes later, Richard appeared in our bedroom doorway. "I guess Rebecca should apologize?" he said.

It was a start.

Rebecca and Richard came into our room. She said she was sorry. We hugged. We cried. Then, apropos of nothing, she said, "On our second date Richard said to me, 'I know that I know how to love because of the love I have for my mother and the love she has for me.'"

I was stunned to hear what Richard had told her about our relationship. He felt as bonded to me as I felt to him. I also realized his comment might have been detrimental to my relationship with Rebecca, who is both competitive and insecure. That remark had set me up as someone she had to compete against and defeat.

Rebecca also told us that night that she'd had anger-management problems until she was fourteen. I wondered who had declared that her anger problems had ended at fourteen.

After twenty minutes of talking and hugging and crying, we said goodnight.

I went to bed that night feeling hopeful that my relationships with both Rebecca and Richard were going to improve.

The following morning, Rebecca passed me in our hallway as I was headed to work out. That afternoon, Richard came to me and said, "Rebecca did not like how you looked at her this morning when you passed her in the hall. If you don't apologize to her and tell her you love her, we are leaving tomorrow. She also wants me to tell you that we are not having any more cathartic makeups."

I did not remember anything significant happening when Rebecca and I had passed each other. I was already in my pre-workout frame of mind, zoned out to the world.

When Richard said I needed to apologize to Rebecca for not smiling, I wanted to knock on her door and say, "I hate you."

Instead, I knocked on her door and when she called out, "Yes," I opened it and said, "Rebecca, I'm really sorry that I did not smile at you this morning. I was dreading my workout and that is all I was aware of. I love you. I love you very much. I'm sorry that I hurt you."

She did not say a word. She just nodded at me as if she were royalty nodding from a balcony at her adoring public.

For the remaining two weeks they were with us, Rebecca and Richard did not emerge from their rooms until I went to bed.

A few months later, Richard called to tell us they had passed the bar exam.

"Congratulations!" Andy and I said in unison. After a few minutes of happy banter, Andy chided, "Richard, you never thanked us for staying with us this summer."

"We had nothing to thank you for," he said.

Andy and I were shocked. Neither one of us knew what to say.

If Rebecca's behavior toward me had softened since that night in the restaurant, if she had been any less combative, antagonistic, or rude since that night, I believe my memory of that evening would have lost its sharp focus in my mind. If I'd had something more pleasant to replace it with, I surely would have done so. But I did not.

The month before my trip to Australia, Andy and I had visited Richard and Rebecca in San Francisco. When they told us Rebecca was pregnant, I'd inwardly shuddered. A baby was only going to make the situation more complicated and fraught. Of course, I acted as if I were happy—thrilled for them and for us. I'd bought Rebecca presents Richard said she would like. I'd bought things he said they wanted for the baby. I had not gotten one thank-you for any of it. Not one.

After every mistreatment by Rebecca and Richard, I felt myself inching closer to the abyss.

24

THAT FIRST morning in Sydney, I roused myself out of bed and out of my unhappy reminiscences about Richard and Rebecca and headed down to breakfast. From there I went to the fitness center.

It was just the way I like it. Empty.

I got on the bike and, with *Wrecking Ball* blasting though my headset, pedaled my hour to nowhere. I finished the final second of my final minute and then just let myself sit, without moving a muscle. I felt terrific. I felt more terrific than I could remember feeling in a very long time. And it was more than just happiness I was feeling. I felt proud of myself.

Here I was, doing the very thing that had terrified me for so long and getting along just fine. Some times were better than others, but I was doing it. And I was learning so much and seeing so much along the way. I had been able to tell within five minutes of his appearing onstage at the second concert in Melbourne that Bruce Springsteen was feeling off. I was seeing the E Street Band members passing through the hotels and interact as regular people with each other. I was even having fun.

As I sat on the bike feeling proud of myself, I thought of Richard. Two days before I left for Australia, he'd had a paper accepted in a law journal. When he called to tell me, I had of course congratulated him. Then I had asked to speak to Rebecca, whom I had also congratulated. I thought it was an opportunity to say something nice to her.

"Yes, thank you—it is quite an accomplishment for us," she'd said, accepting the compliment as if she herself had written the paper.

Sitting on my bike in the Park Hyatt Sydney, thinking about Richard, I felt proud of him all over again. I felt my heart opening. I decided to call him.

It was eleven o'clock in the morning in Sydney, six in the evening in San Francisco. Richard would be home. I would call him as soon as I'd showered and dressed.

I tapped on Richard's name on my iPhone.

"Hi, Mommy," he answered after just a few rings. "What's up?"

"I just finished working out and I was thinking about you and how proud I am of you," I said. "You know I am always proud of you. And I am especially proud of you for having a paper accepted by a law journal."

"Thank you," he said with no intonation, sounding as far away emotionally as he was geographically.

"I was also thinking how proud I am of myself," I said, and then stopped and waited. I was not comfortable going forward without some acknowledgment from him that he was open to listening to me. Until Rebecca, he and I had always been able to finish each other's sentences. Now, however . . .

I waited through the silence.

"Richard, are you there?" I finally asked.

"Yes," he said.

I slid from the bed, where I had been sitting, onto the floor. "Okay, Richard, I'll talk to you later."

"Bye," he said.

I dropped the phone on the gray carpet and curled into a ball. I felt I had lost my son. He did not care about me. He did not love or appreciate or respect me. He had cast me off.

Sitting alone in my room at the Park Hyatt Sydney, I wanted to transport myself through time and space back to Philadelphia. Being in turmoil a world away from home made the situation feel even worse. The familiarity of home, I thought, would help me feel less unmoored, less stranded, less helpless.

I have often thought that being in remission from depression, any minutes or hours or days of relief, is not unlike being a recovering alcoholic. Just as a recovering alcoholic may be only one drink away from falling back into uncontrollable drinking, a depressed person is only one difficult episode away from falling back into despair.

As I sat on the floor in my room at the Park Hyatt Sydney, I could feel myself dangling by my fingertips from the precipice of the abyss. But as I ruminated, my sadness and despair began to mix with indignation and anger.

I had really wanted to be able to get along with Rebecca and Richard. I had tried everything I could to make things better between us. But the more I had tried to please Rebecca, the more aggressive and cruel she had become toward me. I had been a sucker to take such treatment from her, and from my son. I should have stood up for myself at the beginning. I was not going to go on with them like this anymore. I had reached my limit.

I stood up from the floor and walked out onto the balcony overlooking the harbor. My eyes resting on the calm blue water, I tried to imagine a world without Richard. I was actually in a good spot in which to immerse myself in this alternate universe, given that we were separated by 7,500 miles and seventeen hours. I pictured visits with my other two sons, Robert and Ross. I pictured Saturday-morning conversations with them. Then I pictured myself not talking to Richard on weekends. That wasn't difficult to do; already, for months, he had been calling us only sporadically and infrequently.

Staring into the soothing waters of Sydney Harbor, I compared losing Richard to having a limb amputated. I would experience something like phantom pain, a pain generated by the brain and spinal cord—real sensations that might last forever.

What I was doing in Australia was unlike anything I did at home. I was living a surreal life. It felt like an out-of-body experience. I was living an alternate life, a life that was someone else's, not mine. While I was experimenting with changing so many things, big and small, why not change one more? Just as my days in Australia had been up and down, high and low, my world without Richard would have ups and downs, highs and lows. I would miss him. Profoundly. After just a week in Australia, however, hearing strangers say kind things to me that I never heard at home, I knew I would *not* miss being cast as the enemy by my son. At least he would not be able to hurt me anew. I had tried—unsuccessfully—living with Richard and Rebecca. Now, I decided, it was time to try living without them.

I felt myself tiring as I dangled from the edge of the abyss. I needed to pull myself up and hoist myself onto safe, neutral ground. I needed something to distract myself as I came to terms with a future without my son.

25

I LEFT the balcony and walked back into the room. I wanted to get out of there.

As I collected my devices, preparing to head downstairs and be a fly on the wall, my right hip—my problem hip—began to ache. I sat down at my desk to give it some relief.

Suddenly, my curiosity about Max Weinberg, the ear-piece-wearing drummer of the E Street Band, came to the front of my mind. In the few concerts I had been to in Australia, I had noticed that before and after songs a subtle glance passed between Weinberg and Springsteen. In a *60 Minutes Australia* interview with Springsteen I had watched in Melbourne, I'd been intrigued when he said that Weinberg watched his every movement and always knew, before even Springsteen did, what he was going to do next.

I googled Max Weinberg.

I went from one story to another, one YouTube video to another. I clicked and read, clicked and watched. There was so much about him that was fascinating. I was absolutely riveted when I came across this quote from Weinberg: "My drumming is based on the concept of the Hebrew word *seder*. If you're a good drummer, you serve the music. That's the only thing that matters. You must have some sense of order and organization."

I knew the Hebrew word *seder* meant *order*. But I could not understand the connection between the word and Max

Weinberg's drum playing. I put on my headset and played *Wrecking Ball* on my iPhone.

Wrecking Ball was the album I listened to every day when I worked out. The music flowed through me as I pedaled and counted down the minutes until I was done, and by the end my mood was always elevated at least a notch. My mind was so conditioned to feel better after listening to *Wrecking Ball*, in fact, that even when my legs were not pedaling my mood could be improved just by listening to it. I would never resort to such a sloth-like approach if I had not already worked out. But when the endorphins from my morning workout were depleted, listening to *Wrecking Ball* often helped me get back onto solid ground.

Sometimes, however, without the breathing and pedaling to focus on while I listened, my brain wandered and a voice began to reprimand me for feeling so bad. I became impatient with myself and my depression. The sounds coming from the headphones became a cacophony of irritating, maddening noise, and inevitably I ripped the headphones off, aborting the session.

Sitting at my desk in Sydney, it was not only my curiosity about Max Weinberg and the word *seder* that had me listening to *Wrecking Ball* but also the fact that the pall that had been cast on me by my conversation with Richard still had not lifted. One part of me was reading and thinking about Max Weinberg, but another part was wallowing in sadness and anger.

I didn't know the titles of the songs, but I was so familiar with the album that as one song ended, I could accurately anticipate the tempo of the next one.

I listened to the drums. I was having trouble focusing. My focus moved from the music to the lyrics. But I was not paying attention to the sounds emanating from my headset. Instead, I found myself listening intently to a voice in my head.

Your life is falling apart, the voice said with disdain. *Your son is an asshole. He's treating you like shit. You are all alone. And you have nothing better to do with your time than to sit here and try to figure out why Max Weinberg says his drumming is based on the word* seder*? Who cares? You should be out seeing Australia, seeing Sydney. Instead, on this beautiful summer day, you are holed up in your room. All alone. Doing nothing. Just killing time.*

Yes, on a beautiful summer day in Australia when I could be doing anything, I was sitting at a desk in my room at the Park Hyatt Sydney. My daughter-in-law Lindsey wanted me to see the Great Barrier Reef. It was on *her* bucket list. Another friend said I had to get out of the hotel and go sightseeing. Another wanted me to see kangaroos. Another, penguins.

Even if I felt good, I would not want to do any of those things.

I forced my attention back to what was blasting through my headset. It was a hodgepodge. Just sounds. Just noise. Irritating noise.

Then I heard it—the *thump, thump, thump* of Max Weinberg's drums. I was not hearing Bruce Springsteen or anyone else in the E Street Band. Just that *thump, thump, thump*.

Once I focused on Max Weinberg's drumbeats, I detected a pattern. And suddenly, sitting alone in my room at the Park Hyatt Sydney, I was no longer thinking about my life with or without my son—I was simply anticipating each new drumbeat together with Max Weinberg. Max Weinberg and I were tied together in the rhythm. In that predictable *thump, thump, thump.*

Thump, thump, thumpity-thump.

I felt my body loosening and relaxing. I was not in charge. Max Weinberg was in control. Accepting that, my mind felt lighter, more open. There was space. And into that open space came the sounds of Bruce Springsteen and the E Street Band. I recognized the song from one of the concerts I'd just attended, but not the band's rhythm or pattern. What were they doing?

Keeping Max Weinberg's *thump, thump, thump* on the first floor of my consciousness—bolstered and supported by his steady beat—I let the sounds of Bruce Springsteen and the E Street Band bounce freely in my head. I was listening easily, not analyzing or thinking, just feeling the sounds as they came and went.

They were riffing, I suddenly realized. The members of the band were taking turns playing their instruments solo or in duet. Springsteen and the band were being a bit crazy, a bit wild, taking chances doing something new while in the background Max Weinberg continued to play his predictable *thump, thump, thump.*

This musical free-for-all moved through me, its energy lifting me—fueling me, even—as I sat motionless in my chair.

Suddenly, every member of the E Street Band, including The Boss himself, went back to thumping along with Max Weinberg's steady, reliable beat.

And then the song ended. Perfectly synchronized. Not a beat missed.

Just as suddenly as the song ended, I understood. I understood what Max Weinberg meant when he said his drumming is based on the word *seder*. With his steady, predictable drumming, Max Weinberg established order, *seder*, for the band. This allowed his fellow musicians to go off and riff and play and dance, knowing that at any time they could tune back in to his beat—find their way back.

It occurred to me that just as *seder* makes for good drumming in a band, so too does it make for good dynamics in a functional family. A good family offers steady, reliable support to its members so that they can go off and try things, take risks, figure things out. A good family offers support to its members so they have the courage to live life, always knowing that no matter what happens, even if the worst happens, they are not alone. They can always go home or pick up the phone. And when they do they know they will hear the steady, reliable *thump, thump, thumpity-thump* of their parents' voices, and be comforted. Encouraged. Empowered. And they will take a deep breath. They will pause, even if unconsciously. And then they will continue with the song that is their life, a work in progress.

Yes, Max Weinberg was right. There is order, *seder*, in good drumming.

And there is—if we are lucky—order, or *seder*, in life.

For years I had tried to be the dependable drumbeat—the *thump, thump, thumpity-thump*—for Richard. Now, sadly, playing the dependable drumbeat for him had become toxic for me.

26

I TOOK OFF my headset and sat back in my chair. I headed downstairs to the hotel lounge for a meal to quiet my growling stomach. As I hiked to the elevator, it was not only my head that was feeling better after my four-hour dive into all things Max Weinberg but also my hip. The hours of rest had calmed it down.

"It's nice to see you again," the hostess said as I approached her stand.

I was surprised and impressed that after only one meal she was making me feel like a regular.

I ordered the eggs Benedict, as I had the night before. When I find something I like, I always go back for more.

I settled back into my chair and looked around. I did not see anyone I recognized from the Bruce Springsteen entourage—or, as I sometimes thought of it in my more cynical moments, the Bruce Springsteen Money Manufacturing Machine. In these moments, I found myself comparing Bruce Springsteen, the E Street Band, and the human machinery that kept them all going to Disney World.

We took the kids to Disney World once. We found it so creepy, Andy still sometimes will say, "First Prize is one week at Disney World, Second Prize is two weeks." What I found eerie and annoying was that behind the Magic Kingdom's facade there seemed to be a network of undercover spies watching every move that every person in the park made.

Once I stepped too far off the path and immediately a park employee appeared before me and cheerily steered me back.

I did not think that the Springsteen Machine was sinister or creepy. But it *was* apparent to me that the friendly, inclusive-seeming guy who was Bruce Springsteen and the cheerful demeanor of the people who shared the stage with him were carefully orchestrated and carefully guarded. Bruce Springsteen on display onstage was one thing. Seeing him offstage, as a private person, was something that—other than hitting the hotel bar after a concert—did not happen. There seemed to be a lot of smoke and mirrors set up to obscure him. He had a public image of Mr. Nice Guy, and it seemed that this image was protected like a hothouse plant. Nothing was left to chance. He did not casually walk out of the hotel to get into his car. He did not amble from one place to another. Teams were in place to make sure that, unlike at the end of *The Wizard of Oz*, no one was going to pull back the proverbial curtain on the wizard that was Bruce Springsteen and find a nasty old man faking it. No, the Bruce Springsteen Machine was a well-oiled money-making operation. That, it seemed to me in my darker moods, was the purpose of the whole enterprise. And I was as much a dupe as anyone for being sucked in by it.

On the other hand, they weren't hurting anyone. No one was being strong-armed to buy a concert ticket. And, in the end, even offstage, it was fascinating to me to see how these A-list people interacted with each other and with the rest of the world.

I sat back in my chair in the lounge and made a full visual sweep of the room—front to back, side to side, and through the narrow openings in the Chinese-motif accordion scrim that separated the lounge from the lobby. I spotted the young man with the short curly brown hair and earpiece I had seen the previous evening who I now thought of as Springsteen's "advance man." Again, he was dressed in black jeans and a black hoodie. Again, his intense gaze was bouncing from his iPhone to the periphery of the lobby.

The previous evening, he had left the lounge and walked into the lobby just as Barbara Carr was getting there. And as the two stood there talking, the E Street Band had begun assembling around them before heading out the door and leaving for the beach, creating a hubbub of activity that had built to a distracting crescendo, allowing Bruce Springsteen to slip out the door unnoticed. Their decoy mission successfully completed, the E Street Band and entourage had then followed their leader out the door and disappeared too.

As I finished my eggs Benedict, I kept my eyes on the alleged Advance Man for Bruce Springsteen, or AMBS. He traversed the small lobby twice.

I jumped up, unable to contain myself, and headed to the lobby to stake out a spot.

I positioned myself in between the lounge and the lobby. As I leaned against an archway, I saw Jon Landau step off the elevator. The two concierges, standing at their station across from the elevator, smiled at him. As he began to walk toward them, one of them came out from behind the desk and met him off to the side. They were less than two feet from me, but the narrow edge of the archway demarcating the boundary between the lobby and the elevator/concierge section of the room was enough to hide me.

"We'll be checking out at eleven on Friday," Landau said. "I want to make sure you have time to call in the staff you will need."

"Yes, of course, Mr. Landau," the concierge said.

"The group will leave first. When everyone is loaded into the cars, his things will be brought down."

"I will make sure things go smoothly," the concierge said. "I will be sure to be here myself."

Landau ambled into the middle of the lobby. Moments later, AMBS appeared beside him. They exchanged a sentence or two, and then AMBS got into an elevator and disappeared behind the closing doors. Landau shuffled a few steps to the only couch in the lobby and sat down at one end. I sauntered toward the couch, checking my iPhone, hoping to appear like any other distracted hotel guest waiting to meet someone, and sat down at the other end of the couch.

A few days earlier, I had read that Landau, an honors history major at Brandeis University, had begun writing for *Rolling Stone* in 1967. In 1974, after he offered his immortal line about the future Boss—"I saw rock and roll future and its name is Bruce Springsteen"—Springsteen had hired him. He was credited by many for fanning, if not strategically plotting, the rock star's rise to fame. He'd coproduced many of Springsteen's albums and advised him artistically. He had also managed and produced other celebrated singers, including Livingston Taylor, Jackson Browne, and Shania Twain.

It was amazing to me that a young kid with a history degree and no connections could follow his passions and convictions and rise to the top of the music industry. But as much as I admired and respected Jon Landau, as I sat near him on the lobby couch, it was mind-boggling to imagine this large, tired-looking, sixty-seven-year-old man with white hair and too much paunch as the prognosticating rock critic and all-knowing music powerhouse that he was. I pondered the silent but unerringly continuous passage of time and its effect on all of us.

I was bounced out of my reverie by a plop on the couch, one cushion over.

"Where are we going next?" I heard someone ask.

It was Tom Morello.

"We have a choice tonight," Landau said, turning his head to look at him.

He had to see me. I was sitting a foot from Morello. As a fly on the couch, I could not have been better situated.

"No, I don't mean where are we going *tonight*," Morello said. "Where are we going after Sydney?"

I was stunned.

I am by no means a member of the itinerary police. However, even *I* knew the cities in my itinerary and their order. Not that this meant anything to me, since I had no knowledge of the corresponding geography. But as someone counting down the days until I could return home, I was fully aware of the remaining cities on my itinerary and how many days I would be spending in each one.

Sitting on the couch next to Tom Morello, I realized that he was on the clock, punching in and punching out. I suppose it shouldn't have been surprising to me. But he was so electrifying onstage, I'd never thought of him as a guy doing a gig to pay the rent.

"The next concerts are in the Hunter Valley on Saturday and Sunday," Landau said. "We're leaving here Friday. We've rented out a golf resort there."

Max Weinberg stepped off the elevator and was coming toward us. He moved in a slow manner. Not a saunter; he did not look relaxed. It was more like plodding, as if he were concentrating on putting one foot in front of the other to move himself forward. It looked to me like the gait of someone for whom every step to get through the day requires determination and effort. I wondered if Weinberg suffered from depression. Compared to Morello, whose voice and body seemed to be overflowing with energy, Weinberg seemed lethargic. Morello was fifty and Weinberg was sixty-three, but it didn't seem the age difference would account for this much difference in energy levels.

Before coming downstairs, I had read that money had been tight for Weinberg's family when he was growing up; in fact, his father had declared bankruptcy at one point. Before he went into drumming, he had planned to become a lawyer. He just wanted to be financially secure. In 1989, when Bruce Springsteen disbanded the E Street Band, Weinberg had considered going back to school.

Watching him coming toward us now, I wondered if he was grappling with phantom financial demons. I also had read that he had had heart problems and cancer and had undergone multiple hand surgeries as well. I knew that he iced his hands regularly to cope with the pain caused by drumming.

Sometimes when I worked out, the pain in my left calf was so severe that the only way I could pedal through the agony was to pour cold water on it at regular intervals, momentarily numbing it. Of course, I worked out for only an hour. I did not have to endure for three-plus hours like Max Weinberg did during concerts. Furthermore, it was acceptable for me to look like I was in agony when I was pedaling. Weinberg did not have that luxury when he was playing for fans who saw him onstage and larger than life on the giant arena screens. He said that playing with Bruce Springsteen lifted him up and he didn't get tired during shows. But I did not think the Springsteen Money Machine would have approved if he'd told reporters that every time he beats the drum, pain reverberates through his hands.

Looking at him—he was now standing only a few inches from me—I could not help but wonder if he endured the pain of drumming for the money. Even if his net worth was, as reported on Celebrity Net Worth, $45 million, perhaps his parents' financial struggles had made him so insecure about money that he always felt he needed to earn more.

"So, what's the plan?" Weinberg asked Landau, his shoulders slumped.

"Do you mean where are we going after Sydney?" Landau asked. "Or do you mean what are we doing tonight?"

He reminded me of a camp counselor fielding questions from his charges.

"Where are we going tonight?" Weinberg asked, shifting listlessly from foot to foot.

"One of the multiplexes has offered to close down tonight and give us a private showing," Landau said. "There are thirty-eight movies to choose from, including a movie not opening until July 4."

"I want to see *The Wolf of Wall Street*," Weinberg said, suddenly coming to life and looking engaged, even happy.

The reviews I had read about this Martin Scorsese–directed movie had not been at all favorable. I was surprised that Max Weinberg was not more discerning. Surely this master drummer and performer knew the difference between good and bad art.

"And you?" Landau asked Morello, still seated hip to hip with him.

"Whatever," Morello said with a shrug, reminding me of a fourteen-year-old.

The three of them had turned into a father and his two adolescent sons, trying to figure what to do for the evening. It was fascinating to me to compare these people slumped beside me with the commanding, energetic superstars I watched with awe when they performed onstage.

"*The Wolf of Wall Street* it will be," Landau said, and with that he hoisted himself up off the couch, put his phone to his ear, and walked to the other side of the lobby.

Tom Morello slid to the edge of the couch just vacated by Jon Landau, and Max Weinberg sat down beside him. And beside me. It was amazing to me how invisible I was to them.

For a minute or so they just sat together, saying nothing. Then Weinberg turned his head toward Morello and began speaking. But his words were muffled; I could not make them out.

I needed to get closer without bringing attention to myself. I bent over and rifled through my tote. Then I simultaneously lifted it up onto my lap and resettled myself on the couch, closing the six-inch gap between me and Max Weinberg and putting us shoulder to shoulder with each other. My sweatshirt was rubbing up against Weinberg's black leather jacket. I could feel his arm moving as he spoke. My hands still inside the tote on my lap, I nonchalantly looked up and around the room—even looking at them, unaware of me—before circling back to my bag.

I felt as if I had no physical presence. Sitting there feeling Max Weinberg's shoulder, I began to imagine myself as nothing more than a floating spirit. Since I had left home, except for my conversations with Barbara Carr outside the hotel in Adelaide and a seatmate at a concert or two, I had not spoken face-to-face with anyone who was not performing a service for me. In this country, I was not accountable to anyone, anywhere. I could lock myself in my room and never leave, and the only people who would notice would be the drivers who took me from the hotels to the concerts.

My mind was pulled back to the here and now by a jolt to my shoulder from Weinberg as he turned the upper half of his body toward Morello and rested his upper back against my shoulder.

"He came up to me in the bar after the concert the other night and said, 'You know, the tempo in the first song was five beats off by the sixth measure,'" Morello said to Weinberg.

"I know. He spoke to me too." Weinberg shook his head slowly. "I knew we were off. But the sound coming through my earpiece was really bad. I couldn't hear anything."

I could not believe what I was hearing. It had been decades since I had taken piano lessons and thought about a "measure." I immediately imagined a sheet of music, and I remembered that dividing music into measures provides regular reference points to pinpoint locations within a piece of music. I pictured Bruce Springsteen as the "he" strutting into the bar and dressing down his employees with his post-concert critique, identifying the location of the errant beats in the "sixth measure." He was The Boss for a reason. He was relentless, not letting his band off the hook for even five errant beats.

It occurred to me that a good rock band is no different from a good ballet or a fine orchestra. They make what they're doing look easy and effortless, but in reality it is painstakingly difficult. Still, I never would have thought that precision and perfection would be as crucial for a rollicking, raucous rock band as it was for an orchestra or ballet company.

I was also surprised that it was only now, on Tuesday night, two full days after the concert, that Max Weinberg and Tom Morello were discussing this. Then again, the two men had been off the clock since the last concert in Melbourne. Maybe they had not even been together since then.

"Yeah, but ya know, if you go online people loved it," Morello said, shaking his head. "Really, they loved it. And at the beach last night, everyone was coming over and telling me how great the concert was."

I imagined Tom Morello trolling social media sites after a concert to see how fans had judged his performance. Being a rock star was hard work.

A woman about my age, dressed in black and with straight shoulder-length black hair and unforgiving bangs, came into the lobby and looked around. I had seen her in Melbourne in the hotel and again the previous evening in Sydney, and I had wondered if she, like me, was a fan following the tour. But unlike me, when she came over to Max Weinberg, he not only noticed her but stood up and, with a happy, easy smile spreading across his face, kissed her on the cheek.

Ah. She was Max Weinberg's wife.

I had read earlier in the day that the rabbi who had encouraged Weinberg not to give up drumming had married the two of them in 1981. It was nice to see how much more alive Weinberg seemed with her at his side.

A vortex of energy whirled through the lobby, creating a controlled commotion—and in the blink of an eye, everyone but me and a few nonplussed hotel staff was gone. No doubt off for their private showing of *The Wolf of Wall Street*.

I felt left behind. Sitting on the couch, absorbing the conversations of Jon Landau, Tom Morello, and Max Weinberg, I had forgotten I was me.

27

IT WAS seven o'clock when the E Street Band entourage abandoned me in the lobby to go see *The Wolf of Wall Street*. I wanted to get out of the hotel too. I remembered seeing a 7-Eleven down the street; I decided to go there to get some Kit Kat Bars and Diet Cokes. On nights when Bruce Springsteen and the E Street Band were unwinding postconcert with beers in the bar, I would be doing the same with Kit Kat Bars and Diet Cokes in my room.

The early evening weather was so comfortable that it felt like nothing at all. The air seemed weightless and frictionless. The hotel was in the middle of The Rocks, a neighborhood where the first fleet of Europeans landed and settled in Australia. Along the cobblestone streets and sidewalks were restored sandstone and glass buildings filled with art galleries and boutiques with artisan jewelry and one-of-a-kind clothing.

I stepped carefully along the cobblestones, ever vigilant not to stumble or twist an ankle. I imagined a channel in my head from which I had expunged Richard. My life as I knew it in this moment, I told myself, would be no different with him than it would be without him. His existence had no effect on my plans for the evening. If I could obliterate him from my mind as if he had never been born, I would feel better. Not good, but better. I was determined to try to inhabit this surreal world without him. Practice makes perfect—and I did not even need perfection. I did not need my pain level to be zero. I just needed it to be less than it had been for months going on years.

I stood on the sidewalk, watching tourist couples swaying together as they went in and out of still-open shops. As I did, I heard a voice in my head that I had not heard before. *You are amazing*, it said. *What you are doing is absolutely amazing.*

In spite of my unbounded fear, I had come on this trip. Even in the lowest moments, I had not thought of packing up and going home. And today, after being deflated by Richard and feeling myself hanging by my fingertips from the edge of the abyss, I had pulled myself up. I had moved myself forward. All alone—okay, with a little help from Max Weinberg and his drums, but *mostly* alone—I had changed the course of my mood.

How was I ever going to be able to go back to my boring box of a life in Philadelphia, where every single step was an effort? Where I felt like I had nothing to say? Here I was across the world—seeing so much, learning so much. Here I was across the world from everyone and everything I knew, functioning hour to hour, day to day, doing things.

Resting against a lamppost on the cobblestone sidewalk in The Rocks, I felt like I had so much to say. So much to share. I wanted to be part of a conversation. A conversation about ideas. Ideas about how people get through their days. I was not the only one struggling. If Bruce Springsteen could sit down on a stage at the beginning of a concert and say, "An hour ago I had to take a Xanax," then there had to be a lot of people out there besides him and me who knew what it felt like to suffer through a day.

It was okay to struggle. It was okay to be figuring things out. And that is exactly what I was doing. I was trying to figure out how to make my life better. I was trying to figure out how to make myself feel better. I deserved credit for knowing the day I quit my job at CCP that I needed to take control of my own life. No one had been able to help me stay out of the abyss in the past. I knew it was up to me to do it, in one way or another. And now here I was, walking toward the 7-Eleven in The Rocks neighborhood of Sydney, Australia, in search of Kit Kat Bars and Diet Cokes.

Yes, I was amazing. I really was.

When I left the 7-Eleven with my bag of Kit Kats and Diet Cokes, a voice in my head said, *Only a loser would feel happy to have traveled across the world only to spend the evening buying Kit Kats and Diet Cokes.*

With that, my nascent self-awareness and the accompanying feelings of self-acceptance and confidence that had filled me from the inside out minutes earlier began cracking like a shedding skin and decomposed to nothingness.

Still, for a few minutes on a cobblestone sidewalk in Sydney, a new, confident, hopeful me had emerged. A me who felt she could take care of herself. A me who had something to add to a conversation. Just as suddenly as these new-found feelings of hope and confidence had risen up in me, they'd imploded. The feelings had vanished. But images of the awakened me remained.

I began walking along the cobblestones opposite the side of the street I had walked down on my way to the 7-Eleven with my bag of Kit Kats and Diet Cokes. Unlike the gleaming boutiques and galleries I had passed earlier, the storefronts on this side seemed smaller, even quaint. I stopped at a shop with provincial blue wood framing the front window. A white sign with simple black lettering read Louis

Cardini. The inside was dark, except for a softly lit window display with colorful leather handbags, totes, backpacks, and wallets—cherry red, sky blue, leaf green. There was even an orange knapsack. I was mesmerized by the colors and buoyed by their cheerfulness. I had never seen leather backpacks and pocketbooks in such bright, playful colors before. Unlike kangaroo salt-and-pepper shakers or koala shot glasses, a wallet or backpack or tote would be a perfect souvenir to bring home. I decided I would come back when the store was open.

I had turned from the window and taken my first step back toward the hotel when I heard the jingle of bells. I looked around and saw a man in his early seventies holding open the store's blue-framed door. The lights inside had been turned on.

"Would you like to come in and look around?" he asked in a heavy French accent. "I always feel honored when I see people stopping in front of my window."

No doubt he was the eponymous Louis Cardini.

"Oh, no," I said. "That's okay. I'm staying down the street. I can come back when you're open."

I really did not want to bother the man. It was late. He probably had put in a long day and was ready to go home. But also, I don't like going into stores where there are no other customers. It makes me feel self-conscious when salespeople watch me as I look through their merchandise. I feel self-conscious anytime someone is watching me or looking at me. I am particularly uncomfortable when I think someone is analyzing me or labeling me as one thing or another, including a likely sale. I like to be The Watcher, not The Watched. If I accepted the invitation of this French-accented man, I would feel awkward looking at his merchandise. I was not *sure* I wanted to buy something. I did not want the pressure of shopping under duress.

"As you wish," he said. "But I'm in the back doing paperwork. I still have a good-size pile to get through."

I had no place to go and nothing to do. I smiled and walked into the store.

"I will leave you to look around," he said. "I'm just there in the back corner if you have any questions. And please, anything you see I can make for you in any other color that you see."

"Are you Louis Cardini?" I asked—almost rhetorically, as he seemed so sincerely accommodating, even after hours, that I was sure he was the owner.

"I am," he said with a kind smile, as if he were proud to be able to claim the name. "Please, if you would like to put your bag on the counter, you might be more comfortable."

I looked down at the 7-Eleven bag I had forgotten I was holding. "That's okay. It's just a couple of candy bars and some soda."

"As you wish," he said again. And he disappeared through a doorway into the back.

I picked up a leaf-green backpack and opened it. The inside was lined with a lighter green leather with zipper pockets and a pouch for a phone. The price, marked on an easy-to-read tag hanging from the zipper, was less than I had paid for a backpack before I left for my trip. I walked over to a blue backpack and slipped it over my shoulders. It felt comfortable, as if it had been mine forever.

I took it off and tried imagining it in one color after another. Then I saw an orange wallet.

That was it. Orange. I wanted this backpack in orange. How fun that would be!

Louis Cardini reappeared from the back. "If you like chocolates, you must try these," he said, holding out a chocolate sampler box with six delicately molded candies. "I am a chocolate lover and I bring back a supply of these every time I go to France."

"How long have you been here?" I asked, forgetting about the chocolate. Forgetting about the orange backpack I wanted.

"I have been here twenty years," he said, picking up one of the chocolates and putting it in his mouth.

When he first offered me the chocolates, I had cynically assumed they were merely a ploy to soften me into a sale. But watching him quietly savor his chocolate of choice, it seemed clear that his willingness to share with me from his special stash was also an act of kindness from one chocolate lover to another. To show my appreciation for his considerateness, I chose a chocolate from his box.

"How did you come to be in Australia?" I asked before carefully placing the chocolate in my mouth.

"Have you heard of Louis Vuitton?" he asked, looking skeptical.

I nodded. His products were ubiquitous in the hotel. They were also ubiquitous in my hair salon at home.

"I worked there for fifteen years," he said. "I worked my way up from floor sweeper to designer. But then things started to go bad for the company and then for me. The economy was not good in France. So I came here where there was so much room for growth. I started with a workshop in the back of this store. Now I have a factory outside Sydney with twenty people."

"It's just you overseeing everything?" I asked.

"My daughter is in France. She helps me with sales there. But other than that, I do everything from designing to buying and selling. It keeps me young." He selected another chocolate and placed it in his mouth.

He was a lanky man, but he clearly loved his chocolates. And he seemed to be enjoying sharing them with me, just as an aficionado of specialty beers or fine wines might enjoy drinking with a fellow enthusiast rather than drinking alone.

"What brings you to Sydney?" he asked when he had swallowed his second chocolate.

"Oh, nothing," I said. "I'm just here to see a Bruce Springsteen concert."

"That doesn't sound like nothing," he said.

"It's a long story." I gave a small shrug. "I quit my job and didn't know what to do, so I came to Australia to see eight concerts, actually. It hasn't been too bad, I guess. But I haven't really done anything. My friends keep writing and telling me I should go on excursions to see kangaroos and penguins. I pretty much just hang out at the hotel and watch all the things going on there. It's where Bruce Springsteen is staying, so it's pretty interesting. But I do get what my friends are saying."

"If you want to please them and see those animals, just get on the ferry and go over to the Sydney Zoo for an hour and have a couple of pictures taken with a kangaroo and some penguins," he said. "But I think you're being hard on yourself. It sounds to me as if you're doing what you want to do."

I could not believe it. When had Louis Cardini gotten the memo about my being hard on myself? Did it precede me everywhere I went? Was there writing on my forehead that I could not see?

Sales tactic or not, I could not help but smile at him.

"I was wondering if it would be possible for me to buy an orange backpack?" I asked, walking over to the leaf-green one and pointing to the orange wallet next to it.

"Of course." He smiled. "I don't have one. No one has ever asked for an orange backpack or handbag. Occasionally I sell the wallets in orange. Especially around Halloween. But I think it's a splendid choice. Very fun. I can take down your shipping information and I can ship it free of charge in about four weeks."

We completed the transaction, and I was gathering up my 7-Eleven bag to leave when he said, "Excuse me. Please, would it be possible for you to wait here a minute while I go in back?"

I nodded and waited.

When he returned, he handed me two small provincial blue "Louis Cardini" bags with white tissue paper peeking out from the top. "These are for you," he said.

I was not sure if I should look inside then or wait until I got out of the store. But he looked so happily expectant that I did not want to disappoint him.

I pulled out the paper in the first bag and inside I found a beautiful orange wallet, a perfect match for the backpack I would be receiving. In the second bag was a box of six chocolates.

"It's been a pleasure having you in my store," he said. "And, really, I have lived here twenty years and I have never seen a kangaroo or a koala."

"Thank you," I said. "It's been a pleasure for me too. Thank you for opening your store and giving me a private showing, chocolates and all."

We shook hands and I walked out the bell-jingling door. In one hand I carried my white plastic 7-Eleven bag with Diet Cokes and Kit Kat Bars. In the other hand I carried my provincial blue Louis Cardini bags with French chocolates and a supple orange wallet.

Not a bad evening out and about. Not bad at all.

There was no one in the lobby except the check-in staff when I returned from 7-Eleven and Louis Cardini.

Riding up the elevator to my room, I could not block Richard from my mind.

Richard was born on January 10, 1982, at 12:06 p.m. When I heard his first cry, I instantly knew that for the rest of my life I would do anything in my power to help him and support him. Until now, that had been the case. But never before had I felt as if I were sacrificing myself for him. Helping him had always buoyed my own consistently sagging feelings. When I talked to him about whatever angst he was wrestling with, I completely forgot about myself and my own problems. I am a goal-oriented person. I loved him, and his well-being was my primary goal. Nothing gave me more gratification than helping him unravel his predicament of the moment.

It was only recently that I had realized Richard never thanked me with words. I wish I had known to teach him to make a concerted effort to convey his appreciation for me, to me. But, until he became engaged to Rebecca, I always *felt* appreciated by him. When we were together, I could see his gratitude bubble up through his body and spread across his face. In person or on the phone, I felt a gratitude from deep inside him traverse our invisible bond and fill me to the very top. And because I felt what I thought was his profound appreciation, I did not feel anything was lacking from him. I did not miss the Hallmark-like sentiment of an official thank-you.

But when Rebecca came into our lives, the dynamics between Richard and me changed. The fact that she was now Richard's confidant and Number One Person was not what I was upset about. His transfer of allegiance from his mother to his wife was exactly what I had hoped for. I had done my job. I had set him on his way. "You're cooked," I'd said to him when he left for college. The heavy lifting of bringing him up was over. I would remain available for consultations and crises, but by and large he was off and on his own.

Initially, I'd still felt connected to him. I'd still felt I knew him as well as I knew myself. I had been so proud of him. I had loved him so much.

Now, I loved him, but I was not proud of him.

Until Rebecca, my putting his needs before my own gave rise to a synergy that left us both better off. Now, my ongoing efforts to ignore the abuse and rise above it were only leaving me feeling increasingly depleted and depressed.

The doors of the Park Hyatt Sydney elevator opened. I stepped out, turned toward the floor-to-ceiling windows along the corridor, and rested my head against the glass. I thought of something I had learned in Hebrew school decades earlier, an aphorism attributed to Rabbi Hillel: "If I am not for myself, who will be for me? But if I am not for others, what am I? If not now, when?" It is from *Pirkei Avot* (in English, *Ethics of the Fathers*), a compilation of the ethical teachings and maxims passed down to Moses and rabbis who came after him, detailing the Torah's views on ethics and interpersonal relationships. In Hebrew, as I had learned it, the words are mellifluous and poetic—some version of a long haiku (oxymoronic, I know). I would often ponder the didactic conundrum put forth in these deep but simple words: "If I am not for myself, who will be for me?" Sadly, I realized that for me, as I considered this problem with Richard, there *was* an answer to this rabbinical puzzle. If I were not for myself, *nobody* would be for me. And that was just not right.

Feeling unsettled, I lifted my head off the hall window beside the elevator and, carrying my gifts from Louis Cardini and my 7-Eleven bag, went to my room. I put my Diet Cokes in the mini-fridge, placed my two Kit Kat Bars on top of it, and unwrapped the box of chocolates and orange wallet. I placed one of the French chocolates on my tongue and stroked the leather of the wallet. The sweetness of the melting chocolate in my mouth and the suppleness of the leather that was making contact with each and every nerve receptor in my fingertips filled me with a sense of calm.

My eyes closed. Richard evaporated from my consciousness.

28

I WOULD NOT have thought that a bed at a hotel as perfect as the Park Hyatt Sydney would have a wrong side. But it did, and the following morning I woke up on it. I headed down to the dining room with a weary heaviness in my head and heart.

The kind familiarity of the dining room staff was comforting. I sat back in my chair and looked out at Sydney Harbor. I needed to get control of my head. I could not continue to let Richard hijack my mind.

I breathed in. I breathed out. I picked up my coffee cup and took a long sip, concentrating on the bitterness and the sweetness of the warm liquid as it passed down my throat. I took another sip and did the same. I picked up my spoon and scooped some oatmeal and blueberries into my mouth. I focused on the feel of the lumpy, warm cereal sliding down my throat and the squish of the blueberries against my teeth. Over and over, I reined my mind in and focused on the minutiae of the oatmeal and coffee as I consumed it.

It was early. There were no guests in the dining room for me watch and distract myself. So I watched the servers.

"Madam, is there anything I can get you?" my server asked when he noticed me looking around the room.

"No, everything is fine, thank you," I said.

I picked up my newspapers. One after the other, I focused on the stories. When I felt Richard creeping into my thoughts, I focused on the words, the letters, the photographs in front of me until he disappeared. I opened my laptop and wrote to my people. It felt good to be writing to them about my E Street Band sightings. It felt good to have stories in which I thought people would be interested. Whenever I started to think about my oldest son, I concentrated on the feel of the keyboard beneath my fingers. I focused all my consciousness on the word I had just typed.

My being in the moment seemed to be working. But it was exhausting. When I finished writing to the people back home, I crossed my arms in front of me on the table and lowered my head onto them. I was tired. So tired.

"Ma'am, is everything okay? Are you all right?"

I looked up. The man who had served me breakfast was standing beside me, looking down at me with a worried expression. He seemed truly concerned.

"I'm sorry," I said, appreciating that he had taken the time to check on me. "I'm sorry," I repeated, now starting to gather up my things. "I'm fine. Thank you. I will be out of here in a minute."

"No worries. I was just concerned when I saw you with your head on the table. Take your time." He gave me a small smile before walking away.

I packed up my belongings and headed for the fitness center.

As workouts go, it was not a good one. In the nanosecond before I pushed down on the pedal, my legs kept faltering. I could feel my body wanting to stop. I could feel it wanting to give up. But my mind did not. It was determined to get me through, minute by minute. It knew that if I let my body take control and stop my pedaling, I would feel bad about it for the rest of the day. My brain knew that I had enough things about which to feel bad. It did not want one more.

So, because the music wasn't helping, my brain focused on the timer on the control panel. It watched the seconds add up to a minute. One less minute to feel bad about if my body quit.

Finally, after thirty minutes, the endorphins began to kick in and my mind was able to coordinate the beat of Max Weinberg's drumming with the push of my feet on the pedals. When I finally got to the end of the sixty minutes, my mind disconnected from my legs and they came to an abrupt stop. *It's over*, I thought. *I did it. That's all that matters. The worst part of your day is over.*

I had generated only enough endorphins to get me through the workout. When it was over, there were none left to move me forward. I sat catatonic on the bike for some time. Then I dropped my feet to the ground, shuffled to a window overlooking a park, and curled into the window well to watch the scene.

What I saw was identical to what I had viewed the previous day. The sky was blue with puffy white clouds. The sun was shining. Families and couples were strolling along the paths, pushing strollers or holding hands. Children were running circles on the grass and flying kites. On the lake, boaters were rowing in slow motion, as if they had no place to go and merely wanted to move their arms back and forth.

When I'd looked out the window the previous day, I'd been reminded of the painting *A Sunday Afternoon on the Island of La Grande Jatte*, by Georges Seurat. Today, after my uninspiring workout, I watched the people and wondered if they were really happy or even content, or if they were just going through the motions.

As I tried to imagine what was really going on inside their heads, my brain was simultaneously trying not to acknowledge that a Richard Abel existed in the world and also trying to figure how best to handle him.

A burly man came into the fitness center and began grunting behind me as he lifted and lowered barbells. My dark reverie broken, I slid off the window and went into the locker room.

Although it was labeled as such on the door, "locker room" seemed like an absolute misnomer for this deluxe suite of rooms, even though there were, in fact, lockers. The rooms sparkled even as they enveloped me in a cocoon of warmth. The walls and lockers were made of a lustrous dark wood that looked like it was nourished daily with oils. The small white tiles on the shower room floor glistened, as did the larger white ones lining the walls. The grout was applied so perfectly between the individual tiles that from a distance they could have been mistaken for a prefabricated single sheet. But the texture of the grout was not fake and it added a palpable dimension to the wall. I imagined it as an art installation titled *White*.

The hint of fragrance in the air permeating the rooms filled my nostrils, but instead of feeling annoyed as I do by most perfumes and fragrances, I felt soothed. Blissfully, there was no ambient music, just the quiet hum of the HVAC.

I sat down on the wooden bench in the middle of the room and took off my shoes and socks. The tile floor was heated! I pulsed my toes on the floor, breathed in the rarified air, focused my gaze on the light dancing off the tiles of the wall, and listened to the steady, hushed flow of the HVAC.

All that filled my mind were the steady stimuli of four of my senses. When I finally blinked and broke my reverie, I felt my chest moving up and down slowly and almost imperceptibly, as if I had just awakened from a state of hypnosis.

As I showered, I remained focused on physical sensation—the rainforest-like spray of water, the smell of the shampoo and body wash, the deep plushness of the soft white towels. By the time I was dressed in my khaki-gray cotton concert garb and walking out the door of the fitness center, I felt as if I were returning from a laid-back beach vacation. No worries, no cares. It was as if the humidity in the locker room had soaked into my brain and turned my sharp-edged thoughts and feelings into a potpourri of soothing mush.

My stomach was gurgling. I wanted nothing more than to eat. I headed down to the lounge.

When I sat down to eat, the server smiled at me and asked, "The same?"

I nodded and thought of the 1980s sitcom classic *Cheers* and its theme song, "Where Everybody Knows Your Name."

The eggs Benedict were as good the third time as they'd been the previous two. As my hunger pains subsided, my mind, which until this point had been preoccupied with physical survival and the hunt for food, returned to combating a more secondary threat to my survival: my feelings of hopelessness and despair about Richard.

Angst churned through me. I did not feel like sitting in the lounge. I did not feel like people-watching. I had no idea what I did feel like doing, but I knew I could not sit still in my chair any longer.

I left the lounge and went straight to my room, where I threw myself face down onto the bed.

There was really no need for me to move for the next several days that I was booked at the Park Hyatt Sydney. The only people who would miss me were the drivers hired to take me to concerts five, six, and seven.

Lying face down on my bed, I just wanted to get on a plane and go home. As much as I wanted this trip to be over, however, I was no longer picturing home as a familiar place where I was surrounded by people I loved.

Imagining this place called home, I felt a shiver go through me. I was as lonely and despondent as I had been since arriving in Australia—but imagining myself in familiar surroundings did not make me feel any better. Rather, my mind ran an endless loop of the insurmountable problems facing me at home. I did not seem to be able to break the cycle. I did not seem able to even begin to formulate a solution.

I jumped off the bed, an anguished, frustrated, terrified scream rising in my throat—but I subdued my vocal cords. I did not need hotel security bursting through my door.

Today I did not have the energy to be a fly on the wall. I did not even want to go to the concert that night. I also was no longer looking forward to going home.

"It's pathetic," I said to myself. "It's pathetic that you have nothing better to do with your life than chase an aging rock star around the world. Even worse, this aging rock star who lifted you with his smile and his energy, his enthusiasm and humanity and his words, and made you feel like you had a chance is nothing more than a con man. His only concern is making money. Money, money, and more money."

I lay in my bed thinking how stupidly gullible I was to have been fooled by the Springsteen Money Machine. A man who sucked in his adulating, adoring fans night after night, playing a varied assortment of the same High Hopes Tour songs with a smattering of fan requests. I had seen enough. I did not need to be part of his chicanery anymore. I had been duped. Dorothy thought the wizard was a powerful, all-knowing man; then she saw his old, chubby body behind the curtain and realized he was a phony. So too had I seen behind the curtain of Bruce Springsteen and his abetting cronies.

I was done with him. I was done with his concerts. I was done watching him tap his feet and strum his guitar, stirring me and the rest of the audience into a rock-band frenzy of worshiping disciples. The magic was gone.

I did not have the energy to push myself back from the abyss. I did not have the energy to fight off the negative voice. I flopped onto my belly on the bed. My heavy head dropped to the pillow. My eyes closed.

I never takes naps, not even when I am sick. But that afternoon I fell into a deep sleep.

I felt a startle go through me when my eyes opened. Disoriented, I lifted my head to look at the digital clock on the night table. I had been asleep for almost four hours. For over four hours, I had put myself out of my misery. For almost four hours, my mind had felt no pain.

When I sat up, my head felt as if it were filled with heavy, opaque stuffing. I did not feel rested. I felt like crap. Maybe it was jet lag. Maybe it was fatigue. Maybe it was me. Just plain, depressed me. I wanted to collapse back onto my pillow and remain there. I was *not* going to go to the concert that night. I needed to contact the driver to tell him. But I did not have the focus to track down his number to reach him. Besides, he was probably on his way to the hotel already.

I would go down and meet him and tell him that I wasn't going.

I got up and headed for the door. Then I stopped and turned around. I gathered my concert ticket, my passport, my international phone, some cash, and a credit card and stuffed it all into the two oversize pockets of my pants. More options are always better than fewer. It would be better for me to have what I needed in case I changed my mind and decided to go.

My room was some distance from the elevator. My response to physical exertion is mostly always positive. By the time I stepped onto the elevator, the despair and heaviness I had felt in the room only minutes earlier was dissipating. I felt my mind loosening and my momentum building.

Feeling lighter and more open, I let myself be sucked into the vortex of activity swirling through the lobby.

I had never seen the room filled with so many people. I did not see any E Street Band people, but that wasn't a surprise; they were probably at the concert venue already.

I triggered the automatic glass doors that opened to the hotel entrance and stepped outside. "Waitin' on a Sunny Day" rang from my iPhone. The driver was here.

I'll just tell him I'm not going to the concert, I thought.

But as my hand slid into my pocket and I felt my ticket, I stopped. I *had* come across the world to see this concert. I had nothing to lose by getting in the car. If I decided when I got there that I did not want to go in, I could ask the driver to take me back to the hotel.

I located the car and climbed in.

"Hi, Anne," he greeted me. "I'm Joseph."

"Hi, Joseph," I said as I fastened my seat belt. "Just so you know, I might want to leave the concert early."

"Really? I've never heard of anyone leaving a Bruce Springsteen concert early," the thirty-something said, looking at me in his rearview mirror and smiling.

I gave him a limp smile to acknowledge his comment.

"Are you seeing any more of Springsteen's concerts in Australia?" he asked me.

"In the Hunter Valley and then Brisbane."

"The Hunter Valley concerts should be really cool," he said, his voice reflecting excitement.

"I read the venue has only two thousand seats," I said. "Why do they bother doing a concert so small?"

"There are only two thousand *seats*. But it's an open-air venue and there will be twenty thousand people there. They bring chairs and blankets and spread out on the grass. Concerts there require days and days of setup. But they do it absolutely for the cool factor," he said. "It's much more unique and special than playing in an arena. Last year when Springsteen toured here, he played at Hanging Rock—it's a former volcano that's now a national park in the middle of the country."

"How far is it?"

"It's about seventy-five kilometers northwest of Melbourne."

I shook my head. "That seems pretty crazy, to have rock concerts in a volcano."

"Isn't it? They just started doing it a few years ago. Leonard Cohen was their first concert."

I did not know who Leonard Cohen was, but I didn't ask—I didn't want to seem culturally clueless. Instead I said, "You sound like you know your way around music."

Joseph chuckled. "Actually, I'm the only one in my family not involved in one way or another in the music industry."

"What do they do?" I asked, always curious about people.

"My brother works for a company that sets the lighting for concerts in stadiums and arenas. He worked on the lighting for tonight's concert."

"That's pretty interesting," I said, and I truly meant it.

"Do you know it takes two days just to set up the lighting for a concert like the one tonight?"

My eyebrows raised. Once again, I was learning about something I had never even known enough to wonder about. "I had no idea," I said. "I am new to all this."

"Springsteen has a guy whose job is packing and unpacking the lighting equipment they ship for overseas concerts," he said. "It takes up ten shipping containers."

"I'd think it would be easier to use local lighting than shipping all that equipment."

"They don't want to depend on strange equipment. It's a really finely tuned operation. My brother works with the guy responsible for the shipping. This guy personally oversees the packing and unpacking of every piece of lighting equipment. If something breaks in shipping, he's on it immediately to replace it."

"That sounds like a pretty painstaking, stressful job," I said. If Bruce Springsteen complained about being a few beats off in a song, he surely would not be happy if the lighting malfunctioned during a concert.

"That concert you're going to in the Hunter Valley . . ." Joseph looked at me in his rearview mirror. He seemed to be enjoying talking to me as much as I was enjoying listening.

"Yeah?" I said.

"It's in the middle of a vineyard," he said. "It takes two weeks to set up the stage. Two weeks."

"That seems excessive. And after two nights they take it down?"

"Yep." He nodded vigorously. "It doesn't take two weeks to break it down, but it isn't fast either. But the vineyards love it. They get a lot of exposure and they sell a . . . well, let's just say they sell a *lot* of wine."

Before I could ask another question, we arrived at Allphones Arena.

Joseph jumped out of the car and held the door open for me. "I will text you my number. If you want to leave early, just text or call me. I have local jobs tonight, so I'll be able to swing by and get you."

I sat still for a moment. Then I slid across the seat and got out.

"You know what?" I smiled at Joseph. "Just listening to you made me feel better. It's pretty unlikely I'll leave early. Actually, it's much more likely I'll leave late. It is a Bruce Springsteen concert, after all. Thank you."

"That's terrific," he said, returning the smile. "I am really glad. I'm sure Bruce will make it worth your while."

When I stepped onto the sidewalk in front of the arena, I realized that not once during the fifteen-minute ride with Joseph had I thought about Richard. It felt good not to be churning. It also was empowering to see that I could live a life that did not include him, even if only for fifteen minutes. It was a start. It made me a bit more confident about baby-stepping my way toward a solution, whether that solution included him or not. Whatever the answer was, I would consciously and deliberately find my way to it.

As I walked toward the entrance of the arena, my Richard problem shrank to the back of my mind. In the forefront of my mind was Bruce Springsteen and the E Street Band. From deep down within me, I felt excitement bubbling up. Bruce Springsteen had never disappointed me. Bruce Springsteen had never not made me feel like I had a chance.

My steps felt light. My mind felt light. My heart was open and full of hope.

29

THE TWENTY-ONE thousand–seat Allphones Arena in Sydney, the site of my fifth concert, seemed pretty generic. It did not have the homey, quaint feel of the eleven thousand–seat Adelaide Entertainment Center. It also did not have the sweeping magnitude of the outdoor AAMI Park stadium in Melbourne. But it didn't really matter. I had not come to Australia to study stadium and arena architecture. I had come to hear good music and see good shows.

I arrived just as the arena doors were opening, and I easily found my aisle seat—stage left, in the middle of the first section. Two women whooshed in front of me and sat down in the seats beside me. Then, holding two plastic cups of beer, the woman next to me stood up.

"These are great seats," she said, twirling around in a complete circle and speaking as much to me as to the person she'd come with.

I smiled at her, relieved that her beer stayed in its cup.

She was in her early forties and had long blonde Farrah Fawcett–style hair. Her jeans were so tight I did not know how she was able to sit, and she was wearing a white scooped midriff blouse that left little to the imagination.

"I'm so excited," she said, turning to me. "I brought my daughter with me tonight. It's her twenty-first birthday."

I smiled at her and then at her daughter. "Happy birthday," I said.

Her daughter, who was holding a bottle of water, gave me a half smile. Her face implied mortification more than excitement. Like her mother, she was wearing jeans and a white blouse. But the jeans were the loose-fit style and her blouse covered her torso. She was pretty enough with her shoulder-length blonde hair. Unlike her mother, she did not seem to be going for the bombshell look.

"By any chance would you be willing to change seats with us so I can sit in the aisle seat?" Farrah Fawcett's Australian doppelgänger asked me. "You'd be able to see the stage better."

"Thank you," I said, as if she were my fairy godmother and she had just offered to wave her wand and fulfill my deepest wish. "I would like to keep this seat."

"Okay," she said cheerfully. "But I have to tell you, I am going to be running in and out to get closer to the stage. I really want to get a selfie with Bruce."

I was unsure how she was going to manage this. Security guards were already lined up and down along the wooden barrier separating the seats from the pit and the seats on the floor area in front of the stage. But all I said was, "That's fine. I'll move out of your way."

"After the concert I am going to run to the back door behind the stage where the musicians come out," she said. "I am going to try to get Bruce to invite me to an after-party. I heard he does that."

I was pretty sure my half-dressed seatmate was delusional—either because she was high on drugs or just naturally out of touch. I felt sorry for her daughter, whom I would have liked to talk to . . . but not enough to relinquish my aisle seat to her mother.

Suddenly, Bruce Springsteen was center stage, strumming and singing and smiling and tapping the heel of his boot. I jumped up and clapped and smiled and tapped the heel of my boot too. True to her word, Farrah ran past me and down to the wooden barrier. As soon as she got there, the guard sent her back. I was not really paying attention to her, but she seemed to do this every other song, leaving her daughter sitting glum and alone.

Toward the beginning of the show, Bruce Springsteen had announced that Jake Clemons, the band's saxophonist, had gone back to the US because his father, Bill Clemons, had died. Bill Clemons was the brother of Clarence Clemons, who had been the E Street Band saxophonist from 1972 until his death in 2011 from complications of a stroke. Clarence was a close friend of Springsteen's; Springsteen had dubbed him "The Big Man." At every concert I had attended, Bruce Springsteen sang a tribute to Clarence in "Tenth Avenue Freeze-Out," singing the lyric "and The Big Man joined the band" as images of Clarence Clemons and Danny Federici, another deceased band member, filled the jumbo screens on both sides of the stage.

Tonight, after his fifth song, Springsteen sat down at the foot of the stage facing the audience, his feet resting on the steps leading up to it in the center. Everyone in the audience sat down too. It seemed to me that in Australia Bruce had been doing this more than he had in the concerts I'd been to in the US. Here, he'd been doing it at least once a show. During the second concert in Melbourne, he'd sat down twice. Now, after only five songs, he was sitting again. I wondered if he was feeling sad about the death of Bill Clemons; perhaps, I thought, the death had rekindled his grief for Clarence.

"I'm gonna be sixty-fucking-five this year," Springsteen said with a weariness in his voice that matched the fatigue that seemed to have overtaken his body.

Looking at him onstage, sitting there before us—shoulders slumped, elbow resting on his leg—my heart opened up to him. I knew just how he felt. Tired. Very tired. Tired and achy. Tired and achy and old.

It seemed to me that Bruce Springsteen was giving everything he had to put on the high-energy, multi-hour performances his fans paid to see. I sensed it was getting harder and harder for him to maintain the level of physicality for which he is known and revered. His ability to do a marathon-length concert with the energy of a sprint. Despite his aura that suggested otherwise, he was human. For all of us, some days and some nights are better than others. As you age, the frequency of the better ones, the days and nights where you can perform like a superhuman, are bound to become fewer, bit by bit. Aging, it seemed to me from watching the people and dogs I know and love, does not happen in quantifiable chunks. It seemed to be more of a slow, erratic decline.

Sitting onstage, his weariness showing, Springsteen segued from his approaching sixty-fifth birthday to "the toilets in the fine hotel I am staying in."

I started nodding my head. I knew those toilets. To call them "toilets" was a radical understatement. They were like nothing I had ever seen before. I, myself, had been startled when I'd first arrived in my room and gone to pee in the bathroom. An iridescent blue light emanated from within the bowl and on the keypad to the side. I had not spent any time investigating this unusual piece of plumbing equipment, but from what I could tell after scanning the icons on the keypad, the toilet could talk to you, wash you, and even play music.

And now, Bruce Springsteen was talking to twenty thousand fans about these blue-light übertoilets. What was he thinking? This was not a plumbing convention. Where was he going with this? Was he experiencing the early stages of dementia or Alzheimer's? Was Steve Van Zandt going to get a signal from Barbara Carr or Jon Landau to pull Bruce Springsteen onto his feet and thrust a guitar into his hands?

No, no, and no. They let Bruce Springsteen talk on.

"You know, I get up in the middle of the night in these strange hotels," he said. "The jet lag has me not knowing if it's day or night or where I am. Even though it's dark and it's supposed to be nighttime, even with drugs, I'm unable to sleep. As I stumbled into the bathroom in this fine hotel, not knowing where the lights are, worried about falling, I see a blue light coming from inside the toilet and on the keypad attached to it. Who thinks up things like computerized toilets? But man was I thankful for that blue light. Yeah, there really is a blue light coming from the toilet. A blue light. The blue light."

He stood up from the steps at the front of the stage and walked to his microphone. He took the mic from the stand and, holding it to his mouth with his right hand, he raised his left hand high above him and quietly, almost in a whisper, he sang, "Can you see the spirit?"

He sang it again, a little louder, and again, a little louder—"Can you see the spirit?"

A blue light shone down on him.

"Can you see the spirit?" he bellowed.

The next thing I knew, I, along with twenty thousand other fans, was jumping and swaying and dancing, singing and clapping and feeling terrific, as Bruce Springsteen and the band belted out a high-energy rendition of "Spirit in the

Night." It was just how I imagined it would be to be reborn at a gospel revival.

I found myself standing there wondering, *What just happened? What did he do to us?* One moment he was rambling about feeling old and disoriented and about the blue lights on the computerized toilets. Then, like magic, we were jumping to our feet. He had been invigorated. We had been invigorated. Life was good.

I was awed by his creativity in using the blue light on his toilet to elevate his fans into a rock 'n' roll–style revival. Had he known he was going to do this at the beginning of the concert? Had it come to him in the previous song, as he felt his energy waning?

Like any good magic trick, the fun was not in knowing how it was done. The fun was in seeing it performed for us.

He finished the song on the catwalk at the back of the pit, pointed toward the stage, and dropped himself on his back into the crowd and the upstretched arms of his fans. Inch by inch, the fans passed his body toward the front of the pit and the stage.

I had seen him do this at other shows. This time, as always, my heart sped up. I clutched my hands together in front of me and willed him forward with all my mental might. He never seemed to betray any nerves during this maneuver: his smile never waned; his singing did not stop. But tonight, when he dropped back into the arms of his fans, it looked bad, sloppy. His body was not straight-as-a-board taut. It was sagging, and his smile was flickering.

Then again, I was sitting closer to the pit than usual. I wondered if it was simply because I was so close that I could see the strain in him.

After a few minutes, he arrived back across the pit, in front of the stage, and two band mates hoisted him up to a standing position. It seemed to take longer than usual for him to regain his composure.

He shook his head and with a grim smile said, "Thanks for not killing me. It got a bit hairy there for a minute."

When he said this, I suspected it was not because I was sitting closer to the action that his passage had seemed to be difficult. I suspected it had *seemed* difficult because it *was*.

From my seat, I was able to see the audio people off-stage, sitting in front of screens and controlling the sound. A few songs after "Spirit in the Night," I saw Barbara Carr come out from behind the back of the stage. Standing behind the audio people and facing Bruce Springsteen up on the stage, her back toward me, she began clapping and dancing.

Wow, I thought. *Barbara Carr must truly believe in her product. And she must truly like his music.* Despite her daughter's death, she was inspired enough by Bruce Springsteen and the E Street Band to dance and clap and maybe even have some fun.

As the show went on, my Farrah Fawcett seatmate continued ping-ponging from her seat to the waist-high barrier separating the pit and the seats on the floor from the rest of the arena. Each time she got to the barrier, two guards pointed her back to her seat.

Below us, Bruce Springsteen was walking down the stairs across the stage from us and parading through the audience, smiling and singing. People along his path were reaching out their arms to touch him. He stopped beside a fan and took the cup of beer he was holding out for him. Tossing back his head, Springsteen chugged the beer. It was hard to tell who was enjoying the beer more, Springsteen or the fan whose beer he was drinking. Even I was savoring it, and I don't like beer. Bruce Springsteen handed the beer back to the fan, gave him a soft salute as a thank-you, and then continued to sing and dance his way around the bottom perimeter of the stadium.

Farrah Fawcett whooshed past me, exclaiming, "I'm going to get my picture now!" I watched her run to the bottom of the steps, push aside the people standing at their seats in the first row, and fling herself at Springsteen, stopping him in his tracks. Quickly, she snapped a selfie.

Springsteen, ever the professional, smiled even as the security guards pulled her off him and set him free. As one of the guards escorted her back to her seat, I looked over at her daughter. When her eyes met mine, she shrugged and winced.

I smiled back.

"If you go back down, we are going to have to evict you from the concert," the security guard said to Farrah Fawcett when they arrived at our row.

Farrah pushed by me and stood, beaming, at her seat.

"Did you see me?" she asked her daughter.

Her daughter gave her a weak smile. She stood woodenly as her swooning, twirling, half-dressed mother danced on.

Two songs later, the E Street Band held up their instruments to the audience and left the stage single file through the back. An organ was brought onstage. Springsteen handed off his guitar and sat down in front of it; the lights onstage dimmed, and a soft spotlight appeared only on him in his black jeans and black, sweat-soaked T-shirt. He put his hands on the keyboard and, with his head bent and his face as somber as his surroundings, he began to play a string of slow, gently resonating chords.

"Dream baby dream," he sang. The sounds of the organ rose and took flight, carrying his words and a part of his soul to us in the audience.

Dream baby dream
Dream baby dream
Come on and dream baby dream

Tears dripped down my face. The words were so simple, and yet as Bruce Springsteen sang them, I felt my body softening. I felt my mind expanding, as if it was trying to feel what it would be like to dream.

Andy and I once went to see the comedian John Oliver perform in a small theater near Philadelphia, where we were lucky enough to sit in the first row, just a couple of feet from the center of the stage. Midway through the show, a spotlight following him, Oliver began pacing back and forth across the stage riffing about fantasies, dreams, hopes he'd had as a kid. He talked in great detail about the many superhero powers he'd dreamed of acquiring so he could pummel his many bullies. Then he stopped in the middle of the stage. He lifted his right hand and pointed his index finger at me.

I felt a sudden warmth and realized that my entire body was lit up by the spotlight.

"What was your dream when you were a kid?" Oliver asked, walking forward on the stage toward me.

I knew he was speaking to me, but just in case, I turned around to the person behind me. There was no light on him, and he, and everyone in my peripheral vision, was looking at me.

"I'm asking you in the first row here," I heard Oliver say.

I turned back to face the stage. He was staring at me with a smile and a twinkle in his eye.

I stared back at this very funny man who was waiting for me to speak. For a moment I did not know the answer to this simple, straightforward question.

Then, suddenly, it came to me. I did not have dreams or fantasies as a child. I never fantasized about who or what I might want to be when I grew up. I never dreamed or fantasized about things I wanted to do in the here and now either. It never occurred to me to do that. It never occurred to me that was something people did. I was so busy and intent on following my parents' every edict and doing all that they set out for me that I did not have the time or energy to wonder or daydream about anything. I loved them and trusted them and wanted only to do everything they asked of me so that someday they might love me.

And even that desire—for them to love me—was not a dream. It was the distant cousin of a dream. It was a hope. I hoped that someday they would deem me worthy of their love. I kept this hope deep down inside and recreated it into its more pragmatic form, as a goal. I never let my mind go free and daydream or imagine a someday world in which they loved me. I never let my mind go free and daydream or imagine a someday world about *anything*. I hadn't done it as a child, and I hadn't done it as an adult. I had never learned how to dream.

With the spotlight on me and John Oliver watching me, waiting for me to tell him my childhood dream, I just shook my head and shrugged. I did not want to push the limits of his comedic abilities, vast as they were. I did not want to hear him turn my inability to dream into a joke. He got the message. The spotlight moved on.

At the Allphones Arena in Sydney, as Springsteen sang "Dream Baby Dream," my mind loosened. I felt safe. Safe enough to let myself go, safe enough to try to imagine what it might feel like to dream.

As the tightness in my body and mind released, as my brain opened, I kept my gaze tethered to Bruce Springsteen and I kept my ears attuned to his voice.

We gotta keep the light burning
Come on we gotta keep the light burning
Come on we gotta keep the light burning
Come on and dream baby dream

I stood at my seat, trying to feel if I had a light burning inside me. Did I have something I deeply wished for, something I wanted so much that it would keep me moving forward?

We gotta keep the fire burning
We gotta keep the fire burning . . .
Come on and dream baby dream

Fire? Did I have not only a light but also a fire burning inside me? Something so hot, so powerful it would fuel my reach for a dream? Maybe I did.

Come open up your heart
Come on and open up your heart
You gotta keep on dreaming.
You gotta keep on dreaming
You gotta keep on dreaming

His voice faltered on that last "dreaming," as if he himself were overcome with skepticism about his own ability to keep doing it.

Come on dream on,

dream baby dream
Yes, oh yes, my heart was open now. My mind was open. My body was swaying.

Come on darling and dry your eyes
Come on baby and dry your eyes . . .
Come on dream on, dream baby dream.
Yeah, I just wanna see you smile
And I just wanna see you smile
Come on dream on, dream baby dream.

He wiped the sweat from his face with the palm of his hand.

"Yeah, I just wanna see you smile," Bruce Springsteen sang again. But this time as the words floated from him to us, from him to me, he stood up and, holding the microphone in one hand, he moved to the front of the stage.

"Come on you gotta keep on dreamin'," he sang as he held the microphone in his left hand and stretched his right arm above his head and then pulled it down to his side, extolling us to notice and follow his words.

"Come on and open up your hearts," he sang over and over, lifting his arms and dropping them each time as if begging us to really listen to what he was asking us to do.

"Come on darling and dry your eyes," he sang. But now he held his right arm outstretched at his side as if pulling us all in and embracing us. His chest was out, his head tilted back. It felt like he was begging us. Begging us to pick ourselves up, to lift ourselves, to open our hearts and our minds and to try to dream our best dreams, to be the best people we possibly could be.

I wanted so much to do that. I wanted so much to take control of myself and let myself be the best, happiest me I could be. It was okay that I was not that way now. That I had not been able to do it thus far in my life. Bruce Springsteen was standing in front of me telling me with every bit of soul and energy he had that it was okay to open my heart and try to dream.

As he stood there with his arm out, his chest out, his face lifted up, he began to sway. First his head. Then his torso. Then he spread his feet hip-width apart and let his entire body undulate from side to side.

As he urged us—begged us—it seemed to me he was also speaking to himself. He was also urging himself, begging himself, reminding himself to keep on dreaming. To keep the light, the fire inside him burning. To dry his tears and smile.

Maybe he was feeling deflated because of the death of Bill Clemons. Maybe he was reliving the fresh grief of Clarence Clemons's death. Maybe he was exhausted from jet lag. Maybe he was exhausted from touring. Maybe he was exhausted from being almost sixty-fucking-five years old. Whatever the reason, he was struggling to do what he was begging us to do. We were in this together.

"Come on you gotta keep on dreaming . . . Come on dream on dream on baby . . . Come on and dream baby dream."

His face filled the giant screens on both sides of the stage. I could see the lines in his forehead. I could see the lines around his eyes.

He stopped singing and stretched both his arms above him. The music, which had continued even when he had left the organ, played on.

"The E Street Band loves you," he said above the organ's rolling chords. He smiled. He bowed his head. He bowed his body. He turned and, with his arms stretched out, he walked slowly into the darkness of the unlit stage and disappeared.

I stood staring into the darkness where he had been, shaking my head, my hands clasped together at my heart. I had never been a part of anything so beautiful and powerful.

I left my seat and floated toward the exit in a trance. If people were pushing and shoving, I did not feel it. It all seemed surreal, as if I were already living in my newly created dream.

If I talked to Joseph on the ride back to the hotel, I do not remember what we said. I do remember seeing Springsteen's young, hoodie-clad Advance Man waiting outside the hotel when I stepped out of the limousine. But I did not stop. I did not pause. I did not care if he was waiting for Springsteen to arrive. I did not need to hover and wait, hoping to glimpse this superman so powerful that in a single evening, with a single song, he had been able to lift the heaviness in my brain that had been weighing me down as far back as I could remember. I did not need to see him. I held him in the depths of my soul.

In the coming days and weeks, I was going to learn to dream. I wanted to be loved and respected by the people close to me. I wanted to be able to depend on myself to make myself and my life better. I was going to create a dream in which I was not a silent, accepting victim.

I floated to sleep feeling hopeful that I would be able to make that dream come true.

30

THE NEXT morning, as I stood up and turned toward the dining room exit after finishing my breakfast, I saw Barbara Carr's husband running out the door after their three-year-old grandson. Nearby, in the middle of a banquette, at a large oval table, sat a tired-looking Barbara Carr. I was the only other guest in the dining room. I was sure she would not want to talk to me. But there was no way for me to avoid going by her table on my way out.

I left my table and started my way across the dining room, headed to the fitness center. I had the leaden feeling that accompanies my pre-workout lethargy. There was no way I would be able to initiate or maintain a conversation with this woman. The only thing I could think of saying to her was about her daughter who had died. Andy, when I had asked his opinion, had told me not to mention it to her if I ever spoke to her again. He thought it might upset her.

I put my head down and began to walk across the taupe carpet toward the exit.

Mid-step, my feet stopped. Mid-step, I looked up.

I was standing at Barbara Carr's table. She was looking at me and smiling. I didn't know what to say.

"Hi, Barbara," I said.

"Hi, Anne."

She began chatting to me about someone who'd been at the concert the night before. She said his name, but I didn't recognize it.

"You know," she said, "he's very rich. He owns an estate across the harbor over there." She pointed out the dining room's floor-to-ceiling windows toward the harbor with animated drama. "You know, Bruce solicits donations at all his concerts for local food banks. This man gives a lot of money to Australian food banks, and he has invited us to his estate for lunch today." She spoke quickly, excitedly.

"Oh," I said, not knowing what else to say. I was a bit dazed by her liveliness and the larger-than-life scene I was imagining of Bruce Springsteen and the E Street Band and their entourage all having lunch with a rich Australian man at his estate on the coast of Sydney Harbor. "That's very generous of him to give to the food banks," I said, finally thinking of something appropriate to say.

I looked at Barbara Carr. She looked at me.

"You know, Barbara, I read about your daughter. I am very sorry."

She was looking into my eyes. I could feel them connecting with mine.

"Thank you, Anne. Thank you so much for reading about her. It is very hard. It was, as you know, twenty-one years earlier, but it feels like a month ago."

I nodded. I did not know what to say. I tried to imagine the unimaginable. I tried to *be* Barbara Carr, whose daughter had died. And in that moment, I knew that I would never choose to live a life without Richard. Barbara did not have that choice. In light of her suffering, my even considering excommunicating myself from Richard suddenly seemed crass and insensitive. It would be an unspeakable sacrilege.

As if any mother would or could ever truly prefer to live in a world in which her child did not exist. I wondered if perhaps I could continue to be Richard's drumbeat without it causing me to sink deeper into depression.

"Yes," she said, her gaze tethered to mine. "You can see why Wes is so important to us."

Wes, the grandson for whom she'd bought the T-shirt in Adelaide eight days ago. This was how we had connected initially, speaking of her experience as a grandmother.

"We live next door to Weston in Connecticut," she went on, "and my husband and I lie in bed sometimes and say, 'What would we do without Weston?'"

"I read about the wonderful organization you started," I heard myself say. "That Steve Van Zandt and his wife are chairing it." This was the Kristen Ann Carr Fund, whose mission was to fight sarcoma and improve the lives of young adults and teenagers with cancer.

"Yes, Steve and his wife chaired it one year," she said, smiling. "They got the Rascals to play at the benefit that year."

She appeared happier and more energetic than she had only a couple of minutes earlier.

"You should come to our benefit this year," she said.

I looked at her, dumbfounded.

"It's April 5 at Tribeca Grill in New York. You live in Philadelphia, right?"

I nodded.

"Really. Think about it. Really, you should come. I *hope* you will come."

31

AFTER LEAVING Barbara in the lounge, I went to the fitness center and settled onto an exercise bike. As I began to pedal, hope that I would be able to improve my relationship with Richard pulsed through me. I was hopeful that we could get to a point where his treatment of me did not push me toward the abyss. If I could do that, it would be enough.

Sixty minutes later, I got off the bike feeling like I had more energy than the Energizer Bunny—more energy than Bruce Springsteen himself.

I was leaning against the wall, stretching my Achilles tendon, when a woman who worked in the hotel came through the door with a stack of perfectly folded white towels. She was wearing an understated light gray skirt, ivory silky blouse, and a strand of pearls, apparently the uniform of all female employees of the Park Hyatt Sydney.

"I've seen you up here each day this week," she said, stopping and smiling at me.

I smiled back.

"You're a machine," she said, still smiling.

I thought of all the times Andy had told me I was "a machine" when he saw me working out. I always told him, "I *am* a machine." And I didn't just mean during my sixty-minute workout. I also meant in the minutes and moments prior to my workout when, defying every cell in my mind and body, in spite of my despair, I picked myself up off the floor, hoisted myself onto the bike, shut out all the physical, mental, and emotional messages surging through me, and made myself do what I had to do. I did not question it. I did not tell myself I was stupid or pathetic for doing it. I did not tell myself I was a loser for shutting off my brain and working out.

I wished I could be as resolute when I was not working out. I wished I could transfer the discipline I had developed getting myself to work out to keep myself from thinking negative thoughts about everything I did. I wished I could shut off, or even just turn down the decibel level, of the negative voices flowing incessantly through my brain. I had tried cognitive therapy. I had tried erecting mental stop signs every time a negative thought appeared in my head. But I was so adept at negative thoughts about myself that even as my mind's eye was seeing a stop sign for one discouraging thought, another one would float into existence.

It was like the episode of *I Love Lucy* where Lucy and Ethel are working in a candy factory, sitting beside a conveyer belt and wrapping candy as it moves by. When the conveyer belt speeds up, Lucy and Ethel can't move fast enough to pick up all the candies and wrap them without letting others move by unwrapped, so they begin stuffing the unwrapped candies in their pockets, in their hats, in their mouths. Similarly, I was unable to erect the mental stop signs quickly enough to keep up with all the negative thoughts racing through my head. But unlike Lucy and Ethel, who have pockets and hats and mouths where they can hide their unwrapped candies, I had no place to hide the errant thoughts flying past my stop signs.

It does not end well for Lucy and Ethel. They get fired. It did not end well for me and cognitive therapy either. I quit.

"Are you in training for something?" the hotel employee asked.

"A marathon," I said, wondering where this answer came from.

"Really?" the woman said, looking intrigued. "Which one?"

"Life," I said.

When I got back to my room after working out, I remembered that I'd told Barbara Carr I would check my calendar to see if I would be free the night of the Kristen Ann Carr benefit dinner, and I chuckled.

She did not need to know that my calendar was empty from the day I returned from Australia. She did not need to know that the day I quit CCP, the specter of a lifetime of empty days in an empty house was the reason I'd grabbed on to the idea of going to Australia, or that before my trip, unable to think past my departure date, I had given no thought to what I might do when I returned.

As I tried to think about what it would be like to be at such an event, it occurred to me that it might not be such a preposterous or bad idea for me to go to it. Or to at least *to plan* to go to it.

Perhaps it would be a way to keep my Bruce Springsteen energy going when I returned home.

Here in Australia, even when I was feeling down and lethargic, I had never been bored. There was always something on my horizon, around the corner, or down in the lobby that I knew would be interesting. Everywhere I went, I found stories. Stories I could not wait to tell the people back home.

In Australia, too, interesting thoughts came to me so fast that I found myself writing them down on whatever scraps of paper I could find nearby, including hotel napkins. I did not want to forget even one idea.

As my countdown was bringing me closer to my goal of returning home, I was becoming increasingly excited about telling my Australia stories to my family and friends. They may not have been interested in my fly-on-the wall stories about people in Starbucks or Whole Foods, but they would surely want to hear stories about Bruce Springsteen and his entourage.

The April 5 benefit dinner was a month after I returned from Australia. I sat down at my desk and googled "Kristen Ann Carr benefit dinner."

Up popped "A Night to Remember 2013," with image after image of men in black—informal black, formal black—along with women in every permutation of the little black dress possible. I would not have trouble finding a costume that would render me indistinguishable from my surroundings at this year's "A Night to Remember 2014."

I marked April 5 in my empty post-trip calendar. For a month after my return, I could still be the me I was discovering in Australia. A me who was out and about in the world, willing to go anywhere I thought something interesting might happen. A me who was ready to go anywhere I thought I would find a good story.

32

FRIDAY MORNING in Sydney I awoke feeling sad and left behind because this was the day Bruce Springsteen and the E Street Band were checking out. I was not part of their entourage, but they were part of mine. The previous night, I had overheard Jon Landau telling the concierge to prepare for Bruce Springsteen's eleven o'clock checkout. I was not sure what that entailed, but I planned to do my best to find out.

At ten o'clock I left the dining room and went into the lobby. I was hoping for some E Street Band sightings. Immediately, I saw Max Weinberg. He was slouched against the checkout desk, holding a large, unframed watercolor, haggling with the clerk about the items he had and had not removed from the minibar. Jon Landau—as always, when the entourage was on the move—was standing in the middle of the lobby. I saw him motion to a concierge. As the concierge walked toward him, so did I.

"His things are in Room 315," Landau said to the concierge, softly, but loud enough for me to hear. "Check Room 318 also, please."

The concierge smiled, nodded, and walked away. I smiled too. Apparently, Springsteen's room was on the same floor as the fitness center. I had probably walked by it ten times by now. Later, I would have to check out exactly which room it was so I could imagine being Bruce Springsteen sauntering out of that very door.

Tom Morello was now standing beside Landau.

"Where are we going next?" Morello asked.

I was surprised to hear him ask this. Where the group was playing next did not seem to be something about which Tom Morello wanted to think. Itineraries did not seem to be any more important to him than they were to me.

The lobby was bursting with E Street people and energy. I noticed three or four other band members and their wives or partners standing across the lobby.

I followed Morello to the carport, where a minivan with an open back was parked off to the side, and I watched him drop his backpack inside. As he turned back toward the hotel entrance, a gray Mercedes van with tinted windows pulled up to the entrance. Morello got into the van.

I went into the lobby and put my workout bag down next to the check-in desk, then followed the mass exodus of the E Street Band out of the hotel. Most of them climbed into the Mercedes van as I stood and watched. Across the street, a BMW, also with tinted windows, pulled up and Max Weinberg and his wife ran out of the hotel and into the car.

Even as the van and the BMW pulled away, I remained in my spot. I was determined to see Bruce Springsteen exit the building.

A valet walked by pushing a gold-colored luggage cart. Not just any luggage cart—a luggage cart with a black plastic Park Hyatt Sydney garment bag hanging from it. And not just any black plastic Park Hyatt Sydney garment bag—a black plastic Park Hyatt Sydney garment bag with a gray vest showing through the clear plastic of the top half.

This was no ordinary gray vest. It was the gray vest Bruce Springsteen had worn at each of the five concerts I had been to in Australia.

The valet left the garment bag hanging from the luggage cart on the far side of the bell captain's desk, to be watched over by him.

I walked over to the black plastic garment bag with the gray vest inside it. When I got there, I stood and stared. Goose bumps popped up on my arms and chills ran through me. Staring at the vest, the moments and hours I had stood in the audience watching the body buttoned into that very vest came rushing all at once into my mind.

I closed my eyes, took a deep breath, and opened them again. I was filled with feelings of intense and uplifting nostalgia. This was the vest of the man who made good things happen. I wanted to see this man. I wanted to see this special man walking out of the hotel like an ordinary person.

I returned to the lobby. The head concierge and two security guards were standing next to the check-in desk, circled around my workout bag. One of the security guards was speaking into a walkie-talkie.

I walked toward them.

"Is there a problem?" I asked as I reached them.

"Is this your bag?" the security guard with the walkie-talkie asked, lifting his mouth away from the receiver.

"It is," I said. "It was too heavy for me to hold, so I put it over there while I waited outside. Is there a problem?"

"Now that we know it's yours, there isn't," he said with palpable relief. "We saw it sitting here unattended, and we were worried there might be a bomb inside."

"We would be happy to hold your bag at the desk," the concierge said, smiling.

"That's okay," I said. "I can take it."

I claimed my bag and lifted it onto my shoulder.

Satisfied, they smiled and walked away.

I was about to head back outside to wait for Bruce Springsteen, when I heard someone say in a very familiar, very gravelly voice, "Thank you, thank you, thank you."

I looked at the other end of the checkout desk and saw a short man wearing sunglasses, a straw hat, a peach-colored button-down shirt, and white linen pants. He was pulling his own rollaboard.

"Thank you," he said again.

I looked at the staff. Every one of them was smiling at him. I looked back at the man in the straw hat. He was now walking out the open glass doors of the hotel.

I stood immobile for a moment, stunned. When I looked around again, the lobby was quiet. One clerk was standing at the check-in desk, still smiling. I went outside. There were no fancy cars. There was no gray vest in a Park Hyatt Sydney black plastic garment bag.

I went back inside and was surprised by how quickly the activity in and around the lobby had gone from one hundred to zero. Now it was like a ghost lobby.

I walked over to the concierge desk.

"Was that guy in the straw hat and sunglasses Bruce Springsteen?" I asked all three of the men standing behind the desk.

I was hoping that since the short man in the straw hat was no longer a guest, they would give me some scraps of information.

"We cannot say anything about our guests," said the concierge. "Is there anything else I can help you with, Mrs. Abel?"

I stood there for a few moments, thinking about the man I'd just seen saying thank you to the hotel staff on his way out.

It was reassuring to me that when he was not onstage being larger than life, the man I had followed across the world was a regular person who did kind things.

33

AT FOUR o'clock the following afternoon, after a three-hour drive from the hotel in Sydney to the Hunter Valley, I arrived at the Hope Estate winery for my sixth concert.

I walked from the sidewalk across a vast parcel of grass that was quickly filling with cars. When I reached the entrance, I felt as if I were entering something between a carnival and a county fair. Two white makeshift booths surrounded by security guards and ticket takers flanked the gates leading into the venue. Even though the concert was not scheduled to begin until seven o' clock, long lines were already forming behind me.

Signs at the entrance said that no outside food or drinks, not even water, were allowed inside, and that no alcoholic beverages could be removed from the venue on concert days. Fortunately, the security guard did not seem too worried about a sixty-and-a-half-year-old woman sneaking in contraband. When I opened my tote for him to search with his flashlight, he just smiled and waved me forward. At the bottom of my bag, hidden by a section of newspaper, I had snuck in a turkey club sandwich from the clean and never-disappointing Park Hyatt Sydney. I felt quite proud of myself for following my own travel tip to take food when going somewhere new and unknown.

With nothing to do for three hours, I began wandering around the estate.

Rows of small white plastic folding chairs, tied together with cable lines, were set up on the grass in front of the stage. No one was in any of the seats yet. I found my seat in the third row of the center section, third seat in from the aisle.

Behind the seats was the general admission area where people who had not purchased seats could put down blankets and beach towels. Blankets were scattered about, but nobody was on them.

I did not know what else to do, so I sat down on a grassy knoll overlooking the wine booths. People were walking away from the booths clutching the necks of two bottles of wine in each hand.

My heart sank as it suddenly became obvious to me why Hope Estate opened three hours before the beginning of the concert. It was a winery. Their business was to sell wine.

The only thing I did not like about concerts were drunk audience members. They infuriated me. Exceeding their personal space, they pushed, knocked, bellowed, and catcalled, their drinks sloshing and spilling to the floor, first making surfaces slippery and treacherous and then merely sticky and gross. And this was at venues that opened only an *hour* before the concert.

These people were not stocking up on bottles to take home as souvenirs. Signs around the venue made it abundantly clear that no alcohol could be taken from the winery on concert day. As I saw my fellow fans returning to buy even *more* wine, I grimaced. Not knowing how else to make my disheartened self feel better, I gave myself a pep talk: *Even if it's an abominable evening, this too will pass. I will survive. I will not only survive, but also in eight more days I will be on a plane headed home.*

Thinking about going home once again began to lift my faltering mood.

I looked around me. Everyone seemed to be with someone. There were couples. There were small groups. There were large groups. Most appeared to be in their thirties and forties. Some were older. Some were younger.

With each day of my trip, my loneliness had been increasing. Now, two-thirds of the way into it, the loneliness seemed to increase exponentially with each additional day. I was accustomed to spending chunks of my days at home alone. I was even accustomed to spending entire days alone when Andy was traveling. But even during those times I at least periodically saw friends and acquaintances. Never before had I experienced such a sense of isolation as during this trip in Australia.

I was not always conscious of this loneliness. When I was distracted by activities around me or by interesting thoughts and ideas popping into my head, or when I was writing my emails to the people back home, I did not feel so empty and disconnected from the world. But when there was a lull—when my mind was not actively engaged in something, in anything—I felt the thud of loneliness dropping its anchor inside me. With each new day and with each new lull, the anchor felt heavier and heavier. More and more rooted.

By the time I returned to the seating area, every seat in my row except mine was taken. I squeezed past a forty-something couple sitting at the end of the row and sat down. They did not take any note of me. On the other side of me, the rest of the row appeared to be a twenty-year fraternity reunion.

One forty-something man after another was thumping his friend on the back, knocking shoulders, chortling, and alternating between brandishing and swigging from his plastic cup.

I turned to face the stage and sat back in my chair. Withdrawing into myself like a turtle pulling into her shell, I closed my eyes and zoned out. I saw nothing but blackness. The ambient cackling of the crowd became distant and lulled me like sounds from a white noise machine. I sat. I stared into the blackness inside my head. I waited.

Sit. Stare. Wait. Repeat.

When I finally opened my eyes, all the seats in front of me were also filled. I turned to my right. The fraternity reunion was still going strong.

When I had first sat down and seen the rowdy group, I had lumped everyone in the row together. Without noticing the man beside me, without bothering to even look at him, I had assumed he was one of the frat boys. Now, as I opened my eyes and he came into focus, it was patently clear that he was not one of the boys. Like me, he was all alone. Like me, he was two decades older than the fraternity boys. Like me, he was small. Like me, he seemed to be pulled into himself and taking up less space on his chair than would another same-size man.

I smiled at him. He smiled back.

"Are you from around here?" I asked.

"Oh no," he said, sounding surprised that I would think he was local. "I'm from outside Cessnock."

"How far is that from here?" I asked. I had no idea if Cessnock was a town, a city, or a country.

"Oh, it's a good thirty-minute drive," he said to me with quiet conviction.

"Is this your first Bruce Springsteen concert?" I asked.

"It is," he said with a small nod of his head.

"Are you a fan?" I asked.

"No. I don't even know his music."

I was intrigued. "What made you decide to come to the concert?"

"My kids said I needed to get out of the house."

I did not know what to say. I did not want to pry. So I smiled and said nothing.

"I'm sixty-one," he volunteered. "Last year I retired from AusPost."

"What's AusPost?" I asked. I did not think I needed to explain that I was not a local.

"It's the postal service. I was a carrier for forty years."

"Congratulations on your retirement," I said.

"Yes, thank you." He dipped his head. "But then my wife was diagnosed with stage 4 breast cancer. She died four months later." He looked down at his hands, folded on his lap.

"I'm so sorry."

"Thank you," he said, looking back up at me. His lips had turned up into a sliver of a smile. He was trying to cheer up, but his sad, soulful eyes had not come on board yet.

I gave him a gentle smile in return.

"I saw in the paper two months ago that this concert was happening, so I got a ticket. But I got it so late that I ended up paying twice the price that is printed on it." He shook his head in wistful disbelief.

"I'm pretty sure that after the concert you'll think it was worth all the money you paid for your ticket," I said.

He didn't say anything. For a few minutes we both sat facing forward, not speaking. Then I turned back to him.

"Bruce Springsteen is an amazing performer," I said. "One song that is my favorite is called 'Waitin' on a Sunny Day.' He doesn't play it at every concert, but when he does, it is amazing. I hope he plays it tonight so you can hear it."

Looking at this sad man beside me who had come to the concert in an effort to please his children and distract himself from his sadness, I felt nothing but empathy. I knew what it was like to try to distract yourself from that sadness. I knew how many times I had listened to "Waitin' on a Sunny Day" to jolt myself out of my depression. Sometimes I had to listen to it five times before I could muster the strength to stand up and take a step forward in my day. But no matter how many times I had to listen to it—five or three or six times—eventually, it got me up and going. Sometimes, if I imagined Bruce Springsteen at a concert, picking a child out of a concert crowd to join him in the song, I even felt myself smiling.

The man looked at me. "I hope so too."

At that moment, the crowd roared in unison. The man and I stood up. As we did, I saw that he was holding a small rectangular Instamatic camera. I could not remember how many decades it had been since I had last seen a camera like that.

I was disappointed to see that The Rubens, an Australian rock band, was filing onto the stage instead of Bruce Springsteen.

Their music did nothing to alleviate my disappointment; it sounded like nothing more than loud, annoying noise to me.

When they were done, I was let down again when another Australian rocker, Dan Sultan, came onstage.

Except for my postal worker seatmate, who was standing inert, his Instamatic hanging from his wrist, everyone else in the audience seemed to be jumping and clapping and cheering and dancing. The livelier the crowd became, the more sullen and dull I felt. I sat down and closed my eyes.

Suddenly the crowd seemed to become even louder and more energized. I opened my eyes and stood up and saw the members of the E Street Band skipping one by one onto the stage. I felt my heart begin to quicken in anticipation.

"Broo! Broo! Broo!" the crowd was now bellowing. "Broo! Broo! Broo!"

Bruce Springsteen jogged onto the stage, an acoustic guitar in one hand, the other hand raised to the crowd. He was not wearing the gray vest he had worn at the previous concerts. Instead, he was wearing just a gray T-shirt. I wondered if he was dressing down for the more laid-back countryside setting of this concert.

This was the best part of every concert: Bruce Springsteen was present. Bruce Springsteen was with us. Bruce Springsteen was about to hit the first note on his guitar. Everything was ahead of us.

He took his place at his microphone up front in the middle of the stage and began singing,

> *All the people just sucking that wine*
> *Drinkin' wine is their delight*
> *When they get drunk they start a fight*
> *Knockin' down windows and bringin' down doors*
> *Drinkin' half-gallons and asking for more*
> *Wine, wine, wine, Elderberry*
> *Wine, wine, wine, or sherry*
> *Wine, wine, wine, Sweet Loser*
> *Wine, wine, wine, Thunderbird...*

After each call of "Wine, wine, wine," he called out another Hope Estate Winery label.

The song sounded familiar to me. He was altering the lyrics of "Drinkin' Wine Spo-Dee-O-Dee," an old blues song I knew from driving in the car with Andy.

From one song to the next, Bruce Springsteen and the E Street Band went, never taking a break or even pausing to catch their collective breaths. Springsteen seemed much more animated and energetic than he had three nights earlier in Sydney. He seemed more playful than I had seen him since Adelaide. Maybe it was the Hunter Valley golf I had heard Jon Landau talking about in Sydney. Maybe it was that Jake Clemons was back from his father's funeral. Springsteen had given him a solo right off the bat in the first song.

Then I heard the familiar chords and the familiar drumbeat, followed by,

It's rainin' but there isn't a cloud in the sky
Musta been a tear from your eye
Everything will be okay.

I stopped jumping and clapping. I turned to my postal worker seatmate and exclaimed excitedly, "This is it. This is the song I was telling you about!"

He returned my smile, slipped his Instamatic off his wrist, held it up to his eye, and clicked a photo. I turned back toward the stage, jumping and dancing and clapping and crying. It was always perfect and wonderful for me when Bruce Springsteen sang this song at a concert, but tonight it was even more perfect and wonderful. Tonight, I had someone with whom to share it. I so hoped he would be lifted up by the song, at least a little.

When the song was over, I turned again to my seatmate.

"Yes, it's a very nice song," he said quietly. "Thank you for telling me about it."

I hoped he meant what he said and was not just being polite.

In what seemed like a flash, the show was almost over. After two encores, the E Street Band filed off the stage.

"Thank you, Hunter Valley," Springsteen called out. "We'll be back here tomorrow night." He raised his hand and waved. Then he turned and left the stage too.

I turned to my postal worker seatmate and smiled at him. He smiled back, but he did not look exuberant or excited. He did not even look happy.

I hoped that he was feeling more inside than his subdued exterior indicated. Maybe one morning when he was feeling down, he would listen to "Waitin' on a Sunny Day" and feel better. Maybe he would remember how much I said it helped me. Maybe it would help him feel less alone.

I did not say any of this to him. I did not want to risk overdoing it and making him uncomfortable. When he turned and began walking toward the end of the row, I followed behind. Then he was absorbed into the mass of humanity around us and was gone.

I had not made much progress forward when I, and everyone around me, heard a loud whirring coming from behind us. We turned our heads in unison. Rising from behind the stage was a helicopter big enough for only a few passengers.

Being a rock star had its privileges.

34

AS I INCHED my way toward the exit alongside twenty thousand other fans, I called Melissa, my driver for the day, to tell her the concert was over.

I was surprised when she did not answer. I left her a voicemail.

As I hung up the phone, I looked at my watch. I had been so mesmerized by Bruce Springsteen and his band that I had not looked at it since the concert began. I was surprised to see the concert had ended as early as ten thirty—but even so I had been standing for almost seven hours, first on the grassy knoll and then during the concert. My legs and my right hip were aching.

I leaned against one of the empty ticket booths to give my lower body some relief. I shifted my weight back and forth on my weary legs as a blur of people rushed past me and burst into the openness of the grassy, dark parking lot. I did not want to leave the safety of the well-lit area until I heard from Melissa and knew where and when I was going to meet her.

I called her again. Again, she did not answer. Again, I left her a voicemail. I waited and I called. I called and I left voicemails. Over and over and over.

"Ma'am, you've got to step away from here," a security guard eventually said to me. "You have to exit the venue."

"I'm trying to reach my ride," I told him. "I don't know where to go."

"I'm sorry, but you can't wait here or anywhere else on the venue grounds. Everyone has to leave."

He did not seem like someone I was going to be able to convince to break a rule. I stepped away from the ticket booth and out onto the edge of the parking lot. The cars were barely moving.

I could see across the field to Broke Road. It was a two-lane road, which was probably adequate on non-concert evenings. Now, however, twenty thousand fans were in ten thousand cars, and all ten thousand cars wanted to get out of the parking lot and head home. They were backed up in both directions.

I called Melissa again. I did not bother to leave a message. I'd left enough.

The ache in my right hip was radiating and my legs were quivering. I sat down on the grass, cross-legged, and with my elbows planted on my inner thighs I rested my head on my upturned hands. As long as I could sit, I would be all right waiting.

"Ma'am, no loitering on the venue grounds," another security guard said to me.

A platoon of security guards was now sweeping up and down the grassy lot, shooing stragglers toward Broke Road.

"I have no place to go," I said.

"I don't make the rules, I just enforce them," he said with conviction.

"I'm from the States," I said plaintively. "I don't know where my ride is. I'm all alone and I don't know anyone in Australia to call for help. Can you help me find a ride back to Sydney? To anywhere? To the local police station?"

"No, ma'am, I can't. Like I said, you have to vacate the premises and wait on Broke Road."

I stood up and walked slowly to the sidewalk on Broke Road. The traffic was still creeping in both directions. I sat down on the sidewalk, out of the way of a small group of people pacing up and down together, searching for their ride.

What was the worst that would happen? That I'd sit on the sidewalk until morning?

I thought about waiting until daybreak on the sidewalk of Broke Road. It was not darkness that was my problem. My problem was that I was a three-hour drive from the Park Hyatt Sydney, my home away from home. Nothing about the morning light was going to help get me there. I thought of calling the hotel and asking them to send a car for me. At best, that would have me sitting on the sidewalk for three hours.

I pulled out my iPhone and googled "Royale Limousine Service." I called the number listed. My heart fell when I got a voice message, but I did not hang up. Maybe they checked their messages during the night. I waited for the beep at the end so I could scream my desperate plea into the phone. Before the beep sounded, however, a second message began: "If this is an emergency, please call . . ."

My fingers shaking, I tapped in the number. To my surprise, a human being answered.

"My driver abandoned me," I blurted out. "I am in Hunter Valley, and I need someone to pick me up and take me back to my hotel in Sydney. *Now!*"

The emergency dispatcher took down my information, then said, "Let me call your driver and find out where she is."

"When will you call me back?" I asked.

"Within five minutes."

Five minutes later, my phone rang.

"I do not seem to be able to reach her either," he said. "I am not sure what to tell you."

Now I was not only tired and desperate but also pissed. He was an emergency dispatcher, not an answering service. He should have come back with something better than that.

"I am a woman who is sitting all alone on a dark sidewalk because your driver has gone AWOL," I bellowed. "I should not need to tell you how bad it will be for your business if I am attacked and end up, alive or dead, in a hospital emergency room. This is just the kind of story newspapers love to put on their front pages. You had better get the owner of this company on the phone right now. Do not hang up on me. I am sure you have another phone. Use your own cell phone if you must. But get her on the phone, *now*! I am sure she will want to get this situation under control before it is too late. What is your name, in case we get disconnected?"

"Ma'am, my name is Jack," he said. "I will call Anita now."

Joseph, my driver to the Sydney concert, had told me about Anita. She had started the business in 1989, and now it was the largest privately owned limousine service in Australia. You don't grow a successful limousine company leaving customers stranded. I was hopeful that Anita would come through for me.

I could hear Jack speaking on a second phone, and then he came back on the line with me. "Ma'am, I just spoke to Anita. She is going to call your driver and then she will call you."

"I do not want to hang up with you," I said. "If she doesn't call me, I'm afraid I won't be able to reach you again."

"I promise I will answer if you call me," he said. "Let me give you my cell phone number. Will that make you feel better?"

"What will make me feel better is getting into a car and going back to my hotel in Sydney," I shot back. "Let me get a pen so I can write down your number."

I scribbled the number on a napkin. And then, just to make sure, I also wrote it on the back of my hand. Then we hung up.

I waited and waited. Each time I looked down at my watch, I was surprised that only a minute or so had passed. I was tired. I was hungry. I wanted to go home to my real home. Enough was enough. I did not feel like doing this anymore.

"Waitin' on a Sunny Day" jingled from my iPhone.

"Hello?"

"Hello, Anne, this is Anita. I am so sorry about this situation."

"Sorry is not going to get me back to Sydney."

"Yes, of course. I tried calling Melissa and she didn't answer me either. I am trying to find a driver closer to you that I can send. In the meantime, I also have someone calling other companies to see if we can find anyone to come get you. I really don't know what is going on with Melissa. Let me make some more calls and I will get back to you with a plan."

"How long until I should expect your call?" I asked. "I don't like sitting here with no time frame."

"Of course. I understand. I'll call you back in ten minutes, whether I have an answer for you or not. How is that?"

"Okay. I'm sitting here counting down the seconds already."

Surely Anita would be able to find someone in Sydney. That would be only three hours. If I just knew *when* I would be picked up—if I knew there would be an end to this—I would be reassured enough to pace myself and be calm. Hungry and tired, but also calm.

My Australian flip phone rang. I fumbled for it in my pocket.

"Anne, it's Melissa."

"Where are you?" I shouted as I stood up.

"I'm on—"

My flip phone slipped from my hand, landed on the sidewalk, and split into several pieces. I stood there for a moment just staring at it. I could not believe it. I felt like screaming. I felt like crying. I felt like dropping to the sidewalk and pulling myself into a tight, tiny ball.

I had not written down Melissa's number. I had only entered it into the flip phone. I thought of calling the dispatcher and getting her number so I could call from my iPhone. But I did not have the patience, the wherewithal to track them down. I just wanted to connect with Melissa. Now.

"Take a deep breath, take a deep breath," I said to myself. I did not feel like taking a deep breath. Not one. Certainly not two. I was too tired and hungry and angry and frustrated. "Just stay calm. Bend down and pick up the pieces."

Even in the midnight darkness, I could see that my hands were shaking. There was no way I would be able to piece the phone together with such unsteady hands. So, as much as I did not feel like it, I followed my own advice. I stood up straight. I pulled my shoulders back and down. I stared ahead and closed my eyes. I inhaled, filling my belly with air. I exhaled, sucking in my belly until I could feel it tight against my lower spine. I inhaled and exhaled. Then I opened my eyes and stooped down to scoop up the phone and the battery and two other metal pieces that were by my feet on the sidewalk.

"Stay calm," I said aloud. "Stay calm. You can do this. Just do it one piece at a time. One piece at a time."

When we are all together at the beach, Andy and the boys like to do jigsaw puzzles. They spread all one thousand pieces out on the table in the living room, and over the course of the day—or, sometimes, many days—someone, sometimes everyone, stands at the table studying the pieces and fitting them together, bit by bit.

But I hate doing puzzles. Jigsaw puzzles, crossword puzzles, sudoku, any kind of puzzle. It just isn't interesting to me. It's frustrating and absolutely boring. I do, however, like listening to the conversations that happen around the puzzle table. *That* is interesting to me.

Conversation was exactly what I was hoping for as I picked up the pieces of the phone from the Broke Road sidewalk and stared at them in my hand. If I could fit them together, I would be able to have the conversation for which I had been waiting for almost two hours.

First, I fit the biggest piece, the battery, into place. Then, piece by trial-and-error piece, I maneuvered the smaller pieces into place. When they were all together, I hit the power button—and the phone turned on. I called Melissa.

She answered.

"Melissa?" I shouted into the receiver. I felt like Alexander Graham Bell in 1876 when he made the first phone call ever.

"Anne," I heard her say, "I'm on my way to get you."

It was a miracle. I had actually put the contraption together and gotten it working. Even more miraculous was that I was still connected to Melissa.

"Where are you?" I asked, my eyes darting back and forth at the crawling traffic going in both directions as far as I could see. "Where are you? Where should I meet you?"

Instinctively, I started walking. Adrenaline was rushing through me. I looked around for a landmark to give her. There was nothing recognizable in the dark landscape. I could feel myself becoming frantic.

"I see you," I heard her say.

I looked up. I looked around. I saw her stopped in traffic a few car lengths in front of me.

"I'm here," I heard her say in stereo, from my phone and from her car, as she pulled up beside me.

After being abandoned on the sidewalk for ninety minutes, I jumped into the back seat of her car. "Where were you?"

"I was just down the road at a McDonald's," she said, answering my question but not telling me what I wanted to know.

"Why didn't you answer my calls or return my voicemails? Or Anita's?" My voice sounded *almost* as angry as I felt.

"My phone wasn't charged, but I didn't realize it."

"What?" I could not believe what I was hearing. "How long did you say you've been a limo driver?"

"Three months."

I did not say anything. Not then. Not for the rest of the trip. I did not really believe that her phone had not been charged. I wondered if she had fallen asleep after she dropped me off. It was understandable to me that she might be tired. Exhausted, even. Still, whatever the reason, it didn't seem professional.

At 2:45 a.m., after three hours of silence, we pulled into the entrance of the Park Hyatt Sydney. I had never been so happy to be anywhere as I was to finally be there. My home away from home. As I tumbled out of the car, I found myself deciding that I was not going to go back for the second concert at Hope Estate. To have breakfast and work out before I left, I'd have to be up at 6:30 a.m., not even four hours from now. It was just too much. There was no need for me to go. Been there, done that.

I didn't bother to tell Melissa she didn't need to come pick me up the next day. I was still annoyed with her and did not feel like interacting with her at the moment. I would tell her when she came back tomorrow. I had already paid for the trip, after all, so she would be paid whether or not I went. She'd probably be happy to have the day off, or she could book herself another job if she wanted to.

Back in my hotel room, as I slid under the covers, I felt myself melting into the Park Hyatt Sydney's mega-thread-count sheets. I picked up my Bruce Springsteen book from the night table and looked at the clock. It was 3:30 a.m. I opened the book and settled back into my pillow. As I waited for the first word to come into focus, my eyes closed.

I let the book fall onto the bed beside me, relaxed into my pillow, and fell asleep.

35

MY EYES popped open. I turned my head to look at the digital clock on the bedside table. It was 6:30 a.m. My head was clear, alert. Excitement was buzzing through me. It was a concert day. Concert number seven.

Without my willing them to, my feet sprang out of bed and onto the floor. I stood for a moment to assess myself and my general condition. I did not feel as if I had slept for only three hours. On the contrary. I was raring to go.

I remembered returning from the concert only a few hours earlier feeling sure that I was not going back for the second concert at Hope Estate. I also remembered not telling Melissa that I was not going because I didn't have the energy or desire to talk even that much.

Standing by the side of the bed, eyeing the workout clothes that I had laid out for myself the previous morning, I wondered if the real reason I had not informed Melissa of my plans was that I'd subconsciously remembered that more options are always better than fewer options.

I pulled on my workout clothes, packed up my tote, and practically skipped out the door of my room to breakfast.

I *was* going to concert number seven. Logistically, it had to be better than concert number six. I had learned on this trip that the second time doing anything is always easier than the first. I was now familiar with the venue. I would bring a book to help pass the hours of preconcert waiting. And, as it had turned out, the drunk audience members had not been a problem. They had been mellow, happy, and considerate drunks.

And Melissa would surely be on her best behavior.

When I entered the winery and began walking toward the grassy knoll that afternoon, everything seemed the same as the previous day; the food lines, the wine lines, even the porta-potty lines seemed to wind around just as they had the night before. Even my seat was the same: third row, center, third seat from the aisle.

Only the people were different. Beside me, where the retired postal worker had sat the previous day, was a tall blonde woman with a large diamond ring and diamond-studded wedding band. She was wearing spiked black high heels. I was surprised she was able to stand upright on the grass beneath us.

I was peering at her feet when I felt a couple of drops hit the back of my neck. I looked up at the blue sky. I looked up at the spike-heeled blonde woman. She was swaying between me and her husband, red wine sloshing in and out of her plastic wineglass.

I stood up. "Excuse me, ma'am," I said, loudly enough to get her to look at me. "Could you please be careful with your wine? You just spilled some on me."

She looked at me, stunned and aghast, her head moving in small concentric circles from the top of her neck. Clearly, this was not her first glass of wine. She was still staring at me, speechless, when her husband yanked her by the elbow and switched places with her.

"This is a winery. This is a concert. This is our seat," he bellowed at me, his face turning red. "You have no right to tell my wife what she can or cannot do."

The red wine in the plastic glass he was clutching by the stem was obviously not *his* first either. I looked at my watch. It was a few minutes past seven. I looked around for an usher. I did not see any. Two fortyish men had sat down on the other side of me. I thought about asking them if they would switch places with me. It meant they would be giving up a much-coveted aisle seat.

I was mustering the courage to ask them when the crowd suddenly began howling, "Broo! Broo! Broo!"

I looked up at the stage, where Max Weinberg had materialized seemingly out of nowhere and was tapping a steady *one-two-three-four* repeatedly on his drums. Measure after measure, his beat was unwavering. The beat was mesmerizing. I was simultaneously standing on my toes so I could see and tapping to Max Weinberg's contagious pattern.

Then Curtis King, a dreadlocked vocalist and percussionist who usually stands at the back of the stage with the other vocalists, came into view from backstage wearing a purple shirt and gray vest. Shaking a maraca in the palm of his left hand and tapping the same *one-two-three-four* beat with a stick in his right hand, he shimmied languidly to the front of the stage.

With every beat of the drum, with every shake of the maraca, with every tap of the stick, I felt my anticipation growing, *one-two-three-four*.

The previous concerts had begun with an exuberant rush of the band to their places onstage, immediately followed by the energetic entrance of Bruce Springsteen, who quickly ignited the band and the crowd with "a two and a three" and set off the evening with a fast-paced, endorphin-inducing first song.

Tonight, I shook my head in wonderment, not knowing what was happening. Not knowing where we were going. It did not matter. Following Max Weinberg and Curtis King, I was as happy as I could be. I would be perfectly content going nowhere with them, just tapping *one-two-three-four* with them forever.

Then Everett Bradley, another vocalist and percussionist who usually stood at the back of the stage, walked unhurriedly, his bald head shining, to the front of the stage. Like Curtis King, he was wearing a purple shirt and gray vest, but he had a conga drum strapped around his waist. *One-two-three-four*, *one-two-three-four*, *one-two-three-four*, he beat.

The three men onstage, leading us with their *one-two-three-four* beat, did not seem to be in a rush.

A synthesizer joined the beat as Garry Tallent soft-shoed onto the stage followed by a boogying Nils Lofgren and Steve Van Zandt, his signature scarf flowing from his neck, another wrapped snugly around his head. He raised his arms; the move, self-mocking or not, solicited cries of adoration from the crowd. We were all on this ride to nowhere, to somewhere, to anywhere, together. We didn't care about the where; we cared only with whom. We were comfortable and confident, hopeful, happy to put ourselves in the hands of our tour guides as they led us in a relaxed *one-two-three-four* up on the stage.

More E Street Band members ambled to the beat from backstage, some shaking large maracas, others with their bodies undulating. No one was in a hurry. Everyone seemed mellow. Everyone was connected to the *one-two-three-four* beat. If any of us were waiting for anything or anyone, we were not conscious of it. We did not think about a past moment. We did not think about a future one. We were snug in the swaddle of the present moment. We were pulsing hypnotically, measure after steady measure, to our collective *one-two-three-four* mantra. There was nothing but here. Nothing but now. We had no wants. We had no needs. We stood not aimless but open, our collective heart, soul, and mind ready to receive whatever we were given. Whoever stepped forward to lead us, we would follow.

And step forward he did, our leader. There he was, in a black T-shirt and black jeans. The man for whom we had traveled miles. The man for whom we had traversed continents. The same man our hypnotized minds had, until now, forgotten.

He was not boogying; he was not dancing. He did not have a guitar. He did not have a smile. He came toward us with purpose. As if on a mission, he moved closer to the microphone at the front of the stage, one foot taking root on the ground before the other one stepped off. The only thing about this man—the leader for whom we suddenly realized we had been waiting—that indicated to us that he was not a severe and solemn commander was the subtle bobbing of his jutting chin to the *one-two-three-four* beat that was coming to a crescendo as all the E Street Band members lifted their instruments and joined in.

Bruce Springsteen reached the microphone stand and lifted the mic out of its holder. "Where's the *wine*?" he asked, his lips spreading into a smile. "Where *is* the wine?"

Cheers erupted from his people.

He walked to the other side of the microphone stand, bobbed his head, undulated his shoulders, and then raised his free hand and dropped it quickly, like a conductor quieting his orchestra. Immediately, the collective decibels of the band's *one-two-three-four* beat dropped some levels. He moved his head up and down in time with the beat. He looked around. He looked straight at us. We watched him as he watched us. He was not in a hurry, and neither were we. We were exactly where we wanted to be. We were with him. Everything was ahead of us. We did not know what the Everything was. We did not have to know, because we knew that he knew. That was why we were here. To give ourselves over to this man who never disappointed us, who never let us down. Who never forgot, when he was onstage in front of us, that we were counting on him to do for us what we could not do for ourselves: Lift us up. And make everything fun.

"Well, uh, I was out strolling one very hot summer day," he said easily, holding the microphone in one hand and casually holding up his other hand.

He was telling us a story!

He bent over and made eye contact one by one with the people standing in the front of the pit. On the jumbo screen at the back of the stage we could see the wide-open eyes of the chosen people connecting with his. As we watched him looking into their eyes and them looking into his, it was as if we, ourselves, were looking into Bruce Springsteen's eyes. We felt chosen too.

"When I thought I'd lay myself down to rest in a deep green valley," he continued. "In a field of tall grass." He lowered himself to a near-reclining position on the top step leading up to the stage, bending the elbow of one arm to prop himself up as he leaned against the stair riser and holding the microphone to his mouth with his other hand.

"I lay there in the sun," he said, laying his upper body almost all the way back. "I felt it caress my face. I fell asleep." He closed his eyes, wrapped his arms across his chest, and dropped his head back.

One-two-three-four, one-two-three-four, one-two-three-four we heard as we watched Bruce Springsteen sleep peacefully in front of us on the stage. *One-two-three-four, one-two-three-four, one-two-three-four* we heard coming from Max Weinberg and Curtis King and Everett Bradley and everyone else in the E Street Band. It was like a heartbeat. Like we were hearing Bruce Springsteen's heartbeat— *one-two-three-four, one-two-three-four, one-two-three-four*.

We knew it was not because he was tired that he was sleeping. Or because he was hungover or bored. It was not at all like the concerts in Melbourne and Sydney, where he seemed down and badly in need of rest. Tonight, he was relaxed. And he was casting upon us his magic spell.

"I dreamed I was in a land far, far away from my home," he said, eyes still closed.

One-two-three-four, one-two-three-four, one-two-three-four.

He cracked his eyes open. He peered out at us.

One-two-three-four, one-two-three-four, one-two-three-four.

"A land at the edges of the earth," he said, sitting up. "Populated by *strange* animals." He nodded his head as if to acknowledge the veracity of what he was about to tell us.

"Wombats." His deep voice resonated with awe.

One-two-three-four, one-two-three-four, one-two-three-four.

"Kangaroos."

One-two-three-four, one-two-three-four, one-two-three-four.

"Koalas."

One-two-three-four, one-two-three-four, one-two-three-four.

He sat up straight.

"Now, in this land, all the women are beautiful," he said with authority.

The crowd cheered.

"All the men are very handsome."

The crowd cheered again.

"And all the children are exceptional students."

He was not forgetting anybody in this story of his.

"Everyone greeted you in a strange language that sounded like 'ga-*ding*, ga-*ding*, ga-*ding*, ga-*ding*."

Yes, I thought. *That is what the phonemes, the lilts of the Australian accent, sound like. Ga*-ding, *ga*-ding, *ga*-ding. *How does he do it? When does he think these things up?*

"I couldn't remember how I got to this place. How an Italian Irish American mutt like me ended up here."

The high-pitched melody of a solo flute percolated above us like the music of a snake charmer. As it did, Bruce Springsteen's body rippled and unfurled like a snake uncoiling and rising from its basket.

"There I was, taken to a place . . ." Now he was transforming his spoken-word story into a sonorous song. He held on to the microphone stand with an outstretched arm and twirled himself around it until he was facing us.

He stopped. He waited as the high-pitched flute delicately mimicked the pace of his last words and the beat of the drums and the maracas and the stick repeating *one-two-three-four, one-two-three-four, one-two-three-four.*

"After a minute, came a lady. She whispered in my ear . . . something crazy."

He waited. The flute sounded nine mimicking notes. Michelle Moore, a vocalist, stepped delicately and in rhythm to the *one-two-three-four* beat over to Springsteen and stood beside him at the microphone. She leaned sideways toward him and whispered in his ear. Then she danced back and forth, side to side, next to him. Her hair was pulled back and her upper body was wrapped in a multihued pink shawl.

With a sudden burst of energy, Springsteen raised his arm and threw it down with gusto, singing, "She said, 'Spill the wine, take that girl.'"

The entire band joined him. With all their resonant musicality, as if they were collectively stepping on a pedal to heighten the intensity of their sound, they accompanied Springsteen in this chorus.

Three times he sang the chorus. Each time he sang the word "spill," he threw down his hand with such force that the whole of his muscular, sixty-four-year-old body quivered from the aftershock.

"I could feel hot flames. Fire roaring at my back. She disappeared," he sang to us in his gentle story-singing voice.

The flute mimicked the sixteen syllables of this latest part of his story. *One-two-three-four*, *one-two-three-four*, *one-two-three-four* the rest of the orchestra beat reassuringly and calmingly as Michelle Moore turned her back on us and danced a few little steps toward the back of the stage.

"But soon she returned," Springsteen sang to us. "In her hand was a bottle of wine. In the other was a glass."

Michelle faced us and danced the few steps back toward Springsteen, holding out a bottle of wine in one hand, a wineglass in the other.

"She poured some of the wine from the bottle into the glass," he sang. "She raised it to her lips."

Michelle poured some wine from the bottle into the glass. She held the glass up, as if she were going to drink it.

And then? I thought. *What happens next?*

"Just before she drank it," he sang to me.

The flute sounded; the band's beat resonated.

Yes? Just before she drank it, what? WHAT!?

Well, just before she drank it, every single person on the stage coaxed every single morsel that could be coaxed out of their instruments, out of their vocal cords, and joined together as Springsteen raised his arm into the air and pushed it down fist-first like an iron hammer on an anvil, every cell in his body bellowing, "Spill wine, take that girl. Spill wine, take that girl. Spill wine, take that girl."

He turned from the audience and shimmied toward the musicians, his entire body undulating to the rhythm. He dropped his head in the direction of the horns—and off they went. One by one, the horn players came forward and had their time in the spotlight, each one riffing his version of "Spill the wine, take that girl."

As they took turns strutting their stuff, Springsteen's back remained to us. He was dancing. Really dancing. He was dancing at his own concert, making himself one with the music of the trumpets. Our eyes darted between him and the trombone players. We followed his lead and danced, really danced, reveling in the melody, feeling the beat. No one onstage was in a hurry to be anywhere other than the energetic, exploding moment they were in. We were in no hurry either. We knew we could trust Bruce Springsteen when he embarked on his once-upon-a-time story. He had proven to us that sometimes fairytales do come true—that sometimes there is a happily ever after.

But the story was not over. There were more characters who had something to say to us, more members of the band whose time had come to step forward and share with us the gifts of their talents. A trumpeter stepped forward. Bruce Springsteen pounded his feet and flexed his muscles as he grooved and moved to the music and the beat. Another horn player came into the light. And another. Then Bruce called out, "Jake!"—and to the front came Jake Clemons.

We cheered. We danced. We clapped. It was truly a party. A celebratory party.

Next The Boss called Tom Morello to the front. As Morello became one with his guitar, performing physical and musical gymnastics, Springsteen, ever the perfect host, continued to lead us in dance, song, and revelry.

The wine was flowing. The music was flowing. We were flowing. We were flowing from one happy, unanticipated moment to the next.

"Spill wine, take that girl. Spill wine, take that girl. Spill wine, take that girl." Over and over and over and over, Springsteen sang this chorus. Over and over and over and over, he thumped his fist down. We were on a roll. Our momentum grew and grew and grew. We were reaching heights we could never before have imagined. Nothing could stop us. Nothing *would* stop us.

Then our host held up his hand to his band and brought it down quickly—and, but for a hint of the melody and the subtle pounding of the *one-two-three-four* beat, all went quiet.

We watched him. *What magic are you going to perform for us now, Bruce Springsteen?*

He walked to the front of the stage. He held the microphone out toward us. He looked at us with almost no expression. He was not smiling. He was not singing. He was waiting. He was waiting for us.

We sang tentatively. We were on our own now. The band was giving us a background beat, but it was up to us to work together to keep the party going. Our vocals were muffled.

Springsteen remained in front of us, holding the microphone out to us patiently. His mouth was open and slack. His eyes seemed to be taking us in loosely; they weren't focused on anyone in particular.

We continued singing. As we did, our confidence began to build. We were listening to each other, following each other. We were singing together. Louder. A bit louder. Louder still.

We can do this.

"Spill the wine, take that girl. Spill the wine, take that girl. Spill the wine, take that girl."

Bruce Springsteen listened and watched. He waited. His eyelids began to droop and close. We had hypnotized him with our singing.

He pulled the microphone from us.

"Then I woke from that dream and . . ." he said, his eyes opening.

The music stopped playing. We stopped singing. His eyes closed again.

"There's something here," he mumbled into the microphone.

He paused. He opened his eyes. He scratched his head in befuddlement.

"What the fuck?" he muttered softly, slowly shaking his head.

The audience erupted in laughter.

He turned to the band. Raised his hand. Then, as if he were a conductor holding a baton, he dropped his hand.

Max Weinberg began beating the drums; the band joined in. Their tempo was fast and furious. Their energy was nothing like the trancelike state of mere moments earlier.

Springsteen took his guitar and, without strumming a chord, he started singing, "At night I go to bed, but I just can't sleep . . ."

We were on to song number two, "My Love Will Not Let You Down."

Springsteen handed off his guitar, and with the band playing on, he sang his way down the steps of the stage and began parading along the unobstructed path between the pit and the seats. People in the front rows thrust out their hands to touch him, as if he were the pope and they were pilgrims in Rome.

But unlike the pope, The Boss high-fived his disciples. He swigged their beer. He tasted their wine. And he posed for selfies.

From one song to another we went; from one song to the next Bruce Springsteen went—without taking a rest, without even a pause. As he did, so too did I.

I employed all the channels in my mind to absorb and record and participate in all that was happening. One channel was dedicated to my dancing and clapping and tapping. Another to watching Bruce Springsteen's boot-clad tapping foot, guitar-strumming fingers, grinning, sparkling, white-toothed mouth, and glistening, dancing eyes. In fact, each and every member of the E Street Band had one of my mind's channels devoted to him or her, as if each one was the only person performing. I also had a panoramic channel trying to track all the cues being transmitted between and among the members of the band and Bruce Springsteen himself. A nod of the head, a shift of the eye. With each concert, I was becoming more and more aware of how they communicated with each other during a song and from one song to the next.

Before my first concert here in Australia, I had not known when a portion of song was being improvised—that sometimes the players came and went, taking cues from each other and creating a version of a song unlike the original one recorded for an album. I hadn't even known the names of most of the band members. But now, at my seventh concert in Australia, I could recognize when they were playing a standard-issue album song and when they were improvising in the here and now, as if we were in a jazz club.

I had learned so much about this band, these people, in such a short time, without even trying. By being 100 percent present and absolutely absorbed in every single moment, in every single beat these rock stars shared with me and their thousands of other fans, I had become a self-proclaimed expert on the High Hopes Australia 2014 Tour.

36

Riding home from the second Hunter Valley concert, I felt as if I had seen and experienced so much during my trip. I had not seen the koalas or kangaroos or penguins that my people back home were imploring me to see, but I had watched and overheard and studied so many people. People unlike any I had seen before. I had seen A-list celebrities killing time between gigs. I had talked to people from all over the world—not just Australia but also France, India, Indonesia, China, Turkey, and Pakistan. Countries so far from Philadelphia that they had never seemed like real places to me. Now, I could place them easily on the map. The world seemed smaller and more familiar and more relevant to me now than it ever had.

And it was not only the external world to which I felt more connected; I also felt more in touch with my inner world. Myself. When I arrived in Sydney, I had been a mere third of the way through my daunting trip. My anticipated return home seemed a lifetime away. When I had loosened my grip on the reins of my brain, I'd found myself unable to imagine how I would ever be able to last so long, so alone and so far from home. So I had learned to keep my brain reined in. I had learned to bring myself back to the moment I was in and focus on that.

Still, the waves of loneliness that were swelling up within me, their intensity increasing with each additional day, were unlike anything I had ever experienced at home. I would be doing something or other—getting through the day, getting through the hour, getting through the minute—when suddenly I would feel as if I were free-falling toward nowhere. A barren place. A place inhabited by no one and nothing. No one and nothing but me.

These swells of loneliness always took me by surprise, upending my physical and emotional equilibrium. But I was learning that if I did not try to stop it, if I did not argue with it—if I paused and let the feeling fill me, if I paused and acknowledged the loneliness idling unhurriedly in every crevice and cell of my body—it eventually lost its strength and evaporated. It was just a feeling. If I did not hold on to it, it could not hold on to me.

During this trip, I'd had no one to turn to, no one to help me, when I felt terrified or lonely or angry or sad. So, by trial and error, consciously and unconsciously, I had helped myself. And I had not done it in a vacuum, in a world where no one existed but me. On the contrary. Each time I'd been felled by a feeling of sadness, loneliness, hopelessness, or all-out despair, at times combined with jet lag and fatigue, I had motivated myself to put one foot in front of the other, step outside my hotel room, and let myself be absorbed into the excitement, the life, the humanity around me. Whether it was two E Street Band members grousing to each other about Bruce Springsteen dressing them down for being behind a beat or those same two E Streeters performing musical acrobatics onstage or Barbara Carr, an eternally grieving mother, coming out from behind the stage during a concert, dancing and clapping and looking like she was having as much fun as the rest of the audience—I'd seen people coping. I'd seen people coping with life and going on. Doing their best. Having fun.

It was exciting for me to see such talented celebrities making magic onstage for the rest of us. It was validating, even life-affirming, to see them killing time in the between hours as they waited for their next gig.

I had come to Australia to see eight Bruce Springsteen concerts, to work out, and to write. So far, I was accomplishing all three of my goals. I had worked out every single day. Even the day I arrived. I had written every day too. And I had been to seven concerts and had one last one to go.

I was doing it. And in less than a week, I would be able to say I had *done* it. In less than a week, I would be home—and with so many stories to tell.

I felt as if I had spent the better part of an adult lifetime at The Park Hyatt Sydney. Not my chronological adult lifetime, of course, but rather my emotional and psychological growth arc. It was as if The Park Hyatt Sydney were a university. I had checked in a week earlier as an undergraduate; tomorrow, I would be leaving with the emotional and psychological equivalent of bachelor's, master's, PhD, and postdoc degrees. Over the course of my week at the Park Hyatt Sydney, I had become less inclined to question or berate my instinct to want to stay in the hotel and be a fly on the wall. I'd stopped telling myself I was an unadventurous loser for not once venturing into a restaurant outside the hotel, or that I was pathetic for having eggs Benedict every day.

I was doing what I wanted to do. I did not care what people at home would say when I returned without a photograph of a koala or kangaroo. It was okay. *I* was okay.

In fact, I was more than okay. I was learning to accept myself.

37

ON THE eighty-minute flight from Sydney to Brisbane, I felt as good as I could remember ever feeling. During the flight, I pulled out a map of Australia from the seat-back pocket in front of me. My eyes scanned from Perth to Melbourne, then to Adelaide, Sydney, and Brisbane. When I'd looked at a map of Australia before I left home, my eyes had glazed. It had meant nothing to me. Even when I had looked at it before landing in Melbourne on the flight from LA, it had seemed like nothing more than a drawing of an island. Now, each of the cities on the map evoked scenes from my stays there. Australia no longer felt like the "land far, far away from my home" about which Bruce Springsteen had riffed at the Hunter Valley concert.

The great big world had not shrunk. My small world had expanded.

When the flight landed in Brisbane, I followed the Royale Limousine driver to the car. I realized that my mindset was no longer, "One foot, then the other. One step after another." I was not using my highly developed sense of discipline to get me from here to there. I was just going. I was curious, interested about where I was and where I was headed. I was not dreading anything. I was not worrying about anything.

My heart did not even pause when we pulled up to the Emporium Brisbane and I immediately knew it was *not* a hotel where I would be rubbing shoulders with Bruce

Springsteen or any of his traveling village. It was situated at the end of a strip mall. I could see Chinese restaurants, dress shops with gauzy, tie-dyed fashions hanging out front, and a jewelry store with peace-motif baubles displayed in its windows.

Through the limo window, I looked up toward the top of the sun-reflecting glass facade of the hotel, expecting to see a flashing red sign that read Elvis Presley Las Vegas Hotel. Instead, it read Emporium Brisbane.

I circled my way between the mirrored panels of the revolving door and stepped into a small, triple-storied mirrored lobby. There were no chairs or couches. At the far end was a small, mirrored bar with a counter and three stools. I did not see a restaurant or a doorway that looked like it might lead to one. To my left was a mirrored check-in desk with one attendant.

"Are you checking in?" I heard someone ask.

I nodded, letting my totes slide off my shoulders and dropping them to the floor.

Fifteen minutes later, after I'd checked in and dropped my bags in my room, I looked at my watch. It was only four o'clock. Brisbane was an hour behind Sydney, so the hours in my day had increased rather than decreased. I needed to find something to do for the rest of that afternoon and the following day until six o'clock, when I would leave the hotel for my last concert.

I went downstairs to the front desk to ask for ideas about things to do.

A young blond man in his early twenties was standing behind the desk. He wore a gold tag that said, "Concierge" and, below that, "Robert."

"There's a great island nearby to see koalas and kangaroos. You would need to take a ferry to get there. It's an easy day trip," he said.

"I need to be back here by six," I said. "Would that work?"

"Absolutely," Robert said.

I stood tall with excitement. Earlier on the trip, I'd had no desire to follow the suggestions I was getting from everyone at home to go on an excursion to see koalas and kangaroos. There had been other things I wanted to do. Like be a fly on the wall. But here at the Emporium Brisbane, that was not an option. There wasn't even a lobby.

Tomorrow, Wednesday, was my last free day in Australia. Thursday I was returning to Sydney. Friday I was going home! It would be great to see kangaroos and koalas and get my picture taken with a couple of them. It would be fun to show the people at home that I had done it all. Now I had a goal. I had a project. And I had to admit: it would be cool to have iconic proof that I had been to this continent on the other side of the world.

"Would I be able to get my picture taken with the animals?" I asked Robert.

"Oh, yes." He nodded. "You can pay to have your photograph taken holding a koala. But be sure to wear a long-sleeved T-shirt. They have sharp claws."

"How exactly do I get there?" I asked, excited about being able to do something appropriately touristy without it being too much trouble.

"There's a ten o'clock ferry to the island. You'd have to leave here at nine o'clock."

My heart sank. "I have to work out at Goodlife, the health club down the street, tomorrow morning, and I have to be back here by six o'clock in the evening to leave for a Bruce Springsteen concert. Do you still think I can go to the island?"

"Lucky you to be going to a Springsteen concert," Robert said.

"I have to agree," I said, smiling. "You're a fan too?"

"I am. Not too long ago I went on a tour of the US and saw Springsteen and the E Street Band play at Giants Stadium in New Jersey. It was a concert of a lifetime, to be sure. Actually, it was a trip of a lifetime."

"Really?" I said, intrigued by such a bold statement. "What made it so special?"

"Well, I don't have to tell you why Springsteen concerts are special. But on the way home to Australia, I sat next to an amazing woman. And now that woman is my wife!"

"A once-in-a-lifetime trip indeed—going to a Bruce Springsteen concert and meeting the woman who would become your wife." I shook my head in amazement. "Good for you!"

Finally, we circled back around to my day trip to the Lone Pine Koala Sanctuary.

"It will be tight," he mused, "but you can do it. If you're interested, I can book you a place on the ferry and a ticket for the sanctuary and arrange for a nine o'clock taxi."

"Thank you so much, Robert."

"It is my pleasure," he said.

The plan was set.

38

THE FOLLOWING morning, my eyes popped open even before my alarm went off. I was wide awake. I was excited that today was my day to get a photograph with a koala.

I had a terrific workout at Goodlife. On my way out, I hesitated when I saw a bistro with a sandwich menu posted above. Every minute mattered if I was going to make it in time for the nine o'clock cab. But I had no idea where or when I would find my next meal.

"I'm in a hurry, and I was wondering how long it would take for me to get a vegetarian wrap and a turkey wrap?" I asked the barista.

"Three minutes," she said. "I will pass on the order and ring you up while they get it ready."

I reached into my bag for my credit card and noticed that my Australian flip phone was not there. I was sure I had put it in there before I left the hotel. I needed that phone. It had all my Australian contact numbers. My heart began to race. I did not have time to retrace my steps back to Goodlife. But I needed that phone.

I paid for my sandwiches and ran back to Goodlife.

"Did anyone find a flip phone?" I asked the woman at the front desk of the gym. "I can't find mine."

"No. Do you want to go back to the locker room and see if it's there?" she asked, looking concerned.

I nodded and ran through the locker room. I had kept all my stuff with me when I showered, so I didn't need to check the lockers. I ran back to "my" bike, retracing my exact steps. Nothing. I went back to the front desk.

"No luck?" the woman asked.

I shook my head.

"How about if I call your phone? Maybe we'll hear it."

"I don't know the number," I said. "It's a temporary, just for this trip. I didn't need to know my number. Until now."

She nodded.

Without thinking, I lifted my tote and dumped everything onto her reception desk. My passport, Visa card, room key, one remaining concert ticket, cash, headset, iPhone (I used it to listen to music during my workout), sneakers, Lululemon workout clothes, yellow comb, and three empty water bottles were all there. But my flip phone was not.

I felt weak and tenuous, as if even the movement of air created by a person walking by would be enough to blow me over. I had been so careful about planning my morning so that I would be back at the hotel at nine o'clock and be on my way to koala land. All morning I had been increasingly impressed by how smoothly I was executing my plan, even leaving myself time to buy lunch and dinner at the bistro outside Goodlife. But I had not been as efficient and clever as I thought I had been. Somewhere along the way, I had been careless enough to lose my phone.

"If anyone turns in a flip phone, will you please bring it to the Emporium down the street?" I asked the woman at the desk.

"Of course," she said.

I gathered my things and stuffed them into my tote.

"Sorry for spreading out all over the place like this and for taking up your time," I said as I headed out. "And thank you."

I retraced my steps from the morning all the way back to the hotel, hoping I might find the phone along the way. I walked rather than ran, even though it was nine o'clock, the time I was supposed to be getting into the cab. I no longer felt like rushing to the koala island just to get a picture. I suddenly felt exhausted.

It made sense that I would be. It also made sense that my fatigue, however masked it had been by adrenaline, coffee, and endorphins, would make me forgetful and careless enough to lose my phone.

Fair enough, I thought. *Everyone's entitled to a mishap. No one is always at the top of her game.*

I thought of the concerts when Bruce Springsteen had seemed tired and had faltered. Even this A-list celebrity was not always at the top of his game. Of course, Bruce Springsteen always rallied. He always pulled himself up, pushed himself onward, and created a once-in-a-lifetime concert experience for every single one of his adoring fans.

I quickened my steps, keeping my eyes to the ground. Maybe I could still make it to the ferry if I did not find the phone on the sidewalk and had to go to my room to look for it.

"Great, you're here," Robert said when I came through the mirrored revolving door into the lobby. "The cab is outside, waiting."

"Did anyone find a flip phone here?" I asked. "I lost mine this morning."

"Not that I know of," he said.

"I'll go check in the back," the other front desk person, Timothy, said. He started walking toward the door behind the check-in desk.

"I'm going to go up to my room and look around," I told Robert. "Will you call my room if Timothy finds it?"

He nodded. "Absolutely."

But Timothy had already reappeared from behind the mirrored wall.

"No luck," he said, looking disappointed.

"Thanks anyway. Do you think you can hold the taxi just a bit longer?" I asked, walking backward toward the elevator.

"No worries," Robert said. "We'll take care of that."

The red lights on the digital clock in my room said 9:10 when I walked in the door. I dropped my workout bag and went into the bathroom, hoping to find the phone on the vanity or the ledge above. No luck.

There was a possibility that I would be fine without the phone. I could probably get help contacting the drivers here in Brisbane, and in Sydney too. But, standing in my room in the Emporium Brisbane, my eyes scanning for the phone, I became even more determined to find it. I did not want to take any chances screwing up my return home. I did not want to put myself in jeopardy of missing a call from a driver or from Qantas. I had worked too hard and waited too long for the day when I could finally go home. If I could not find the phone in the room now, I would spend the day figuring out how to contact my drivers. Nothing was more important to me than going home. Not a trip to a koala sanctuary. Not even my eighth Bruce Springsteen concert.

Instinctively, I breathed in a deep breath and then let out an even deeper breath. My shoulders softened. My neck loosened. As my loose neck moved in a slow, easy circle, my eyes fell on the recalcitrant flip phone, sitting conspicuously on the bedside table.

I just stood there and stared at it. How could I have not spotted it as soon as I walked in the door? I picked up the phone, shaking my head. I was tired. Not a bad, lethargic tired. Just physically and emotionally exhausted from keeping myself moving forward. I had not stopped pushing myself, mentally and physically, since I had left home. I was entitled to be tired. I was entitled to a few brain lapses.

I grabbed the phone, packed up my laptop, vegetarian wrap, iPhone, passport, concert ticket, credit card, driver's license, and Australian cash, and hurried to the elevator. The game of getting to the ferry in time was not over until it was over. It was not over until I got there and found it was either still docked or already sputtering off toward the horizon.

"I'm guessing from the expression on your face that you found your phone?" Robert asked as I stepped off the elevator.

I nodded and broadened my smile. With their sincere, warm, and easy manner, the Emporium Brisbane staff had already endeared themselves to me.

"Any chance the taxi is still here?" I asked, sure that it was not.

"It has not moved a centimeter. The driver is a friend of ours."

"Thank you," I said, and ran out to the curb.

"Thank you for waiting," I said when I got into the taxi. "Do you think we can get to the ferry by ten?"

"It shouldn't be a problem," the driver said. "Unless we run into traffic. But rush hour should be mostly over, so I think we're in good shape."

I sat back in the taxi and let my body go limp. For the first time all morning, I could just be. For the first time all morning, I did not have to be rushing anywhere or doing anything. *Koala photo op, here I come*, I thought. *Then a concert tonight.*

I heard a chorus of sirens. They did not sound like the sirens at home. They reminded me of sirens I had heard in movies about the Holocaust. A cold chill ran through me.

The cab driver pulled to the side of the road just as an ambulance and police cars sped by. Traffic was stalled as far as I could see in front of us and as far as I could see behind us.

I did not feel at all agitated or annoyed that we were falling behind schedule. The shriek of an ambulance siren always humbles and terrifies me. Nearby, someone is in distress. Nearby, someone's life has potentially been shattered.

After some minutes, the taxi driver called his dispatcher and asked what was going on.

"I'm sorry, ma'am," he said when he hung up. "There was a bad accident. It's hard to say when this will clear up."

I nodded. The koala sanctuary did not seem so important now.

"I have a thought," he said with a look of delight. "If you don't mind walking a bit, I could have the dispatcher send a cab to meet you."

"That's a great idea," I said, smiling.

The dispatcher arranged for a taxi to meet me ten blocks away.

"Thank you so much," I said to the driver. "Thank you for all your help."

"My pleasure." He got out of the car and opened my door for me.

"How much do I owe you?"

"Nothing," he said kindly. "I'm sorry I could not take you all the way. I'm sorry you have to walk."

"No, really. First you had to wait for me at the hotel. Now this. And you had such a good idea about how I might still be able to make it."

He smiled.

I dug through my bag and found my cash. "Thank you," I said, handing him a twenty-dollar bill.

"No worries. Thank *you*," he said, smiling. "I appreciate your kindness."

I hoisted my tote and began my trek toward my waiting taxi.

As I plodded into view of the designated corner ten minutes later, a man jumped from his cab and ran toward me.

"Anne?" he asked when he reached me.

I nodded and smiled. I was not as anonymous as I thought.

We arrived at the ferry dock at ten fifteen, fifteen minutes after the ferry's scheduled departure time. But the ferry was still there.

"Bravo," said a man standing on the dock. "I'm Frank, the ship's steward. I bet you're Anne."

I had been surprised to see the ferry still docked. I was even more surprised that Frank knew my name.

"I am," I said. "How did you know my name? And how come the ferry is still here?"

"When you weren't here, we called Robert at the Emporium since he was the one who made the reservation. He called the cab company, and they told him about the accident and that you were on your way."

"Thank you so much for waiting," I said. "I didn't expect to get here in time."

"Unfortunately, accidents happen," Frank said. "I'm glad you're here." He took my ticket and ushered me up the gangplank.

"Thanks, Frank," I said. "I'm glad I'm here too."

39

WHEN THE ferry docked at Lone Pine Koala Sanctuary, I followed the tree-lined, shady path leading up the hill, hoping it would take me where I wanted to go. I had two and a half hours to get my iconic koala photograph and be back on the ferry by two o'clock for the return trip.

Sure enough, at the top of the hill, the path opened onto a lush, green park. Among the trees ahead, I could see a snack bar, a souvenir shop, and restrooms partly camouflaged by the wooded surroundings. There was also a signpost with arrows, each one pointing to a different attraction: cassowaries, kangaroos, koalas, wombats, koala photos. I followed the arrow pointing toward the koala photos. I had heard Frank, the ship's steward, say that there was usually a long line for the koala photographs. I was relieved to see only five groups of people in line when I got there.

The people ahead of me oohed and aahed and giggled as they cuddled the koala. No one seemed bothered by the sharp claws about which Robert at the Emporium had warned me. After the third group of people had been photographed, a park employee handed a new koala, Tango, to the woman supervising the photo shoots and took the other one away. I was reassured to see that these animals seemed to be well cared for and not overworked.

When it was my turn, I stepped into the photo spot—a patch of fallen leaves and wood chips with a backdrop of verdant eucalyptus trees. I handed the park employee my glasses and she placed Tango on my chest. He fit perfectly. I wrapped my arms across my belly to support him and leaned my head down toward his, as if I were cuddling a baby or my Chihuahua, Ryan. It felt good to be so close and cozy with another living creature.

Click, click, click, and *click.*

I did another pose wearing my glasses.

Click, click, click, click.

"You and Tango look like a matched set," the park employee said as she lifted Tango off my chest.

I looked at Tango. I looked down at me. My gray-khaki oversize T-shirt and matching drawstring pants—my concert uniform—were the same color as Tango's fur.

I walked to the souvenir store to pick up my photographs. Above the cashier, a sign said, "Koala is Aboriginal for 'no drink.' Koalas get the water they need in the eucalyptus leaves they eat."

My photographs were amazing. More than amazing. Especially the one with my head resting on Tango's. Mission accomplished—and so efficiently. I had two hours to spare before the ferry departed.

I walked out of the souvenir shop. As I headed back to the path down to the ferry, I passed an arrowed signpost and stopped. Beside the signpost were square glass vessels—like gum dispensers, only these were filled with kangaroo food. I fed the machine a dollar and filled my hands with whatever it is kangaroos eat. Then I followed the signs toward the kangaroos.

They were enclosed in a large, grassy area with piles of logs and tall trees. I did not know how big kangaroos were, or if there were different varieties. These kangaroos were small. Standing, they were barely three feet tall. It was a hot day. Many were lying, splayed on their sides, in the shade of the trees. A few were walking about, slowly, no doubt hoping that those of us who had come to visit them in their home had brought house gifts.

I sat down on a log in the shade, next to a kangaroo who was asleep on his or her side. Another one was standing a few feet from me. I pulled a few treats from my pocket and held out my hand. The kangaroo stepped over and pecked the food from my palm. I offered a few more.

With each offering, the kangaroo seemed increasingly comfortable with me. It was no different from befriending a dog. The kangaroo did not have a pouch, so I guessed it was a male. I rubbed the top of his head and behind his ears as he ate the treats. Again, it felt good to be touching and patting a living creature, and I realized how much I missed my three little dogs.

I looked up and saw a young couple approaching.

"Would you mind taking a picture of me with this kangaroo with my iPhone?" I asked, waving them down.

The young man took my iPhone.

Sitting on the log, I bent down and leaned into the kangaroo, who was now sitting beside me. I wrapped my arms around the middle of his body in a hug and looked up with a smile.

The young man took a couple shots from a standing position and then kneeled and took some shots at eye level with the kangaroo and me.

"I think you'll like these," he said as he handed me back my iPhone.

I looked at the photographs. The kangaroo and I seemed so natural and comfortable together. We could have been lifelong companions. "Wow!" I exclaimed. "These are terrific. Thank you so much."

Koalas *and* kangaroos. This day trip had truly exceeded all expectations.

Halfway back to the trail leading to the ferry, I came to another signpost with arrows. I studied it—and it took my breath away.

On the left side of the signpost were twenty placards with arrows pointing left. Beside each arrow was the name of a city and its distance in kilometers. On the right side of the signpost were twenty placards with arrows pointing right. Beside each of these arrows was also the name of a city and its distance in kilometers. Arrows pointing to my left included Sydney—the closest at 734 kilometers—Cairo (14,407 kilometers), New York (15,496 kilometers), and Dublin, the farthest at 16,668 kilometers. Pointing in the other direction was Surfers Paradise (82 kilometers), Jakarta (5,446 kilometers), Jerusalem (14,066 kilometers), and Toronto (15,027 kilometers).

I was in awe that Anne Abel, a person who heretofore had not liked to travel or to be alone, was standing excitedly, alone, on a spot 15,496 kilometers from New York. Anne Abel, kangaroo-hugger and koala-cuddler, was standing all alone 15,496 kilometers, give or take a few, from home. *This* was the iconic Australia photograph to top all iconic photographs.

I stopped the next person coming down the path and he took a series of photos of me and the signpost.

I strolled back to the ferry. The steward let me onboard even though it was early. I dropped my tote and sat down on a deck chair. I closed my eyes, leaned back in the chair, and lifted my face toward the sun. Its soothing warmth embraced me. I felt good, so good. My mind was not fighting with itself. It was not fighting with me. My mind was letting me be. It was letting me be me.

A deep sense of relief permeated both my body and my mind. I was at peace.

40

THAT EVENING, on the twenty-minute drive to the Brisbane Entertainment Center, I felt myself filling with excitement. Tomorrow I would be able to say, "Bon voyage, Anne Abel, you are homeward bound." I had been looking forward to going home since the day I'd booked the trip. I was excited to see Andy. I was excited not to be alone day after day. I was excited to share my stories with my family and friends.

I was also excited, of course, that I was going to a Bruce Springsteen concert. The seven concerts I had been to in Australia had been blockbusters. Each concert had been completely different. Mostly, they had varied in the way Springsteen had released his energy. Some he'd begun in high gear. Others he'd worked his way up. Sometimes he'd gone up and down.

Always, he'd delivered heartwarming, soul-soothing, goose bumps moments. But each time he'd done it in a different way.

Riding to the concert that night, I told myself there could be only a finite number of ways Bruce Springsteen and the E Street Band could present and perform their High Hopes Tour songs. I did not think they would be able to add a new or novel twist to this final concert in Australia.

I knew, of course, that Springsteen was not going to come out onstage and mechanically run through a set list of songs from the album mixed with sign requests from the audience. I knew he would make sure that all twelve thousand of us in the audience had a good time. But I had never heard of an extraordinary baseball player hitting a grand slam or even a home run every time he went to bat. Bruce Springsteen was an extraordinary performer, but I didn't expect him to hit a musical grand slam, or even a musical home run, every time he took to the stage. Not every night had to be spellbinding.

But that's the thing about magic—the thing about Bruce Springsteen. One moment you're sitting with your feet on the ground, your butt in your chair, thinking about what you're going to eat after the concert, what you're going to do the next morning; then Bruce Springsteen appears onstage. And when he does, you jump to your feet. You clap. You dance. You jump. You sway. Goose bumps pop up all over you. You are not thinking about the past moment. You are not thinking about the next one. You are simply and wholly in each and every moment, following every footstep, every heel tap, every strum, every word, every muscle ripple of the man with the smile—sometimes beatific, sometimes mischievous, sometimes mournful, sometimes soulful.

As you follow this man with the smile, as he anchors you to each moment, he is also anchoring himself to you. You do not feel alone. Feelings blossom from deep down within you. Some make you gleeful. Some make you sorrowful. Some make you wondrous. You do not think about why you feel these ways. It does not occur to you to break out of the moment, to try to understand what is happening to you. It is enough that you are in this place, at this time, with this man, with these people, ensconced in this feeling. You do not think that you have been cast under a magnificent spell. A spell that awakens every single cell in your body. A spell that fills every single cell in your body with pulsating life.

You are not thinking about feeling alive. You *are* alive! You are alive in the here and now. You are alive with this man, with these people. You want for nothing. You have it all.

That night, after I'd found my seat at the Brisbane Entertainment Center and settled in, I saw a figure come to the microphone at the center of the dark stage. A dim light shone down, and the figure became a shadow. The shadowed figure of Bruce Springsteen. He began strumming on his guitar, a steady and unvaried *strum*, *strum*, *strum*.

Soon, the cry of a trumpet joined Springsteen's *strum*, *strum*, *strum*. The circle of dim light from above grew to include the man whose trumpet was sending forth a mournful melody while Springsteen's strumming remained in the background, consistent and unchanging.

I was holding my breath. I was taut with anticipation.

The steady and unvaried *strum*, *strum*, *strum* of Bruce Springsteen's background beat anchored me even as I floated on the sad, soulful sounds of the trumpet.

The notes of the trumpet gradually became weaker and weaker, until eventually they melted into nothingness. The light went dark on the trumpeter.

But we were not alone. We were not abandoned. Bruce Springsteen was still here with us. Steady and unvaried.

"Well, you can tell by the way I use my walk," he began singing gently, calmly.

> *I'm a woman's man, no time to talk*
> *Music loud and women warm*
> *I've been kicked around since I was born*
> *But now it's all right, that's okay*
> *You may look the other way*
> *We can try to understand*
> *The New York Times's effect on man.*

A chorus of soft voices came forth from the dark.

"Whether you're a brother or whether you're a mother . . ."

The dim light from above illuminated Curtis King, Cindy Mizelle, and Michelle Moore, who were all standing at the front of the stage beside Springsteen.

Whether you're a brother or whether you're a mother
You're stayin' alive, stayin' alive
Feel the city breakin' and everybody shakin'
I'm a stayin' alive, stayin' alive
Ah, ah, ah, ah, stayin' alive, stayin' alive
Ah, ah, ah, ah, stayin' al-i-i-i-ve

The tempo was quickening. The decibels were increasing. There was a pause. A moment of hesitation.

The singers were not singing. Springsteen was not singing. Springsteen was not strumming. And for a moment, an infinitesimal fraction of a moment, I felt my heart stop. For an infinitesimal fraction of a moment, I was suspended, untethered, unmoored. For an infinitesimal fraction of a moment, I felt uncertain.

What is going on? I wondered. *What is happening?*

Then Springsteen tapped the heel of his boot, loudly saying, "Two, three, four"—and a chorus of strings, a serenade of violins, came floating from the back of the stage.

Strum, strum, strum, Springsteen accompanied them.

Lights illuminated the back of the stage. Weaving their bows along the strings of their violins were eight young women dressed in black, sitting in a row. The intensity of their sonorous melody increased with their tempo as they kept pace with Springsteen.

Springsteen backed up the violins as their notes swelled, lifting the melody higher and higher. He sang, "Well, now, I get low, and I get high . . ."

The stage lights brightened and every single member of the E Street Band joined in.

And, if I can't get either I really try
Got the wings of heaven on my shoes
I'm a dancin' man, and I just can't lose
You know, it's all right, it's okay
I'll live to see another day
We can try to understand
The New York Times's effect on man . . .

The musicians were playing. The vocalists were singing. The violinists were stroking their bows over their strings.

Together, they repeated the chorus.

Whether you're a brother or whether you're a mother
You're stayin' alive, stayin' alive . . .

The trumpeter came forward and the light shone down on him as he belted out his melody to Springsteen's steady but now animated *strum, strum, strum.*

A trombone player stepped to the front and the light shone down on him as the trumpeter stepped back.

Jake Clemons had a solo. Tom Morello had a solo. Springsteen's eyes were closed as he nodded his head in tempo with the music, as he soaked up the sounds of his band members.

As every person onstage played and sang with every cell of their being, intensity and emotion exploding from the stage, Bruce Springsteen sang:

Life goin' nowhere, somebody help me
Somebody help me, yeah
Life goin' nowhere, somebody help me, yeah
I'm stayin' al-i-i-i-ve
Life goin' nowhere, somebody help me
Somebody help me, yeah . . .

The Boss sang these words with the conviction of someone who had been there.

Except for the violinists and Max Weinberg, everyone onstage joined Springsteen in a line as they continued playing their instruments. Their music was desperate. It was imploring. It was soulful. It was explosive.

Life goin' nowhere, somebody help me
Somebody help me, yeah
Life going nowhere, somebody help me, yeah
I'm stayin' al-i-i-i-ive.

The singing stopped. The music stopped. The stage lights dimmed.

I did not know, as I stood in the Brisbane Entertainment Center listening to this first song of the show, that what I was hearing was not in fact a Bruce Springsteen song. I did not know that it was a cover, a Bruce Springsteen version of a song by a group called the Bee Gees. I had never heard of the Bee Gees. I had no idea that this band, formed in 1958, was the third most successful band in Billboard-charts history after The Beatles and The Supremes.

Of course, eighteen months earlier I had never heard of Bruce Springsteen either.

Standing in the Brisbane Entertainment Center, carried away by the first song of my eighth and last Australia concert, I did not know that Bruce Springsteen was tipping his hat to the Bee Gees, a group who emigrated to Australia from England in the late 1950s and settled in a town twenty miles from Brisbane. I did not realize, as I clapped and swayed along with Springsteen, that this song, bare in all its desperation, was originally a smooth disco song with a light, tinny backbeat and no dark edge to it. I knew only that I felt enveloped by the music, validated and emboldened by the words, by this anthem that was reminding me I was not alone in the struggle called life.

If, when the last notes of the song had been played, when the light momentarily dimmed, the concert had ended, it would have been enough. But, of course, the evening was just beginning, and I felt thankful so much was yet to come. I felt grateful to be in the hands of a master performer, a man with compassion, a man with empathy, a man with a smile that melted my cares away. A man who did not promise life everlasting but who promised life in this moment.

A man who, in this moment, was onstage performing for me.

Bruce Springsteen took the microphone off the stand and began pacing back and forth, slowly, across the front of the stage.

"How do you stay alive?" he asked slowly and with gravitas as he placed one foot in front of the other and walked steadily, methodically across the stage.

"How do you stay alive?" he asked again, turning around and placing one foot in front of the other and walking steadily, methodically to the other side of the stage.

"How do you get through the day and stay alive?" he asked. He was holding the microphone close to his mouth, moving across the stage, making eye contact with audience members sitting in his line of vision.

The audience was silent. The audience was rapt.

"How do you stay alive? How do you get through the day?" he incanted as he lumbered back and forth across the stage.

"How do you get through the day and stay alive *inside*?" He sounded like a revivalist preacher.

Yes, I thought, *making it through the day, physically, is often a struggle. But getting through the day and feeling anything inside but heavy dread at the end, dread that morning will come and you will have to do it all over again—that is the most demoralizing aspect of the struggle. I try, and I try, and I try. I try to do all the things I think I should do to be a good wife, mother, friend, person. Then I get to the end of the day and I feel a dull sense of dread inside me. I feel I have accomplished nothing. That nothing I did matters. That I do not matter.*

"We have come all this way to ask one question," he said, stopping and turning to face the front of the stage. "Have you got the spirit?" he sang in an ethereal, high-pitched voice. "Have you got the spirrrrrit?"

Two, three, four, and Preacher Bruce Springsteen and the E Street Band jumped into a full-throttle, fast-paced, energizing rendition of "Spirit in the Night."

I recognized the song. It was from his 1973 debut album *Greetings from Asbury Park, N.J.* I was not sure what the song was about. It seems to be about a young man and a young woman on a Saturday night, taking a bottle of rosé up to Greasy Lake where there were some "gypsy angels." I assumed that once you were in the presence of gypsy angels, whether they were figments of your imagination or real, wonderful things were possible.

> *And they dance like spirits in the night (All night) in the night (All night)*
> *Oh, you don't know what they can do to you.*
> *Spirits in the night (All night), in the night (All right)*
> *Stand right up now and let it shoot through you*

As I stood in the audience letting the sights and sounds fill me, I *felt* a spirit. I felt infused with lightness. I felt infused with a spirit of possibilities. It felt possible that I could get through the day *and* feel alive inside.

A few songs later, Springsteen waded into the pit, chose a few signs that fans were waving in the air with song requests, and took them back to the stage. "We can do more fan requests, or we can do something special," he called out. "It's up to you. Fan requests?"

There was a groundswell of cheers and claps.

"Something special?"

There was a louder wave of cheers and claps.

"Okay." He turned to face the band for a moment. Then he took his place at the microphone. "Two, three, four," he said, tapping his heel.

And they were off, playing one song after another from the 1973 album *The Wild, the Innocent & the E Street Shuffle*—the second studio album Springsteen and the E Street Band released.

I recognized some of the songs, although I did not know they were all from one long-ago album. What I did notice was that the band was riffing. One song after another, I noticed Springsteen give a single, subtle nod to one player after another. Each time he did, the player stepped forward and played his or her instrument as if they were in their own solo show. One and then another, sometimes two or three or four of them together. I could see them simultaneously playing and watching, waiting for a sign to step back or continue.

Bruce Springsteen and the E Street Band were having a grand time together, and I was having a grand time watching them having so much fun.

After a number of songs, I heard a chorus in the audience calling, "Broo! Broo! Wake up, wake up!"

It was not the affectionate "Broo!" I was accustomed to hearing at concerts. Song after song, I saw more people getting up and leaving. And their seats remained empty. Apparently, they had left for good, disappointed and annoyed with Springsteen's "something special."

I was sure Springsteen was aware of the small uprising. If he had not noticed or heard himself, his village of support staff could have somehow informed him about it. In any case, the band played on. And on and on and on. They played and riffed on and on and on, seemingly oblivious to the quiet exodus of some of the audience.

Then, all of a sudden, they were playing "Waitin' on a Sunny Day." And after that, the songs went on and on and on. If anyone still in the audience had been unhappy about going down memory lane with *The Wild*, Springsteen was more than making it up to them. The songs did not stop. Each one spun out more energy than the one before.

Suddenly, Pearl Jam's Eddie Vedder—who had also been onstage in Melbourne—appeared beside Springsteen and joined him and the E Street Band in a loud, raucous, spirited rendition of "Highway to Hell," a song I would later learn was written by the hard rock Australian band AC/DC. When the song ended, Eddie Vedder left the stage, followed by the band members and then Springsteen.

"Broo! Broo! Broo!" the fans called, back to a full-throated enthusiastic chant now that the dissatisfied concert-goers had left.

I looked at my watch for the first time since the concert had begun. They, we, had been going nonstop for more than three and a half hours.

"Broo! Broo! Broo!" shouted hopeful fans.

And out he came to his microphone in the middle of the stage. Hanging from his neck was a harmonica; in his hand was an acoustic guitar. He was wearing a black V-neck T-shirt, and sweat was coming through the shirt and glistening on his brow.

"Thank you so much," he said to the audience, giving them time to cheer.

"Whoa!" he said, as if he had just run a marathon. "Damn!"

More cheering from the crowd.

He spoke casually to the crowd.

"We had a chance to go south along the coast, way past Surfers Paradise. We've been here before but never had a chance to go. It's so beautiful. Waves you can surf for like half a mile."

The crowd cheered and catcalled.

"Don't tell anyone about this shit," he said. "People will all be coming down here. I'm telling you, keep it a secret. It was just paradise."

As he spoke, I noticed for the first time that he looked tanned. I had not noticed his tan at earlier concerts or even during this concert. Not until now. He looked tired. But at peace.

"Whew," he said, as if he had just run *another* marathon. "Well, last but not least, The Thunder for Down Under."

He was referring to "Thunder Road," a song from his 1975 album *Born to Run*.

Tonight, he began with his harmonica and a few faint strums on his guitar.

"Screen door slams," he sang faintly.

Mary's dress sways
Like a vision she dances across the porch
As the radio plays

His fingers seemed to strum the guitar strings as an occasional afterthought. He seemed deep in reverie.

Is he thinking about the thousands of times he has sung this song since 1975? I wondered. *Is he thinking about the people with whom he has sung it? The places?*

Roy Orbison singing for the lonely
Hey that's me and I want you only
Don't turn me home again
I just can't face myself alone again

His competent voice was telling the story on its own.

Don't run back inside
Darling, you know just what I'm here for
So, you're scared and you're thinking
That maybe we . . .

Bruce Springsteen, his eyes still closed, hesitated. As if on cue, the audience took over, gently but clearly in command of the words and the melody: ". . . ain't that young anymore."

Bruce Springsteen nodded in approval, eyes still closed, and listened to his fans.

Show a little faith there's magic in the night
You ain't a beauty but hey you're alright . . .

Eyes closed, The Boss took over.

Oh that's alright with me . . .

He was barely playing the guitar. His voice seemed to go from singing to speaking to earnest preaching.

My hands were clasped together in front of my heart. I was swaying in tandem with Bruce Springsteen in my own open-eyed, tearful, happy reverie.

We got one last chance to make it real
To trade in these wings on some wheels
Climb in back
Heaven's waiting down on the tracks
Oh-oh come take my hand
We're riding out tonight to case the promised land
Oh-oh-oh-oh Thunder Road, oh Thunder Road, oh
  Thunder Road.

His voice was imploring, gaining strength as it got louder.

Tears dripped down my face. Though I had seen him perform this song many times, I had never before heard it or felt it as I did tonight. Tonight, I saw myself as some version of the character Mary. Tonight, in this song, I saw myself with Bruce Springsteen. I had taken his hand and let him lead me out of town to the promised land when I decided to go on this trip. He did not know I existed. He did not know that he had guided me through so much in the last few weeks.

Well, I got this guitar
And I learned how to make it talk . . .

He sang low and slow, strumming a rush of notes on the guitar.

This man and his talking guitar had saved me. We were at the end, but I was not afraid. I was ready to set off on my own.

So Mary climb in
It's a town full of losers
I'm pulling out of here to win

Springsteen played a few measures on his harmonica. Then he dropped it and let it rest on his chest, hanging from his neck.

With his eyes still closed, he hummed and hummed and hummed the melody.

Then he broke into, "La-de-da, la-de-da, la-de-da."

He sounded like he was singing the end of a lullaby. His voice was soothing. His voice was calming. At the end of the song, he opened his eyes.

"Australia, the E Street Band loves you."

He stretched his arms out to the audience, his guitar in his right hand. He turned slowly, bidding adieu to everyone in the audience. Then he took his harmonica from around his neck and slipped it to a fan standing at the front of the pit.

"We'll be seeing you," he said, holding up his arms in tribute to his fans.

Then he walked to the back of the stage and disappeared down the stairs.

I stood motionless in front of my seat, staring at the spot where I had last been able to see him. It was hard to believe that almost four hours had gone by so quickly. It was hard to believe this was the end of the road for me. It was hard to believe that I had done it.

Now I was a world traveler. A world-traveling Bruce Springsteen fan. I had met the enemy—abject loneliness—and I had survived. Day after day, I had grappled with difficulties both emotional and physical, and I had moved past them, on my own. I had not fallen into the pit of depression and been unable to crawl back out. I had teetered on the precipice, yes, but each time—through a combination of my own strength, the kindness of strangers, and the magic of Bruce Springsteen—I had righted myself.

41

THE DAY of my departure from the Emporium Brisbane, my alarm was set for 5:30 a.m. But at 5:20 a.m., after fewer than three hours of sleep, my eyes opened.

During the trip, my feet had often jumped onto the floor as my eyes were opening. Not today. Today, I pushed myself up to a sitting position on the bed and just sat. I was tired. Very tired. My body felt heavy. My mind felt heavy. The only thing left on my Australia itinerary was to head home. This was the day I had been looking forward to since I had booked the trip. Yet here I was, sitting on the bed, feeling befuddled and worried.

Did I want to go home? Yes. I had accomplished all I had hoped to do on the trip. I had been more victorious on this trip than I could have ever hoped for. I *felt* as if I had learned so much.

But what exactly *had* I learned? I was frustrated that I did not know how I would explain to my people at home how much I had experienced.

I thought about my friends and family who so often shook their heads in condescension and made derogatory remarks at me. Thinking about returning home, I suddenly felt like Cinderella when the clock struck midnight and she once again became the mistreated stepdaughter. Unlike Cinderella, my wish was not to go to a ball. My wish was to connect with people. I wanted respect. I wanted empathy. I wanted compassion.

I also wanted acknowledgment of my courage. My courage in going twice to Sheppard Pratt for inpatient treatment. My courage in undergoing three regimens of ECT. My courage in going to Australia. All of these things had terrified me. But I had not let my fear stop me from doing them. I had done them because I wanted to claw my way out of the abyss of depression. Because I wanted to be the best me I could be.

I wanted my friends and family to appreciate how hard I worked to try to keep myself afloat.

Sitting on my bed in the Emporium Brisbane, waiting for my 5:30 a.m. alarm to ring, my mood continued to darken as I thought about my people at home. I remembered an email I had written to them during my trip, trying to explain why my wanting to write was valid, justified. Remembering it, I felt annoyed that I had felt the need to justify myself to anyone. And I was annoyed that so many of my people back home had rolled their eyes and dismissed me for wanting to write, and for wanting to go to Australia. The only thing they acknowledged about me or were interested in about me was my depression.

From the moment I began my trip, I had been counting down the days until I would return home. Now that it was about to happen, I had a sick feeling inside me. I feared that when I returned home, my friends would be unable to see me or relate to me outside the box of depression.

My days in Australia had not been utter bliss. I had been up and down. Lonely and dejected. Upset and sad. But I had also been uplifted.

"Is there anybody alive out there?" Bruce Springsteen sometimes called out during his shows, speaking directly into his microphone and staring out into the audience.

Whenever he asked this question, I felt as if he were lifting me up off the ground. He was acknowledging that we all feel dead sometimes. And he was reassuring us that it wasn't going to happen on his watch.

There had been so many moments in Australia when, despite my feeling depressed or sad or lost, I had pushed myself to move forward. Sometimes I'd done it by researching Bruce Springsteen and the E Street Band members. Sometimes by perching as a fly on the wall among the bevy of A-listers sharing my space. Sometimes by allowing strangers to reflect back to me a broader view of myself.

I wanted to go home. I really did. After almost four weeks in Australia, my hope was to go home and not lose the energy and determination I had worked so hard to acquire in Australia. My hope was that my friends and family would support and respect me in this.

And after almost four weeks in Australia, I'd learned something important: with enough dedication, a hope could be turned into a dream.

42

WHEN THE driver pulled up to the curb of Sydney International Airport for my flight to LA, I felt an unsettling sensation rising inside. I realized I was about to burst into tears. Instantly, I sucked in my stomach and tightened the muscles around my eyes. I did not want to alarm the driver. I did not want to make a scene. I just wanted to get myself on the plane and go home.

The driver took my suitcases inside the terminal to the stack of luggage carts.

"Thank you," I said, still pushing down sobs of joy.

He smiled, turned away from me, and took one step in the direction of his car. Then he turned back around and looked at me. "Would you like me to help you with the luggage cart?"

The sobs welling up in me dissipated. I felt myself beaming. I knew I did not have the patience or the concentration to unravel the convoluted directions for securing a cart.

"Thank you so much," I said, handing him my Visa to pay for the cart.

He got me a cart and loaded it with my overweight suitcases and overstuffed totes. Then he turned and walked away.

I grasped the handles of my cart—and burst into tears. Leaning forward on the cart, I sobbed with relief and happiness. I was finally going home.

As I began to push the cart forward, I heard a chorus of voices inside my head cheering, *You did it. You are amazing. You are one amazing woman who is on her way home.*

Over and over, the voices cheered me onward to the check-in counter.

"I'm here for the flight to LA," I said, presenting my passport and my ticket and leaning my upper body on the counter.

"Wonderful, let me check you in," the agent said. "When I'm finished, one of our representatives will take you to the express security line."

The express security line did not look express, but I didn't mind. I took my place at the back of the line, happy to be there. Elated to be there. I was going home.

The line moved slowly—very slowly. Behind me was a silver-haired woman in her mid-to-late seventies; she was impeccably but understatedly dressed in a flowing gray skirt and matching sweater set. Our eyes met and she smiled at me. I smiled back.

"This is quite a long and slow-moving line," she said. "We're going to be here a while. Where are you headed?"

"Home," I said with relief. "To Philadelphia."

"How long were you in Australia?" she asked.

"Almost four weeks."

"Were you here on vacation or for work?"

I hesitated. It was not vacation. It was not work. I did not want to misrepresent myself. I also did not feel like explaining myself.

"A little of both," I said, finally.

It was not too far-fetched to say that keeping myself out of the abyss was work for me. But I added "vacation" to distract her from the "work" part of my answer. People seemed more interested in talking about vacations than work. I would tell her about the concerts.

"What do you do?" she asked, surprising me.

"I'm a writer," I said. The words came out before I could think about them.

"Why did you come *here*?"

I wondered if she was a private eye. "I followed Bruce Springsteen's concerts here."

"Oh, how marvelous. Are you writing his biography?"

I laughed. "Oh, no," I said, shaking my head and still smiling. "I didn't know who he was eighteen months ago, never mind being a biographer of his or anyone's."

"You didn't know who Bruce Springsteen was eighteen months ago?" she asked, looking incredulous.

"No," I said, "I'd never even been to a concert before. Not until eighteen months ago, when I went with my son and daughter-in-law to a Bruce Springsteen concert just so I could spend time with them."

"And now you're in Australia following him?" she asked, smiling.

I nodded.

"Alone?"

I nodded again.

"Forget about writing Bruce Springsteen's story," she said. "You should be writing your own story. I know I'd like to read it. You sound fascinating."

"Thank you for your kind words," I said.

I felt myself standing taller. It was amazing to me that this stranger seemed so interested in my story.

"Where are *you* going?" I asked.

"I'm going to Manchester." Her face turned somber. "My husband's brother died, and I'm going to give some TLC to my eighty-five-year-old sister-in-law."

"Oh, I'm so sorry," I said.

"Thank you, yes. He was ninety-one. He died yesterday, suddenly, after having a heart attack. I'm on a bereavement ticket. The quickest way for me to get to Manchester on a bereavement ticket is to go through Dubai, of all places."

I nodded. I did not know what to say.

"Two years ago, when my husband died, my sister-in-law did the same for me. We're lucky to have each other, even if we do live so far apart."

"I can't imagine anything more difficult or horrible than losing a spouse," I said.

"You're right. It isn't easy. But it happens." She shrugged. "You figure out a way to go on."

The line began to move; I realized we were being sent into different queues. "I hope your sister-in-law can find comfort in your presence," I said.

"Good luck to you with your writing," she said. "What's your name?"

I hesitated, unsure why she was asking.

"Tell me your name so I can keep my eyes open for your book," she said.

When I hesitated again, she stopped heading toward her queue. I stopped heading toward mine.

"Ladies, you have to keep the lines moving," an airport person told us.

She looked at me, smiling and still not moving.

"Anne Abel," I said. "A-B-E-L."

43

I WAS SO tired, so relieved, so calm on the flight home that I slept most of the way. When I arrived in Philadelphia, I followed the arrows toward baggage claim. Toward Andy.

I stepped onto the down escalator, carefully, with my heavy carry-on bags. I grabbed the black railing and steadied myself. Then I lifted my eyes and saw that below, at the bottom of the escalator, was Andy.

Tears began dripping down my face. It was all I could do to keep myself from letting the bags slip down my arms onto the stairs and start running. I stared into Andy's eyes as I descended closer toward him. At the bottom, I slid one foot and then the other off the stair and onto the floor—and then I dropped my bags and ran the few feet into my husband's arms.

I pressed myself into him, squeezing us together as tightly as I could. As I did, a quiet, peaceful, content happiness filled my body. I was exactly where I wanted to be. I had arrived. I did not need to take one more step. I let Andy's gentle, secure hug radiate through me. The physical connection was sublime. I was not alone. I mattered to someone. To Andy. And oh, how Andy mattered to me.

As I felt myself melding into him, I realized I had not touched or been touched by another human being since I had kissed Andy goodbye. How lonely and empty the lack of human touch had made me. How I had ached, unconsciously, to be touched by my husband.

Over the weeks, as I had become more familiar with Bruce Springsteen's songs, I'd noticed that whenever I saw something or felt something, one of his song lyrics describing what I was experiencing would flow through my head. Each time, I marveled not only that he had similar feelings and experiences to mine but also at how poetically and articulately he expressed them. Standing at the bottom of the escalator in Philadelphia International Airport's baggage claim, the chorus of his 1992 song "Human Touch" began streaming through my head:

> *Tell me in a world without pity*
> *Do you think that what I'm askin's too much?*
> *I just want something to hold on to*
> *And a little of that human touch*
> *Just a little of that human touch.*

It was not until this moment, wrapped in Andy's arms at the bottom of an escalator after nearly a month away from him, that I realized the truth and reality of Bruce Springsteen's words.

Andy and I unwound ourselves from each other, and he picked up my bags.

"Let me take one," I said.

"No, I'm fine," he said as we began walking to the baggage carousel.

"Oh, Andy," I said when we got to the still-empty carousel. "It was an amazing trip. I am so glad I went. And now I am so happy to be home."

Andy smiled. "That all makes me happy."

"I never want to go off alone like that again."

"That makes me happy too. I missed you. The dogs missed you."

I hugged him.

When we'd finally recovered my bags, made our way to the car, and gotten on the road, I bubbled over with excitement. "Andy, I have so many stories to tell you. To tell everyone."

He smiled, his eyes straight ahead on the road.

"Isn't it amazing that except for the last one, I stayed in the same hotels as Bruce Springsteen and the E Street Band?"

"It is," he said amiably.

"One night when I was waiting outside the hotel bar after a concert, Bruce Springsteen walked by me, so close that I could have put out my hand and touched him, easily."

He didn't say anything. Andy is careful about everything he does. Driving is no exception. His hands were at ten and two on the steering wheel, his eyes on the dark road ahead of him.

"You know, Bruce Springsteen is actually pretty short. It's funny, onstage he doesn't seem short at all. But in person, he really is."

Andy nodded.

We rode in silence. I looked at the blue digital clock on the console. It was 1:30 a.m. I had no idea what time my body thought it was. I did not even know if I was tired or not.

I leaned back in my seat. I did not feel like trying to talk anymore. I knew Andy did not like to be distracted from driving, and I did not feel like speaking into a vacuum.

I turned on the radio. A golden oldies song came blasting through the speakers.

"Wow, you were really grooving," I said with a chuckle.

"I think it comes on louder when it's turned on than it was when it last played," he said, sounding apologetic.

"There's nothing wrong with grooving to loud music," I said cheerfully. "Do you mind if I turn it to E Street Radio?"

I had stumbled upon SiriusXM's E Street Radio the previous summer. I'd quickly learned that the channel primarily played Bruce Springsteen songs—albums, concerts, covers of Springsteen songs by other musicians. They also had a schedule of shows, some with call-ins, as well as a host who always talked about some topic related to Bruce Springsteen. Whenever I got into my car, I turned on the radio and blasted the music. I loved it.

"Go ahead," Andy said.

I changed the channel.

"Oh my God!" I said. "I can't believe it. This is 'Tenth Avenue Freeze-Out.' Bruce Springsteen played this song at every concert in Australia. At first, I had no idea what the song was about. I couldn't understand the lyrics. But it was really fun. He would go out into the audience. I found myself jumping and clapping and feeling really happy when he did it. Then I finally figured out that one of the lines he was singing was, 'It's okay to have a good time.' I felt so good when he said that. It was really validating for me to hear him say those words. And I think of them often. That it's okay just to have fun and not be doing anything productive."

"I don't know how you can like a song if you don't know or understand the lyrics," Andy said.

I turned and looked at him. "I don't know, I just let the music go in me without thinking about it. I'm just feeling the music, I guess. The tempo, the tone. I'm just absorbing it. Eventually, after I hear a song often enough, little by little the words become clear to me. But mostly I just feel the beat and hear the melody."

By the time "Tenth Avenue" was coming to an end, we were driving up our driveway.

When I walked into the kitchen from the garage, it looked like I had never left. My Mr. Coffee was on the counter, ready for me to press the button in the morning. Beside it was my Chihuahua coffee mug, my favorite. Beside that was a cereal bowl and my box of oatmeal.

"Everything looks perfect," I said, turning toward Andy, who was wheeling in one of my suitcases. As I turned, I saw a vase of yellow roses and a plate with two chocolate chip cookies from Whole Foods—my absolute favorite cookies—sitting on the table.

"Wait, let me get the dogs from the mudroom," Andy said.

He let go of my suitcase and opened the door—and out they came, almost flying.

They landed at my feet, jumping and barking. Even Ryan, the Chihuahua, who is typically the unflappable, even-tempered senior member of our four-legged gang, was going crazy.

I forgot about my arthritic knees, I forgot about my arthritic wrists—I bent my knees and melted to the floor, not giving a thought to how I would hoist myself up. The dogs were all over me. Jumping into my lap. Jumping up to lick my face. Jumping and barking, their tails flitting back and forth like windshield wipers.

"I missed you too," I said. "It's so good to see you."

It *was* good to see them, to feel them, to pull them close to me. I looked up at Andy, who was watching us, beaming.

I beamed back. I felt as if my entire house were hugging me, telling me it was happy to have me back.

When the dog licks on my face began to feel like a sponge bath, I raised my hands to Andy, and he pulled me up onto my feet.

I turned around, taking in our kitchen and family room. I stood there and absorbed the comfortable familiarity of the room. The room in which I had spent so many hours—too many hours—feeling terrified of my upcoming trip. It had been my cocoon, my nest, that I had been so terrified of leaving. Now, I had gone and come back. Now, images of the places I had been in Australia streamed through my head. The vast, scary, world seemed a lot smaller, a lot less scary and a lot less unknown. My home of thirty years felt like a cocoon no longer; now, it felt like a launching pad.

"Andy, it really is good to be home," I gushed. "To be with you. And the doggies. I have so many stories to tell you. And I weaned myself off all the pain meds Dr. Ashburn had me on, and off the Ritalin Dr. Bhati insisted I take." Dr. Ashburn was my pain management doctor and Dr. Bhati was my psychiatrist.

"Anne, it's six in the evening in Sydney, but it's two o'clock here in Philadelphia," Andy said wearily. "I know you're excited to be home. I'm excited too. But I don't have the advantage of being on Sydney time. I'm going to go to bed." He walked over to me and gave me a kiss. "Good job. You did it. And now you are home."

I smiled as he turned and walked out of the room—but the dogs looked at him and back at me with a hint of trepidation. Typically, their allegiance was 100 percent to me. Now they seemed confused. Andy had been their person for the last three-plus weeks, and a dog's allegiance is primarily based on who gave them their last treat.

I stood up, went into the mudroom, and pulled out some chewy biscuits.

"Chase, Megan, Ryan," I said as I doled out the treats one after the other.

A few rounds of treats later, they would have followed me on foot and by dog paddle across the world to Australia if I had commanded. Instead, I asked them to follow me up to bed. I wanted to be with Andy. It did not matter what time it was in Sydney or Philadelphia.

I led my choo choo train of dogs up the stairs and put them on the bed. I washed up and slid into bed, sandwiched between Andy and the dogs, who were nestled against my back and in the crook of my bent legs. It was so good to have the bodies of my two-legged and four-legged creatures warming me from the outside in and from the inside out.

I synchronized my breathing with Andy's.

Two inhales and two exhales, and I was asleep.

44

I WOKE UP the following morning as the winter daylight began streaming through the bare branches outside our windows. The dogs were eager to get downstairs and outside so they could come in and eat. I followed them, the caboose to their happy, hopeful train.

I pressed the button on my Mr. Coffee. I filled the pot with water for my oatmeal. I cut up strawberries; I washed blueberries.

It was so fun doing the ordinary tasks of my life. It was hard for me to imagine just how bad I had felt so many mornings as I slogged my way through these tasks, metaphorically putting one foot in front of the other as I prepared my breakfast. I knew I had felt bad. Very bad. But now, back at home sweet home at last, it was impossible for me to conjure that abject desperation.

I was *happy*, I realized. I was happy I had gone. I was happy I had returned.

As soon as Andy stepped into the kitchen, I jumped up from the table.

"Andy," I said, excitement bubbling up in me. "It's Sunday. Let's go downtown this afternoon to a movie, and then go out to dinner to celebrate that I am home."

Andy stared at me. "Dinner at a restaurant? That doesn't sound like you."

I smiled. "Well, it's how I sound now."

"I can't," he said, gathering his cereal and raisins. "We have a job candidate coming in tomorrow. There's a lot of disagreement in the department about him. We're having a meeting early tomorrow morning to try to smooth things out among ourselves. And I have six papers to read before we meet."

I did not say anything. I did not know what to say. I understood that life had gone on while I was away—that Andy had commitments and obligations. Still, I felt disappointed by his lack of interest or involvement in anything I said. He'd had more than three weeks to do nothing but work. It seemed to me that *today* he could slow down for a day, a morning, an hour, to focus on me.

"Andy?" I said, not sure exactly what I else I was going to say but hoping to somehow let him know how much I wanted to spend some time with him and tell him about my trip.

"In addition to the six papers I have to read," he added, "I have more than twenty-five emails from yesterday that I didn't look at because I was busy getting ready for you. I need to read them and respond to them before the next batch starts arriving."

He ate quickly, then pushed his breakfast dishes aside, opened his laptop, and began reading and tapping.

I looked at the clock. It was eight thirty. At nine o'clock I could call Ross and Robert, who both lived in Boston. At noon I could call Richard in San Francisco. In the meantime, I'd read the paper.

When I looked up at the clock, it was ten. I'd gotten caught up in the stories in the paper.

I called Robert. No answer. I waited for the voicemail beep.

"Robert, it's Mommy. I'm home. It was amazing," I chirped. "I can't wait to talk to you. Please call me. I love you. Bye."

I called Ross. No answer. I waited for the voicemail beep and left the same message.

I sat back in my chair at the table. I could feel my excitement and energy waning, even as I rested against the chair back. I felt tired. Maybe I was feeling depleted because of jet lag. Maybe I was feeling depleted because I had just returned from a three-plus-week trip to the other side of the world, where I had never gotten more than four hours of sleep on any given night.

I decided to work out, hoping it would energize me.

When I finished my sixty minutes of pedaling, I did not immediately open my eyes. I did not immediately do anything. I sat on my bike, Bruce Springsteen's *Wrecking Ball* blasting though my headset, and let myself be. My inhales and exhales slowed. The pounding of my heart slowed to thumping. The thumping of my heart turned to soft beats.

I opened my eyes and looked through the window beside my bike, out at the trees and driveway. A scene I knew so well. My workout was over. My trip was over. I looked at the big round wall clock with its green hands. It was noon. Richard, in San Francisco, would be awake by now.

I tapped on his name in my iPhone, my heart speeding up with anticipatory excitement.

"Hi, Mommy, what's up?" Richard answered after only a few rings.

"I just got home last night!" My voice rose with every word, buoyed by my excitement.

"Oh, that's right," he said. "How was it?"

"Richard, it was amazing," I said, not sure how to begin trying to explain myself. "I stayed in the same hotels as Bruce Springsteen and the band at three of the four hotels. The first day, in Adelaide, I was waiting in the lobby outside the elevators, hoping to see him, and I ended up meeting his manager of thirty-four years and talking to her. Then, in Melbourne, she singled me out of the concert crowd of thirty thousand people. And she has a really sad story, and . . ."

I stopped speaking. I had a sense that Richard was not listening.

I began counting the seconds of silence between us. Richard did not say a word.

"Richard, are you there?"

"Oh, yeah, sorry. Rebecca was just saying something to me. That, uh, sounds great."

I strived for a "casually concerned" tone. "Is everything okay?"

"Oh, yeah, everything's fine. Rebecca just woke up and she was telling me she's decided to go to a nine thirty yoga class and she wants me to drive her. So I've got to go."

"Okay, I won't keep you," I said.

"Sure. Well, I'm glad you had a good time and I'm glad you're home," Richard said, sounding relieved that I understood that he had to get off the phone. "I love you. Bye."

"Bye." I didn't bother to say anything about love, because he had already hung up.

I was not surprised by this turn of events. There was no reason Rebecca could not have driven herself to the local yoga studio. Furthermore, I was 100 percent certain that if I had not been speaking to Richard, she would have remained curled up in bed with no intention of going anywhere or doing anything. She'd just wanted to interrupt our phone call.

I was not surprised, but I *was* disappointed. I was annoyed with him for not offering to call me back. I was annoyed with how dismissive he had been. I was annoyed enough to not want to talk to him. So I did not ask him to call me back after he dropped Rebecca off.

I decided I would think about the situation between us later. I did not want to spoil the happiness I was feeling that, after a job well done in Australia, I was finally home.

Not long after I hung up with Richard, Robert and Ross each called me back. Unlike Richard, neither one was distracted by a competing wife or girlfriend, but like Richard, neither one seemed interested or willing to talk about my trip. They asked no questions, and when I ventured to tell a quick anecdote, neither one showed any curiosity or interest. So I asked them instead about *their* last three-plus weeks. Then it was, simply, "Bye, I love you."

My three boys seemed to have less interest in my trip to Australia than they usually had about my daily trips to the dog park. When they were growing up, living at home, my entire focus had been them. What they were doing. What they wanted to be doing. How I could help them. If they were happy, I was happy. If they were sad, so was I. If they had a problem, there was nothing more important to me than helping them solve their dilemma. And I'd never asked for a thank-you or a formal show of gratitude of appreciation because I hadn't needed one—because I'd always felt it in their presence. Heard it in their voices. Seen it on their faces.

Now, however, they were adults, living their lives apart from me, and when I talked them through issues on the phone or gave them gifts, I could not see or hear any appreciation.

More importantly, I could not feel it. I had not taught them to think of me as someone who wanted to feel appreciated by them as much as the servers at restaurants who they always thanked profusely. Equally important, and equally disappointing, I had not taught them to see me as a person who wanted to be seen and acknowledged.

45

THE NEXT morning, when my eyes opened, I saw a white ceiling. I did not know where I was. I did not what day it was. I barely knew who *I* was.

I blinked and turned my head to the side.

I was lying on my back in my bed. Yes, now I remembered. I was home. And it was Monday.

I went down the steps and into the kitchen. Andy was sitting at the kitchen counter, eating his Muesli-sprinkled yogurt. He looked up from his iPhone and over at me. "What are you doing today?" he asked.

In the months between quitting my job at CCP and leaving for Australia, I'd gotten annoyed when Andy asked me this question. I'd told him every time, curtly, that I was doing nothing.

Usually, that was not actually the case. I volunteered teaching English to immigrants at the Sisters of Saint Joseph Welcome Center every Wednesday. I often had doctor's appointments. I often tried to write. But all those plans felt meaningless, vacuous, and pointless. I felt like I was doing nothing, even when I was not. And when Andy asked this seemingly appropriate question, it made me feel even worse. (Ironically, at dinner, no matter what I had done, even when I didn't go out of the house, I had stories for Andy. More stories than he had for me, after going to the University of Pennsylvania and talking with students, professors, and administrators all day.)

This morning, however, I was excited when Andy asked me about my plans for the day.

"Beverly is coming over this morning," I said, smiling. "I got her a coming-home present." I was excited to see my friend.

"That should be fun for both of you," Andy said.

"Oh," I said, my smile fading, "and this afternoon I have an appointment with Dr. Bhati. I've been dreading this appointment my whole trip."

"It won't be bad," Andy, ever the optimist, said. "Your visits are never long. He'll probably just want to hear about your trip. You won't have any trouble filling up the time."

"Yeah, but he kind of intimidates me." I scrunched up my face. "He's so arrogant. He always acts like he has the answer. And frankly his insistence on that third round of ECT was a mistake. He thinks he knows what's best all the time, and he gets kind of aggressive if I question him or don't agree right away. I just don't feel comfortable with him."

"Just remember, he's working for you. You're paying him. His job is to please you."

Andy has a way of cutting through the noise of a situation and seeing it for what it is. He was right. Dr. Bhati worked for me. But it did not feel like he did. Not at all.

Two hours later, when Beverly's gray Prius puttered into my driveway, I ran outside. I was standing with my arms open when she stepped out of the car.

"It's so good to see you," I said, wrapping my arms around her. "How are you?"

"Pretty good—can't complain," she said, sounding as if she actually wanted to do so.

"Come in," I said, almost skipping toward the house.

I had set out kangaroo mugs that I had bought at the 7-Eleven for tea, and I'd put her present, wrapped in red tissue paper, on the kitchen table. I could not wait to give it to her.

She sat down at the kitchen table.

"This is for you," I said, pointing to the red tissue paper beside her.

She looked at it. Then she looked away and out the window across from her.

Beverly had her own one-woman company teaching people how to use their computers and troubleshooting tech problems. She had been helping with my computer for five years and we had become friends.

Often, when she came over, we spent more time talking about our kids and our concerns and angsts than we did about my computer. Which was fine with me. I needed the camaraderie as much as, if not more than, the computer help.

I poured hot water for tea into the kangaroo mug beside Beverly. She nodded indifferently at the kangaroo mug. "This must be from Australia." She didn't sound like she cared if it was or was not.

"Good guess," I said, undaunted by her current lack of enthusiasm and warmth. I had more than enough of each for both of us. "I bought them in a 7-Eleven down the street from my hotel in Sydney. At first, I thought they looked like tacky junk. But after a week there, I thought they would be the perfect things to help me remember my week there. It really was amazing."

I poured myself some tea in a matching kangaroo mug and sat down at the table across from her.

"Can you believe I stayed in the same hotels as Bruce Springsteen and the band? My—"

"You know, before you went, I thought you'd back out and not go on the trip," she interrupted me. "When you *did* go, I kept waiting for you to give up and come home. But you didn't. So, good for you." Her tone was as dismissive as her words.

"Uh, okay. Thanks?" I took my hand off the handle of my kangaroo mug and sat back in my seat.

Before I could continue telling her my story about meeting Barbara Carr, Beverly leaned forward in her seat and smiled for the first time since she had arrived. "You've missed a lot of stories at the dog park."

Without any encouragement from me, she began gossiping about the park where we both walk our dogs, bringing me up to date on all the two-legged and four-legged happenings. She went on for thirty minutes. When she was finished, she stood up. "I have to go. I need be at a client's house in ten minutes. We can't all spend our days being Bruce Springsteen roadies."

"Don't forget your present," I said as she was walking out the door. I ran back to the table, grabbed it, and brought it to her.

"Sure," she said, taking it from me. "Welcome home."

Without a hug or a smile, she got into her gray Prius and tossed the unopened present into the back seat.

As I watched her roll down the driveway, I was disappointed. Not only because she had not opened the gift, or shown any interest in it, or given me any indication that she appreciated my thinking about her when I was Down Under—but also because she'd given no indication that she even knew who I was. If there is one thing I am not, it is a quitter. I do what I say I am going to do. I do what I set out to do. Beverly should have known me well enough to know that.

Staring at the empty driveway, I found myself wondering who Beverly thought I was. All these years, I had assumed that in spite of my depression, Beverly respected me and saw me as a person who did not back down because something seemed difficult or frightening. She knew how terrified I had been of going to Sheppard Pratt both times and having ECT there, and as an outpatient a third time. She knew I hadn't let my terror keep me from doing what I thought would help me. She knew how hard I worked to keep myself moving forward, one foot in front of the other. Didn't she?

I thought she did. I had assumed she did.

Now, two days back from Australia, I felt like someone who had once again persevered. I felt like someone who had accomplished her own version of Something Remarkable. And I realized that Beverly did not know me.

More importantly, I realized she did not *want* to know me. Not *this* me. Not the real me.

But this was the only me there was now.

46

IF I WAS anxious when I got in my car, headed for my three o'clock appointment with Dr. Bhati, any fears, apprehensions, or misgivings I was experiencing evaporated when I turned on E Street Radio. It was not only the fact that I was listening to Bruce Springsteen that changed my mood as I backed out of the garage, but also that they were broadcasting the first of the two Hunter Valley concerts I'd attended.

Immediately, I felt as if I were back at that concert, standing on the grass beside the retired mailman whose wife had recently died. As I navigated the familiar, tree-lined streets of Philadelphia, I once again felt connected to that man who'd come to see Bruce Springsteen because his kids had urged him to get out of the house.

I turned up the volume and felt the sound waves reverberating through the body of my car. When "Waitin' on a Sunny Day" began blasting through my speakers, I remembered the retired postman holding his Kodak Instamatic up to take pictures of Springsteen playing the song, and I grinned.

Most of all, I was happy because I could still feel the energy I had gotten in Australia. I was disappointed that Andy, my boys, and Beverly had not wanted to hear my stories—but even their lack of interest had not depleted my energy.

As soon as I stepped into the waiting room of Penn Behavioral Health, I wanted to take myself and my energy and turn and run. As usual, the waiting room was so full that it was standing room only. As usual, the television hanging from the top of the wall at one end of the room was blaring.

I began reminiscing about my past two years as Dr. Bhati's patient.

"You need ECT immediately," he said after listening to me only briefly during my first appointment.

"I can't do it right now," I protested. "I'm teaching."

"You have to quit," he commanded. "You need to begin the ECT treatments next week."

"Dr. Bhati," I said, "the only thing that has been keeping me going besides my daily workouts is teaching at CCP."

And at the time, that was true. Three times a week, I had a place I needed to be. I had lessons I needed to plan. Papers to grade. And I had a couple of students in each of my three classes who were trying hard in the hopes that a CCP degree would help them improve their lives. I'd been meeting with each of them once or twice a week to encourage and guide them. I did not want to quit and let them down.

I told Dr. Bhati I would do ECT in the summer, after the semester was over.

"You will regret waiting," he said, narrowing his eyes and shaking his head.

It was clear he didn't like my arguing against his protocol. But I stood my ground and got through the rest of the semester. And when two of my remedial students won awards and invited me to the presentation ceremony, I felt proud watching them walk to the stage and accepting their awards. I was glad I had not given in to Dr. Bhati and quit teaching to begin ECT—glad I had not let my students down.

One week after the semester ended, I dutifully began my third regimen of ECT, this time as an outpatient. Every Monday, Wednesday, and Friday morning, Andy drove me to Pennsylvania Hospital in downtown Philadelphia for the procedure.

But unlike the two regimens of ECT at Sheppard Pratt, where I began to feel blissful as I counted backward from ten and then blanked out to a happy oblivion, this time I experienced terror every single time.

Toward the end of the summer, several sessions short of what he had intended, Dr. Bhati became concerned about my increasing loss of memory and aborted the ECT treatment.

Mentally, I did not feel one bit better than I had beforehand.

Physically, I felt much worse. Jaw pain arrived with a vengeance. My upper left jaw throbbed every minute, day, and night. The throbbing reverberated like a hammer on my skull.

On the Friday of Labor Day weekend, Andy came with me to my appointment with Dr. Bhati. I was in excruciating pain.

"Andy," Dr. Bhati said. "You're a Wharton professor. You have connections. You should call the head of the neurology department at Penn and get Anne an appointment."

Andy did exactly that, but even though I was working with the head of the neurology department at Penn, I continued to suffer from Level 10 pain in my jaw for the next two and a half months.

Then, finally, a colleague at CCP told me I should see a pain-management doctor. I had never heard of this specialty.

As soon as I told my story to Dr. Ashburn, the pain-management doctor, he said, "We saw this all the time when I was an ECT anesthesiologist. Sometimes the mouth guard is not enough to protect the jaw from the jolt of electricity. I can't say I can get you down to zero-level pain, but I am sure that within three weeks you'll be down from the ten it is now to a two or a three."

He was true to his word; he prescribed a new round of medications, and my condition improved.

It was a monumental relief, mentally and physically, when Dr. Ashburn was able to figure out a cocktail of drugs that, for the most part, took away the pain. But these drugs sucked out every ounce of saliva from my mouth, making it difficult for me to eat and speak. I had never before appreciated or even thought about saliva, but when it malfunctioned, I yearned for those days of ignorant bliss when I could speak and eat without a thought. Teaching at CCP, always with a water bottle in one hand, there were times that while forming a word in my mouth, my lips stuck to my teeth and my tongue adhering to the roof of my mouth, I wondered how I was going to utter the next syllable. But as awkward and uncomfortable as dry mouth was, it was far better than the pounding jaw pain I had suffered for three months.

Soon after my first visit with Dr. Ashburn, I had my monthly appointment with Dr. Bhati. He hadn't even closed his office door before I blurted out that I had finally found relief from my jaw pain.

"Dr. Ashburn told me that severe jaw pain it is not an unusual side effect for ECT patients," I told him.

Dr. Bhati sat down in his desk chair and looked at me as if I hadn't said a word. He didn't look surprised, he didn't look pleased, and he didn't seem the least bit interested in my news.

I told him the five medications Dr. Ashburn had prescribed for me. He wrote them down.

"How are you feeling with the depression?" he said.

"Not good," I admitted. "I'm struggling."

"I'm involved in a couple of clinical studies right now," he said. "We could include you in one of them and try you on a new drug."

I was already on five new medications. My mouth was so dry I could barely speak, and no doubt my poor teeth would soon be rotting. The pain was finally under control—I could put my head on my pillow at night and not be kept awake by the *thud, thud, thud* in my upper left jaw—most of the time. He could not possibly think it was wise to add another drug to the mix. Especially one with no track record.

I looked at him, stunned.

He stared back at me. Finally, he said, "Yeah, I suppose this isn't a good time to be experimenting with you."

Then, I had thought he was trying to help me. I had seen him as a professional who truly believed in what he did. He truly believed that he could help people with drugs, with ECT. The fact that I had tried more than twenty antidepressants and never found any of them helpful had not discouraged Dr. Bhati's belief that there was something out there, or something coming along, that would be the magic pill for me.

"Anne, Dr. Bhati is ready for you," a nurse said to me, startling me out of my reminiscence.

I walked across the waiting room toward Dr. Bhati's office. He was standing with his hand on the doorknob, waiting for me.

I walked inside and sat down in the chair across from his desk. I was hoping that he had forgotten about my trip. If he did not mention it, neither would I. Our appointments were fifteen minutes long—just enough time to discuss how I was feeling and what effects the medications I was taking were having on me. We did not typically discuss my life. The only reason he knew about my trip was because the day I decided to quit CCP and go to Australia, I happened to have one of my routine appointments with him and I'd told him my plans.

He closed the door, sat down in his desk chair, and picked up a pen and pad of white-lined paper. "When did you get back?" he asked, ready to write.

I took a deep breath, trying to calm myself. I reminded myself not to overtalk. It was better to say too little to Dr. Bhati than too much. Frankly, I was not sure why I was even here. As I'd mentioned to Andy, I had weaned myself off the Ritalin, the only medication Dr. Bhati had prescribed for me, during my trip. I did not want or need anything from him anymore.

"Early yesterday morning," I said. "Really early."

"So, how was it?" he asked, leaning toward me a bit.

I wanted to be careful. I was not here to tell him stories about my trip.

And then, suddenly, I realized the reason I *was* here.

"I weaned myself off the Ritalin while I was away," I said. "Actually, I also weaned myself off the pain meds Dr. Ashburn prescribed last year for my jaw pain."

"And?" Dr. Bhati tilted his head slightly to the side.

"And what?" I was determined to make him work for whatever it was he was going to get from me. If he had to work to get me to talk, maybe he would back off and let me go.

"Well, how do you feel?"

"I feel great. Really great. I have enough energy and I do not have any residual jaw pain. It feels great to be off all those meds. They were better than the pain, but they took their toll on my body with the dry mouth and the constipation and dizziness."

"Uh-huh," he said, making some scribbles on his pad. "You didn't tell me how your trip was."

Is it not obvious? I wondered. I had gone off my meds. I'd said I felt great. Would either of those things be possible if I'd had a miserable trip? I stared back at him, unsure how to answer his question succinctly.

"Amazing. My trip was amazing." There—I had answered his question truthfully and succinctly, just as I had wanted.

"I see." He scribbled more and then looked up and peered at me across the room. "What did you do there?"

"I went to eight concerts, I worked out, and I wrote."

"What else did you do?"

My heart skipped a beat, two beats. I felt my body tightening. What *did* I do?

"Did you do any sightseeing?" he asked.

As I shook my head, I could feel my mood and my energy dropping. I did not feel like telling him the story about my cuddling Tango the koala. I was afraid if I did, he would make me feel worse.

"That's a long time to do nothing alone," he said.

"I love being a fly on the wall, and I spent a lot of time doing that in the hotels. As it turned out, I stayed in the same hotels as Bruce Springsteen and the E Street Band, so it was interesting people-watching. It was fun watching other people in the hotels too."

"So that's what you did? Watch people?" he asked, his voice a mixture of skepticism and disapproval.

"Yes. And, like I said, I wrote."

"What did you write about?"

I hesitated. What could I tell him I wrote about? I was embarrassed to tell him that I wrote emails to twelve people who asked me to write to them about what I saw, did, thought, and felt during my trip. I leaned my head back against the wall.

I didn't want him to think I was a self-absorbed narcissist. I didn't want him to think what my father had said to me when I told him I was writing a short memoir as my MFA thesis at the New School for Social Research: "Why would anyone want to read about what *you* think about anything? You say you write about yourself because you know yourself best. You don't. You know yourself from a very narrow perspective."

When I had my first piece published, I asked my father if he wanted to read it.

"I'll read something you write," he replied, "when you get a Pulitzer."

I had been taken aback and hurt then. But now, thinking about what my father had said, I felt angry. Angry at him for being so cruel to me.

And here was Dr. Bhati—another authoritative, self-assured man, another man who made me feel as if I had nothing to add to a conversation, not even a conversation about myself.

But then, sitting there with my father's words from more than a decade earlier filling my head and infuriating me, I realized Dr. Bhati was *not* my father. He was someone who had *asked* me to tell him a story. Unlike my father, he had said he wanted to hear this from me. Understanding this, I felt empowered to tell my story. Here and now.

I lifted my head and looked him in the eyes. "I wrote about me and about what I saw."

"Okay, so tell me something interesting about you and what you saw that you wrote about."

"You really want me to tell you a story from my trip?" I asked, feeling myself getting excited.

"Yes, that's why I'm asking," Dr. Bhati said, reassuring me.

The excitement took control of my mind and body. I was finally being asked to tell one of my stories!

"Well, the first day there, I was standing in the hotel lobby across from the elevators, and some E Street Band members walked by on their way to the arena for that night's concert. I even got pictures taken with a few of them. After they left, I stepped outside the hotel to feel some warm summer sun. I overheard a conversation going on right behind me. It was between a man and a woman. I could tell that the woman was older—like, my age—and the man younger. When the man said goodbye to her, I turned around and began talking to her. Well, it turned out she was Bruce Springsteen's manager of thirty-four years!"

As I spoke, I inched forward to the edge of the chair. Dr. Bhati was simultaneously scribbling and nodding. Occasionally, he looked up at me and smiled.

I forgot that I was talking to my psychiatrist. I forgot that I was being psychologically prodded and analyzed. I forgot about everything that did not have to do with my story about Barbara Carr. About her singling me out in the Melbourne stadium of thirty thousand fans and calling me down to say, "Anne, don't you remember me? I'm Barbara Carr." About her daughter dying at the age of twenty-one. About my speaking to her in Sydney about this despite Andy's advice not to, and how appreciative she was that I had. About her telling me how difficult it was for her, still, twenty-one years later. About her suggestion that I come to New York in April for the yearly fund-raising dinner they had for a medical research organization they had established in memory of her daughter.

"Andy and I are going in a few weeks," I said excitedly, just as Dr. Bhati's phone rang.

"This is my boss," he said, putting down his pen and picking up the receiver of his desk phone. "I have to take it."

I sat back in my chair. I felt exhilarated.

"I'm with a patient," he said into the phone. "I'll call you right back."

He hung up the phone and turned his swivel chair so that he was facing me again, and he looked at his watch.

I looked at my watch and let out an audible gasp. I had been in Dr. Bhati's office for forty-five minutes.

I slunk down in my chair. I had done exactly what I had not wanted to do. I had failed to stick to soundbites about my trip. I had lost my resolve and told a story.

Dr. Bhati reached across his desk for his prescription pad and wrote something on it. "Here, take this prescription." He held the slip of paper out toward me. "It's for a sedative."

My heart stopped. I believe it truly stopped. When it resumed, I bolted straight up and sat forward in my chair. I stood up and hung my purse on my shoulder.

"Dr. Bhati," I said, taking one step toward him. "I did not go all the way to Australia to come back to West Philadelphia to be sedated."

I did not wait to see his reaction. I did not wait to hear him tell me to make another appointment for a month from now. I walked to the door, opened it, and left.

47

THE KRISTEN Ann Carr benefit dinner was on a Saturday night at the Tribeca Grill in Manhattan a month after my return from Australia. When the cab pulled up in front of the restaurant, I jumped out and stood facing the entrance. It was now or never.

Body humming with anticipation, I suspected I knew just how Bruce Springsteen felt in the moments before he appeared onstage. Nervous. Excited. Ready.

When I stepped into the restaurant, three young women, all wearing black, were sitting at connecting tables. They looked up at Andy and me and smiled.

"Oh my God!" the woman at the first table said, her entire face beaming. "I love your dress."

I stopped in place and just stared at her, unsure that I had heard her correctly. I was wearing a beige linen dress with a calm, meditative black owl sketched on the front from my neck to my knees. I looked down at myself and then back up again at her.

"You look absolutely terrific," she said, leaning forward on her table.

In my peripheral vision I could see the other two women smiling and nodding. I let her words and her excited persona settle in my brain.

"Thank you," I finally said. "Your words mean a lot to me."

"Absolutely," she said. "Welcome to A Night to Remember." What's your last name?"

"Abel," I said—tentatively, but also relieved that I had someone kind and not intimidating to talk to.

"Perfect," she said, making me feel as if I had said the exact right thing. "You're in my group."

She opened the lid of the recipe-like box in front of her. "Here you are, the very first ones. You are VIPs. You can take these tickets and go to the bar. As VIPs, you can also go upstairs. There's a silent auction table, and later there will be entertainment and speeches up there." She studied me again and gave an approving nod. "I really love that dress on you. I don't think there are too many women who could pull that dress off as perfectly as you do."

Her kind words lifted me. I smiled at her as Andy took the drink tickets.

Together, Andy and I ventured past the welcome table and into a room with windows facing the street. The bar took up half of the room, all the way to the back. As VIPs, we had been allowed to come in before the "regular" ticket holders. But already, the line for the bar was five people long.

Everyone was laughing and talking and tossing about the name Bruce Springsteen as if he were their best buddy.

"Yeah, when I saw Bruce at the Stone Pony . . ."

"Bruce was talking about the time . . ."

"Were you there that time Bruce . . ."

Everyone was invoking his name. But after saying his name, the stories trailed off. And the line at the bar did not seem to be advancing.

"Let's go upstairs," I said to Andy.

I didn't know what was upstairs, but I had seen what the first floor offered, and I was ready for something else.

I had no idea what I was hoping the evening would be. Broadly, I was here because I had not known what else to do with myself. I had not known another way to keep my Bruce Springsteen Australia energy alive. Committing to coming to this dinner a month after my return had bought me another four weeks of actively planning my way toward a Bruce Springsteen event—another four weeks of energy. But as Andy and I climbed the stairs up to the second floor, I realized I had no idea what I would do the following morning to keep my energy up, to keep me feeling like the me I wanted to be.

At the top of the stairs, we walked into a large room, empty of people. In the back was an elevated platform and a drum set and some microphones. To our right, there were three tables with a dozen or so items spread across them that constituted the silent auction.

I walked slowly along the tables. There was a sketch of Bruce Springsteen, a Springsteen-autographed album cover, a pair of tickets to an upcoming Mets game, tickets to a Yankees game, more Springsteen-autographed album covers, and then a sign that said, "Be a cohost with Dave Marsh on E Street Radio's Wednesday morning *Live from E Street Nation*."

I stopped and turned to Andy, who was one step behind me.

"I didn't know why I came here until now. I want to bid on *that*." I pointed at the sign.

At that moment, before Andy could say a word, Barbara Carr appeared in front of us.

"Anne, it's so good to see you. Thank you for coming." She shook my hand, making me feel as if we were friends from way back.

"Barbara, this is my husband, Andy," I said.

They shook hands.

"Anne and I met in Adelaide," Barbara told him. "It was brave of her to venture to Australia, all alone, to see our concerts."

Andy smiled and nodded.

I was amazed that she not only recognized me but also remembered my name and story.

"It was lovely seeing you again, Anne," Barbara said. "It was nice to meet you, Andy. I hope you both enjoy the evening."

And she was off.

I watched her slip into the crowd. Then I took Andy's hand and led him back to the silent auction table.

"Andy," I said, letting go of his hand. "*This* is why I came here. I *want* it."

"Okay," Andy said. "Let's try to win it."

I knew Dave Marsh was Barbara Carr's husband. But I had never listened to his radio show; I did not even know he was a radio host. When I was in my car, listening to E Street Radio, I only ever heard music—the Springsteen albums and concerts they always played. Even so, I wanted to win this. I wanted to win it very badly.

As it turned out, Bruce Springsteen was not in attendance. He was in Texas, playing at the March Madness game. Some musicians I did not recognize took their places on the platform at the back of the room and began playing.

The people who had been in line at the bar were now forming a crush around the stage. I was in the first row, exactly where I always want to be at any live performance; I had staked out my spot early on. Andy was at the back of the crowd, keeping tabs on the silent auction table and checking on our bid.

After the music, Dave Marsh stood at the microphone and gave a long-winded, slowly spoken, boring speech about the Kristen Ann Carr Foundation's accomplishments in the last year. Then he stopped.

For a few moments, he said nothing. He seemed to be taking long, calming breaths, as if gathering the strength to continue.

"It was Kristen's dying wish that there be a foundation to research sarcoma and to help the young people afflicted by this disease," he said, his voice faltering. "I miss her every day. But I take comfort in knowing that we have fulfilled her wish. We are making great strides and hoping that someday no one will have to suffer like she did."

Tears were dripping down Dave Marsh's jowled face. Tears were dripping down my face and onto the face of my calm, meditative owl.

"Kristen, I love you," Dave said.

The crowd was silent, nodding and smiling in commiseration, as Dave shuffled off the stage and was whisked out of the room.

Food was set out along one side of the bar. There were also servers walking around and offering hors d'oeuvres and flutes of champagne.

I was too nervous and excited to eat. Various E Street Band members, and their wives and girlfriends, were weaving through the crowd—and here, they seemed to be a totally different species from the people I had observed and followed onstage and off throughout Australia. In Australia, in the hotel lobbies, they had looked and acted like any other people waiting for their group. If their gaze had passed by me, I'd felt that I'd registered with them—if not in their consciousness, then at least in their unconsciousness. Somewhere deep inside, they knew there was a human being nearby, taking up space. And onstage, of course, they'd all seemed so full of energy and enthusiasm. So inclusive of every one of the thousands of fans in the audience.

But here at the Kristen Ann Carr dinner, with their wives and girlfriends on their arms, the E Street Band members kept their eyes cast down toward the ground. Here, the E Street Band members refused to look at anyone but each other. It was as if they would turn to ash if they glimpsed or made eye contact, even briefly, with anyone in the crowd who was not one of them.

And maybe they would; they all looked exhausted. More exhausted than when I'd seen them in the hotel lobbies in Australia. Which made sense. They had been home less than a month since returning from New Zealand. In a few days, they were beginning their six-week High Hopes North America Tour in Cincinnati. They probably could have used a free Saturday night just to hunker down at home. Instead, they were here at a nonpaying job-related event. They were fulfilling a professional obligation, no doubt counting the minutes until it would be okay to leave. They were no different than any other worker, invited to an after-hours event by a boss or supervisor. I felt sorry for them.

Meanwhile, Andy had put in our maximum bid: $1,025. And last he had checked, we seemed to be winning.

My feet were not accustomed to being squeezed into tiny, dainty shoes, and they were screaming at me to sit down and give them some relief. I found an empty banquette in the corner of the room and slid all the way in until I was up against the wall. I noticed some E Street Band members and their partners lurking nearby, casting furtive looks toward my table.

The table in front of my banquette was cleared, and then another person came by and put a white tablecloth over it.

"Ma'am," a young woman said to me. "You're going to have to get up and move from here."

"What?" I asked. I could not believe she was going to force me out of the only empty seat I'd been able to find.

"You're going to have to find somewhere else to sit. We're setting up this table for a group." She looked behind her at the small coterie of E Street Band members, who were shifting back and forth on their feet.

"There is no place else to sit," I said. "That's why I sat here."

"Ma'am, you have to leave," she said. As she spoke, she became more adamant, as if empowered by her own commands.

"I am not leaving here," I said. "There was no reserved sign here when I sat down. I have as much right as anyone else in this room to sit here."

"I'm not asking you," she said. "I'm telling you."

"And I am telling *you* I am not leaving. You can find your supervisor and tell her that I absolutely refuse to leave. If you want me out, you will have to carry me away."

My feet were killing me. I could not stand and wait indefinitely for the silent auction to be over so that these people could sit at the table. They could sit down with me. I wasn't going to bother them. Except for the first concert in Adelaide, when they had passed through the lobby on the way to the concert, I had not bothered them when they were hanging out together in the hotel lobbies and bars in Australia. I was a fan, but not a cloying fan. I had been respectful of their off-stage presence in Australia. And tonight would be no different.

The woman no longer looked strong or empowered. She looked frustrated. I watched her walk away into the throng of people, leaving the E Street Band members looking confused.

A few minutes later, she arrived with a stack of dishes and white cloth napkins. Place setting after place setting, she put together the table until this table for six was set for five. Three E Streeters and their partners came toward the table and sat down. All of them shifted ever so slightly away from me. The men were better musicians than I am. The women were no doubt people of note in their own right. But, tonight, at the Kristen Ann Carr dinner, I thought we were all here to help raise money for the foundation. At this event, my money was no less important than theirs. At this event, I was no less important than they were.

Watching them avert their eyes from me, I wondered if these same people who sang and danced and made music onstage before thousands of fans might be less skillful, less comfortable than I was talking to a stranger. I let them nibble at their food, eyes cast down and away from me, in peace.

"Anne . . . Anne," I heard someone say.

I came out of the trance I had gone into in order to remove myself from the five people at my table and looked up. It was Andy.

"You won. You won!" he announced with a beaming smile. "You got the cohost gig!"

I jumped out of my corner of the banquette. I didn't feel my aching feet anymore. My mind had detached from my body.

"Oh my god, Andy! Thank you so much! I am so happy. It's just what I wanted. It's just what I need. Thank you for getting it for me!"

I was so happy. And hopeful. I had bought myself a project, another event to plan toward. Being a cohost with Dave Marsh on *Live From E Street Nation* would be a way to keep my Bruce Springsteen energy going.

48

IT SEEMED crazy, but at the same time not crazy at all. It seemed bizarre, and yet also fitting, that in six months—exactly a year after I had quit my job and decided to go to Australia—I was going to be an E Street Radio cohost.

I had come home from my trip with so many stories. I also had come home with a desire to be part of a conversation about the transformative power of Bruce Springsteen and his music, something I felt but did not completely understand.

I wanted to tell my story about being inspired to go to Australia when all the treatments I had tried in order to keep myself out of the abyss had failed me. My entire adult life I had been compliant with doctors and mental health professionals, dutifully trying every treatment they suggested for my depression. None of them had worked. But, over the course of my twenty-six days in Australia, I had begun to hear my own voice. The people I'd met in Australia had seen me as heroic. Many young people had told me they wished their own mothers were as "courageous" as I was. They had helped me begin to see myself in a new way. And Bruce Springsteen's concerts had empowered me. Many of his songs were therapeutic. I saw myself in his songs, and in much of what he said and emoted about himself. They made me feel that if he could go on, so could I. Meanwhile, I had also learned that I could have fun. I had come up with my own regimen—one that had not only helped me to stay out of the abyss but had also taught me about the transformative power of music and storytelling and connection.

And I wanted to talk about it.

Live From E Street Nation aired live on Wednesday mornings for two hours, beginning at ten o'clock. On the Wednesday after I won the auction, I had an 11:00 a.m. doctor's appointment. Instead of leaving at 10:30 as I normally would, I got into my car at 9:55 and began driving there early so I could hear more of the show.

At ten on the dot, a man announced, "Welcome to *Live From E Street Nation* with your host, Dave Marsh."

I expected to hear Dave Marsh's voice. Instead, I heard three Bruce Springsteen songs. Only after the third song ended did the voice from the beginning of the show say, "And here he is, your host, Dave Marsh."

There were a few seconds of silence. A few seconds more. The suspense was building. I found myself holding my breath in happy anticipation as I steered along the familiar streets.

"Yeah, hello," a voice finally stammered. "This is Dave Marsh."

There was a pause. More silence.

"The traffic was foul today. That's why I'm late," he said, slowly. "New York traffic is obscene."

He sounded truly annoyed. As if New York rush-hour traffic was an attack on him and him alone.

"It should not take two hours to travel a distance that can easily be done in thirty minutes," he continued.

I could not believe it. Was this man really affronted about a phenomenon that was a fact of life for New Yorkers? Was

Dave Marsh really complaining about New York's rush-hour traffic as if that were a valid excuse for missing the beginning of his show? I felt annoyed. Not about the traffic but about *him*. Even if a fluke traffic jam had caused him to be late, he should be accepting responsibility and apologizing to his audience, not whining about it.

After his traffic preamble he began yammering about vinyl versus digital—something about which I knew nothing. Normally, in my desire to know about all things music, I would have been excited to learn something new. But Dave Marsh's voice was monotonous and slow. I found my mind wandering off as he mumbled one slowpokey sentence after another. Each time he paused and began a new sentence, I pulled my well-disciplined mind back to his barely audible words. But after only a few beats, after only a few syllables, my mind would drift off again. He was that boring and unintelligible.

Finally, relief came in the form of a Bruce Springsteen song.

After the song, the phone lines were opened so callers could weigh in on vinyl versus digital. I was hopeful that finally I would learn something. But no matter what a caller said, Dave took umbrage.

"It never ceases to amaze me how imbecilic people are," Dave barked before disconnecting a call with a man who was touting digital for its versatility.

Another caller began by saying, "Dave, I so agree with you. Vinyl is much more elegant than digital."

"You are putting words in my mouth," Dave yelled at him. "I never used the word 'elegant' to describe vinyl. I wouldn't use that word because it isn't right. Get yourself a dictionary."

There was silence where once there had been a connection between two people.

"I think I've had enough calls for now," Dave said. "Vinny, let's hear a Bruce song. Let's here 'Radio Nowhere.'"

When the song came on, I did not recognize it. Moreover, I could not listen to it. Even as it blasted from the speakers in my car, I did not hear it. My hands were gripping the steering wheel and shaking. My body was trembling in my ergonomic car seat. I was terrified. I was terrified of going on the show and being yelled at by Dave Marsh. It seemed that no matter what anyone said, he slammed the person as wrong. He was a tyrannical know-it-all.

I focused my attention on the radio. "Radio Nowhere" ended. Dave Marsh was back.

He took a call.

"I'm taking a friend who doesn't like Bruce Springsteen to a concert this spring," a young man said. "What album should I have him listen to in order to change his mind?"

"What kind of jerk are you?" Dave demanded. "Why are you wasting your money on someone who isn't smart enough to appreciate Bruce?"

The young man began to stammer.

"*Live in New York City*," Dave interrupted, "is the album he should listen to."

There was a pause.

"Vinny, is there a full moon or something?" Dave said, derision in every syllable.

It was painful for me to listen to my future cohost. Painful and boring. I turned off the radio. I drove a few blocks. I turned it on again. I needed to listen to this inane show, this vitriolic man. I tried to reconcile him with the man at the Kristen Ann Carr dinner who had cried over the loss of his daughter. Tried to think of him as the husband of Barbara Carr, who had moved me so deeply when she spoke about the loss of their daughter. Listening to him on the radio, though, it was hard to imagine he had any emotion other than anger.

For the rest of my ride, I alternated listening to him for a few minutes and then turning off the radio in an effort to build up my tolerance for this curmudgeon of a man.

Knowledge is power. I needed to learn. I *wanted* to learn.

At least I had my first assignment as a future cohost of E Street Radio.

When I got home, I downloaded *Live in New York City* and sat on the living room couch with my dogs and listened to it. It was a very high-energy set of songs, many of which I had heard before. I liked the album, but I had no idea why Dave Marsh had suggested it. I went to Wikipedia for answers.

I learned the record had been recorded at concerts on June 29 and July 1, 2000. *Live in New York City* was also the name of a concert film done by HBO, featuring the first-ever major televised Bruce Springsteen concert. It marked the reunion tour of Bruce Springsteen and the E Street Band—their first concert tour together in eleven years—which turned out to be very successful. I assumed that was why Dave Marsh had selected it as the album that could convert a nonbeliever into a believer and a member of Bruce Springsteen's adoring flock.

I turned off the music and began to think about Dave Marsh. In order for me to succeed as a cohost, in order for me not to be shut down in the first minute, I needed to overcome the obstacle that was this man. According to the ancient Chinese general, military strategist, writer, and philosopher Sun Tzu, "Know thy enemy and know yourself; in a hundred battles, you will never be defeated."

So I decided to learn all I could about Dave Marsh.

Meantime, I would keep my energy going for the rest of April and May by going to Bruce Springsteen and the E Street Band concerts.

Over the next two months, I went to concerts in Pittsburgh, Albany, and Hershey, Pennsylvania, as well as two at the Mohegan Sun in Connecticut.

On the first Sunday morning in June, days after my last High Hopes concert and a week before Andy and I were planning to go to the Outer Banks of North Carolina, I pulled out the Arts section of *The New York Times*. On the front page, above the fold, was a story about *Holler If Ya Hear Me*, a musical previewing on Broadway inspired by the lyrics of rapper Tupac Shakur.

I had never heard of Tupac Shakur. I spent four hours reading about him—his murder in Las Vegas in 1996, his whole story, and his music, including the song "Dear Mama." I listened to that song over and over and over. It was one of the most beautiful songs I had ever heard. Each time I listened to it, I cried.

I envied Tupac Shakur's mother. I envied her for having a son who had so loved and respected and appreciated her. I was profoundly moved that a twenty-year-old Black rapper could write words that spoke to me, a sixty-year-old white Jewish woman.

As I sat down and read about Tupac Shakur and listened to "Dear Mama," Steve, our skinny, skateboarding, twenty-year-old dog walker arrived.

"Steve," I said as he was leashing up the dogs. "Have you ever heard of someone named Shakur Tupac?"

I knew that when Steve was not walking dogs, he composed electronic music.

He laughed. "I think you mean Tupac Shakur, and yes."

"Oh my god, he's amazing," I said. "I mean, he *was* amazing."

Steve laughed again.

"Can you help me send two songs to my sons?" I asked.

"Sure," he said, dropping the leashes and coming to the kitchen counter, where I was standing in front of my laptop. "What two songs?"

"I'd like to email 'Dear Mama' and Bruce Springsteen's cover version of 'Dream Baby Dream' to my sons with the message, 'Please listen to these two songs and think of me.'"

"That'll be easy," he said.

I hoped Tupac Shakur would show my boys how I wanted them to think of me and how to appreciate me:

And after my boys listened to "Dear Mama" and thought about me as they listened to the words, I wanted them to listen to "Dream Baby Dream" and hear what I was so desperately trying to do for myself now, just as I had always encouraged them to do for themselves when they were growing up:

Dream baby dream
Dream baby dream
Come on and dream baby dream . . .
We gotta keep the fire burning . . .
Come on and open up your heart . . .
Come on darling and dry your eyes . . .
I just wanna see you smile
Come on and dream baby dream

49

AS ANDY and I headed to our house on North Carolina's Outer Banks, he was, as usual, at the wheel for the eight-hour drive while I read. I read newspapers. I read magazines. I read silently, I read aloud.

Halfway into the trip, I picked up the latest issue of *The New Yorker* and began reading a review of a concert in New York by a sixty-three-year-old musician named Chrissie Hynde. I had also read about Hynde in *The New York Times* a week earlier. She was a founding member, and guitarist, as well as the lead vocalist, primary songwriter, and only constant member, of The Pretenders, a rock band formed in 1978. Like most women of her generation, it was difficult for her to stand out front and on her own as a rock musician. For decades she hid behind the mantle of The Pretenders. But she had just recently released her first solo album, *Stockholm*, and had performed in New York.

I picked up my iPhone and called Rob, the ticket broker who had gotten me my Australia concert tickets.

"I'd like to go to a Chrissie Hynde concert," I said to him. "Can you tell me where and when she's performing?"

Five minutes later, Rob called back. I put him on speaker. "She just finished her US tour. She'll be in London at the Royal Albert Hall on July 6."

"Great," I said. "Please get me a ticket."

Andy looked at me. "You're really serious about learning everything you can about music."

"London is a lot closer than Australia," I said. "I'm not sure what I need to know or want to know. I just know I have between now and October 18 to get it all done."

I scribbled "The Pretenders" in my pocket notebook. Then I downloaded *Stockholm* and *The Best of The Pretenders*. The remaining time in the car passed with me aware of nothing but this new music wafting out of the car's speakers.

As my cohosting date advanced toward me, I began to have nightmares of going on E Street Radio and being insulted and ridiculed by Dave Marsh. But sometimes, as I was researching and learning and going to concerts and listening to music, I found myself daydreaming. Before I could rein my wayward mind back to reality, I would start to imagine Dave and me having a respectful, back-and-forth dialogue.

I knew that I needed to do my best to go on that show and tell my story. I needed to do my best to keep myself from being bullied by Dave Marsh.

My first morning at the beach, I woke with the rising sun. I opened the sliding glass doors so I could hear the ocean, and I sat down at the breakfast table with my newspapers, my iPad, and my iPhone.

When I had finished my oatmeal and berries and read the Arts sections of my four newspapers, I pulled my iPad in front of me on the table.

"Bruce Springsteen Rock & Roll Hall of Fame," I typed into Google.

Up popped a twenty-one-minute YouTube video. I watched, spellbound, as a man named Bono introduced Bruce

Springsteen. I had no idea who Bono was—but it did not matter. He was talking about my favorite aging rock star, back in 1999, when he was not quite so aging.

"He got rich and famous with no drug busts, no golf, no bad-hair period, even in the eighties. No public brawling."

Yes, Bono, whoever he was, was talking about my man.

"He's played every bar, every stadium . . . His eyes see through to the souls of his fans."

Bono talked for five minutes, sometimes serious, sometimes not. He mentioned different Bruce Springsteen albums and their significance. I played and replayed and wrote down every word, underlining the albums to be downloaded for future listening.

Next was a three-minute video montage of photographs and videos and songs of and by Bruce Springsteen. There was nowhere else I wanted to be. Nothing else I wanted to be doing. Who knew learning could be such fun?

As the video ended, Bruce Springsteen came onstage. He and Bono hugged. Bono handed him his Hall of Fame trophy and left Bruce Springsteen alone at the podium.

"Let me warn you. My albums take two years—my concerts three hours," he said. "So this speech may take a while."

It was not surprising to me that a man who could write and perform beautiful lyrics could also write and deliver a masterful speech.

"I've stood on this stage and inducted into the Hall of Fame James Brown, Roy Orbison, Creedence Clearwater Revival, and Bob Dylan"—I stopped and played and replayed the video as I wrote down the name of each musician he mentioned in my notebook—"whose music was a critical part of my own life. I hope my music will serve my audience half as well. If I've succeeded in doing that, it's been with the help of many kindred spirits along the way."

He thanked his mother for buying him his first guitar for sixty dollars. Sixty dollars she scrimped together. He thanked her for teaching him that work was fun and rewarding.

"This is for you, Ma," he said, holding out his trophy. "It is a small return for the investment you made in your son."

I envied his mother.

Then he went on to his father, who had died that year.

"I want to thank my dad," he said. "What would I have conceivably written about without him?"

It was no secret that Bruce Springsteen's father, a depressed alcoholic, did not approve of his son's career. "Get rid of that guitar and get a real job," he would yell at his son late at night when the young man got home after a gig at a bar.

Some years before he died, however, his father knocked on his door and asked for forgiveness.

"If everything had gone great between us, it would have been a disaster," Springsteen continued. "I would have written happy songs. I tried that in the early nineties, and the public didn't like it."

He mentioned one person after another, including all the members—past and present—of the E Street Band, his managers, his wife, and, finally, Clarence Clemons, his saxophone player. He spoke about the night Clarence walked into the bar where he was hanging out in Asbury Park and how, after hearing Clarence play, he knew he had found his saxophone player.

"But Clarence is more than that," Bruce Springsteen continued as the camera showed Clarence in the audience. "Something happened when we stood side by side. Some energy, some unspoken story. For fifteen years, he has been a source of myth, light, and enormous strength. Night after night, Clarence filled my heart. So many nights. So many nights. I love it when he wraps his big arms around me."

Bruce Springsteen's Rock & Roll Hall of Fame induction took place in March 1999. Clarence Clemons died from complications of a stroke in June 2011. As I watched Springsteen's acceptance speech and his words about his friend Clarence, I could not keep myself from overlaying a foreshadowing of the tragedy of Clarence's death.

When Andy walked into the kitchen, still half asleep, I looked up from my iPad.

"I just watched Bruce Springsteen being inducted into the Rock & Roll Hall of Fame," I told him. "He was introduced by a man named Bone-o."

"It's Bono," Andy corrected me.

"Have you heard of him?" I asked.

"Of course," he said. "He's part of U2."

I looked down at my notes from the video. "That's what I hear. I have a lot to learn."

I Wikipedia'd Bono and printed out the pages. I downloaded three U2 albums.

Usually, I work out at eight thirty or nine, immediately after breakfast. But it was already noon by the time I looked up from my iPad.

Instead of heading for my exercise bike, I leashed up the dogs, put on my headset, and, with my iPhone in a pouch on my waist, I headed to the beach.

We had owned our beach house for a decade. It was ten feet from the beach, but I never went there. The sun was dangerous. It was hot. And I do not go in the ocean. But on this morning, I took my dogs, and we went.

For one and a half hours, the dogs and I walked along the water. As they frolicked at the edge of the surf and dug in the sand for crabs, I splashed in the shallow water, blasting U2 through my headset.

When it was time to turn around and head home, I played Bruce Springsteen songs to energize me for working out when I got home. Toward the end of the walk, two of the dogs lay down in the water, exhausted and hot. For some time, I coaxed them forward.

Eventually, I picked one up in each arm and carried them home, all the while dancing in the sand to Bruce Springsteen and the E Street Band.

The following morning, I googled "Bruce Springsteen inducts into Rock & Roll Hall of Fame." Up popped a YouTube video of him in 2004 inducting Jackson Browne, a singer that I didn't know. Bruce Springsteen was funny, and he was serious, as he talked about meeting Jackson Browne in the early 1970s in New York City.

"Jackson was kind enough to let someone he didn't know—me—get up onstage and play a song," Bruce Springsteen said. "Later, he was gracious enough to let me open for him."

It was hard for me to imagine Bruce Springsteen as an unknown someone took a chance on in letting him on his stage. It seemed that Jackson Browne was not only a kind man but also a man with good instincts.

"In the seventies post–Vietnam War era, no album captured the fall from Eden, the long, slow burn of the sixties, its heartbreak, its spent possibilities more than Jackson's masterpiece *Late for the Sky*," Springsteen said. "It's a beautiful body of work, essential for making sense of the time. 'Before the Deluge' still gives me goose bumps and raises me to cause. There was not more searching, loving music made for and about the times."

I googled "Late for the Sky" and found a 1974 review in *Rolling Stone* by Stephen Holden.

I laughed to myself as I read the first few sentences.

"Like Browne's two previous albums, *Late for the Sky* contains no lyric sheet. The three or four hours required to make a full transcription will, however, be well worth the effort for anyone interested in discovering lyric genius."

I was glad it was 2014 and not 1974. All I had to do was search for the lyrics of the songs on Google and the genius of Jackson Browne's words were there for me to see. I printed out the review and then Wikipedia'd "Jackson Browne" and printed out those pages. Then I downloaded the albums *Late for the Sky*, *The Pretender*, and *Running on Empty*.

Andy came into the kitchen, still wet with sweat from working out. "I walked in here this morning when I woke up and you were in another world," he said. "You didn't look up once from your iPad. I don't think you even noticed I was here."

I looked at him, stunned, for a moment. It was hard to imagine that in our small, cozy kitchen, I would not have noticed him. "Don't take it personally," I said. "I just got caught up watching and reading."

"Who are you onto today?" he asked.

"Jackson Browne? Have you heard of him?"

Andy laughed. "Good morning, Rip van Winkle, I'm glad you've woken up from your nap. Yes, I've heard of Jackson Browne."

For the first time since I had sat down for breakfast at six thirty, I looked at the clock. Again, it was noon.

"Yikes!" I jumped up from my chair. "I can't believe how late it is. Doggies, it's time to go to the beach."

"Are you taking them on another death march?" Andy asked, smiling.

"Maybe not so far," I said, clearing my breakfast dishes from the table. "We'll see how we feel."

I leashed up the dogs, slathered my body in sunscreen, put on a hat. Pulling the eager dogs behind me, I raced across the hot sand to the water.

My burning feet cooled by the ocean, I tapped on *Late for the Sky* and our walk began.

Step by wet, sandy step, I listened as the most beautiful words and music filled my head. I forgot what Bruce Springsteen had said about it being a post–Vietnam War album and all that implied. I heard words and music and songs about love, life, and death. The words were simple, the verses short. The music seemed perfectly paired with the lyrics.

As I listened to "For a Dancer," a meditation on death, my steps slowed until I finally stopped. Death, to me, is such a frightening thing. I hate all goodbyes. I hate that one moment when you are with someone and the next moment when you are alone. Death is the final goodbye. I know it is part of life. I know it is inevitable. Knowing all of this, of course, does not help me with my fear. But listening to

Jackson Browne sing about it in such a poetic, honest way was comforting to me.

Every day, I read the Arts sections of my four daily newspapers. Every day, I studied a new musician.

I watched a YouTube video of a musician or band being inducted into the Rock & Roll Hall of Fame. I Wikipedia'd the musician or band. I printed out the pages and added them to the stacks on the dining room table. I downloaded the music. I took the dogs for three-hour walks on the beach. For the walk out, I listened to the musician of the day. For the return walk, I listened to Bruce Springsteen.

I studied Roy Orbison, Creedence Clearwater Revival, Bob Dylan, James Brown, Michael Jackson, The Jackson 5, Cream, Kiss, The Clash, Avicii, Bon Iver, Jay-Z and Beyoncé, Eric Church, Liz Phair, Talking Heads, Vampire Weekend, "Weird Al" Yankovic, and the Wu-Tang Clan.

Anytime I read about someone being important in the history of rock 'n' roll, I included them in my daily study. I researched Aretha Franklin, Bob Dylan and *The Basement Tapes*, Bob Dylan & The Band, David Bowie, Darlene Love, Elvis Costello, Elvis Presley, Ike & Tina Turner, Kanye West, Kendrick Lamar, Kip Moore, Marvin Gaye, The Notorious B.I.G., Sam Cooke, and the Traveling Wilburys, just to name some. During that summer and early fall, I also saw Jay-Z and Beyoncé, Avicii, Tom Petty and the Heartbreakers, Elvis Costello, and Jackson Browne in concert.

I had initially planned to study only rock music. I needed to learn all I could to protect myself from Dave Marsh and to hold my own as a cohost. But as I learned more, I became curious about other genres, particularly those that influenced nascent rock 'n' roll.

I had also thought I would be able to categorize each musician in a specific genre. The more in-depth my study went, however, the more I realized that every genre blended into the next. I listened to blues, gospel, R&B, soul, some opera, some jazz, and a lot of rap. (I was so excited when I learned that *rap* stands for "rhythm and poetry.")

I also bought any book about music that was reviewed or referred to as "important" in the newspapers. Among the many books I added to my bookshelves were *Musicophilia* by Oliver Sacks, *Yeah! Yeah! Yeah!: The Story of Pop Music from Bill Haley to Beyoncé* by Bob Stanley, *Rocks Off* by Bill Janovitz, *The History of Rock 'N' Roll in Ten Songs* by Greil Marcus, and even *The Birth of Tragedy* by Friedrich Nietzsche. I wanted to learn about rock and the genres that came before and after it, as well as how to place Bruce Springsteen's music therein.

Typically, I skimmed each book to get a sense of what they were about. Then, I carefully read the introductions, acknowledgments, chapter titles, and indexes. I always looked up "Bruce Springsteen" first in the index. Those pages and the few pages before and after, I read, underlined, and marked with yellow stickies. I often found Dave Marsh's name, alongside those of music and cultural critics Greil Marcus and Lester Bangs, in the acknowledgments. This was always a happy, gratifying highlight for me. It reassured me that I was on the right path with my evolving and all-encompassing autodidactic music curriculum.

I also read everything that I could find about Dave Marsh. In a 2013 article in *Progressive Christian*, writer Tim Suttle described Dave Marsh as "a grumpy rock and roll journalist . . . known for his cynically jaded writing style and his strong (often negative) opinions of legendary rock bands. (He . . . considered Queen a fascist rock band and called the Grateful Dead 'the worst band in creation.') Marsh is irascible and likes to rip on rock icons . . ."

My heart stopped when I read that. If Dave Marsh insulted Queen and the Grateful Dead—what was he going to do to me?

50

WE LEFT for New York on Tuesday evening after Andy got home from work. It was still rush hour, and somewhere in my consciousness I heard Andy cursing about the traffic. Sometime later, I heard him talking about back roads and alternative routes.

At some point, I looked out my window and saw we were on a curving, rolling, tree-lined country road and not the flat, smokestack-studded, billboarded Interstate 95 that we usually took to New York. I heard these things. I saw these things. I filed them in my mind's data bank. But, headed to New York the night before my Wednesday-morning cohosting of *Live From E Street Nation* with Dave Marsh, none of these things mattered. All that mattered to me was that I do a good job. I wanted to be able to hold my own with Dave Marsh. I wanted to engage Dave and the callers in interesting conversations. And I wanted to tell some of my stories.

I was also aware of the fear I was feeling about the following morning. The fear that Dave would slam me down in the first minutes. The fear that he would make me crumble in front of the extensive network of people who tuned in every Wednesday to hear the show. The fear that, even with all my preparation, with all my stories, Dave Marsh would reject me. I was terrified of failing as cohost of *Live From E Street Nation*.

This fear was different from the fear I had experienced in the weeks and days leading up to my Australia trip. Before my trip, that fear had increasingly immobilized me as my departure date neared. It was all I could do to heave myself onto my exercise bike each day. Packing had been a nonstarter. It was not until a snowstorm forced me to leave a day early that my fighting instinct had kicked in and I'd gathered my items into my suitcase. I had needed a new mental health plan. And my new mental health plan was Australia.

There was nothing I needed to do in advance, other than pack, to help me succeed with my goals of writing, working out, and seeing Bruce Springsteen in concert. There was absolutely nothing for me to do before my journey except worry. So, worry I did.

I was as terrified of cohosting as I had been of going to Australia. But the first time I heard Dave Marsh snarling away on his Wednesday-morning show, I had immediately decided that the ammunition I needed to stock up on for this fight was knowledge. The problem with this strategy, I realized each morning when I began studying a new musician, was that I had absolutely no idea what my focus should be. I had no idea what Dave Marsh would be prattling on about on the particular day I came to the studio.

At the end of some of the shows I listened to, Dave would announce the following week's guest. Usually, it was some rock musician who was in town for an event. Once it was Steve Van Zandt. I had been disappointed on the Wednesday before *my* show that he had not mentioned me, although I did find it understandable that he did not think I was someone who would lure people to turn on their radios. He'd also failed to announce what topic he would be discussing on this week's show.

So now, as we drove toward New York, I was as unsure of what my focus should be as I had been when I had embarked on this terrifying project. Glimmers of facts and songs and concerts and books were cascading randomly through my overstuffed brain. In twenty-four hours, it would be over: I would be standing, or I would be slain.

Since winning the silent auction, I had felt pressured by my limited time. I'd had only four months to learn everything and anything I could that might help me sound smart to Dave Marsh—or, rather, smart enough. Smart enough that he would not tell me I was an imbecile and turn off my microphone. Smart enough for him to engage with me in a conversation. Smart enough that he would let me tell my stories.

In the car headed for New York, I had two canvas bags stretched taut with the Wikipedia pages I had printed out over the past few months. Behind me in another canvas bag were my books, their pages studded with Post-it Notes for quick reference. I pulled out one page after another from my canvas tote, reading each one aloud. That Andy was sitting beside me, listening, made my speaking the words I was reading seem less strange. But Andy was incidental in this endeavor; I was reading it out loud for myself. I was reading out loud because it seemed to me that the more senses that I could involve in this task of learning an encyclopedic amount of information, the more chance I had of succeeding. And a side benefit was that it kept my brain occupied and in the present moment.

I finished reading the Wikipedia pages for Kiss, shoved them into my canvas tote, and randomly pulled out another stack.

"Here's Dave Marsh's Wikipedia," I said.

"Are you sure you want to read that?" Andy asked. "It might be better if you put him out of your mind and think instead about what you might want to say about Bruce Springsteen."

"I'm not going in there with any pretense that I'm a Bruce Springsteen expert," I countered. "I'd like to be able to talk a little about how he affected me. But I won't be able to do anything if I can't stand up to Dave Marsh. The more I know about him, the better I'll understand him and maybe see him as less terrifying and intimidating."

Andy frowned. "Anne, you don't have to do this. If you're that scared, you could just not go. Or you could just go and watch what happens in a radio studio. This isn't supposed to be torture for you."

"I'm doing this," I insisted. "Even though I'm not sure what *this* is. But I'm going to show up tomorrow morning and do my best to tell some stories and be part of a conversation with Dave and the people who call in." I looked directly at Andy, whose eyes were focused straight ahead on the narrow, winding road. "What I really wish is that it was tomorrow at this time."

"You're in luck, then," Andy said. "Because no matter what you do, no matter what happens, in twenty-four hours it will be over. And, Anne, you'll be fine. You've got good stories. You've learned so much about all things music. I'm sure you will be able to hold your own with Dave Marsh. You can always resort to my mother's trick: just imagine him naked."

I wrinkled my nose. "I really wish you hadn't put that image in my mind. Now I have to expunge it somehow."

I turned on E Street Radio and sat back and tried to make my mind go black and blank. But I couldn't. My brain was not having it. It did not want to relax. It wanted to continue preparing so it would be at its best.

I turned off the radio and pulled out Dave Marsh's Wikipedia page from the canvas tote again. I held the stapled pages in front of me like a medieval king about to read a proclamation: "Dave Marsh began his career as a rock critic and editor at *Creem* magazine, which he helped start. At *Creem*, he was mentored by close friend and colleague Lester Bangs. Marsh is credited with coining the term *punk rock* in a 1971 article he wrote. . . . He has written extensively about his favorite artists, including Marvin Gaye, whose song 'I Heard It Through the Grapevine' he chose as the number one single of all time in his book *The Heart of Rock & Soul: The 1001 Greatest Singles Ever Made* . . ."

We arrived at The Peninsula hotel at nine. After dropping our bags in our room, we went directly to the dining room for dinner. Uncharacteristically, I was not hungry. My stomach was clenched too tight to be able to accept any food into its chamber. I sat across from Andy and watched him eat one slow, meticulously gathered forkful of salmon after another. I watched him sip his daily glass of red wine.

I wished I were Andy. I wished I had a life that did not involve doing one thing after another for which I had no qualifications. One thing after another where I seized the opportunity and then tried to figure out how to do it *as* I did it. I was sixty-one years old. I wished I had a skill that I had perfected over my lifetime and was good at by now.

But I did not. So, here I was.

That night I was so nervous I couldn't fall asleep. When I looked at the clock and saw it was 4:00 a.m., I thought, *That's it. I am not cohosting. I don't need this shit.*

Immediately, I fell asleep.

51

TWO HOURS later, at six o'clock, I woke and remembered I was in New York and that it was Wednesday morning. I also remembered that I had decided I was not going to cohost at E Street Radio.

Lying in bed, I did not feel like doing anything. I did not feel like working out. But more than anything, I did not feel like lying awake, unable to sleep, in a dark hotel room.

I sat up on the edge of the bed. Putting my body on automatic pilot and shutting off my brain, I grabbed my workout bag and headed for the fitness center. I did not think about E Street Radio. I did not think about Dave Marsh. I knew that if I thought about those things, I would lose the will to move forward. I would crumble right there in the elevator. So I thought only about getting myself onto the exercise bike.

I had not eaten since lunch the previous day. I had slept for only two hours. My head felt as if it weighed as much as the rest of my body.

When I reached the bike, I hoisted myself onto the seat. I took a deep breath and began coordinating my feet to pedal their first revolutions. As my feet pushed and pulled, my right index finger tapped the music icon of my iPhone and then on the recording of Bruce Springsteen and the E Street Band's 2012 Apollo Theater concert. These days, it was the only thing I listened to when I worked out.

The concert had been a warm-up date for the band's upcoming Wrecking Ball Tour. It was the first official performance for Bruce Springsteen and the E Street Band following the death of Clarence Clemons. And it marked the debut of Jake Clemons.

I first heard about it listening to Dave Marsh yammering on the radio. The following morning, I had listened to it as I started my workout. As I began huffing and puffing and pushing and pulling the pedals, feeling sluggish and uncertain if I would be able to last sixty minutes, unsure if this would be the day my legs stopped and my body rebelled, a full minute of audience applause flowed through my headset, as if cheering *me* on.

Springsteen plays many roles in this concert album: gospel preacher, soul singer, folk singer, and rock star. He begins mournfully, which is perfect for the first several lackluster minutes of my workout. Then his tempo rises, and as it does, I always feel my energy rising too. I feel stronger. I often increase the level of my workout a bit and then a bit more.

By the end of my sixty minutes that day, I was pedaling two levels above the level on which I had begun. Bruce Springsteen's Apollo concert had blasted through my headset the whole time. And the heaviness in my brain had lifted and dissipated into nothingness.

I know, I thought. *I'll go on the show and say what my favorite six songs are. That's all I have to do. Just say my six favorite songs. If I do that, I will have accomplished my goal.*

The concreteness of my plan, its specificity, calmed me *and* excited me.

I can do this, I thought. *I will do this.*

By going on the show and sharing my favorite six songs, I would be continuing a tradition with which Dave was familiar. So many of the music books I had paged through over the summer had used lists of songs to tell the history of one thing or another. Sean Wilentz's *360 Sound: The Columbia Records Story*, for example. In it, he covered the 264 greatest songs from Columbia Records, beginning with the 1890 performance of John Philip Sousa's "Washington Post March" and working chronologically up to Adele's 2011 "Rolling in the Deep."

When I returned to the hotel room after working out, Andy was already showered and pulling on a maroon V-neck sweater.

"What are you going to wear?" he asked with a smile.

I did not answer.

"You know, to be on the radio?" he said. "I was making a joke."

"I know you were," I said. "But it isn't a joke. I thought about this a while ago. I'm wearing nice jeans and a blue sweater."

"That sounds like you," my husband of thirty-six years said.

And he was right. Blue was my color. Also, my monochromatic blue outfit would look good enough and ordinary enough that no one would think twice about it.

On Monday, two days earlier, I had received an email from Vinny, the producer of *Live From E Street Nation*. I did not know what a producer did, but one of his tasks, it seemed, was to attend to details. In his email he'd said to arrive at the SiriusXM lobby, located on the thirty-sixth floor of the

McGraw-Hill Building at 1221 Avenue of the Americas, at 9:30 a.m. There would be passes and name tags waiting for Andy and me at the building's ground-floor security desk.

At 9:00 a.m., Andy and I were standing on the steps of the hotel, waiting for the valet to hail us a cab. What should have taken a few minutes, however, was taking much longer. It was raining. And raining and raining. The cabs were scarce, and we were not the first ones in line.

Five minutes passed. Ten minutes passed. With each passing second, with each passing minute, my already-fast-paced heart rate rose.

"I have an umbrella," Andy said. "Do you want to walk?"

I looked at my three canvas totes filled with Wikipedia pages and books. Andy was carrying two of them; I was carrying the third. I looked down at my ballet flats. I imagined taking them off and walking barefoot on the puddled sidewalks of New York City as my Wikipedia pages turned soggy and illegible from the steady downpour.

No, I did not want to walk. Not yet.

Finally, it was our turn and a cab arrived. I followed Andy into the back seat. As I shut the door and he gave the driver our destination, I leaned back in my seat and let out a deep breath.

One minute went by. We moved a few inches. Another minute went by. We moved a few more.

"The rain isn't helping rush-hour traffic, today, is it?" Andy said to the driver.

The driver nodded. "This is New York."

I shook my head. Over the months, I had contemplated and anticipated many things about this morning. But I had not anticipated getting stuck in traffic. I had not anticipated being late.

We moved a few blocks. We moved another block. Then we stopped. We stopped and we did not move. It was now nine twenty.

"How much farther is it?" I asked Andy.

"One short block and one long one," he said.

"I'm walking." I pulled my ballet flats off my feet and stuck them in my tote.

But just as I unlatched the cab door, it lurched forward—and it did not stop until we had arrived at 1221 Avenue of the Americas.

I pulled my ballet flats back on and sprang from the back seat of the cab with my tote full of Wikipedia pages. I ran ahead toward the entrance as Andy paid for the cab. The rain was so strong and steady that by the time I had run across the plaza to the building's entrance, my black leather ballet flats were filled with water. I took them off, shook them out, squeezed the remaining water out, and walked into the lobby to wait for Andy.

As I looked up from my bare, wet feet into the lobby, I stopped as if frozen in place. The "security" Vinny had mentioned in the email was not some wooden desk with a guard watching people as they passed by. It looked like a replica of any TSA airport-security checkpoint, with a metal detector and a conveyer belt for personal belongings. A guard was sitting at a table just a few feet before the metal detector and conveyer belt, just like the guard at the airport who matches your ID with your face and then marks your boarding pass. And, like any TSA airport-security checkpoint, the line to pass through was so long it wound around itself.

I had worked so hard in preparation for this. And now it looked like I would be spending the morning in line at security.

Oh my god, how I wanted to give up then and there—just collapse onto the wet, slippery stone floor and die.

"Wow!" Andy said, coming along before I could act on my desire to give up.

"We've got to get to the guy at the front and tell him . . ." I was already moving forward.

"Tell him what, Anne?" Andy asked, catching up to me. "That we are special and should go ahead of everyone else?"

I did not disagree with Andy's sentiment. On the other hand, the worst the guard could do was snarl at us and send us to the back of the line. We had nothing to lose by asking, except for our self-respect. And, right now, it seemed that being late for *Live From E Street Nation* would hack down my self-respect a lot more than being sneered at by a security guard and everyone in line for appearing entitled.

"It's just nine thirty now," Andy said, pointing at the clock on the wall. "Even if this line takes fifteen minutes we'll still be there in time." Without waiting for me to reply, he pivoted and walked to the back of the line.

I knew he was right. But I had to try. It was worth taking a chance. If I succeeded, we'd be right on time. If I failed, I would accept with grace the sneers of all involved and take my place beside Andy at the back of the line.

"Sir," I said to a burly, middle-aged white man sitting behind a high square wooden table. On the table was a landline, a loose-leaf notebook, a manila folder, and an iPhone. "I was supposed to be upstairs at SiriusXM at nine thirty to cohost an E Street Radio show, and—"

"Ma'am," he said, "I'm going to have to stop you right there. I'm not sure of the particulars of your story. But I am sure I have heard some version of it dozens of times this morning, and it is"—he looked at the iPhone in front of him—"only nine thirty. I'll have to ask you to get in line like everyone else."

I smiled. I nodded. I had tried. And he had done his job. But I could not believe that after all the months I had planned and prepped for this morning, I would be late. Maybe even miss the show. I felt dejected and defeated.

I had never screwed up this badly. My terror disappeared. Disappointment filled its place.

I turned and looked for Andy. He was not the last one in line anymore.

"Ma'am," I heard as I began to walk toward him in line.

I ignored the voice. Half the rain-soaked people in this crowded lobby were ma'ams. I kept walking.

"Ma'am," I heard again.

This time the voice sounded stronger and closer. I stopped and turned. It was the guard who had been sitting at the desk.

"You said you are expected upstairs at SiriusXM's E Street Radio?" he asked.

I nodded.

"Do you work there?"

I smiled. "No, I'm a visitor."

"What is your name?" he said, opening his manila folder.

"Anne Abel. My husband is with me too. Andy Abel."

"This is a list of all the visitors coming to the building this morning and where they are going." He showed me the list. "I don't have your names down for E Street Radio."

"What?" I said, letting my canvas tote full of Wikipedia pages slide off my shoulder and down my arm and land with a thud on the floor.

"I also don't have any badges prepared for E Street Radio guests for this morning."

At that moment, my knight in shining armor gave up his spot in the advancing line and appeared by my side.

"Andy, this man says we aren't on any list for E Street Radio," I said, my voice quivering. "They have no record that we are supposed to be allowed up."

The guard smiled at Andy sadly and nodded.

"Can you call up there?" I asked.

"I can, but they never answer," he said. "Give me a minute."

We followed him to his desk. We watched him pick up the receiver of his landline and punch in some numbers. We waited. I don't think I was breathing.

"I don't know what goes on up there, but they never answer calls from here," he said, hanging up.

I began breathing again, only to have all the air in my body sucked out of me. I could not believe it. The slow cab ride had been the least of our problems. Vinny had sent me an email giving me directions to pick up badges at the desk, but apparently he had not followed through and sent our names to anyone downstairs. The fiasco was no longer my doing. Even if we had arrived thirty minutes early, we would have been stranded in the lobby. Now was the time to admit defeat and go home. I was ready to turn and head back to the hotel.

"Wait," Andy said, pulling out his iPhone. "I think I have Dave Marsh's cell phone."

"What?" I said, suddenly standing straight.

"The night you won the auction, the woman who was helping me gave me his number and I put it in my contacts."

I could not believe it.

"Dave?" Andy said, holding the iPhone close to his ear and mouth.

He paused.

"This is Andy Abel. My wife, Anne, is supposed to cohost with you this morning. Vinny told her there would be passes for us at security but there aren't. Now we're late and they won't let us up."

He paused again.

"Okay, great. Thank you."

"What did he say?" I said, my lungs filling with air.

"He said he's gonna call Vinny."

"Call Vinny? Where is *he*?" I asked.

It was nine forty-five; I'd assumed Dave would be in the studio by now.

"I have no idea," Andy said. "I'm just telling you he said he'd call Vinny."

"Wow!" I couldn't believe it. "Thank you so much, Andy. Even if we're late, at least it wasn't our fault."

We walked back to the line. We were headed for the rear when the twenty-something blonde woman in a short, tight black skirt and stilettos who had been behind Andy raised her hand toward us.

"Come take your spot," she said.

We thanked her profusely and shuffled forward, waiting and hoping to get some kind of signal, some kind of communication, from Vinny.

We had not advanced much when the guard from the desk came to us.

"Vinny, the producer for E Street, just called me. He's sending down your passes. But I'll let you go up if you clear the metal detector before they arrive."

How my heart soared. For Andy. For the guard. For the blonde woman behind us. I felt so happy and so relieved that there was no room inside me to be angry or annoyed at Vinny for screwing up. At 9:47, just as we were about to reach the metal detector, someone got off an elevator and handed the guard a white envelope.

"Here you go," he said when we reached his desk. "You're all set."

Within a minute, we had loaded our canvas totes onto the conveyer belt, passed though the metal detector, and were standing at the bank of elevators.

I could feel my heart going *thump*, *thump*, *thump*. It was thumping harder than it ever did when I worked out.

52

WE ARRIVED at SiriusXM Radio on the thirty-sixth floor and the elevator doors opened.

My eyes blinked, instinctively protecting themselves from the shock of brightness assaulting them from outside the elevator. I stepped out. If this was in fact a lobby, a space out of which other rooms or corridors led, then surely this was the lobby for heaven.

The room, an atrium, was easily six or seven or more stories high, and entirely white. Not just white but a shiny, high-gloss white. The shiny glossy whiteness was rendered even more so by the bank of windows at the top and by glass walls circling the perimeter of the top third of the room. A set of matching semicircular banquettes sat side by side in the middle of the room. Across from them was a high circular white reception desk. Behind the desk were posters for Dick Cavett, Howard Stern, and some rappers I did not recognize. I did not see one for Bruce Springsteen.

"Can I help you?" a mid-twenties woman with spiked black hair called from the reception desk.

As I walked toward her, I noticed off to my right, down a short corridor, a door with a sign that said HOWARD STERN in bold black letters.

"I'm here to cohost *Live From E Street Nation* on E Street Radio," I said. "Vinny's expecting us."

"What's your name?" she asked.

When I told her, she clicked her mouse and looked at the computer screen on the side of her desk. I held my breath.

"There you are," she said, smiling at me.

"And you're Andrew?" she said, turning to Andy.

He nodded.

"Have a seat on the couch. I'll call Vinny and let him know you're here."

It was already ten o'clock. The show was supposed to be starting now. As I headed to the couch and sat down, I was nervous—very nervous. And my nervousness at this point had nothing to do with Dave Marsh or going on the radio. At this point, I was simply nervous that time was ticking away. Nervous that I was not going to get to cohost. Everything had gone wrong, thus far, with the arrangements. I had no confidence in Vinny, Dave Marsh, E Street Radio, or SiriusXM Satellite Radio, or that this was going to work out.

Five huge Black men in baggy white basketball shorts and baggy white T-shirts stepped off the elevator and bopped together slowly to the couch beside us. I noted the heavy gold chains around their necks as they sat down.

The receptionist smiled at them and picked up the phone. Apparently, they needed no introduction or clearance.

Apparently, they were also important, because in less than a minute a young woman with blonde hair in a short black skirt and bust-hugging T-shirt came into the lobby and, with a big smile, ushered them out of sight.

Just after they disappeared, a man, about forty, came into the lobby and walked toward Andy and me.

"I'm Vinny," he said, putting his hand out. "I'm sorry about all the confusion this morning. It happens sometimes. But don't worry, Dave's running late. He's not here yet. So you haven't missed a thing."

I did not know if this was good news or bad news. I was glad I had not been late and made it seem as if I had not taken my mission to cohost seriously. I was glad I had not missed any of the show. I was also worried that, the way things were going, Dave might not show up at all. My trust in everyone had been depleted.

I followed Vinny down a corridor and into the E Street Radio studio.

In all the months I had thought about cohosting, in all the months I had prepared, not once had I stopped to think what the E Street Radio studio might look like. In the middle of the cramped room was a U-shaped table with eight microphones hanging from the ceiling above it and eight swivel chairs below them. On the wall at the front of the room was a board with flickering red lights and toggle switches and digital readouts. Between the wall and the U-shaped table was a smaller table with a microphone and a control panel.

For months I had been listening to Bruce Springsteen's concerts and albums, in all their glory, on E Street Radio. As I had listened, I had imagined Bruce Springsteen onstage. I had imagined the thousands of cheering, singing fans. How was it possible that so much energy and excitement and enthusiasm could come from a small, dark room like this? Once again I felt like Dorothy in *The Wizard of Oz*, pulling back the curtain and discovering the almighty wizard was really just a little old man.

"Excuse me for a minute," Vinny said. "I'm going to put on some music for our listeners while we wait for Dave to get here."

He walked to the table, put on his headset, and pulled some toggles on the control panel in front of him. As he took off his headset, I heard a Bruce Springsteen song blasting out of them. The rousing Springsteen music that filled E Street Radio was all in the flip of a switch.

"Take a seat at the table," Vinny said. "That's where Dave usually sits." He pointed to the microphone at the bottom end of the U-shaped table. "The microphones aren't on. No one outside the studio can hear us."

I walked over to the seat to the right of where Dave would sit. Andy took the seat beside me. I began to empty my totes, putting the pages and pages of research printouts in deliberate, neat stacks in front of me, and the books in a stack beside them. The purposefulness of my hand motions was calming.

"I have some good news." Vinny smiled. "I am going to tell our listeners that we have a special surprise today."

I was fantasizing he would say that *I* was the surprise.

"Joan Jett is joining us for the second half of the show," Vinny said.

I looked at Andy. He shrugged, pulled out his iPhone, googled Joan Jett, and handed it to me.

"An American rock singer born in 1958," I began reading.

In all the reading and studying and researching that I had done over the past months, Joan Jett's name had not popped up. Of all the musicians I had researched and listened to, *she* had to be the one to share the studio with me today!?

I sat down in my chair to read the rest of the Wikipedia entry.

"Good morning, Dave," I heard Vinny say before I had read the second paragraph.

I looked up from the iPhone as Dave shuffled in and slouched into his seat beside me. He was wearing a black leather jacket, black slacks, and a black turtleneck.

"I can't believe it," he mumbled, looking down at the table. "I got out of the train station this morning and turned right when I should have turned left. I must have gone five or six blocks before I realized I was going in the wrong direction."

This was the man who had been late for the show the first time I listened because he had not expected rush-hour traffic going into Manhattan during rush hour! And now, today, he had not been with it enough when he got off the train to turn in the right direction? When he left the house in the morning, did Barbara Carr worry that he would not find his way back?

"Dave, this is Anne and Andy Abel," Vinny introduced us. "Anne is cohosting with you today. She won the auction last spring."

Dave did not look at me. He did not look at Andy.

"Vinny, I'm going into the bathroom before we begin," he said, standing up.

I jumped up from my seat. "I have to go too."

"I'll show you where the women's room is," Dave said, not looking at me.

I did not tell him I knew where the bathroom was. I followed him out of the studio and down the corridor.

"Dave," I said, as we came into the SiriusXM atrium, "would it be okay if on the air today I just said what my favorite six songs are? That's all I want to do. I just want to say my favorite six songs."

By now we had reached a fork in the road: the women's room on the right and the men's room on the left.

"You can say your favorite *hundred* songs," he said with a growl, his back toward me. "I don't care."

He went his way, and I went mine.

I was not at all put off or offended or hurt by Dave's surly, even rude, response to my request. I was just excited—*really* excited.

If I had thought about it, I would have been surprised that I was not nervous. But I was not. I was not scared. For months and months, I had been absolutely terrified of this day. I had not been terrified about cohosting a radio show that was broadcast throughout the United States and Canada. I had been terrified of cohosting with Dave Marsh. But now I had met my dragon face-to-face. I had asked him if I could just say my favorite six songs. And, through a puff of flame, my dragon had growled an *I-don't-care-what-you-do* yes.

It was more than I could have hoped for, that Dragon Dave would not care what I say or do. That he would leave me alone and let me say my bit. That he would be too apathetic to listen—too apathetic to insult me.

Once I'd said my piece, I would sit back and be quiet. He would have his show back. I would have my dignity. It would be a win-win.

53

WHEN I returned to the studio and took my seat in front of my microphone, I was not worried about anything. I sat in my chair, not looking at Andy, not looking at anyone. I sat in my chair, breathing slowly and calmly. It was showtime. I was ready.

Dave sauntered into the studio and sat down at his microphone. He did not look at me. He did not look at anyone. He stared down at the table.

"Dave, ten seconds," Vinny said. "Five seconds, four, three, two, one, air."

It was just like in the movies! I looked at Dave, my eyes wide with excitement.

"Wow! Great to be here," he mumbled, not sounding at all like he meant it. "Sorry about the madness."

I expected him to start telling the tale of his wayward journey to work.

"We have Anne Abel here," he said, still looking down. "I've been told some bits and pieces that hint at some stories Anne has to tell, and it sounds like some of the best material I've ever heard on this show. I'm serious, Anne."

He was still not looking at me or at anyone. And he was speaking in his characteristic monotone. So it took me a moment or two to realize that his actual words were different than any I had ever heard him utter. It took me a moment or two to realize he was not putting me down or insulting me. It was, instead, the opposite.

As the airwaves went silent, waiting for me to respond, I found myself confused. Not by Dave's pleasant introduction but about how he knew more about me than my desire to just say my favorite six songs. Then I remembered back to the day in April when I had spoken to someone in the Kristen Ann Carr organization to set up my cohosting date.

This was before I had heard the show. I was very excited that I would be cohosting—and as I do sometimes when I am excited, I had told the woman about meeting Barbara Carr in the hotel lobby in Australia, before backtracking and giving her a three- or four-minute story about quitting my job and deciding to go to Australia to keep myself from falling once again into the abyss of depression. She had not said anything when I finished talking. There had been a long silence. I felt terrible. I had talked too much. I had been inappropriate. I was embarrassed. I apologized for taking up her time. I thanked her for arranging the cohosting date, and then we hung up.

Now, sitting in the E Street Radio studio, the microphone an inch from my mouth, the room silent, my heart soared with gratitude for this woman. She must have said something to Dave. And, even more surprising, Dave had listened. At least enough to introduce me.

"Well," I said, looking at Dave even though he was looking down and not at me, "I've been listening to you these last several months, and I know you don't say nice things a lot of times."

I was completely in the moment. I had said exactly what had popped into my head. I was saying the words my subconscious Anne Abel mind was sending me. I was being me, 100 percent me. I was being 100 percent honest.

Dave laughed. Vinny laughed. I smiled. Vinny smiled at me. Dave kept staring down at the table in front of him. Ordinarily, I would have found it disconcerting to speak to someone who was not looking at me. I would think the person did not want to speak with me. But on this morning, in this radio studio, the rules of etiquette seemed different than they would have on an ordinary morning in an ordinary room. So, in a universe where the audience was listening but not watching, I did not let Dave's lack of eye contact, his insistence on staring down at the table, keep me from looking directly at him while simultaneously positioning my mouth an inch from the hanging microphone.

"You're a critic," I said.

He began to mumble a couple of syllables.

"You're a critic," I said again. "It's your job to call people on things and say what you honestly believe."

"Yeah," Dave said. "I'm pretty incorrigible. I know that."

He was not looking at me, but he was smiling. That was more than enough encouragement for me to launch into one of my stories.

"Okay," I said. "I didn't know who Bruce Springsteen was two years ago. I didn't know what music was."

"What do you mean you didn't know what music was?" he said, surprising me with a response. "You mean you didn't know what pop music was?"

"No, I knew nothing about music. Growing up I had a job to do and that was to survive and be a good and dutiful daughter. I didn't know what rebellion was. Where I came from, rebellion was not an option."

I paused. I waited for Dave to say something. He didn't. I looked at Vinny. He was looking at me, his eyes open wide.

"Two years ago, on an impulse, my daughter-in-law and son came from Boston to Philadelphia to go to a Bruce Springsteen concert. My daughter-in-law had just read a *New Yorker* article by David Remnick. She's been a lifelong Bruce Springsteen fan for all of her twenty-eight years, and when she read that Bruce Springsteen was sixty-three, she thought she'd better see him before it's too late. They asked me if I wanted to go with them and I said, 'Why would I want to go? I don't like crowds, I don't like music, and it's past my bedtime.'"

Dave nodded, seemingly to himself.

"Well, the morning of the concert, as I was working out—I work out every day; I suffer with severe depression, and working out is the only way I can even hope of getting through my day—I decided I wanted to go to the concert to be with them. I went. The rest, as they say, is history. And this morning I want to talk about my favorite six songs."

"Whoa," Dave said. "We want to hear the history."

"Well, one October, after having one desk too many thrown at me at the Community College of Philadelphia, where I had taught for five years, I walked out the door and thought, *I'm never coming back*. But as I was on my way home, thinking about my empty house, I began to panic. As I mentioned a few minutes ago, I suffer with severe depression, and I was terrified of falling into the pit of depression. I needed to think of something to do. Almost immediately I thought, *I know, I'll go to Australia in February and see Bruce Springsteen concerts*. Even though I hate to travel and I hate to be alone, and even though eighteen months earlier

I hadn't known what a Bruce Springsteen was, that's exactly what I did."

"That's quite a story," Dave said. "I have never heard anything like that. Tell us, did you enjoy Australia?"

I imagined his downturned eyes boring a hole in the table.

"To be honest, I don't do the F-word. I don't do 'fun.'"

He and Vinny smiled.

"I didn't do the F-word until I came across Bruce Springsteen, that is," I clarified. "I always try to understand why I feel the way I do, why I like things. It helps me understand myself if I know what other people think and feel about things, and . . ." I suddenly felt like I was going off track. "That's not what I want to talk about," I said.

"It sounded interesting, but I know, you want to talk about your favorite six songs," Dave said. "Go for it."

Talk about getting a green light to continue. A double green light. I was not cohosting as much as hosting, which was good, because I had a lot to say.

"My first song is 'Dear Mama,' by Tupac Shakur."

Dave still did not look at me, but as I named that first song, he straightened into an upright position. It was the first time I had seen him not slouching.

"Well, in June, I opened the Sunday paper and started reading about the new Tupac Shakur play, *Holler If Ya Hear Me*, opening on Broadway."

"Yeah, that was something," Dave said, nodding.

"I had never heard of Tupac Shakur before that. But I listened to the first song mentioned in the newspaper article, 'Dear Mama,' and I listened and listened and listened to it. Then I read and reread and read again the newspaper article, looking up everything I didn't know, which was pretty much everything. Remember, until Bruce Springsteen, I knew nothing about music."

"That's hard to believe," Dave said.

"Really, it's true," I said matter-of-factly. "Anyhow, I spent all day researching Tupac Shakur and listening to his music. Mostly I listened to 'Dear Mama.' It was amazing to me that a rapper who was murdered when he was twenty-six could write about his mother in a way that resonated with me, a sixty-year-old white Jewish woman. I have three adult sons, and I wish they were like Tupac."

Dave and Vinny chuckled.

"I wish they appreciated me the way Tupac wrote about appreciating his mother in that song." I nodded. "Well, I downloaded *that* song and Bruce Springsteen's cover version of 'Dream Baby Dream' and I sent them to my sons, saying, 'Listen to these songs and think of me.' I worked really hard to raise my sons differently than I was raised. But I did not teach them to appreciate me."

"*That is* what 'Dear Mama' is about, appreciation," Dave said, nodding in agreement.

It was clear he also liked "Dear Mama."

"Anyhow, the Sunday I found that article in the paper, I got so carried away by it that it was late afternoon before I went to work out. Usually, I listen to Bruce Springsteen when I work out. But after listening to Tupac Shakur all day, I was thinking that Tupac was much more special than Bruce Springsteen. To be honest, I was disappointed by this. But then I started to work out listening to Bruce Springsteen, and I thought, *Bruce Springsteen is just as special*."

"That's a really good connection," Dave said. "A great connection. They are two very special people. You know, Bruce wrote a song about his mother too."

"I know," I said, not hesitating even for a moment. "'The Wish.' He played it in Australia at the Hunter Valley concert."

"No, he didn't. He doesn't play that song very often. Vinny," he said, not looking up at Vinny, "when's the last time Bruce played 'The Wish'?"

I looked at Vinny. He tapped a button on the control panel in front of him and in under three seconds—I had no idea how he did it—he looked up, first at me and then at Dave. "Dave, it was the Hunter Valley concert."

"Okaaaay, let's listen to it now," Dave said.

Vinny tapped some buttons. Then he took off his headphones as "The Wish" played on the air. Vinny and Dave began a quiet banter. It was not intended for me, which was fine. I suddenly felt as if I had not taken a complete breath of air since we had gone on the air. I sat down, breathed in, breathed out, and looked at Andy. He lowered his hand below his chair and gave me a thumbs-up. I was doing it. I did not know what I was doing, but still, I was doing it.

Vinny put on his headphones.

"Ten seconds, Dave. Five seconds, four, three, two, one, air."

"When was that concert?" Dave asked no one. "Last February?"

"Yes," I said. "February 23."

My instant recall did not surprise me. I was taking it moment by moment.

"Yeah, we were just talking about that concert Anne was at in Australia," Dave said. "It was quite a night."

Frankly, Bruce Springsteen's "The Wish" would not have made it onto a list of my favorite four hundred songs. The reason I remembered it at all was because as he sang it, I had imagined the mother he was describing—imagined her listening to it. Other than that, it was forgettable, in my most humble opinion.

"So, Anne, you went to Australia alone?" Dave asked. Still not looking at me.

"I did. As I said, I don't like to travel, and I don't like to be alone. I also don't like hassles. I got myself a travel agent who figured that out pretty quickly. 'Well,' she said, 'if you want this to be a trip of lifetime, you should go in a Qantas cabin.' I said, 'Yeah, whatever. Okay.' Then my daughter-in-law said, 'What's a cabin?' I said, 'What difference does it make? I'll soon find out.'"

"We know what a cabin is," Dave said.

I had never noticed his proclivity for using the royal *we*.

"Yeah," I said. "When I got back from Australia, there was a five-page story about cabins in *The New Yorker*. But that is not what I want to talk about."

"Okay. Well, you were in the midst of telling a story about your six songs. We only got to your first, Tupac's 'Dear Mama.'"

"'Dream Baby Dream' is the next song on my list," I said, pleased that he had used the word *story* to describe my list of songs. "I like that song because . . . um, um . . ." I did not know how to begin to explain how the song and Bruce Springsteen's rendering of it had resonated with me and lifted me. I thought of the concert in Sydney where I had first heard it. "Um . . ."

"Because that's what the music and words of that song taught you to do: to dream," Dave said.

I looked up at him. He had said it perfectly. He had said exactly what I was trying to say. He could have made it sound trite and obvious. But he did not. Not at all. He made it sound like the miracle of music. He made it sound as if my choice of "Dream Baby Dream" was a testament to Bruce Springsteen. A testament to me. Dave Marsh made it seem like an affirmation of the power of music.

"Thanks. You put that really well," I said. "Every time I hear 'Dream Baby Dream' I'm filled with the hope of unseen possibilities, and I'm filled with energy. Now I want to talk about the song 'High Hopes.'"

And talk about "High Hopes" I did. I talked about it my favorite way, which was to start at the very beginning.

"The first time I heard 'High Hopes' was January 14 of this year. I kept getting emails about Bruce Springsteen's new album coming out, and I just ignored them. Then, on January 14, I finished working out, and without getting off my bike I checked my emails. There was the song 'High Hopes.' I tapped on it and listened. It was a cold January morning. As I listened to the lyrics, 'I want to have a wife, I want to have two kids, I want to look in their eyes and know they stand a chance,' I thought of our dog walker, Janice. She smokes. She was also pregnant. And I thought about Janice's baby and what chance he'll have. And then I thought, *That's what being a parent is all about*. Bruce Springsteen got it exactly right. For me, it is what being a mother was all about. It was about doing for my kids when they were growing up and giving them what they needed so that when they went out into the world as young adults, they would be able to strive for what they wanted to achieve. I'm not saying they turned out perfectly. Being a parent is an ongoing thing. But, like I said, for me, Bruce Springsteen really got it right with this song. I know, I know," I said, my brain taking a quick detour, "this isn't Bruce Springsteen's song, originally. It's by The . . . Suicides?"

"No," Dave said. "I want to say The Stranglers, but that's not it either. Hhhmmm . . . It was The Saints. Which is not at all like strangulation or suicide."

"Yeah," I said, picking up on his dark humor. "My husband says that when they do forensics on my computer and see that I googled 'Suicides,' they'll have a lot to say."

"Okay, so what number are we up to?" Dave prompted me. "Number four?"

"Well, as part of my attempt to understand Bruce Springsteen and why I like him, I became interested in all kinds of music. I listened and read about lots of different musicians and genres. I also love reading reviews of all kinds—even restaurant reviews, and I don't like going to restaurants—but there were lots of concert reviews in the paper over the summer. I guess summer is a big time for concerts. Anyway, if I read a good review, I got a ticket and went. One of the concerts I went to was a Jay-Z and Beyoncé performance. Remember, the first concert I ever went to was a Bruce Springsteen concert, at the age of fifty-nine. The Jay-Z and Beyoncé concert was the first concert I went to that was *not* a Bruce Springsteen concert. It was not like anything I could have imagined, and I'm talking not just onstage but the audience. But that's not what I want to talk about now. Anyhow, as I listened to songs by Jay-Z and Beyoncé, I came across Beyoncé singing 'Ave Maria.' I think it is one of the most beautiful things I have ever heard. Sometimes when I was walking my dogs at the beach, I would put that song on repeat and listen to it for thirty minutes straight. Her voice is so ethereal and lifting. It made me feel like I was floating in air."

"Yeah, Beyoncé is a good singer," Dave said.

I waited for him to say more. He did not offer more commentary. I could not help but wonder what he really thought about Beyoncé. Was he abiding by the maxim "If you can't say something nice, don't say anything at all"?

"Okay, number five," Dave said.

"I know critics hate this song, but 'Waitin' on a Sunny Day' is my next favorite," I said, hoping to take some vitriol out of his response to the song.

"Critics don't hate that song," he said. "Fans hate that song. As a matter of fact, it's my favorite song on that album."

I was surprised. At the same time, I was not done making my case.

"Well, I've read what critics say about this song, and it's not good," I said.

"Critics are there to disagree, including me."

"I can trust you on that," I said.

"Better than anyone else you know," Dave said.

"Well, I do love that song. I love the words. I love the melody. Most of all, I love how Bruce Springsteen performs the song at concerts. The way he chooses a child from the audience and gently coaches him or her. And the kids are always so good. I also love how the audience gets so happy for the child and for themselves. That song has a special place in my heart. Before I went to Australia, I was feeling really down. Despondent. Some mornings the only way I could get myself to move from the breakfast table was to blast 'Waitin' on a Sunny Day' over and over and over on our family room speakers and pick up my Chihuahua and dance with him. It always helped me. Isn't that what music is all about?"

"That is exactly what music is all about," Dave said. "Now I want to play for you, Anne, a song by Joan Jett that I think you will like. It's called 'Good Music,' and it's just what you were talking about."

Vinny tapped some buttons, and within two seconds the song was blasting through the studio. It was hard for me to hear the words and it was also hard for me to focus on hearing the words. My mind felt like it was expanding and contracting as random music facts and songs seemed to flood it and then recede. As the song neared its end, however, I was able to decipher the chorus and I understood why Dave had chosen this song.

I need good music—good good music
It always feels good to hear good music
I know I would die without good music.

"If you want to know what I listen to when I'm down about whether the world works," Dave said, "that's it."

He did not look at me. Still.

"One night I talked Joan Jett into going with me and Kenny Laguna to see a Bruce show at The Meadowlands," he said.

One of the many things I had noticed about Dave from listening to him on the radio was that he loved to name-drop. Sometimes it was "Bruce," sometimes "Stevie," sometimes "Van," as in Van Morrison. Usually, it was someone whose name I did not recognize. Kenny Laguna was one of those.

"Joan arrived at the show just as Bruce appeared onstage and the crowd went completely insane," Dave said, staring down at the table. "Joan looked at me and said, 'I want that someday for me.' And I'll tell you, she deserves it."

He continued talking about Joan Jett and what a talented musician she was. I was only half listening. I did not know anything about Joan Jett. I did not care about Joan Jett. I cared about telling my story. Dave was rambling. I was waiting for my moment. At the very least, I wanted to say my sixth song. Right after I heard Dave say, "Steve Van Zandt," I butted back in.

"I want to talk about my sixth song, 'I Am a Patriot,'" I said.

"I heard Jackson play that song live the other night," Dave replied.

"I did too," I said. "But let me back up. Last summer, I watched Bono introduce Bruce Springsteen into the Rock & Roll Hall of Fame. Then I started watching everyone Bruce inducted. I listened to them and studied them, including Jackson Browne. I fell in love with his album *Late for the Sky*, which got an amazing review by Stephen Holden in 1974 in *Rolling Stone*. Then, last weekend, Andy and I went to York, Pennsylvania, to see Jackson Browne in concert there. I didn't think it was a very good concert." I paused briefly, remembering my dissatisfaction that night. "After listening to Jackson Browne's music all summer and loving it, I was disappointed by his complete lack of energy and rapport with the audience at his concert. Nobody in the audience seemed to have much energy either. No one danced or swayed. Nobody clapped. Three women near me were texting and playing Candy Crush for most of the two-hour show. Toward the end of the show, I left my seat to stand on the side of the auditorium so I could close my eyes and try to get into the music, even sway to the beat."

"Yeah," Dave said. "That concert in York was the first concert of the tour. I went to the third concert of Jackson's tour the other night. I thought it was fine. Fine for a beginning-of-a-tour concert. But after the concert, Jackson told me he was not particularly enthusiastic about the York concert you went to. Now I want to get back to what you were saying about the night Bruce inducted Jackson into the Hall of Fame. I actually forgot Bruce inducted Jackson. I was there that night. What I remember about that night was, I happened to be sitting behind Prince. And when Jackson came out to take his bows, Prince was the first person in the whole place to get up and begin applauding. That is a tribute. A real tribute. It was also the night that Prince got inducted. So it was a real artist-to-artist tribute."

I was so busy imagining Dave Marsh at the Rock & Roll Hall of Fame, sitting behind Prince the night Jackson—and Prince—were inducted, that when he stopped speaking, I did not say anything.

"You know," he said, "you should see more Jackson shows. He's not really celebrated as a live performer. But I've been seeing him perform since—hhhmmmm, I think 1973. I'm not a big singer-songwriter guy, certainly not California singer-songwriters. But Jackson's a real rock musician. Which is an accolade from me. Not from everybody, but for sure from me. You should give him another chance."

"Well, anyhow, I wasn't really that impressed with his York concert," I said. "But at the end he sang 'I Am a Patriot.' I loved the words, and it's my sixth song: 'I am a patriot and I love my country / Because my country is all I know / I want to be with my family / People who understand me / I've got nowhere else to go . . .' I love the words because they're so honest and true. People like what they know."

"I hate to say it," Dave said, "but whenever I hear the expression 'People like what they know,' I can't help but think it's a problem."

"Of course it's a problem—it's a big problem," I said. "That's why people need to travel. And we won't talk about if your family understands you. I googled the song and saw that 'Little Steven' wrote it. I have to be honest: I didn't know that Little Steven was Steve Van Zandt. And when I saw that he was the one who wrote it, I thought it was really cool that I liked the song so much and that I have liked Steve Van Zandt from way back."

"What that shows," Dave said, "is that your taste is authentically your taste. You know what you like and you're consistent."

If I had not been listening to every word Dave said, if I had not been so in the moment, I might have wondered if the surly Dave I had tried to make myself listen to for so many months—the same surly Dave I had followed toward the bathrooms before the show began—had been snatched by aliens in the men's room and switched out for a kinder, gentler doppelgänger Dave. But I was not wondering about the transformation. I was just in the moment, listening and responding.

"I'm going to make an offer to Anne on the air right now," Dave said, *still* staring at some spot on the table down in front of him. "For all I know, Joan isn't going to show up. If that happens, just count on you're gonna be talking for another hour, okay?" he said.

"Sure," I said. "Whatever you say."

"You had a couple of other stories you wanted to tell, and I want you to tell 'em. So, let's hear 'em."

I was not sure when I had told him I had more stories. Maybe I had said something while the music was playing; if I had, I'd been so in the moment that I didn't remember doing it.

"Dave, I'll make you an offer," I said, unable to fully comprehend that Dave had just ceded the microphone to me, if not the show. "If you just let me tell this last story, I won't say any more."

"Anne, I'm serious," he said. "We all want to hear your stories."

I stared at him for a moment, astonished. This man who had terrified me for so many months, the man I'd been afraid would shut me down the first time I opened my mouth, was telling me that he and everyone listening to the show wanted to hear my stories. I could not help but think how ironic it was that my family and friends did not want to hear my stories but this curmudgeon did.

"Okay," I said. "One afternoon in Australia I read in a book I had brought with me that Max Weinberg said that he thinks of the Hebrew word *seder* when he thinks about his drumming. I know the word *seder* means *order*. It's also the word used to describe the ritual dinner at Passover. But I could not figure out the connection Max Weinberg was making between that word and his drumming."

I looked at Dave to see if he was listening. He was looking straight ahead and down. It was hard to tell. I looked at Vinny. He was looking at me, expectantly.

That was all I needed.

"I was feeling pretty down that afternoon. My hip was hurting me, so I couldn't even go out and walk around to try to lift my spirits. Instead, I put on my headset and began listening to *Wrecking Ball*, which is what I used to listen to when I work out. But my mind was being really difficult, and the same music that usually lifts me and gets my body moving when I work out—on this afternoon, it sounded like a hodgepodge. Just irritating noise." I shook my head. "I focused on Max Weinberg's drums. I listened and listened and listened.

Soon my feet were tapping in rhythm with the drumbeat. Then I expanded my listening to the rest of the band. I don't remember what song it was, but it was one I had heard on other albums and in concerts, and I recognized that the other musicians sounded different this time. They were going off on these musical rambles. As I listened, I realized they were . . . I'm not sure what you call it. I think it's called riffing?"

"You mean improvising?" Dave asked.

"Yeah, isn't that called riffing in music?"

"It is," he said, nodding to no one.

"Well, that afternoon I realized that the drumbeat is like the backbone of the band. It's steady, constant. Other musicians can go off and take a chance and experiment and try new things knowing that when they want to come back, they can listen to the steady beat of the drum to guide them. And, because I am always thinking about family and people, I thought about how the drumbeat in a band is like a good family. In a good family the parents are strong and give the kids confidence and let them know they can go off and try their things and rebel. They can do whatever they need to do. But, when they need it, they can come back to the solid family structure, just like Max is the solid structure within the band with the drums. When the movie *Get On Up* came out this summer, I read that James Brown had screamed at his band that he wanted every instrument to sound like a drum."

Dave was laughing but still not looking up.

"I wasn't sure what James Brown meant when I read that," I said. "Anyhow, a few days later, one of my sons called. His wife was pregnant, and they had just heard the baby's heartbeat for the first time, and my son said, 'It made me feel so proud.' And I remember at that moment thinking, *That's why the drum is so important. It's such a primal sound. You hear a heartbeat, and it goes right to the core of your being. There's a rhythm, a beat, with so many primal things, like sex.* And I realized that's why James Brown wanted every instrument to sound like a drum."

I sat back in my chair and looked at Dave.

"Well, James's musical role in rock and roll history, rock and soul history, was to shift the emphasis from melody to beat," Dave said. "That was his single greatest accomplishment, in my opinion. And he had a number of great accomplishments. And you're a hundred percent on it. I always think of Max in the E Street Band as gravity."

"Yes," I said, sitting up straight. "That's a great word."

"Everybody can go wherever they want to go, and eventually Max's gravity is going to pull them back to the center," he said. "That strong center."

"That's what I meant about giving the band members the freedom to go off and riff," I said.

We were having a conversation. I had been excited when I finally understood what Max Weinberg meant about the connection between his drumming and the word *seder*. Now I was excited not only to be sharing my thoughts with Dave but also to hear him respond with his own thoughts.

"And that's *a lot*," Dave said, "because of what Max doesn't do. He doesn't elaborate a lot. Max is very straight ahead, and people think that means that it reflects a limit of what he could be doing. But everybody who's ever heard him play in his jazz band knows that isn't true. For a long time, people thought he just does one thing. But it's a *big* thing. What Max does is give Bruce the freedom to turn his back on the band and go be Bruce. It's literally true that without Max Weinberg, Bruce would not be that free. So I think everything you just said is completely true, and particularly germane to the E Street Band. Max is a solid drummer. The E Street Band has not been particularly innovative as a rhythm ensemble. It's all four-beat or waltz time."

Dave paused. He laughed. I waited. I knew he was not done.

"Everett Bradley coming in has opened that up. And now there are some cross-rhythms. It was a nice thing to hear in this last tour. It was an important thing for me to hear. Okay, it looks like we have some callers. And, Anne, you just jump in whenever you want. You're not a guest here, you're a host. Say what you're thinking, because you're good at that."

"Dave, it's Bill from Boston," Vinny said, looking at Dave.

"Hello, Bill," Dave said.

"She mentioned the word *seder*," Bill said.

"'She' being Anne Abel," Dave said.

Bill went off on a ramble about Bruce Springsteen's concerts being like a seder. "You'll be at a concert and hear a song you've heard before a hundred times, but on this night it's different."

It seemed he was making a connection between the song being "different" and the first of the Four Questions asked at the beginning of the Passover *seder*: "Why is this night different?"

"That's where I thought she was going with the word *seder*," he said. "Then she went somewhere completely different."

"The 'she' being Anne Abel, I will remind you, again," Dave said.

Dave let the guy ramble on about Steve Van Zandt being a fellow Massachusetts citizen, having grown up in Winthrop, Massachusetts, until he was seven.

"Yeah, he's such a pilgrim." Dave laughed. "He's not a very good Puritan, but he can be a pilgrim. Thanks, Bill."

"Does that make any sense to you, Anne?" Dave said.

It did not make any sense to me. The guy was an idiot. I wondered if Dave was trying to get me to insult callers like he did. But I was not going to do that.

"Well, actually, it made me think of something else," I said, trying to be both honest *and* kind. "Would it be okay if I talked about concerts being liturgical?"

"Yes," Dave said with force. "The only thing that's not all right is you keeping asking permission. You *have* permission. I'll say it again. You *have* permission." He let out a hardy laugh.

"Well, you're Dave Marsh and *I'm* just Anne Abel," I said, figuring it could not hurt to play into his larger-than-life ego.

"Well, then, listen to me. For the rest of the time we're on air, you have my permission."

That was exactly what I'd hoped he would say.

"Got it," I said. "So, another story I want to talk about is that we belong to a gigantic synagogue outside Philadelphia. I haven't been there since my middle son, who is thirty or thirty-one, was confirmed. It's a huge congregation. On the night before Yom Kippur, the holiest night of the year, the cantor stands in front of the two thousand congregants in a long white robe. There are beautiful stained-glass windows, and everyone's dressed in their most elegant white clothes. The cantor has a beautiful voice and the whole thing is breathtaking and inspiring and uplifting. A few times now, I've seen Bruce Springsteen and Cindy Mizelle, in the chorus, sing, 'Raise your hands, raise your hands'—I don't remember the name of the song—and get everyone in the audience to rise.

And I wondered, what makes Bruce Springsteen and the E Street Band different from the cantor singing and reaching out to his people? What are the similarities and what are the differences?"

"You know," Dave said, without even pausing a moment to think, "the mass was originally *sung*, not just pronounced. So, in terms of worship, a Bruce concert and a mass are not that different. They're both, in a sense, liturgical. But I've never been to a synagogue . . ."

I did not say anything for a moment. I was surprised that this apparently cosmopolitan man had never been inside a synagogue. Did he not have any Jewish friends? Had he never been invited to a Jewish wedding or even a bar mitzvah? The man had an apartment in New York City!

"I didn't mean to compare the cantor's singing with Bruce's and Cindy's in a Jewish sense," I interrupted. "I meant it as a religious experience in general. How is Bruce and Cindy singing and urging the audience to rise similar to and different than a religious leader doing the same with a congregation at a religious service?"

"Yeah, yeah, yeah, I know," Dave said, sounding frustrated. "That's the reason I was saying a concert is in some ways liturgical. The liturgy of public worship is conducted according to a formula. Similarly, there are things Bruce has got to do at certain times at every concert, in one way or another. If it's not 'Waitin' on a Sunny Day,' it's gonna be something else. He's gonna get those kids out of the crowd. And so there's a bunch of things like that that I think are part of theater. And religious ceremony is theater. And in theater you've also got to have these strong moments which define things that happen—to define the characters, to define whatever's turning the plot."

"I see," I said. "And because it reaches people—as we were saying about drumming—in a primal way, these strong, defining moments go right to a person's core." I was trying to sound like I was building on what Dave was saying, but I knew that I was not. "I read about this thing called 'The Tingle Factor' on the BBC website."

I paused. I could not tell if Dave was listening.

"I don't know what 'The Tingle Factor' is," he said, not sounding like he cared to know either.

I was not deterred.

"According to 'The Tingle Factor,' music is a shortcut to emotion. I'm not going to say if that's true or not. But someone told me to read Nietzsche, which I didn't. But I did read the back of the book." I quickly leaned down and pulled the book in question out of my canvas book tote by my feet. "And it explained . . . Well . . ."

I was thinking I had gotten myself into a topic too convoluted and esoteric, and about which I knew virtually nothing, and that I should stop. But I pressed on.

"Nietzsche said that between the two central forces of art . . . Do you want me to continue?" I asked, looking up from the back of the book at Dave.

"Yeah, but I don't know what the heck you're talking about," Dave said. "What's the book?"

"*The Birth of Tragedy* by Nietzsche. I think it was his first."

"Whose first book?" he asked.

I was in deep. Very deep. Not a classic kind of E Street Radio conversation. But now I wanted to continue.

"*Friedrich* Nietzsche," I said with the same ease and confidence as all the times I had said "Bruce Springsteen."

"Oh, okay," Dave said.

I let out a deep sigh. "But first I want to tell the story of how I found out about it. I met this woman in her eighties in the airport on my way back from the Jay-Z/Beyoncé concert. One thing led to another, and she told me how proud she was of her son-in-law and grandchildren, whom she was on her way to spend a week with in Maine. Her daughter had died five years ago. Well, I ended up emailing her son-in-law. I just wanted him to know how wonderful she seemed and how proud she was of him and his kids. And I told him why I was in the airport, coming back from the Jay-Z/Beyoncé concert, and that I was fascinated by music and its power. To my surprise, he wrote me back; he suggested that I read Greil Marcus, the music and cultural critic; Friedrich Nietzsche; and Oliver Sacks. And I did. I was so excited when I found *your* name on page 9 of Greil Marcus's book. It made me think I had come full circle and was in the right place, if he was writing about you."

Dave smiled.

Two months earlier, when I'd found Dave's name in the Greil Marcus book, I had marked it with two Post-it Notes. I had hoped I would be able to work my finding his name into our conversation on the show. The smile on Dave's face now was exactly what I had hoped to see if I had a chance to mention it.

"Anne Abel, I said it already," Dave said. "You're a whiz. If you didn't know about music two years ago, you've certainly made up for lost time. Okay, folks, Vinny's gonna play some music and we're gonna take a break. Then we'll be back with Anne Abel and also Joan Jett."

Vinny pressed a button or two and took off his headset. Dave got up and walked out of the room. I collapsed onto the back of my chair. I looked at the clock on the wall for the first time since we had gone on the air. It was exactly eleven o'clock. We had been on the air for fifty minutes. I could not decide if it felt like we had been on much longer or much shorter. Every cell in my brain had been going full throttle. I felt exhilarated.

I took a deep breath and turned to Andy.

"Good job," he said with a big smile. "Really good job."

I smiled. I had been so in the moment during the show that I could not remember the sequence of the conversation from one minute to the next, but I did know I had covered a lot of topics. It had all seemed to flow so naturally. It was as if all the things I had read and listened to, all the concerts I had gone to, all the things about which I had thought over the past several months had been lined up deep inside me, ready to bubble up into words when the time was right. I knew the material so well that it had all just come to me as needed.

54

DURING THE break at eleven o'clock, Vinny cued up a series of Bruce Springsteen songs. I decided to take a quick bathroom break. When I got back to the studio, Andy was no longer sitting at the U-shaped table but was in a chair away from the table in the corner. My stacks of papers and my book-filled tote had been moved down to the last microphone at the table, the spot Andy had previously occupied.

My eyes met Andy's and he nodded. No one had to explain that I was being sidelined for the main act, Joan Jett. I took my seat just as Dave shuffled into the room, his eyes cast downward. As soon as he took his seat, a woman with a black shag haircut in black jeans and a black leather jacket walked into the studio with a similarly dressed man.

"Joan Jett," Dave said, jumping up from his seat and going to her. "Give me a hug. Kenny, good to see you."

Dave and Joan hugged. Dave and Kenny shook hands. Then Dave took his seat and Joan and Kenny followed him to the table. Joan sat at the microphone where I had been sitting in the first hour. Kenny stood between Joan and Dave but a step back. As Dave introduced Andy and me to Joan and Kenny, Vinny said, "Dave, ten . . . five, four, three, two, one, you're on the air."

Dave introduced Joan and Kenny to the audience, announcing that Joan was going to be an honoree that night at a concert benefiting Little Kids Rock, a philanthropic organization that provides music education and instruments for children in New York City. Dave had clearly been given the task to be this organization's public relations spokesman. Joan and Kenny joined him as they all talked about their own childhoods and how important music and art had been for them.

As they spoke, I found my mind wandering, and I realized how tired I felt. I had used a lot of energy the previous hour accomplishing my mission of being part of a conversation with Dave Marsh. I was aware that now, it was Joan Jett's show. And I was perfectly okay with that.

I kept my ear half tuned to Dave and Joan's conversation. Dave was praising Joan obsequiously and Joan was respectfully demurring. They talked at length about Joan's being nominated for the Rock & Roll Hall of Fame. Then, using music jargon like *fade-outs* and *outros*, they talked about the technicalities of producing a record. Then Dave said Joan had been honored at the Rock & Roll Hall of Fame's Women in Music, and my attention snapped back to the conversation.

"It's always been really uncomfortable for me to say, 'I, I, I accomplished this,'" Joan said. "Nothing in music is *I*. Music is a collaborative project."

"Chrissie Hynde," I said, my voice soft and tentative, "at the age of sixty-two, finally put out her first solo album, *Stockholm*, last June after being a founding member of The Pretenders."

Dave was looking down, as usual, but Joan Jett was looking at me.

"I read that the music industry is really hard for women to break into," I said, my voice now strong as I sat up straight and spoke into the microphone.

"It's hard for *men* to break in," Dave said quickly. "It's almost impossible for women to break in."

"I was actually thinking of Barbara Carr," I said, referring to Dave's wife.

"She's one reason I know that," Dave said.

"Is that something you experienced?" I asked Joan Jett.

"It's always been really difficult," Joan said, not looking at me. "It's just that it's hard for me to say, 'I deserve this day. I deserve to be in the Rock & Roll Hall of Fame.' To say, 'I did it. I stood up for women.' I mean, it might be true—I did stand up for women—but I don't feel like I should . . ."

She seemed to be faltering.

"You don't feel like you should be thanked for it?" I asked.

"Yeah, in a way."

"You also know," Dave said, "when you go onstage at night . . ."

"That's the thanks I get," Joan said. "If the Rock & Roll Hall of Fame happens, I'll be very thankful. I'll have a great time. If it doesn't, I'll be okay."

I could not tell if she was being humble because she did not want to annoy the men in the industry or if she was being sincere.

Apropos of nothing, Dave said, "You looked great onstage with Nirvana."

I had heard of Nirvana, but that was the extent of my knowledge on that topic. I did not know if Nirvana was a person or a band, even.

"Did you know Kurt?" Dave asked.

"I'd met him," Joan said, "but we weren't close friends."

"You actually predate punk," Dave said. "It's hard to believe, given how primal some of your early records were. You were way ahead of the time."

"Well, we formed our band The Runaways in late '75," Joan said.

"*That is the moment*," Dave said with more excitement than I had ever heard from him.

"That is the moment when I think Lester Bangs coined the term *punk rock*," Joan said.

I sat up. I sat up very straight and tall. "Actually," I said, looking directly at Dave, "it was Dave Marsh who coined that term. Dave, it was *you*!"

Dave lifted his eyes from the table in front of him and, for the first time all morning, looked at *me*.

"Anne, you're absolutely right. I'm the one who's in the dictionary if you look up *punk rock*."

"There you go," Joan said. "I'm sorry about that. That's a really big thing."

Joan was talking to Dave. She was looking at Dave. But Dave was looking at me. Dave Marsh was smiling at me. "Like I said, Anne," Dave said. "You're a whiz. Can you believe she's only been a rock fan for six months?"

My heart soared.

Dave and Joan talked. Dave and I talked. The three of us talked.

"It's almost time to sign off," Dave said after getting a sign from Vinny. "Joan, I'm looking forward to seeing you honored tonight at Little Kids Rock. I hope to see you inducted into the Rock & Roll Hall of Fame this year. Thank you for stopping in today." He turned to look at me. "Anne, I want to say it on the air, here and now. You're the most knowledgeable guest I've had on this show. Anytime you want to come back and be a host with me on the show, you have an open invitation."

"Thank you, coming from you that means a lot," I replied. "I absolutely accept."

Dave shook my hand and shuffled out of the room with Joan Jett and her entourage.

I looked at Andy.

"I did it," I said. "I can't believe I did it."

Andy smiled. "You sure did!"

I shook my head in disbelief. Since I had won the cohosting gig, my hope had been to be part of the conversation. I had never dared to dream that after the show I would feel this happy and proud. I felt more confident than I had ever felt before in my life.

55

I WENT to Australia because I needed structure and focus—because I was hoping to avoid falling into a deep depression, again.

Before my trip, my life consisted of trudging through each day, using self-discipline to combat the depression as best I could. I did not go to Australia looking for anything, or expecting anything, other than to harness some Bruce Springsteen energy to keep myself out of the abyss. Harness that energy I did—and something unexpected, something I hadn't even known was possible, happened as a result. I came back from Australia with a ball of that positive energy inside me.

But I was worried about losing this ball of energy once I returned home. I was worried I would not be able to maintain or protect it. And indeed, when the people at home refused to see me or validate me, I could feel my ball of energy diminishing. It wasn't only that my friends and family didn't want to hear about my experiences in Australia. It was bigger than that. When I returned from Australia, I realized for the first time that these people had always been dismissive toward me. They had never appreciated how hard I worked to try to keep myself out of a major depression. And when I did fall into one, they did not appreciate the extreme and terrifying measures I took—like ECT and inpatient treatment—to try to recover.

It wasn't until I came back from Australia with things to say that I understood no one wanted to hear me. No one wanted to hear how transformative the trip had been for me. No one cared that as terrified as I had been of going on the trip, I had gone and come back stronger. No one was interested in knowing *me*. This was particularly apparent because it stood in stark contrast to the appreciation and admiration I'd received from strangers during my trip.

While I was in Australia, I began to see myself through the eyes of these people. It was the first time in my life that people looked at me with a sense of interest and admiration, even awe. Like the young man who told me he wished his mother was more like me. The positive words I received throughout my trip planted the seeds of a positive view of myself.

This nascent positive view of myself enabled me to walk away from people like Dr. Bhati, and Beverly, and other friends and acquaintances who depleted my ball of positive energy.

Before Australia, I needed to regenerate my energy every day with vigorous workouts. But even this energy was impossible to sustain. It might last seconds or minutes; if I was lucky, it could last a couple of hours. This ball of energy I had now, in contrast, was undying and self-sustaining. It was unlike anything I had ever felt before.

In the months and years after Australia, my ball of positive energy guided me to people and experiences that sustain my energy. And my newfound self-respect made me determined to have a voice—to be part of a conversation.

To tell my stories.

Credits

Badlands
Words and Music by Bruce Springsteen
Copyright © 1978 Sony Music Publishing (US) LLC and Eldridge Publishing Co.
All Rights Administered by Sony Music Publishing (US) LLC, 424 Church Street, Suite 1200, Nashville, TN 37219
International Copyright Secured All Rights Reserved
Reprinted by Permission of Hal Leonard LLC

Working on a Dream
Words and Music by Bruce Springsteen
Copyright © 2009 Sony Music Publishing (US) LLC and Eldridge Publishing Co.
Copyright Renewed
All Rights Administered by Sony Music Publishing (US) LLC, 424 Church Street, Suite 1200, Nashville, TN 37219
International Copyright Secured All Rights Reserved
Reprinted by Permission of Hal Leonard LLC

If I Should Fall Behind
Words and Music by Bruce Springsteen
Copyright © 1992 Sony Music Publishing (US) LLC and Eldridge Publishing Co.
All Rights Administered by Sony Music Publishing (US) LLC, 424 Church Street, Suite 1200, Nashville, TN 37219
International Copyright Secured All Rights Reserved
Reprinted by Permission of Hal Leonard LLC

Dream Baby Dream
Words and Music by Alan Vega and Martin Rev
Copyright © 1979 Saturn Strip Ltd. and Revega Music Co.
All Rights for Saturn Strip Ltd. Administered by BMG Rights Management (US) LLC
All Rights Reserved Used by Permission
Reprinted by Permission of Hal Leonard LLC and Revega Music Co.

Drinkin' Wine Spo-Dee-O-Dee
Words and Music by J. Mayo Williams and Granville "Stick" McGhee
Copyright © 1949 UNIVERSAL MUSIC CORP. and MICROHITS MUSIC CORP.
Copyright Renewed
All Rights Reserved Used by Permission
Reprinted by Permission of Hal Leonard LLC and Microhits Music Corp.

Waitin On A Sunny Day
Words and Music by Bruce Springsteen
Copyright © 2002 Sony Music Publishing (US) LLC and Eldridge Publishing Co.
All Rights Administered by Sony Music Publishing (US) LLC, 424 Church Street, Suite 1200, Nashville, TN 37219
International Copyright Secured All Rights Reserved
Reprinted by Permission of Hal Leonard LLC

Spill The Wine
Words and Music by Thomas Sylvester Allen, Harold Brown, Morris Dickerson, LeRoy L. Jordan, Charles W. Miller, Lee Oskar and Howard E. Scott
Copyright © 1970 Far Out Music, Inc.
Copyright Renewed

All Rights Administered by BMG Rights Management (US) LLC
All Rights Reserved Used by Permission
Reprinted by Permission of Hal Leonard LLC

My Love Will Not Let You Down
Words and Music by Bruce Springsteen
Copyright © 1998 Sony Music Publishing (US) LLC and Eldridge Publishing Co.
All Rights Administered by Sony Music Publishing (US) LLC, 424 Church Street, Suite 1200, Nashville, TN 37219
International Copyright Secured All Rights Reserved
Reprinted by Permission of Hal Leonard LLC

Stayin' Alive
from the Motion Picture SATURDAY NIGHT FEVER
Words and Music by Barry Gibb, Robin Gibb and Maurice Gibb
Copyright © 1977 CROMPTON SONGS, REDBREAST PUBLISHING LTD. and UNIVERSAL MUSIC PUBLISHING INTERNATIONAL MGB LTD.
Copyright Renewed
All Rights for CROMPTON SONGS Administered by SONGS OF UNIVERSAL, INC.
All Rights for REDBREAST PUBLISHING LTD. and UNIVERSAL MUSIC PUBLISHING INTERNATIONAL MGB LTD. Administered by UNIVERSAL MUSIC – CAREERS
All Rights Reserved Used by Permission
Reprinted by Permission of Hal Leonard LLC

Spirit In The Night
Words and Music by Bruce Springsteen
Copyright © 1973 Sony Music Publishing (US) LLC and Eldridge Publishing Co.

Copyright Renewed
All Rights Administered by Sony Music Publishing (US) LLC, 424 Church Street, Suite 1200, Nashville, TN 37219
International Copyright Secured All Rights Reserved
Reprinted by Permission of Hal Leonard LLC

Thunder Road
Words and Music by Bruce Springsteen
Copyright © 1975 Sony Music Publishing (US) LLC and Eldridge Publishing Co.
Copyright Renewed
All Rights Administered by Sony Music Publishing (US) LLC, 424 Church Street, Suite 1200, Nashville, TN 37219
International Copyright Secured All Rights Reserved
Reprinted by Permission of Hal Leonard LLC

Human Touch
Words and Music by Bruce Springsteen
Copyright © 1992 Sony Music Publishing (US) LLC and Eldridge Publishing Co.
All Rights Administered by Sony Music Publishing (US) LLC, 424 Church Street, Suite 1200, Nashville, TN 37219
International Copyright Secured All Rights Reserved
Reprinted by Permission of Hal Leonard LLC

Tenth Avenue Freeze Out
Words and Music by Bruce Springsteen
Copyright © 1975 Sony Music Publishing (US) LLC and Eldridge Publishing Co.
Copyright Renewed
All Rights Administered by Sony Music Publishing (US) LLC, 424 Church Street, Suite 1200, Nashville, TN 37219
International Copyright Secured All Rights Reserved
Reprinted by Permission of Hal Leonard LLC

High Hopes
Words and Music by Tim Scott McConnell
Copyright © 1987 UNIVERSAL - GEFFEN MUSIC and
BONE DOG MUSIC
All Rights Controlled and Administered by UNIVERSAL - GEFFEN MUSIC
All Rights Reserved Used by Permission
Reprinted by Permission of Hal Leonard LLC

Good Music
Words and Music by Joan Jett and Kenny Laguna
Copyright © 1986 LAGUNATIC MUSIC AND
FILMWORKS, INC.
All Rights Administered by SONGS OF UNIVERSAL, INC.
All Rights Reserved Used by Permission
Reprinted by Permission of Hal Leonard LLC

I Am A Patriot
Words and Music by Steven Van Zandt
Copyright © 1984 BLUE MIDNIGHT MUSIC
All Rights Administered by ALMO MUSIC CORP.
All Rights Reserved Used by Permission
Reprinted by Permission of Hal Leonard LLC

Music Supervisor: Jonathan Finegold
Music Coordinator: Jack Graubard

The music supervisors would like to thank:

Dave Bechdolt
Todd Ellis
Michelle Ritter
Martin Reverby
Tony Barlo
Andalyn Lewis
Stephen Pielocik

Acknowledgments

THANK YOU to Jonathan Finegold and Jack Graubard of Fine Gold Music and to Leslye Davidson, Esquire, for their superhuman efforts to secure licensing for the lyrics in this book.

Thank you to Nell Casey, who saw the first draft of this book and helped me move it forward.

Thank you to Barrett Briske for her devoted and painstaking care with this book.

Thank you to my new friend Donna Gray. I first heard of Donna and Bruce Funds, the generous organization she founded, in 2014. We finally met through this book. Thank you for caring and helping to make this a better book.

Thank you to Jeanne Gemmill Griffin for introducing me to myself. And thank you for your support and advice, expert and otherwise, every step of the way with this book. And with me.

Andy, thank you for being you. Your patience, thoughtfulness, and unwavering support lift me up every day. That combined with your brilliance and humor make you a perfect person in my book. And this is my book.

About the Author

Eric Michael Pearson

ANNE ABEL is an author, storyteller, and influencer. Her first memoir, *Mattie, Milo, and Me* (2024), about unwittingly rescuing an aggressive dog, was inspired by her Moth StorySLAM win in New York City. Her second memoir, *High Hopes*, was inspired by her Moth StorySLAM win in Chicago. In January 2025, she was featured in *Newsweek*'s, "Boomer's Story About How She Met Her Husband of 45 Years Captivates Internet." She holds an MFA from the New School for Social Research, an MBA from the University of Chicago, and a BS in chemical engineering from Tufts University. She has freelanced for multiple outlets over the course of her career.

Anne lives in New York City with her husband, Andy, and their cavapoo puppy, Wendell. You can follow her on Facebook, Instagram, and Tik Tok: @annesimaabel.

Looking for your next great read?

We can help!

Visit www.shewritespress.com/next-read
or scan the QR code below for a list
of our recommended titles.

She Writes Press is an award-winning
independent publishing company founded to
serve women writers everywhere.